MARK
DR...

Ruin Mist Chronicles

BOOK FOUR

ROBERT STANEK

Mark of the Dragon
Ruin Mist Chronicles Book 4
Copyright © 2005 by Robert Stanek.
First Edition, November 2005

Reagent Press
Published by Virtual Press, Inc.

Cover design & illustration by Robert Stanek
Cover illustration copyright © 2005 Robert Stanek
Inside illustration copyright © 2005 Reagent Press

ISBN 1-57545-091-7

REAGENT PRESS

Reagent Press Books by Robert Stanek

Ruin Mist Chronicles
Keeper Martin's Tale, Book 1
Kingdom Alliance, Book 2
Fields of Honor, Book 3
Mark of the Dragon, Book 4

Ruin Mist Dawn of the Ages
Rulers of Right, Book 1
Knights of the Blood, Book 2
Wardens of the Word, Book 3

Ruin Mist Chronicles (Dark Path)
Elf Queen's Quest, Book 1

Ruin Mist Heroes, Legends & Beyond
Magic of Ruin Mist
Sovereign Rule

Magic Lands
Journey Beyond the Beyond
Into the Stone Land

Magic Lands & Other Stories

Praise for Ruin Mist & Keeper Martin's Tales

Learn more at www.robertstanek.com

Enter the world of the books
www.ruinmist.com

Meet the Characters

Adrina Alder
Princess Adrina. Third and youngest
daughter of King Andrew.

Amir
Son of Ky'el,
King of the Titans.

Ansh Brodst
Captain Brodst.
King's Knight Captain.

Ayrian
Eagle Lord of the Gray Clan.

Cagan
Sailmaster Cagan.
Elven ship captain.

Calyin Alder
Princess Calyin.
Eldest daughter of King Andrew.

Delinna Alder
Known as Sister Midori after joining
the priestesses.

Geoffrey Solntse
Lord Geoffrey.
Lord of the Free City of Solntse.

Jarom Tyr'anth
King Jarom, ruler of Vostok,
East Warden of the Word.

Liyan
Brother Liyan. Presiding member of
East Reach High Council.

Mark
King Mark. The Elven King of West Reach.

Nijal Solntse
First son of Geoffrey.

Noman
Keeper of the City of the Sky.

Queen Mother
The Elven Queen of East Reach.

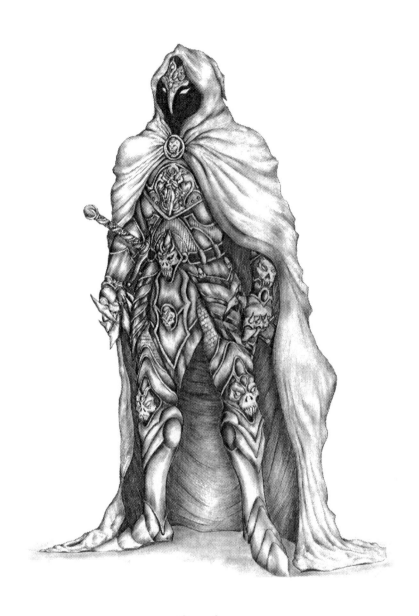

Sathar
The dark lord.

Seth
Elf, first of the Red,
protector of Queen Mother.

Tsandra
First of the Brown.

Vadan Evgej
Captain Evgej. Former Swordmaster,
city garrison at Quashan'.

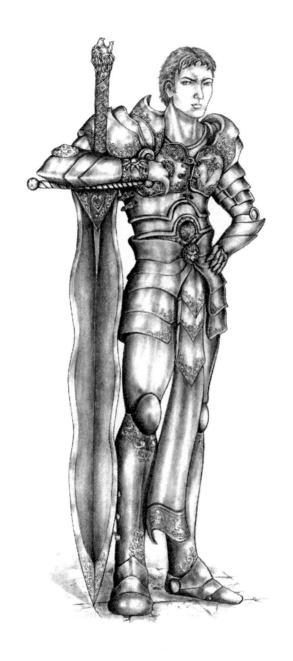

Valam Alder
Prince Valam. Only son of King
Andrew.

Vilmos Tabborrath
An apprentice of the forbidden
arcane arts.

Xith
Last of the Watchers.

Chapter One

With the death of Keeper Q'yer, the battle in the great hall began. Midori and Catrin were slow in recovering from the pain inside. Lord Fantyu, although close-by, was not quick enough to stop their assailants from reaching them. A mailed hand cuffed Catrin and knocked her backward. The large figure laughed as he watched her fall, tumbling down the tiered rows. He grabbed Midori by her long hair and pulled her close to him, close enough so she could feel his breath against her face, and the foulness of it revolted her.

The council members were in panic. They ran blindly toward the great doors, following each other to their deaths. Lord Serant could only watch as they were easily cut down, their blood running bright across the floor. His goal, as well as Captain Brodst's, was to get to safety with Calyin and anyone else who could follow. Although he did feel sorrow in his heart for the deaths of the others, he did not have time to wait for old men, and their end only made it easier for him to leave the chamber without regrets.

Lord Fantyu drew his sword and swiftly ran Midori's assailant through. The expression on the warrior's face went from shocked dismay to horror as he watched the tip of the blade thrust out of his abdomen. Lord Fantyu quickly withdrew his blade and delivered a slapping blow to an attacker that moved toward him from the side. His elbow was quick to follow, as was his sword. He grabbed Midori by the hand and pulled her away. "But Catrin?" she yelled.

Lord Fantyu ignored her words and retreated to the rear of the chamber, where Lord Serant and Captain Brodst had set up a defensive position. They had turned the long, oaken conference table onto its side and strewn the way with chairs piled high, standing at the ready, waiting for any aggressors to come their way.

Geoffrey watched and waited, conferring calmly with the two at his side. He pictured in his mind how the battle would unfold. He was unconcerned for his safety due to the presence of the four men who stood before him; he was absolutely confident of their ability to defend him.

Father Joshua withdrew his hand from Talem's face a third time and looked dead into the dark priest's eyes. "You will pay for your treachery!" he bellowed. Talem was by no account able to argue with him; his world spun before him, in dazzling shadings of black and white.

Lord Serant angrily glared around the hall. "Where was Pyetr? Damn it!" he cursed under his breath. His search stopped when he came upon the four kings, sitting relaxed in the same place they had occupied earlier. A very large contingent of guards was gathered around them, which did not move to join the fray. They stood at the ready with weapons waiting.

Lord Serant's eyes fell to the door that lay behind them; the ante-chamber was beyond. He wondered if they realized the door was there. He nudged Captain Brodst and carefully brought his attention to the door. Both realized what it meant, but they had no way to reach it.

The primary problem with that exit was the considerable number of foes they would have to engage to get to it; nevertheless, there were fewer men in the way of their escape in that direction, no matter how the two thought about it. The more Lord Serant pondered the possibility, the less he favored it. It was not worth the risk; there had to be another way.

The sentries, though outnumbered and overwhelmed, were holding their own. Of twenty, only ten remained. They watched with horror as the enemy continued to come at them in waves. Weapons danced in their hands with the sweat of their lives pouring into their every move. If they failed a block or parry, they were dead, and this they knew and understood very well.

"Damn it, Pyetr!" cursed Lord Serant aloud again. His heart raced with anxiety; his mind spun with possibilities, working through various plans of escape while his sword arm agitatedly held his weapon at his side. Anger and frustration suffused his face. He was forced to stand and watch and wait.

Similar thoughts were crossing Captain Brodst's mind. He too looked for any possible way to escape, and if luck befell him he would find a way past the kings' soldiers. For the first time, his attention moved to the keepers who still stood confused. The priests of the Father, who were not as quick to react as Father Joshua had been, stood directly adjacent to them.

Although he realized that they would be the next logical target for the foe, he held no hopes of assisting them. He must keep his thoughts clear. He did not need the extra baggage. The priests could hold their own for a time; the Father would not easily relinquish their positions on this plane. The keepers, however, were as useless as the High Council had been. He saw a similar fate for them.

Strength of will returned to Midori as she shook off the last of the effects of the dark priests' powers over her. She could not believe she had fallen for their mind tricks. She could not believe what she saw. She clutched her ceremonial dagger firmly in her hand. Her eyes fixed clearly, precisely on the front of the chamber.

Thoughts now raged within her. She sought out Father Joshua, but he was nowhere to be found. She knew none of the other priests of the Father by name. She did not, however, let that distract her from her search among them for one that would suit her needs.

Her eyes went wide with excitement and anticipation. "Catrin," she reached out in thought. The Mother had truly smiled upon them. She saw life within Catrin; Catrin was alive.

A gasp of dismay came from Lord Serant's lips as he watched the last of the sentries fall. It became obvious to him who the leader of the attackers was as he watched the last few rounds of melee. He fixed a cold, icy stare upon the leader and waited for the moment when the attack would come. "Pyetr!" he screamed out in his mind, "Damn it, man, hurry!"

He sighed in relief as his eyes fell upon a small contingent that took a position between him and the intruders. Lord Fantyu had taken up a position there with his men. Nine stood defiantly waiting. Lord Fantyu offered him a reassuring nod; the attackers would have to come through him first.

An idea came to Lord Serant; he turned and glared at Chancellor Volnej. His hand swiftly, subconsciously brought his blade to the chancellor's throat. "This is all your doing! Is it not? You traitorous dog!" he yelled as he spit in the chancellor's face. "You are not worth killing! I should feed you to a pack of wolves and let the vultures pick at your carcass after they are finished!"

Chancellor Volnej swallowed harshly, his face registering confusion. He didn't understand what Lord Serant was saying—a traitor. He was no traitor. "What are you saying? Are you mad?"

Chancellor Van'te was also confused. "Lord Serant, you must be mistaken. I have known the chancellor for a number of years; there is no way he is a traitor. Our enemy lies out there, not here!"

Lord Serant was abashed and confused. "Chancellor Volnej is a traitor; I can prove it!" he stated, his voice quavering uncertainly.

"Lord Serant, please! I beg you, do not act foolishly. Think about what you are saying," begged Chancellor Van'te.

Chancellor Volnej said nothing further in his defense. The tip of Serant's blade at his throat that did not move was more than enough to hold his tongue. He did not want to infuriate the obviously stressed lord with even the slightest provocation.

Chapter Two

Prince Valam Alder departed Leklorall, capital city of East Reach, with few regrets. In his mind, he tried to understand all that happened since he went with Queen Mother to Shalan's tower. The tower that symbolized the heart and soul of the people of East Reach. The tower that only Queen Mother could enter—except that he had entered the tower and now the tower was no more.

He thought about the child of east and west, the bearer of light and remembrance. The one who was also the child of past and present, the bearer of darkness. The one who also hid the angel of life and the key. Was this his child or another?

The thought of having a child suddenly hit him. It was strange to think about. He, the lord and prince of the south, was to be a father. Would he be ready when the time came? Would he know what to do? Would the queen even let him see the child? Was she even with child? Was this so certain?

Soshi had told him once that she was with child but later said she had been mistaken. Thoughts of Soshi, his first true love, brought thoughts of the old blind woman who said she'd lost her sight for the greater good. "The old ways are all but forgotten now," the old woman had told him. "The old gods were not gods at all, merely creatures of power, great power." When she blinded him with the white powder, she said that she gave him a gift. It was Soshi though who took the blindness from him so that he might see truth.

He wished he could see truth now and he longed for Soshi's soothing ways though he knew he should not. Still, first love was an enduring love and his desire did not fade as the morning did. Later he could only picture Queen Mother's face in his mind's eye.

Seth strode up alongside Valam. "There, Valam, that is where the Eastern Plains begin," he said pointing to the line where the trees and the gentle sloping hills were replaced by the tall grasses and flatness of the plains. The plains stretched beyond the horizon into the distance. Its stark beauty was in its vastness and simplicity.

Valam's response was slow as he returned from his reverie. "It seems so endless."

"At times, I think it is."

"Yes, it has a beauty unique to itself," whispered Tsandra to Seth and Valam; she had walked up quietly behind them to look out over the vantage point. "Seth," she began, directing the thought only into his mind, "Please leave us for a moment." Seth didn't refuse her request; he smiled and returned to their small encampment.

"Valam, I haven't until now had an opportunity to properly beg your forgiveness. I do so now. Please forgive my shortsightedness. I acted without thought. I know it is something that is not easily forgotten, and even less easy to forgive, but I say this from within my very center. I am truly sorry."

Valam started to turn around to face her, but she stopped him. "No, please don't. I could not finish if you did."

"But I do not understand. You have done nothing to offend me."

"Shh, listen. I, most of all, should have known that you would do nothing to harm our queen intentionally. I betrayed your friendship, but what I can never forgive myself for was that I also acted out of jealousy. I—"

"What are you—jealous?"

"I know it is wrong, but I am in love with you."

"Love? What? Wait—stop a minute—say that again."

"I am sorry. I have said too much already. Come, we should go."

Brushing the tears from her eyes, Tsandra retreated from the hilltop, leaving Valam completely baffled. He watched her go; he wanted to scream at her but did not. He remained alone on top of the hill and tried to rethink his actions.

He watched as the others saddled their horses in preparation to rejoin the trail, then walked down the hill to join them. In minutes they were back in the saddle trotting toward the plains, leaving behind no signs that they had ever stopped here. They traversed the short distance to the grasslands quickly. It was almost instantaneous, as Valam crossed into the tall grasses, that he began to feel a peculiar sense grow within him.

His eyes began to search the plains rapidly back and forth. He had sensed this feeling once before though he could not place it. His eyes followed down the line to Seth, Cagan, Evgej, Liyan, and finally Tsandra. Their eyes answered his unspoken question; they could also feel it.

With the passing of two days on the plain, the sensations only increased. The air began to grow colder and stronger, reaching sharply through their heavy riding clothes. Seth called a halt late in the afternoon. He held his hand up high, until the last of the group had formed and stopped.

"What's wrong?" asked Valam, wondering why they had stopped

so soon. Seth pointed to a spot on the plains where the wind blew up dust in patches. A whisper of thought entered their minds. Valam had heard the sounds shallow within his mind before. He strained to concentrate only on listening. He could tell the sounds were words, but they were too weak to understand.

"I am Brother Seth, first of the order of the Red!" said Seth, reaching out with his mind. Valam perceived the thrust of Seth's energies like an explosion within his mind. He clenched his teeth tightly and immediately covered his ears. Evgej's reactions also brought his hands speedily to his ears. Although the action did nothing to curb the intensity of the burst of sound in their minds, it did appease their senses.

"Come! It is Brother Teren!" exclaimed Seth as he firmly swatted his steed with his tethers. The two groups of riders raced towards one another. It was not until the other group was in clear view that Valam realized that it was composed mainly of men. By the size and outfitting of the group, he estimated that it must be a scouting party, which Valam hoped to mean that the camp was close at hand.

"Supplies at last!" shouted Mikhal as he approached. He dropped to his feet quickly and knelt, with his head bowed in reverence. He did not allow the icy snow slapping his face to deter his moment of silence. "My prince, you live!" he shouted with a joyful voice, as he stood with his head still bowed.

Words fluttered to Valam's tongue; he knew the man, but couldn't remember his name or title. He tried to think carefully, although quickly, searching for a name to match the face, but he was puzzled and Chancellor Van'te wasn't there to whisper in his ear. What was the man referring to? Of course, he was alive. Valam tried to picture a name for the face he saw, "Mikhal," flashed into his thoughts.

"Prince Valam, we thought you dead. We thought the storm took you. Oh, thanks be to the Father!" shouted Captain Mikhal. Images spun through the captain's mind. His thoughts carried him back and swept him away.

"A storm *is* going to take us if we don't hurry!" whispered Liyan into Seth's mind.

Seth turned to face Liyan. "Yes, you are right. I sense heavy snows. An odd season, is it not?"

"More than that, I suspect," directed Liyan into Seth's mind alone.

"I am Captain Mikhal; this is Lieutenant Danyel'," said the captain as he watched **Valam** search for words.

"Captain Mikhal, yes, 'Lieutenant Danyel,' curious," said Prince Valam. "It is good to **find** you."

They rapidly went through the remainder of the introductions. As Brother Teren took the lead, the winds suddenly changed directions, bringing in a gale from the northeast. The new wind had an instant chilling effect as it touched bare skin. Evgej and Valam wrapped their cloaks tightly around them.

Evgej didn't much care for the cold; as it touched his face and hands, he cursed it. He would much rather be in the warmth of his southerly homeland. Quashan' was rarely visited by harsh cold, and even more rarely with snow. As the group turned in a northerly direction, his teeth began to chatter.

Snow descended from the sky in large flurries. Evgej was growing agitated in the saddle. He had to keep moving around to gain warmth. Evgej could see from Valam's staunch features that he wasn't reacting to the cold as much.

"Do you think he will come before the snows fade?" whispered Seth into Liyan's thoughts.

"I believe we must wait to see, but if he is a wise man, he will wait."

"Yes, as would I."

"These snows are out of place and time. They will soon trap us indoors; let us hope these men have built adequate shelters."

"We have nothing to fear; Keeper Martin and Father Jacob are smart men."

"The weather along the coast should be considerably milder than here," commented Liyan, as he squinted in the face of the heavy snowfall; a mild, tingling sensation against his face spoke of the cold without; otherwise, he did not feel it though he did think it a dark tiding.

Valam drifted back in thought. Images wandered through his mind as life-size pictures against the white backdrop of the snow. He saw the Queen-Mother in those images, and he whispered out the name she had told him only he could call her. He was careful to use the mind controls Seth had taught him to mask his open thoughts, so his words did not drift into the others' consciousness by mistake.

Brother Teren raised a gloved hand high. Although the gesture was scarcely visible, it was seen by the rider behind him and was passed on to those behind him. Thus, the signal to halt was passed to the rear. With a dour countenance, Teren dismounted and led his mount back to Seth and Liyan. The walk was more a formality than a necessity, for he could have directed his thoughts to Seth or Liyan instead, which would have been more forceful than his spoken words.

Seth's response was just as exaggerated; he wished to continue, no matter the odds. A delay in the open plains could prove fatal; they could be snowed in indefinitely. They would continue on, even if they must travel into the night.

"Not much like home anymore, is it, Seventh?" called out Captain Mikhal to the man who rode close at his side. Danyel' waved his head negatively in response although snow wasn't that unusual a sight for him. He had spent many long winters in the northern sectors of the kingdom. It wasn't that he liked it or disliked it—mostly, he was indifferent to it.

Although Teren could no longer see his way, he could feel it. He had visited this prairie many times, as had the snows. His native sense of direction was extraordinarily strong, an important attribute of any good scout, He knew where the camp of men lay along the coast, and the Father willing, he would lead everyone to it.

A startled emotion flowed to Tsandra, who had been riding solemnly with those of her order. She steered her horse mid-group and charged without thought, issuing rapid summons for those of the Brown to follow her and prepare.

Her thoughts reached Seth and Liyan in disarray, and caused the remainder of the group to come to a sudden halt. Seth was confused, as was Liyan; they didn't understand what Tsandra had perceived. Seth sent questions to her mind, but her thoughts were scattered and unreachable.

Valam raced his mount toward Seth; his voice wavered as he shouted his questions. Tsandra's words had been sent frantically. They had been in the words of Seth's people, but he had only caught a few words. As Valam approached, it became obvious to him that Seth was also confused, yet he asked again anyway, "What is it? What did she see?"

Seth's response was that he did not know either, but she had told them to wait until she returned. So they would wait until she returned.

"Can you ask her again?" queried Valam.

"I have tried but her thoughts are unreachable."

"Unreachable?"

"She is confused."

"Confused?" asked Valam, adding when Seth didn't respond to the thought that lay heavily on his mind, "Is this what you call mild snows?"

"This is an odd storm. I assure you the coast is clear and tranquil compared to this. The sea breezes are much more forgiving than those of the plains."

Brother Teren, also of the Brown, charged after Tsandra, screaming out, "No! Don't!" to her mind, but her thoughts were closed. He spurred his mount several times, chiding it to go faster. "What are you doing? No, don't! Leave him alone!"

Tsandra released her right leg from the stirrups, carefully securing her left. She leaned outward and downward with her arms, ready to snatch up the tiny scurrying form as it raced away. She grabbed the figure, with its legs still flailing the air as she picked it up, and tucked it close beside her, sending her followers out in all directions in search of any others.

The child muttered something Tsandra didn't understand, biting her hand immediately afterwards, causing her to release her grip. Tsandra jumped from her mount and chased the child. Her feet slipped as they hit the icy ground. As she grabbed the tiny figure again, she fell face first.

"Brother Tsandra, I implore you. He means no harm. He is my

shadow," forced Teren into Tsandra's mind.

"What do you mean shadow? Why is he following us?"

"He is not following you. He is following me."

"Why?" demanded Tsandra.

"He always does. Let him go, and I'll explain."

As Tsandra released the boy, he scurried away, his short legs weaving a blur, very quickly carrying him to a distance where he felt safe. Teren pushed thoughts and images into Tsandra's mind as they hurried back to the group. Tsandra recalled her warriors and movement slowly restarted; the dark storm attained full fury during the delay and was not dealing with them kindly.

"Explain?" demanded Tsandra into Teren's mind, letting him know that it was a subtle order, which she as the first could make, and that it demanded a quick, precise response.

"He is an orphan. He has been following me for a very long time. Do not let his size fool you; he is quite capable of surviving on his own. He has endured worse storms than this, and the fact that you sensed his presence was not an accident, as you would think. He wanted you to notice him although I don't know why."

"Why haven't you found him a suitable family to dwell with?"

"He would not go. Again, you only sensed him because he wanted you to. Most often, I only know he is there by a presence at the edges of my awareness."

"Nevertheless, I caught him, didn't I, where you couldn't. I could have helped him."

"He was only playing with you."

"Playing with me?"

As Tsandra rode angrily away, Teren didn't regret her later scorn. There was no worse place she could send him to and no better.

Contrary to what Tsandra thought, Teren really loved roaming the plains, even in the face of storms such as the one they now endured.

Cagan, who wouldn't have missed this trip for anything, was having second thoughts. Clumps of thick, wet snow fell upon them, sticking and forming tiny mounds and layers on clothing, equipment, and everything else it touched. He was mutely thinking that if he had remained at the capital, he could at the very least have watched the wind fill the sails of his craft while it was moored at the docks. He would have run the sails up for the occasion. But now instead of rolling waves beneath his feet, he had saddle sores.

The snowfall grew so thick that Teren thought it better to dismount and lead his horse rather than ride. There was nothing he could mistakenly lead them into along this open span. He felt closer to Mother-Earth as he walked across the thick grasses of the plains and it allowed him to maintain his sense of bearing. The animal also needed a reprieve. It was instinctively cautious about traveling under such foul conditions. Being led reassured it.

The pack animals were becoming heavily bogged down under their burdens. The group was forced to stop frequently and remove the mounds of snow from them, most especially from the protectors over the animals' eyes. The snow still had a wetness to it that made it cling to everything it touched. An animal that could not see would not move, no matter how much it was coaxed.

The thick grass they traversed still afforded them fair traction even with inches of snow piled deep onto it, but ever so rapidly the last signs of the grasses were disappearing. Teren stopped the group again and went back to counsel Liyan and Seth. Although his eyes chanced upon Tsandra, who was close-by, he did not acknowledge her presence in his conversation with the two. His suggestion was to construct a shelter here where they stood, while they still had the means and the illumination of day. Although the odd storm obscured the light, it was still better than it would be after dark.

Chapter Three

With the arrival of Nijal and Shchander, the curious company was complete. Xith, Amir, Noman, and the others would now go to the last place the dark lord would expect. They would journey straight into the heart of darkness itself to confront the darkness sweeping the land before the darkness confronted them.

Crossing the Wall of the World at night was a dangerous gamble but a gamble that was accomplished without accident or incident. The company entered the thick woodlands of the Western Territories, traveling day and night for two full days before slowing the pace. The distance did little to quell Xith's nerves. His mind was continually on edge since Vilmos left them. He had failed. He had tempted fate and lost; its sting upon him was as a thousand lashes against his innermost self. He had altered the paths, and they were now lost to him. He felt the convergence sweep in, but nothing beyond.

Yet most puzzling among his many disconcerted, disconnected thoughts was the whereabouts of Ayrian. Although intuition told him Ayrian was not dead, he could not conceive another fate for him. In his mind, Ayrian slowly ceased to exist as hope of his sudden re-appearance waned. He was greatly saddened by this because Ayrian was the last of the mighty eagle lords.

The thoroughfares they traveled, although they were the primary connection between the kingdom and the outlying cities of the territories, were wildly overgrown in many areas. Progress along them with a carriage was slow and tedious. Xith sat absent-mindedly holding the reins in much the same manner that he had chastised Nijal for previously, watching the team of horses plod along the path.

Amir rode beside Noman, honing his muscles with a series of tiny contractions and relaxations, being careful to stretch them after they became fatigued; thus, he maintained his awareness and he was not the only one in the company to feel increasing unease. He took every opportunity, although they were few, to wrest his sword from its sheath. Nijal was often his companion, willing or not, but most times willing. Shchander sometimes joined in with Nijal, making it two against one, to give Amir a challenge, but he was most comfortable watching.

Noman was also content to observe. He spent most of this waking hours reflecting on the turnings of the Path. He enjoyed the intellectual conversations he and Xith would have late in the evenings, which as of late had been of varied lengths, usually lasting well after the two should have retired to get adequate sleep for the next day's travels. Sometimes he would secretly cast the sticks, playing at the game of Destiny though he knew he should not.

Since their passage into the forest, the company had switched their practice of traveling in darkness, for the path was extremely treacherous at night even with the talented Amir leading the way. Noman put to full use the hours that would have been wasted. He sent Amir to search for any signs that they were being followed or tracked. He sent Nijal and Shchander in search of game for their food stocks, as the supplies were running short. Both searches were fruitful.

Adrina whiled away days in relative solitude within the confines of the carriage. Nijal seemed to ignore her presence since Shchander's arrival, not that she blamed him. She could see that the two were old acquaintances, and they had much catching up to do; nonetheless, she felt left out.

She picked up scattered bits of Shchander's stories of Imtal through Nijal, only enough to arouse her curiosity but not enough to quench it. She was very glad to hear that Calyin and Lord Serant were in the Great Kingdom. From time to time she would unconsciously massage the fingers of her hand, soothing away a pain that was no longer there. Nijal remained the only one who knew of the mark upon her. She told no one else and made sure Nijal didn't speak of it.

Within the cover of the forest, Xith allowed Adrina to open the central window's curtains. The view of the forest as it passed by was often beautiful, pristine, and peaceful. The smell of the evergreens with a touch of moisture from the morning's dew powerfully massaged her senses. A feeling of happiness flowed within her.

Under the thick shield of the forest, nightfall became apparent only as the last of the shadows merged and became a mass of blackness, which also signaled a halt to the day's trek. Amir, Shchander, and Nijal worked out a suitable place for them to stop, one that offered sufficient concealment. Camp was set up in a matter of minutes; no time was wasted in obtaining food or rest. The watch shifts had long since been worked into a routine and all knew when their turn would be.

Morning arrived crisp and clear although no one within the

forest's domain knew it. Amir greeted the bird's joyful salutes to the new day with one of his own, which brought immediate silence to the area around him. He had breakfast sizzling over a makeshift spit before anyone else awoke—two fat rabbits, whose juices oozed down into the hot coals, producing an aroma that permeated the camp.

Feeling a presence behind him, Amir whipped around quickly. "Morning," quietly intoned Nijal, with a smile on his lips. Amir knowingly shook his head and returned Nijal's greeting. "Good, very good. Keep up the practice, but next time don't disturb the ground you walk over."

"What? You didn't even know I was there until a moment ago."

"You broke a twig three steps back, but you are getting better," said Amir, handing Nijal a piece of meat. Amir watched Nijal eat, studying his movements before he ate. Noman and Xith soon joined them around the small fire; without a word they sat down and divided the remainder of the first rabbit between them.

"Where is Shchander?" asked Xith of Nijal.

Nijal shrugged his shoulders. He didn't know. The last time he had seen Shchander was when he had relieved him from first watch. Nijal didn't let the thought slow down his appetite. He hurriedly finished the large section of leg and grabbed another one.

As usual Adrina was the last to arrive; her face was pale and her eyes still had sleep in them. Nevertheless, she had a cheerful smile on her face as she sat down next to Nijal. She wasn't particularly hungry this morning, even though the aroma of food brought a desire to try some. She picked at a piece of meat while the others ate, and then handed the remainder to Nijal, who didn't refuse it, and just as quickly finished it.

"How many days do you estimate until Zashchita?" asked Amir, making conversation with Xith more for Nijal's benefit than his own.

"At the very least a passing."

"Two weeks is a long time."

"And Krepost'?"

"I would count on an almost equal amount of time."

Nijal asked "We are going all the way to Krepost'?"

"Yes, we are."

"But, I thought—"

"Nijal, don't worry. I can see it on your face."

Nijal frowned and drank from his water skin. The water tasted good although he would have preferred something else. Afterwards, he passed it to Amir, which was the polite thing to do. "But two turnings?" said Nijal, dishearteningly. "It's—"

"Such a long time," completed Noman.

"It will be gone before you realize it has passed," added Xith.

"Shchander," said Adrina, "come and eat."

"What's wrong?" she said again, waving to him to join them.

Amir readily detected something out of place. He dropped the skin of water to the ground without thought and stood drawing his blade as he did so. Nijal was next to follow him toward Shchander. Xith and Noman responded by whisking Adrina away in the opposite direction.

"I wouldn't do that if I were you," spoke Shchander.

As his words fell upon the air, men stepped out of the forest's cover. They were clad in distinctive heavy leathers and the poise of their weapons in their hands spoke of their skill. Amir slowly moved backward towards the center of the camp, not taking his eyes off

Shchander, unsure whether or not Shchander supported the attackers.

Nijal moved in behind Amir and covered his back. He watched as Xith, Noman, and Adrina also moved back into the middle of the camp as their avenue of escape also closed. The four stood, watching and waiting, as the men approached, with Adrina carefully maneuvered into relative cover between them.

Chapter Four

Geoffrey's elite group paused a moment before charging into battle. Each whispered the free man's creed in their thoughts, "I am a free man, and I will die as such." The first four men moved as one, dividing the onslaught precariously between them. Quickly they defeated the attackers, splitting them into pairs that they picked apart with their four blades.

"I beg you again, Lord Serant," said Lord Fantyu. "No offense is worth a man's life, and right now we need every person here to join the fight to win our freedom. Chancellor Volnej could not be your traitor. Did you not know that King Jarom had his parents executed when they returned to Vostok?"

"I thought they lived here in Imtal until they passed."

"No, that is false," simply answered Chancellor Volnej. "King Jarom had them put to death for treason. They loved your kingdom and for it they died. Do not dishonor their memory with your words. I beg you. I am no traitor. I love this land also. I would die for it, but please do not let my end come thus. It would bring shame upon my family, and there would be none to clear my name."

Geoffrey scowled at King Jarom, who was no more than fifty yards away, seated smugly behind the wall of his men. Words flowed from the king's mouth and a large contingent of his bodyguards moved to join the battle at the front entrance. Geoffrey and the governors reacted immediately and met them mid-way.

Sheer numbers soon overpowered them as the small force was faced with two enemy detachments coming from different directions. Geoffrey cursed and spat into the man's face in front of him, but the warrior didn't hesitate in his attack. Geoffrey offered a wry smile, and responded with a block.

Lord Serant, although puzzled, didn't have time for further consideration of the chancellor's words; his thoughts immediately returned to the fight. His thoughts had never left the front entrance to the hall; subconsciously, he had been weighing his options. He watched as the assailants poured into the chamber uninhibited; the last of Geoffrey's men had fallen. Geoffrey was alone; now was the time to act before it was too late. He had entirely given up hope of reinforcements arriving in time, if at all.

Lord Fantyu was through waiting. Before Serant could stop him, he vaulted over their blockade and charged for the door. Captain Brodst was quick to follow him, with sword in hand. He had already carefully considered the odds and had decided his own fate.

Sister Catrin shook the wavering images from her thoughts and stood. The blow to the head had done her more good than harm. She was absolved, cleansed of the dark priests' treachery. A thought stuck out in her mind, crossing from her subconscious to her conscious. She surveyed the room and gathered her bearings.

Midori's whereabouts were first priority on Sister Catrin's list as she was the first to the Mother and must be safeguarded at all cost. If Midori was safe, her next priority was Calyin. The keepers and priests offered her no concern, although she did reprimand them. "Buffoons!" she yelled.

Her thoughts paused a second more on the priests. Father Joshua—where was Father Joshua? She searched around the chamber but found no sign of him. Movement caught her eye, a struggle. She now knew where he was; unfortunately, the enemy had already taken him.

Although extremely fatigued, Geoffrey raised his blade again to defend. The shine in his eyes faded to the darkness of his weary soul. His companions fought valiantly, but they, like him, were only mortal. He did not grieve their loss. They died as they had lived, and for that he was thankful.

Lord Serant was faced with an ominous decision. He no longer expected support to come, so now he must act, but with wisdom. Princess Calyin calmly stood at his side, also carefully watching and waiting. She knew how to defend herself; and if the time came, she was sure that she would make King Jarom feel her wrath.

Lord Fantyu sidestepped the first attacker to charge; as he did so, he pushed the man directly into Captain Brodst's waiting blade. The warrior fell to his knees clutching the blade as he went down. Captain Brodst retracted his blade and stepped over the body to Lord Fantyu's side.

Catrin's mind worked quickly and similarly to Midori's. She held no hope of reaching Father Joshua. Although he would have been the most suitable, she turned to the other priests. She did not take back her words of moments ago in any way; she only did what had to be done.

Midori had identical intentions running through her mind as she rapidly assessed each in turn. The priest with the strongest will was her choice. She thought he would be a good choice, even more than Father Joshua. Now she had only to reach him. Sister-Catrin had chosen the same priest to link with, but Midori was the first to reach him, and he willingly conceded to the link of the Mother and the Father; together they would unite the two wills and unleash their powers upon King Jarom's forces. They would make him pay.

Chancellor Van'te and Chancellor Volnej, although up in years, held fast to their positions beside Lord Serant and Princess Calyin as they all sought to escape. They held their blades, a short sword the captain had discarded, and a long dagger from Lord Fantyu as they followed Lord Fantyu and the captain, lagging only a short space behind them. They stood proudly, defiantly, in the separation between Lord Serant and Lord Fantyu, waiting and ready.

A defensive position only served a purpose as long as it held the hope of adding to one's resistance. Lord Serant no longer saw such a purpose for the spot they were in. He saw only an end if they remained—a sure, absolute one. His mind was clear although it was alive with scattered observations. Movement was the only alternative he saw that remained for them.

Midori felt a whirlwind of power collide in her center as her will joined with that of the priest beside her. She prepared mentally for the ripping force of the Mother and Father to flow through them as they became one. Although she had never felt it before, she knew it must come. She waited, holding her breath in anticipation; it did not come. Shocked, she backed away from the priest, her eyes wide with disillusionment.

Midori, in disbelief, formed the union again. She quickly completed the link, only momentarily pausing before she joined. She felt the force of wills connect within her, as she had before, but the warmth did not flow to her. She saw no images in her mind; the link quickly fell away, and she knew unequivocally at that moment that the Father and Mother had abandoned them.

"Now!" screamed Father Joshua, with all his strength, to his compatriots as he was being subdued. He reached out for the will of the Father, which he could not find. He attempted to scream a warning to his brethren, but a gloved hand sealed his mouth. The priests of the Father descended into the swarm of invaders, pushing them back momentarily.

Lord Serant seized the opportunity. He grabbed Calyin by the hand and clutched it tightly, indicating that she should follow him closely, and that he loved her. Carefully, he scrutinized the field before him. He made a direct line to the right of the hall, straight for King Jarom, and, he hoped, freedom.

Lord Fantyu was quick to note the direction Serant was taking. He and the captain held a line safeguarding Lord Serant and Calyin's passage, slowly moving alongside them, while the two chancellors prepared to block to the right although the only thing ahead in the direction they moved was a large group of King Jarom's body guards, who stood steadfast at their positions.

As they made a headlong charge towards the group, it became obvious that King Jarom had not anticipated such a maneuver, as his attentions were directed to the priests' demise. He was taking great pleasure, as one by one they fell before his men. His voice boomed throughout the hall with his hideous, raucous laughter. The others seated beside him did not share in his joyous mood. King Peter and King Alexas sat with faces rigid, afraid to look about the hall but not ashamed of their deeds either. They were quite grateful that Andrew rested with the Father, for now they had no one's revenge to fear. King William held his head low in shame; he had had no choice but to concede to King Jarom's wishes.

King Jarom's guards were slow to move and react, as their king had ordered them not to move and they greatly feared his scorn. They did not move to engage until Lord Serant and the others were fully upon them.

Father Joshua managed to raise his voice about the hall one more time before he was belted across the head, and his world faded to black before his eyes. "Ywentir, never forget!" His words were enough to incite fury into the keepers' hearts, and enough to motivate their disheartened spirits, and the final spell dissolved.

Lord Serant said a hurried prayer to the Father as he saw the keepers stir to action. Lord Serant told Calyin to follow the two chancellors wherever they took her and to stay with them at all cost. His voice fell on the last word as he dove, arms and sword stretched wide, onto a group of guardsmen, knocking three of them down with him.

Lord Fantyu masterfully pummeled with the hilt of his sword while blocking another blow with his blade, the hilt catching his would-be assailant directly in the face.

As he blocked the second, he brought his knee up into the man's groin, followed by an elbow to the back of the head. Captain Brodst cleaned up to the right, while Lord Fantyu attacked again to the left, his overbearing power with a sword readily apparent as he sent blows of metal against metal, bringing the edge of his sword always to flesh.

King Jarom's verbal abuse against his men was enough to stir them into frenzied, thoughtless attacks. Serant was quick to his feet. He didn't waste any time, as he covered the two chancellors and Calyin's retreat. He could see the door was within their reach as he turned back toward King Jarom. Only four men separated him from revenge, which his honor demanded that he have.

Lord Fantyu felt a sudden cold feeling that sent chills running up his back. Numbness swept over him. He bit his cheek; his sword did not falter as he followed through, bringing another of the enemies down before him. He felt the blade withdraw from his back, and winced, but he continued to fight.

"Don't be a fool!" yelled Captain Brodst to Lord Serant, "Get out of here now!" He pushed Lord Serant out of the way and engaged the two who stood before him. As he turned to sweep through with his sword, he saw the blade withdraw from Lord Fantyu, but he could not move to help him. Anger flowed through him and into his hands, as he hammered down with all his might on the foe before him.

Lord Fantyu moved in close beside Captain Brodst. His energy visibly slowed as blood dripped from his mouth. "Go! I'll cover you!"

"I will go nowhere! I'm here to cover you, remember," spoke Captain Brodst as he blocked.

"Like you covered my backside!" said Lord Fantyu, sounding harsh, but not meaning it. "Go before it's too late!"

"If I go, you're coming with me," said Captain Brodst, as he blocked again.

"We'll stand and fight together, my friend."

"Yes," said the captain as he watched Lord Serant hack down the last man who stood between him and the door, safely making his exit.

"Are you ready?" asked Lord Fantyu, as he watched a group of warriors break through the disarray in the center of the chamber. He elbowed the captain to gain his attention in that direction momentarily. Geoffrey of Solntse yet lived. He was buried amidst a mass of bodies. Only the glimmer of his full-handed sword raised high caught Lord Fantyu's eye.

Lord Fantyu was slow parrying, and a blow glanced across his shoulder, slicing through his mail, but not wounding him. Captain Brodst paused, and instead of attacking, he opted to defend quickly both right and left, taking the brunt of two attacks momentarily to give his partner a reprieve. "Have you said your prayers?" asked Captain Brodst, indicating they should push forward to where Geoffrey stood.

"Yes, I am ready to go, but not until I take a few more of them with me," grunted Lord Fantyu, as he struggled to maintain his balance.

"If we go, it will be together!" added Midori, as she and Catrin finally managed a short retreat to the spot where the two stood. "Through there—" she further added, indicating the door to the antechamber. "Yes, but first we will help out our friend," said Lord Fantyu. "We cannot abandon one with such skill and bravado."

Chapter Five

"Brother Teren, I believe we must continue on. We cannot afford to stop now. We will push through the night if necessary."

"Yes, I back Liyan also. As you have told us, you promised Keeper Martin and Father Jacob we would arrive within the week. They need these supplies we bring."

"Brother Seth, Brother Liyan, I hear your wisdom, but you do not know the nights on the plains. It will be unbearable."

"We will endure; we must endure. I believe you can get us safely to the coast. I trust in you."

"As do I," added Seth.

Brother Teren, devout in his commitment, pulled the hood of his cloak up tight around his face and walked back into the face of the storm. The wind blasting south only added to the tumultuous flurries surging from the skies overhead. He noticed a conscious twinge of power against his will and cast a feeling of impatience back at Tsandra.

At a lethargic pace, the party began moving again. Teren was very careful to insure that the entire group was behind them as they did so. As he reached his thoughts back to the last section, he was sure all was in order, and he increased the pace ever so slightly.

Seth urged his mount to move onward though the beast would

have preferred to remain still. He whispered to Liyan and then moved back to where Valam and Evgej rode. Seth voiced concerns to Valam over their previous debate. Evgej was quick to add that he was also concerned.

"This storm, what will it be like when it is at its full fury?" asked Evgej.

"Its power comes and goes. It is a natural cycle."

"This is not natural," directed Liyan to the three.

"What do you mean?" asked Valam.

"Brother Seth and I have been discussing this storm and its origins. I believe it is not natural, that it is an omen. A dark omen."

"Have you spoken with Brother Teren about this?"

"We have considered it, but will wait till a better time."

Evgej offered a scowl, to which Valam quickly appended, "I think we should have that discussion now. Brother Teren knows these plains."

Liyan nodded to Seth. Seth rode off in search of Teren. Shortly afterward, Liyan joined the brothers of the Brown. Valam could see the elder riding alongside Tsandra. Tsandra cast glum stares in Valam's direction as the night moved quickly in about them, carrying with it more cursed cold.

The snowflakes became crystalline as all the moisture in them solidified. Contrary to what Seth had hoped, the snow did not stop, nor did it slow; it maintained its barrage on them ever so efficiently.

The bite of the cold, especially in places that they could not adequately cover, grew beyond numbness to pain. Valam removed the gloves from his hands and touched the warmth to his face. A burning sensation swelled through his cheeks and nose. No matter how tightly he wrapped his hooded cloak about him, it did not shield his face.

Valam and Evgej were at a disadvantage as the darkness fell about them. They did not have the gift of Seth's kind to communicate amongst themselves with thought. He doubted his tongue would move if it were necessary; or perhaps, he thought, it would freeze solid mid-sentence if he attempted to speak.

Captain Mikhal and Lieutenant Danyel' followed closely behind Valam and Evgej. Cagan made up the fifth of their tiny group. In front of and behind the five stretched a long caravan of horses and riders although they were the only such grouping amongst the entire party. They rode with a length of rope between them to mark their distances as visibility faded to obscurity. The others had no need for any such bonding. They had their link.

Liyan searched the sky with his eyes, looking for patches of scattered heavenly light, but he saw only blackness. He cast a sour feeling to Seth's mind, to which Seth responded with an equally glum expression. After hours of riding through the darkness, Liyan felt as if they had only moved inches; to him it was if the winds held them at bay and for each step they moved forward it pushed them back an equal measure.

A feeling of despair surged amongst them and even though they would not admit its presence, it was there. They were as weary as the animals they rode upon, especially those heavy with packs. Liyan's propensity for thought was muddled by his exhaustion, another feeling which was pervasive; luckily, his other faculties were still mostly intact. Common sense told him they must stop now, and Liyan answered its call.

"Brother Teren!" he called out with his mind. "We must rest, the animals as well as ourselves."

"If we pause, we will not be able to begin again," answered Teren.

"As you said earlier, this I know."

"If it is your will, then it is so."

"It is."

"Then so be it," responded Teren in thought, while he reached out and touched the minds of those who followed him as one. "My brothers, we will wait out the storm here."

"Can we survive the night here?" asked Liyan, of only Teren's mind.

"If it is the Mother's will."

Tsandra approached the foremost group. "Why do we stop now?" she demanded of Liyan; the words were a spontaneous reaction to Teren's thought. She did not even consider the possibility that it was Liyan's idea that they stop until she reached out with her words to his center. As she did so, she bit back further comment.

"How can we endure this cold?" asked Seth, as he dismounted. Scattered sparks of light lit the sky as torches were raised on the extreme ends of the party. The lights were drawn together as the group formed a closely packed circle.

"The answer, Brother Seth, is beneath your feet."

"The snow. How brilliant!" answered Seth as he touched Teren's mind and Teren's thoughts. "What of the animals?"

"With luck, they will survive also."

Seth returned confused thoughts; Teren had obviously been in this situation before. Teren led the way and the others followed his example. He raised two mounds of snow around him and formed them into walls. Teren explained as he moved through the steps. He positioned the junction of the two walls into the wind, raising it upward to shield him from the chilling effects of the wind.

Cold, tired bodies moved cold, tired hands in a fevered attempt to raise a shelter from the storm. The first thing they did was to release the burdens from their animals and then they followed Teren's example. Teren showed them how to form the walls together, connecting in a series of staggered angles.

The work stirred warmth into their muscles. Seth paused a moment and slumped down beside Teren and Liyan. Valam and Evgej also took a moment's reprieve and joined them. Evgej closed his eyes as he sat down; the warmth returning to his body felt so good. "Do not let the lull of warmth blind your thoughts, Brother Evgej," whispered Teren, "the warmth will carry you off into the winds of the night."

"Say that again," said Evgej, drowsily.

Teren touched the palm of his hand to Evgej's brow. He held it there only a second before he removed it.

"Valam, Seth, remove the gloves from his hands. Liyan, pull off his other boot," thought Teren into their minds quickly, as he removed Evgej's right boot. "Quickly remove his cloak. Seth, remove your gloves as well. Follow my example." Teren washed Evgej's foot in the snow, massaging the foot with his hands. "Seth, can you feel the will within him?"

"Are you mad?" screamed Valam, "The snow will kill him!"

"Valam, please just listen to me, or else Evgej will die."

"Yes, but it is shallow."

The urgency of Teren's message within Valam's thoughts was all the proof he needed of Teren's sincerity. From then on, he did exactly what Teren told him to do. "Evgej, can you feel this?" asked Teren as he pinched Evgej's foot.

"Yes," responded Evgej.

"Can you feel this?" asked Teren again.

"Yes."

Teren looked to the others; he had not touched Evgej's foot a second time. "Keep massaging his hands in the snow," Teren told the others while he talked to Evgej. "Can you feel the movement of your fingers?"

"Yes."

Teren told them to stop, and asked the question again.

"No."

"Good, good!" responded Teren. Teren continued to work frantically over Evgej, directing the other three as he went. "This is exactly what I feared. We must be astute during this night, or none of us will reach the morning." Teren carefully chose words to remind all present of the effects of the cold against their limbs and their lives. Forcefully, he reminded them to remember above all else to keep moving. "Do not let your bodies slow. Guard your will. Maintain close watch over your mount. Do not let it wander away, but make sure it also stays mobile. Be wary. If one bolts, all the animals will bolt."

"Will Evgej be all right?" asked Valam. His mind bristled with thoughts, none of which were pleasant. He wondered how Captain Mikhal and Lieutenant Danyel' fared, as they also were not used to severe cold weather. He blamed himself for Evgej's condition; common sense should have told him to ensure Evgej was wary.

"Yes, I believe he will be fine, but we must keep him warm," responded Teren while he directed into Evgej's mind another question.

"Ouch!" yelled Evgej, "That hurt!"

"Good! Keep moving your toes."

The amount of wood they had for burning only amounted to a scattered stockpile of torches, which would provide little heat even if they threw every last one into a pile and burned them. Besides, they needed to save the torches and a dwindling stack of wood used for cooking. It wasn't much, since most of their food stocks were dried, but at best they could warm their ale over it, which is what they decided to do. They were given the opportunity to get warm liquid into their bellies before they settled in to endure the remainder of the long night.

Fortunately, the cold had not deeply touched many others. Valam surmised from what he saw that Seth's people had a much greater tolerance for the cold. Valam dreaded the many sleepless hours that lay ahead. As he saw Captain Mikhal and Lieutenant Danyel' move from the long line huddled around the dwindling fire, he motioned for them to join him.

He was sitting alone. Seth and Liyan had helped Evgej to the fire. The three were still there, sitting around it. He could see from the expression on Evgej's face that life was returning to his veins. Captain Mikhal and the lieutenant followed Valam's lead and sat upon their packs, to avoid sitting on the cold earth.

The walls of snow shielded them well from the chilling effects of the wind, but the storm's rage still found its way to them. "How do you think Keeper Martin and Father Jacob fare?" asked Valam of the captain as more of a conversation opener than anything else although he was interested in hearing more about the two.

"They are tough men. I am sure they are fine," replied Mikhal.

"Do you know much of these plains?"

"Yes, we have been very thorough in our scouting."

"Then you were on a scouting expedition from the camp when we met you?"

"Well—"

"Yes," responded Danyel'.

"How many days had you been away from the encampment?"

The captain paused, and then Danyel' answered the question, "I had been gone from the camp three days when I met Brother Teren. He had seen something that piqued his interest and asked our group to ride along. Unfortunately, Keeper Martin sent Captain Mikhal in search of my group when we did not return to camp on time. They met up with us just hours before we met your group."

"Then, Captain Mikhal, you probably know best how affairs are at the camp. Are spirits good? How goes the training?"

"Training goes well."

"Have you been able to carry on Seth's training?"

"Yes, you would be surprised at the enthusiasm. After the initial confusion, or should I say rather bluntly, disdain, a certain fascination caught most everyone."

Valam nodded his head in approval. Silence fell between them, and Captain Mikhal muddled over thoughts in his mind. He considered telling Valam of Keeper Martin's plan to return to the Great Kingdom if supplies did not come. He didn't know how Valam would take news like that. He just hoped the keeper and Father Jacob would hold out an extra week as they had planned although tomorrow would mark the seventh day of his absence.

"Tell me more of the lands in the vicinity," requested Valam, ever shifting his thoughts to concerns for the future. "Seth has told me a little, but I want to hear it from a viewpoint I can relate to. Have you seen signs of the enemy?"

The captain and the lieutenant took turns depicting all the details they could recall about the countryside they had explored. Valam was very careful to note each detail they gave him; his mind fed on them. The picture he created in his mind helped him feel more at home here, even under these inhospitable conditions.

As the last embers of the fire fell, Seth, Liyan, and Evgej, with help from the other two, moved back to join Valam. Full feeling had returned to Evgej's joints and limbs. He felt much better although he did still feel rather foolish. He had felt fine until Teren had started prodding him.

Evgej smiled a half-smile, and offered Valam the remainder of the warm ale in his skin, which Valam only accepted after Evgej assured him that it was the third skin that had been forced upon him, and he could not drink any more for some time. As Valam sipped the warm drink and its warmth spread through him, he was reminded all the more of the cold that was present all about him. Only a few more hours to go, he told himself.

The beat of Valam's heart increased as the first, tiny vestiges of light appeared on the horizon. In that instant, Valam thought to himself that he had never seen a more beautiful sight. But as he watched, the tip of the sun broke the horizon, and he realized an even greater sense of elation. For the first time in what seemed an eternity, he saw the blue of the sky.

"Evgej, isn't that magnificent!" exclaimed Valam. "Evgej?" shouted Valam when no response returned. "Evgej? Seth?"

Valam jumped to his feet, "Evgej? Seth?" he yelled wildly. He strained his eyes to focus in the coming light. He squinted. Captain Mikhal and Danyel' stood a short distance away. Liyan sat next to him, his concentration lost while he wrung his hands, trying to keep them warm, but Evgej and Seth were gone.

Valam moved down the line of forms in the immediate vicinity, first to the right, and then to the left. He shouted their names again, stirring Liyan from his thoughts. "Liyan, where are Seth and Evgej?" Liyan shrugged his shoulders; it was evident he was also puzzled. He had not noticed their absence either.

With the coming of morning and the life-giving essence of light, the camp quickly sprang into a bustling hub of activity. The snow stopped. It was a miracle. There was much to be done, but the first order of business was to rescue the supplies from beneath the white blanket where they were buried. Teren was quick to order an accounting of all, including animals and equipment.

Tsandra watched him with contempt in her eyes, but in her heart different feelings were stirring. She almost felt sorry for him. Such a desolate place to endure one's life. What a waste, she thought to herself. The brightness of the sun seemed to return feeling to her cold, tired body immediately. She checked over her own mount and her personal effects. The animal had survived the cold better than she had.

As the minutes swept by, the darkness was swallowed by the brightness of the new day. Valam's eyes continually adjusted to the changing light. His search for Evgej and Seth had taken him along their makeshift shelter, peering into every corner he chanced upon. He finally found them at the far end of the wall. Seth stood upon a large mound of snow, with Evgej beside him.

"Evgej, Seth!" shouted Valam.

Evgej was quick to note Valam's mood and he replied, "We're fine. Idle minds and hands are a waste, that's all." He stooped down and patted the mound of snow beneath their feet, which must have been a full ten feet high. Valam felt foolish for not noticing them, for as he walked towards them they were totally in the open. If he had been looking up or even straight ahead instead of down, he would have spotted them easily.

Valam clambered up to the top of the mound. As he reached the summit, he shielded his eyes from the glare of the white cover all around them. Valam released a gasp of amazement as he looked about, "Wow!"

Teren's voice called out to Liyan, Seth, and Tsandra's minds. "Five dead, and eight beasts gone." He spoke simply; nothing more needed to be said. Teren, as did the other three, held their heads for a moment of silent prayer, and then moved on to other matters. They counted their good fortune; the dark storm could have claimed them all.

Teren counted his good fortune twice. The snows had ceased, the morning sky was clear and bright, and with luck they would reach the coast by late afternoon if his estimate were correct. But first they must excavate the camp. The wind had piled the snow several feet deep in many areas, even with their protective walls. It would be some time before they would be ready to travel again.

Chapter Six

"Shchander, how could you?" shouted Nijal, "I counted you a friend."

"As do I," said Shchander.

"But why this treachery?"

"It was not I," said Shchander.

"Who then?"

"Think about it," said Shchander, subtly indicating those around him.

The distance separating the two forces diminished as the others closed in. Amir swept forward in a crazed fervor. As he sought to gain a clear opening, he met and matched the blades of the attackers many times. Angrily, hand over hand, he swung his blade back and forth circling his body from left to right, back to front, with finesse and ease.

Although his blade covered a full 360 degrees around his body in the blinking of an eye, his assailants did not hesitate to engage him. As a group, four men circled him warily while the remainder of their compatriots moved inward. Their attacks were swift, accurately timed, and precise. Simultaneously, four blades reached for him, only to be just as swiftly denied their target.

Xith drank in the energies around him; he cursed himself for not fully gathering a reserve. He had let his guard down; he would not let it happen again. Energy seeking to come to life touched his fingertips but was not yet alive with power.

Surprise was tough for Noman to handle. His response, however, was in no way slowed. He quickly tossed up a shield about the inner circle, which was effectively sealing them from attack by any projectile.

Nijal had been decisively cut off from guarding Amir's rear by a clever ruse. An additional group composed of a complement of four, guarded his every movement. His prowess with a sword did not match Amir's, but he held his own and kept them at bay.

Amir raised his blade high and thrust, quickly followed by a block left and right. He ducked to avoid the attack from his rear, whipping around to knock the blow upward. Followed immediately a second time into the opening in the attacker's defense, he recoiled as metal striking metal resounded.

The blow should not have been blocked; how could it have been? He gathered his senses close in his mind, and then cleared his thought to a new way of thinking, adapting always as he had learned from the plentiful lessons Noman had given him. He was impressed by his new opponent's prowess.

Xith poised with energy raging within him. The magic was clear and clean at his center. He needed only to give it form. For an instant before he did so, his thoughts slipped to Vilmos. "Oh, the waste," he whispered, "such waste."

Nijal sucked air heavily as perspiration dripped down his face. It was all he could do to defend. He didn't have time to attempt even a simple jab; his mind was fully focused on survival. His sword arm swung through block after block, switching from a clockwise rotation to a counterclockwise rotation as the attacking force necessitated.

Nijal's blade clashed heavily against one of his opponent's glaives and the sting knocked him back. A series of attacks left and right knocked his blade from his hand. Suddenly, Nijal felt as if his heart had stopped beating.

Noman raised his hand to stop Xith from releasing his magic. "Wait," he told Xith. Noman raised his voice loftily to Shchander, "Point well taken. I accept."

"How did you know?"

"You are clever but not overly so. Your desire gave you away."

Dismayed, Nijal accepted his sword as it was returned graciously to his hand. He was beset with confusion. He couldn't comprehend what Shchander had done. Warily, he maintained his distance from the warriors who stood immediately around him, staring at him with coy expressions on their faces.

Amir sheathed his weapon without another thought and without hesitation. "You fight well," he complimented the swordsmen around him, "as one." Amir moved to a position beside Noman, patiently waiting, but yet wary. Wary not because he doubted Noman's abilities, but because it was in his nature, and intuition told him to act thus. He made sure Adrina was close at hand.

"These men are well-trained, as I have told you," explained Shchander.

"I know, my friend, but the point is that we need to move quickly and maintain a low profile."

"If you will not take us with you, then we will be forced to take you with us," said Shchander, raising his sword to join his compatriots, as such was his conviction and his promise. They raised their weapons as well, moving quickly to re-engage.

Noman noted the determination set into Shchander's features and responded in kind, "My mind is set. I can see now that we must travel together." He paused, and then as Shchander smiled and lowered his weapon, Noman exclaimed, "Take them!"

Adrenaline pumped through Amir's veins as he withdrew his sword from its sheath. He looked forward to another test against such worthy fighters. Having learned from the previous encounter, he noted in his mind their movements. He would not make a similar error again, but he also noted in his mind that these were not true enemies, and he would not be severe with his weapon's edge.

Nijal was hesitant to react; these were men of the same blood as him. They were no enemy. He could not raise a weapon against an ally; it was against his code. The dilemma beset his mind, but it did not delay him from defending as he felt the swish of a blade nearly rake the side of his head.

"Shchander, give faith, my friend. Noman knows what is best; this I believe with all my heart."

"The test of swords never hurt a man, especially not a free man. Provide me this jest."

"You always were a man of words," grunted Nijal as he strained under the weight of a blow. He was wild and arcing in his defense, wielding his blade like an apprentice.

Amir studied the four within his mind, contemplating the tensions in their muscles, trying to reach into their minds and feel when they would attack. Shifts in the air about him, smells potently clinging close about him, sounds of agitated hands tightly clenching, or the expirations of breaths heavy into the air, all spoke of their movements in Amir's mind. He circled and moved, blocked or guarded, independent of their individual movements. Now he was fixed on the four as if they were one because now within his mind they were.

Noman reassuringly put a hand on Xith's shoulder; he was more intrigued now that he knew it was only a test between them. A test that he was sure would be anything but easy. He was captivated by the complexity of the fighters' movements. It had been a very long time since he had seen men with such promise, and although he was confident that Amir would win the challenge, he looked forward to watching.

Instinctively Amir edged closer towards Nijal, seeking to use Nijal as a cover for his backside. A similar notion passed through Nijal's thoughts, and he slowly led his assailants in Amir's direction. Amir followed through with a clean series of blows, while Nijal absorbed the necessary blocks.

As Shchander joined the strife, it was nine against two. Under the circumstance, even Amir's skills were being worn away although he was enjoying every moment of the challenge. He had not been so thoroughly tested since they had left Solstice Mountain. He recalled the last hours there with disgust.

"Give up, my friend," said Shchander, "do you not recognize the training?" Shchander maneuvered to split the two up again and divide their defenses once more. For now, the two could hold them at bay while they came in at them, taking each attack as a wave. It was clear: the swordsmen were also taking care not to cause serious injury.

Nijal knew what Shchander was referring to, but he answered slyly anyway, "No, I never had the time to learn from him." Nijal sighed in relief after the words left his mouth, as the edge of a sword sliced the air just short of his neck. One of the swordsmen winked at him, which angered him. Amir quickly returned the favor, and the swordsman lost his air of haughtiness.

"That is a shame; you have his prowess, you could have had his knowledge also," chastened Shchander as his block clubbed Nijal's blade heavily. Two other swordsmen followed suit immediately with a thrust, while a third attempted to knock the blade from Nijal's hands.

"I chose a different path; this you know," said Nijal as he winced from the pain of the stinging in his hands. Amir poured his strength into his blade and drove back his attackers again.

"Yes, but you know oft times he is right."

"In no case does that give you absolution. We will fight."

"Then so be it," said Shchander as he drove in with his blade, blocking up, while two other swordsmen attacked Nijal. Amir whirled around to face Shchander. At the same time, Nijal displaced the sword from Shchander's hand. The sting of it was evident on Shchander's face as it grew red with surprise and rage. "Don't be so gregarious when you fight, my friend. You lose your concentration."

Shchander very graciously bowed to the victor, picked up his sword by the hilt, and said, "We are finished here." Shchander motioned to his compatriots to lower their weapons and follow his retreat, which they did without contest. Shchander sheathed his sword and walked away without further delay.

"For that, there will be no need. You have doubly proven your worth," said Noman, raising his voice loftily. "Come. We must make haste. It is time we departed this place."

A broad smile lit Shchander's face, and the faces of his fellows. Nijal moved to embrace Shchander, "You are correct, though. You have learned well in my short absence."

Shchander nodded his head in response. He was too tired to speak any more now. He understood that Nijal implied his skill of leadership as opposed to his skill of arms. One of the swordsmen motioned to catch Shchander's attention, and he waved back, signaling it was permissible to retrieve their mounts and supplies.

"Come," said Nijal, indicating Shchander should follow him. Nijal went to see to their own animals. The two then assisted Amir as he reconnected the team to the carriage; Adrina was already seated inside, ready to go. She smiled at Shchander, as he passed by, and for the first time, she accepted his presence and approved of it.

As they departed, Xith wasn't the only one scouring the heavens for a presence just on the edge of his consciousness. He was certain that his use of magic had given their position away to someone or something unseen. He could see that Noman felt it as well, as did the mighty titan, Amir.

Chapter Seven

Dark shadows suddenly fell over the hall; scattered thoughts brought hesitant glances to vaulted windows set high along the east and western walls. The windows were designed to fill the chamber with light from dawn to dusk. It could not already be nightfall, thought Captain Brodst. "Had the battle lasted that long?" he wondered.

"Geoffrey. We must reach Geoffrey first!" yelled the captain.

The four surged forward, straight into the onslaught of their assailants. Captain Brodst wasn't surprised at all as he watched Midori hold her own in battle. She had, after all, learned from the same master he had although matched daggers offered no reach compared to a full-handed sword.

Lord Fantyu bit back the pain in his side, and vaulted into the enemy. At least now the invaders were dividing. King Jarom had ordered all available men to chase down and capture Lord Serant and Princess Calyin. The scorn rang evident in his words as his voice boomed over the top of the cacophony of battle.

Geoffrey was also grateful for the slight reprieve, but the advantage was still on the side of the enemy. Words muddled in his mind as his frenzied thoughts slowed. He still did not think he would survive, nor did he hope to, but now he would surely take more of the vile wretches with him.

As the mass of bodies thinned out, Geoffrey saw Lord Fantyu and the good captain for the first time. "Flee!" he shouted to them, "Flee!" although now with both exits fairly secured, he knew the opportunity was gone. Captain Brodst lowered his head for a moment; they were going nowhere.

Midori reached out with her mind, straining to find the will of the Mother. Her consciousness still spun with disbelief at the absence; how could the Mother abandon them in their time of need? As dark shadows lighted over the hall a second time, she hesitated, but slowly her attention was drawn westward, up the raised rows and beyond to the vaulted windows. The sun was indeed setting.

Wearily, Lord Fantyu raised his sword; the clash sent his body reeling. His knees wanted to collapse under his weight, but he strained to hold on. A second blade reached for him; Fantyu moved to block, but he was too slow to recover. He moved to dodge, but he was struck full in the mid-section. Although the gleam of victory was in his opponents' eyes, Lord Fantyu did not lower his gaze.

Captain Brodst's eyes were wide with rage as his blade crushed downward; the two forces collided. Brodst's blow was clearly stronger; he drove through, severing the opposing weapon unmercifully from the other man's hands. The contempt was evident upon his face as he plunged the tip of his sword deep. He watched as the man fell, careful to move around him as he toppled, making his way to his next foe.

Catrin grimaced as she dodged an attack. She was quick to send her daggers home into the man's gut, thrusting upward to reach his heart. Her first blade found its mark as did the second. She laughed as his blood ran bright down her hands to the floor. She held no pity for his soul; she would make them pay for their evil deeds.

Geoffrey sidestepped a blow while he parried a second. He fought to gain back the offensive, but he couldn't get any blows past the two who blocked his every move. A third moved to his side. Geoffrey stopped just short of tossing an elbow into the man's chest. "Captain Brodst, you old son of a wood troll!" he yelled.

Lord Fantyu wavered as his thrust was knocked harmlessly back at him. He perceived a presence to his left and right, Midori and Catrin, but he knew they were too late. He was beyond their help. His countenance held firm, almost regal, as he raised his sword to counter one last time. A surge of adrenaline swept over him as he launched himself full onto the enemy before him.

Two blades sank deep, piercing cleanly through, reaching outward, as Lord Fantyu fell upon the other. A trickle of blood pouring from his mouth spoke of his demise, but the smile held to his lips as he looked into the eyes of the one who lay beneath him. His aim had been true. He breathed in his last breath.

A tear fell from Midori, rolling crystalline down her cheek. She knew without a doubt that Lord Fantyu had passed. The remorse on her face was quickly banished, as she immediately moved to re-engage. She had paused only an instant to say a prayer to the Mother and to the Father. She hoped they would still hear her words even if their will did not walk through her.

Both Geoffrey's and the captain's minds were jolted with a burst of speed and anxiety. They had seen Lord Fantyu fall; similar thoughts moved through their minds. The military mind within them carefully tallied the odds: now they only numbered four.

Midori raised her voice to a pitched, venomous screech, the effects of which were not lost on those around her. Even the most stalwart of figures cringed as the sound pierced their ears. Steadfast,

Midori turned the instant's hesitation into an advantage as she lunged. Daggers level, she descended upon her prey, evil justice in her eyes.

King Jarom stood and turned to face Midori. "Kill her!" he shouted to his henchmen, "Kill her now!" Jarom feared those of the Mother as much as he feared the dark priests, both of which had their uses at the proper time. But now was not the proper time, and he had no use for their sort. He would have his fun with the priests they had captured.

He chuckled as he watched his men turn with new vigor. The attack was taking longer than he had planned, but he liked its progression thus far. In a short while, the kingdom, all its subjects and domains, would be his. He would make sure there were no heirs, apparent or otherwise; even now his servants sought out all those of royal lineage.

"Finish this. I grow weary!" he barked at his remaining bodyguards save two, which he motioned should stay. Afterwards he also sent his captain to urge those following Lord Serant and Princess Calyin. King Jarom smiled and turned to the other kings. All save one were calm. "Do not fear, King William, I hold no grudges."

King Jarom smiled as he walked over and patted King William on the back. "All is forgotten," said Jarom as he lifted his jeweled stiletto from its sheath. King Jarom fiddled with the blade in his hand while he stood behind King William. He watched as William thumped his fingers against the tabletop. William lurched in his seat as Jarom placed his hands back onto William's shoulder. William sighed in relief and his heartbeat returned to normal.

Catrin spun around and clipped the arm of her opponent, her

blade visibly raking into his leathered armor. The man's blade fell to the ground as the tendons in his hand were severed. A gasp of pain came from his mouth. Catrin was quick to follow through with a second slice to the jugular, ending the dispute.

Geoffrey signaled a series of short, defensive retreats so the four could better handle the additional onslaught, which, when coupled with those streaming in from the hall, was utterly overwhelming. It took concerted effort just to make the retreat effective. His eyes sought out a place in the room, which offered little maneuvering; his only hopes were to draw out their demise.

Captain Brodst began kicking chairs at those who covered their retreat, carefully making sure to maintain his balance as he dropped back over the body-strewn floor. As he had a few seconds to think, he reflected that he did not regret his life; he had lived fully. He hoped with all his heart that the lord and the princess had found escape.

Catrin staggered backwards as she slipped across the floor. One of her daggers fell from her grasp and bumped across the floor. She was quick to recover and turned in wild retreat, striving to catch up to the others. As she turned, she caught a blade mid-shoulder, which stunned her to her knees. Her hand stretched out, but no one could help her now; she was beyond them.

Midori stopped cold, and whipped the blade in her hand around to feel the tip between her fingers. She scoffed as she withdrew her hand, and flung it at the warrior who stood so gallant retracting his blade from his victim. The blade caught him clean, low on his neck, just above his armored collar.

The three withdrew all the way to the farthest reaches of the room, fighting their way up the raised platforms, up the rows of benches, to where they did not know. All options suddenly came to a halt as they reached the far wall; there was no place left to go. Geoffrey grimaced as he realized that he had backed into the wall.

"Till the end!" he shouted, as he threw his blade aside. He reached his hands out wide, ready to embrace all those that came near. He hurled himself downward, putting all his strength into the vault, and adding all his weight to the force. As he slammed head first into the closest two, they sent a shock wave rippling down to the last bench, knocking them down along with all in their path.

The waning light suddenly gave way as the last rays of light disappeared with the sun beyond the horizon. The room fell to darkness and shadows, as the glare from the windows above faded with the light. A loud ruckus broke to a roar, immediately following.

"Till the end!" shouted Geoffrey, as he lifted himself up off the floor, bringing his fists into contact with anything available. He flailed wildly about himself, hitting anything and everything around him. A brawl broke out around him, and as none could see in the darkness, no one knew who was hitting whom.

"Get them! Kill them!" shouted Jarom, infuriated. He moved close to the two guards beside him, quickly groping his way back to a chair, and a feeling of relative safety. His curses grew above the noise of the fighting, inciting anger into the minds of those who listened. His voice raised, ranting and raving louder, demanding torches be brought in at once, threatening all who failed him with immediate punishment.

Minutes later, the first torches were carried in from the adjacent halls. King William smirked at the collapse of Jarom's bravado, which even in the shadows was garish. King Jarom was quick to plant the apex of his stiletto dead center between William's eyes, sending him reeling backwards, flailing his arms, dead as he dropped.

Geoffrey had edged his way out of the fight, under the cover of darkness, moving skillfully on his hands and knees. As the torchlight brought sight to those around him, he was caught. He poised his eyes pleading up to the heavens, raising his hands, and shrugging his shoulders.

"Not this day!" he yelled to Jarom as he leaped to his feet and up to the captain and Midori, who had been standing at the ready, waiting in the darkness for whatever came their way. Geoffrey clasped his hands together, "Up you go!" he indicated to Midori.

"Where?"

"Hurry, put your foot into my hands. Don't ask questions. Just do it."

The puzzled look on Captain Brodst's face vanished as realization hit him. His countenance changed to an expression that said, "Are you kidding?" But he was quick to assist Midori up to the sill. Afterwards, he stood motionless for a heartbeat. His eyes moved to those that were only seconds away from them. Captain Brodst interlaced his fingers and said, "Go!"

Geoffrey shrugged his shoulders, "No. Set your blade there, and be quick about it!" Geoffrey had snapped it at the captain like an order, to which Captain Brodst was quick to respond, not because he wanted to, but on impulse.

"But where do we go from there?" asked Captain Brodst, as Geoffrey boosted him up. As Captain Brodst moved upward, clenching his fingers against the wall, pulling himself also upward, his face reflected his confusion. His face also reflected his gratitude.

"The choice is yours!" shouted Geoffrey in response, as he grasped the captain's sword.

Chapter Eight

The city of Zashchita lay only days ahead of them at the far edge of the forest; in retrospect, it seemed to be cut out of the forest. A few leagues away from its lookouts, the forest began anew. Noman knew this, as he knew the sun would rise in the morning. Vast ranges of forests cut across the face of the territories—too much—thought Noman. He looked forward to the time when they would reach the sea and cool, coastal breezes.

The humidity in the forest seeped into his skin and his soul. He breathed in the moisture from the air around him. Three days of rain filtering through the trees had set all in gloomy moods except Adrina. It wasn't because she rode inside the carriage, which was dry, but because the rain brought fond memories. She liked the slight feeling of sadness the raindrops gave her; in an odd sort of way, the sadness actually lifted her spirits.

Adrina thought about the words Noman spoke to her when they stopped. She dwelled upon them. A pain in her stomach caused her to wince, and she leaned her head out the carriage. The fresh air against her face made her feel better, but the queasiness still did not go away. After she got rid of her lunch, her stomach settled down, at least temporarily. Her hands swept down to the mark upon her belly. "Tnavres," she said quietly to herself, "Tell your master, I will never do what he asks."

The carriage jolted to a sudden halt, and Noman jumped down from its seat, as did Xith. In front of them, Amir and Nijal also dismounted. Storms had knocked down a group of trees that blocked the road before them. Noman quickly calculated the options; the forest was too thickly overgrown with underbrush to move around the trees, especially for the coach. The choice remaining was the obvious one, move the trees, which would not be an easy task.

Amir yelled to Shchander and his men to move up from the rear and assist, but by the time he yelled, they were already coming. Hours of toil and sweat later, their combined might moved the first tree a few feet. Amir looked to Noman in frustration but would not give up.

He scratched his head and told the others to put their backs into it this time. On his mark they began again, grunting and groaning as the eleven of them strained beneath the tree's weight, which was going nowhere. Nijal stopped and stripped down his gear, as if it would help, as did the others. "Again," signaled Amir.

Sweat pouring down his face, but with no lessening of determination, Amir called them to a halt minutes later. As he slumped down, spent, the others also rested. After a brief respite, he stood and slapped his hands together, spit into them, and rubbed them together again.

Anger was evident on his face as he motioned for them to give it another try. The others followed without hesitation or complaint, putting every last ounce of their strength into one last attempt. Success lighted Amir's face as they moved the tree from the ground, albeit only inches; slowly they walked it back. They had moved it about a foot when it became clear it was stuck and wasn't going to budge anymore.

Xith and Noman called them to a stop. They decided that they would try magic to levitate the carriage across, as opposed to wasting the entire day trying to move the trees. "Unhook the team," called out Noman. Adrina stepped out of the wagon to watch the spectacle.

Xith looked to Noman. Both had hoped to avoid the use of magic or its forms for as long as possible as much as possible. It might give away their position, a thing they did not want to happen, especially if the enemy did not know where they were. He slowly began building energy within himself, taking it in from the energies around him. Odd, he thought to himself, the energy wasn't as strong here as he would have expected.

Amir looked amused as he watched Xith struggle to gather the power within him. He watched and thought about the problem and came up with a new solution. He signaled to Nijal and pointed to the carriage. Shchander hesitated, but his men joined in without him. Amir and Nijal picked up the rear of the wagon while the other eight lifted the midsection and the front. They squatted and lifted in unison, surprised at how light it seemed compared to the tree.

With a few groans and grunts, they made it over the barrier of trees and placed the coach on the opposite side. Noman was quick to laugh at the simple resolution of the dilemma, but also quick to stop Xith from drawing in any more energy. Xith stopped, looked, and took a second look before he realized what had occurred, but he was also quick to grin in relief that the obstacle had been overcome.

In a short while, and after a short rest, they were moving along the trail again; thoughts of the rain, the humidity, and Zashchita, were for the moment forgotten. Shchander and Nijal broke into light conversation about their home city of Solntse, and the grudge between them also lifted. Nijal insisted that Shchander retain the title of captain. Nijal was fairly settled on the fact that he was not ready to return to Solntse any time soon to regain his office; and if Nijal had his way, Shchander would return to Solntse once they safely reached Krepost' on the edge of Statter's Bay.

Noman was perplexed. Concern played heavily on his face as they rode on, bringing a furrow to his brow. It was something Xith had said to him just as they had departed that had sparked the consternation. His fears caused him to lose track of everything around him as he turned inward. There was a presence in the farthest reaches of his thoughts that he could not grasp.

A shadow passed over the sky above unnoticed. Xith rode in the coachman's seat beside Noman, still a little miffed at the proceedings. Xith fiddled nervously with his fingers, the touch of them against each other was wrong.

A breeze, albeit slight, began to stir, moving through the trees with a whisper. Subtly, the temperature began to change, and the air around them became cooler as the humidity dissipated. Noman and Xith were not the only ones fidgety; the oddities around them played on Amir's senses, made more perceptive by his blindness.

Adrina drew in a quiet breath; the sudden coolness brought on drowsiness. She watched the trees pass with their leaves of green, brown, and gold. Her eyes grew heavier and her breathing slowed, and then she drifted off to a light slumber. Her thoughts were mostly pleasant as she shifted to a deeper, peaceful sleep.

The trail became dense and twisted; large overgrown patches were in rich abundance. Thick shadows formed beneath the trees and as they moved deeper into the shadows the light of day slowly faded. The trees around them spoke of ancient times; their forms grew as thick and tangled as the path.

The harbinger of night fell quickly upon them although it was far from dusk. They found themselves huddling closer together. Even Adrina, who was sleeping soundly now, suddenly felt solitude, a great separation between her and the world around her. Spontaneous reactions brought many hands to the hilts of weapons held yet in their scabbards.

They waited with bated breath, fingers playing restlessly against hardened metal, minds filled with images of looming horrors. Gloom sank into their souls, creating specters in the trees. Without realizing it, they slowed to a lethargic, careful pace.

Minutes became hours as the seconds ticked past, a heart beat at a time, a breath at a time. Every sound caught the ears of the listeners—a trodden stick, a moving branch, the breeze rustling through the trees. Nervous eyes darted from side to side in anticipation.

Shchander motioned for his companions to split up and ride alongside the carriage, four to a side, while he went to the front. He cast his eyes towards Noman and Xith, shrugging his shoulders. He wanted to ask, "What is it? What is wrong?" for surely they must know the answer, he thought, yet his mind told him not to break the silence.

Xith returned Shchander's gesture—he did not know. Something weighed heavily upon him although he could not touch it. Absent-mindedly, he rubbed his palms with his thumbs. The minute spark of energy created as he did so trickled across his thumbnails.

Ahead, the growth around them grew sparse, but the darkness did not dissipate. It loomed around them, clinging to their souls. A clear disjoining lay ahead and as they passed it, the shadows seemed to lift. Then as suddenly as they had come, the dark clouds overhead scattered.

"Help me! Somebody, please help me!" screamed Adrina. Her body was fixed with convulsions, "Help me!" she whimpered.

The coach came to a sudden halt, and Adrina was jolted backwards into the padded seats. She lay there trembling, afraid to move. "Make them go away!" she yelled. "Make them go away!"

Two large figures unfurled the doors to the carriages and leaped inside. They stared blankly at one another. The coach contained no one save them and Adrina. "Princess, there is nothing here. You are alone."

"No, they are here!" she cried, her eyes pleading with them to listen to her.

"Adrina, are you unwell?" yelled a familiar voice.

"Xith, please send them away! Make them leave!"

"Please," said Xith, "leave her alone." Xith indicated that the others should leave and he took Adrina's hand and led her outside. "What is it, dear?" he asked sympathetically.

"Please send them away. Make them go!"

"Them?" asked Xith, pointing to the two who had just returned to their mounts.

"No, not them. They are there," said Adrina, pointing to the inside of the carriage.

Xith peered into the interior of the coach, "There is no one there. It is empty."

"No," cried Adrina bursting into tears. "They came for me. They want me to go with them."

Xith was confused and worried. He glanced at Noman, subtly

asking, "Is there something there?" Noman stepped down from the buckboard, and inspected the carriage. Afterwards, he shook his head negatively. He saw nothing. "You must have been dreaming, my dear. Everything is fine now, I assure you."

"No, it is not," replied Adrina. "They have come for me because I won't do what he asks."

The way she said it sent chills down Xith's spine. He looked to Noman again for assistance, then to Amir and finally Nijal. Nijal took Adrina's hand and returned with her to the coach. As Nijal stepped into its confines, Adrina froze cold, her face fixed in a mask. "No," she repeated. She would not step within.

"Adrina, I assure you there is nothing here," said Nijal, sitting. Adrina held firm. Nijal stood and took her hand, pulling her inside. Adrina became hysterical. She started screaming and shouting frantically, tears welling up in her eyes and streaming down her cheeks. "Please, no," she said pitifully.

Nijal held her hand warmly, caressing it, soothing her, slowly coaxing her to step in. "There, there," he whispered to her as she leaned her head against him. One small step at a time, he drew her into the carriage, and they started anew although all were a little shaken. They would be very glad to have this section of the forest far behind them.

The remainder of the day proceeded smoothly. They set up camp just as dusk came on. Xith was still puzzling over what Adrina had said. He tried to help her by talking about what she had dreamt, but Adrina would not talk about it. Fear was still evident in her eyes, and she did not want to be left alone this evening. That was clear.

Nijal took the cushioned bench across from Adrina as they lay down to retire for the evening. He watched her as she lay there for hours with her eyes wide open. "What is it?" he asked softly.

"Nijal, can we sleep outside tonight?"

Nijal thought about it for a time, and as he did so, Adrina said, "I will not get dirty. I will be fine on the ground. I do not need special comforts." Nijal agreed, but he would not allow her to simply lie on the ground. He woke Shchander and his men, and the ten of them gathered a nest of pine needles for Adrina to rest upon. The light seemed to return to Adrina's eyes as she lay down to sleep.

✳ ✳ ✳

Father Jacob paced nervously in his command tent. He was alone. Captain Mikhal had left in search of the seventh, and Keeper Martin was gone, to where he wasn't sure. If he were not a holy man, his curses would have been foul. He did not like the dilemma he was faced with. How could they leave, but how could he justify not leaving? He had given his promise to King Jarom and to Prince Valam, but he had also given new promises to Keeper Martin.

"Why did I let him leave?" rang his voice loudly about the empty command tent. The page outside the tent quickly entered and stared at him. Father Jacob waved him away. "Be gone!" he yelled. As the page retreated from the tent, Father Jacob caught a glimpse of the sky outside; it was as foul as his mood, which sent him deeper into his rage.

He walked over to the table and stared blankly at the half-filled charts strewn across its surface. He cast them aside and unrolled several more from a trunk near the table. His heart fell heavily as he examined the coast of the kingdom. The next chart contained hastily written remarks that Jacob couldn't decipher—winds, currents, times, and cycles with blank spaces and question marks, which Jacob assumed were estimates, or better yet, guesses.

Fatigue suddenly overwhelmed him, as it had often of late. He slumped into a chair, sitting motionless until his breath returned. He again threw the charts aside, cursing Keeper Martin as he did so; immediately, he unrolled a piece of parchment and began hurriedly scribbling.

Hours later, as he finished the scroll, he placed it with the other scrolls of his account, careful to secure them with lock and key in a small chest, which he placed back into the larger trunk. The page hesitated before entering, clearing his throat to ensure that it was okay to come in.

The page set Jacob's lunch on the table, meager as it was. Rations were extremely low even for one of Jacob's stature. Jacob had insisted on equal rations for everyone including himself. With his face set in a mask, Jacob ate and for a time cleared his thoughts of all matters, even those of a pressing nature. As he finished, the page came back and took the plate, exiting without uttering a word.

The food sat thick and warm in his belly. Jacob sat still for quite some time, staring emptily at the wall of the tent. Anxiety and exhaustion coupled with internal turmoil brought him to the verge of collapse yet again. He had not slept in days, as was evident by the hollow shells of his eyes.

"Was it all for nothing?" he asked himself as his world faded to blackness. The camp was at the brink of depleting its last food stores; the little they had would only last a few more days at the most, and that only if they continued the strict rationing. They had only enough wood to maintain meager fires for cooking and little else. Water was the only thing they had in abundance.

Images played through his mind. He recalled distinctly the day they departed Imtal, the sojourn to Quashan', the trek across the dark waters, reaching the Eastern Reaches, but most clear in his mind were the emotions in Keeper Martin's face as he triggered the ancient device and disappeared. Jacob could not tell if it was surprise or shock or horror; nonetheless, Martin was gone now, and he, Jacob, was alone.

Chapter Nine

As Lord Serant broke into the courtyard, clutching Calyin's hand followed by the venerable chancellors, his mouth fell agape. In astonishment he watched as the sun was swallowed by darkness, piece by piece. Frenzied thoughts ran through his mind. Thoughts of escape suddenly became secondary.

Calyin jolted to a halt as she stumbled into her lord. "What is it?" she asked, before she registered what was evident. She raised a hand to her mouth. A flicker of movement caught her eye on the far side of the courtyard as she peered heavenward.

Chancellor Van'te sank to his knees because of the agonizing pain in his side but also from awe. Chancellor Volnej quickly followed. "Father?" he cried, the word springing from his lips before he could cut it short.

The air turned cooler and a light breeze moved in as the shadows swept toward them. On the far side of the courtyard, a figure ran toward them, exhaustion clearly showing on his face. Lord Serant paused, also regarding the figure moving toward them. From a distance, Lord Serant couldn't tell positively who the figure was. He did not know whether to flee or stand and fight.

As the figure approached, Lord Serant became certain that it was Swordmaster Timmer, as he had thought. The swordmaster dragged his right leg and draped his sword over his shoulder as he moved toward them, surprise and relief on his face.

"My lord, you are safe!" he hailed. "Thanks be to the Father."

"Swordmaster Timmer, what has happened? Where did they all come from?"

"I do not know, my lord, but we shall make them pay for the treachery; this I promise."

"Where are the garrison troops? The palace guards? Pyetr?"

"A few of the guards were with me, as you know. We have fought our way from the armory. I am afraid it was the first to be taken; only a few of my good men survive. We escaped the ambush. They are pushing into the inner castle as we speak. We did not know where you were, my lord."

"The garrison troops, are they not in the city?"

The swordmaster shrugged his shoulders; he had dispatched men to inform them, but they had not returned although he thought that the garrison troops had surely seen the siege. "Where were they?" he thought to himself. "Come, we mustn't delay here. It is not safe," spoke Timmer, eager to move from the vulnerable position of the garden area.

"Where is Pyetr?" demanded Lord Serant.

"I do not know; come my lord, princess," said Timmer with concern in his voice. He cast his eyes often to the sky as they retreated.

"Where is there safety?" asked Lord Serant. "Is the whole of the palace under attack?"

"I am afraid it is. There are so many. Damn it, where are the reinforcements!" Timmer cursed. "Are there others yet in the great hall?"

"I pray so," said Serant in hushed, reverent tones.

"We will reach them, don't worry. It will be just a matter of time as reinforcements arrive."

"How many men do we have now?" asked Lord Serant.

"Scattered pockets, I am afraid. We were taken by surprise. Vile treachery, I tell you. We had no warning."

"In all?"

"Several detachments, four squads in all, managed to escape with me; they are within the palace now."

"Is that all?"

"I am afraid it is. They descended upon us in a swarm from all directions. It is a miracle that any of us escaped at all."

Lord Serant hung his head; his thoughts were grim. He stopped just before they reentered the palace, looking at the shadows play upon the sun. It is an unnatural thing, he thought. It can only be an omen, an omen of ill tidings. He raised a defiant fist at the sun, and shook it angrily. He swore under his breath; he would make all who were responsible pay.

Movement through the halls proceeded slowly and cautiously; constantly they changed directions, moving away from the sounds of fighting. Slowly, they were being led around in a circle, being pushed back out into the courtyards. They were too small a group to venture an encounter. They could escape only if they avoided engagement.

As they entered a section of the old palace, ascending many floors and backtracking through the old private hallways and corridors, Calyin took the lead since she knew this area the best. Although she had not wandered these paths for many years, she still knew every detail from the time she had spent in them during her childhood. She brought them to a place where they could look out at the front courtyards, which lay behind the palace gates, and see the square just opposite the wall.

The sights from both views were ominous. A large contingent of black-clad warriors poured from the square through the gates. Within the courtyard was turmoil, a sea of bodies moving and clashing, mostly waves of black with tiny sections bearing the green and gold of the Great Kingdom. Lord Serant staggered back from the window, confused and dismayed. Fatigue swept through him, a sudden weariness that came from his soul.

Carefully circumnavigating the open passageways, Calyin brought them back to the old sections of the palace and to windows that looked down into the courtyards of the armory and a section of the garden. Although they noted no movement and no signs of the enemy intruders, the scene was nevertheless startling. Fields of bodies lay scattered across the grounds as if they had fallen from the sky.

Lord Serant closed his eyes. He considered plans for escape, which seemed the only alternative left to them. The odds were definitely not in their favor. He wondered about the fate of those they had left behind in the hall. He thought them perhaps lucky. They did not have to look at what he saw now.

Suddenly, Chancellor Van'te clutched Serant's hand. "How did my brother die?" he asked. The weariness of his voice spoke volumes.

Lord Serant said with great sincerity, "He died with honor, honorable sir."

"Good," weakly responded the chancellor a glint of pride in his eyes. "Good-bye, my friends."

Van'te collapsed, still holding Lord Serant's hand as he fell. Lord

Serant remorsefully closed the old man's eyes. The last expression fixed on the chancellor's face was happiness, and Serant felt that the chancellor had indeed found peace.

"Look!" cried Calyin, as she stared out the window, not in disrespect for the chancellor, but because her eyes had welled up with emotion. "There!" she said pointing. Although the sky was shrouded in darkness, a beam of light bathed a section of the courtyard. In the midst of the light sat the white gazebo of the garden. They took this as a message and hurried to that spot.

Oddly, when they came upon the open walkways, none thought to look for danger before entering, for in such beauty they knew there could be only safety. Shadows lingered in the air above them. As they drew nearer, the ray of light diffused and became many patches of light, one of which was on a window high above, though none of them was aware of this.

As the day turned into night, all the warmth was drawn from the air by restless breezes. The small company stood upon the dais of the gazebo and gazed upon a raven-hued sun. Its light was no more. They did not look at it, knowing that they might be blinded.

"Please forgive my transgressions this day, Father," crossed each of their lips more than once in the moments that followed; but still they waited, standing still upon the platform, for the thing that had brought them here had not yet arrived.

Shards of glass struck the stone of the palace and plunged downward. Raised eyes could make out the figures stepping onto the ledge even in the darkness. Those that remained constant saw the others emerge from secret places within the courtyard as the force that drew them gathered all.

Timmer raised his sword in his trembling hands, facing those that approached. Lord Serant was quick to catch movement out of his periphery vision. He stepped in front of Calyin, raising his sword, placing himself between those that approached and his beloved.

"Your weapons will do you no good. We have long since passed and they will do you no harm," spoke a voice, crisp and clear, with melodic hints of song in the words. Hesitant, Serant, Timmer, and the chancellor lowered their blades. Calyin's stance had not changed at all. She had noted the arrival but was not afraid.

"Who are you?" demanded Lord Serant.

"Listen close, and listen well," bade the voice again, wavering in rises and falls as it spoke. "We have only a short time before we must leave. Do not fear us, but do heed us."

"But—" interrupted Serant.

"Foolish one, be still. Wait and I will tell. With three you are free and you are seven. Find it destroyed by the first, and you will endure the second."

"Yes," said another, as Lord Serant made it clear that he wished to speak.

"What is it we seek?"

"He that is learned, and he that is wise, and he that you despise."

"Find the place of old. There then will your answers lie," chimed another.

Lord Serant attempted to speak again, and another began to speak. Her words flowed cool and soothing, gentle to their ears, "When you find him, he will know."

"How do we escape?"

"You have only to try."

"Where is it we must go?"

"Through the rain and towards the sleet, beneath the toil and the heat, downward, inward, outward, upward, under your feet."

A minute tracing of light fell from the sky. The figures raised their hands to the questioning eyes and crept back to the places they had emerged from. As the figures receded, so did the other creatures that had been drawn. Vile were their faces as the glee and hopes of tasty morsels faded.

"Wait, do not go!" yelled Lord Serant. "But what of Imtal? I must stay."

A faint voice echoed back to him. It was hard to hear the words, and he strained to decipher them. It almost sounded as if the words had been, "Go you shall," yet it also could have been, "It will fall." As he thought about it, he decided perhaps it was both.

Under the light of a dawning day, two figures moved across the rooftop, followed by a third. It was the reflection of light from steel that brought their attention to the small group in the gazebo. Calyin started as she studied the pair closer. A sputtering of the wind caught strands of long, dark hair, and blew them as they did her own. "Midori!" she exclaimed.

Timmer squinted and stared. His eyes were old and untrue, but judging from proportions in the changing light, one was a woman or a very thin man. Chancellor Volnej was sure as he looked closer, as was Lord Serant—the long, flowing black hair was a distinctive trait of all three sisters.

The fastest way to reach them was to move straight through the central towers, which is what they sought to do. Lord Serant took the lead and Timmer took the rear, hobbling along but still able to move surprisingly quickly. The stairs were more difficult for him, but with Volnej's assistance he was able to make the climb at a fair pace.

"The roof, how do we get to it?" he demanded of Calyin, without thinking of the effects of the bluntness of his words. His anxiety was at its peak, and the aggressiveness of his soul had taken over his actions. Calyin glared at him and walked around him, taking him to a window that offered a ledge.

"Take care," she whispered to him while kissing his cheek as he moved out of the window onto the ledge.

"Stay with her!" he barked back at the other two, who had been unsure of what to do.

Without giving it another thought, he turned to look for the others to mark their progress, nearly falling from the ledge as he did so. Calyin shuddered as she watched him inch along the edge, slowly disappearing. Lord Serant cursed the slickness of his boots and his own shortsightedness as he stumbled a second time, clinging to the masonry above only by his fingertips.

Out of the corner of his eye, he watched the progress of the third as well as the first two. It was difficult at best to make out the forms without stopping to turn to look at them, but he did not have time for that. He was sure that one was Midori and the other the captain. The closest window they could escape into lay midway between him and them, but the other was now only a few feet away from them. He thought about shouting a warning to them but decided not to do so lest they be discovered.

He waited until they had passed the corner. Perhaps then the time would be right. He checked the sword sheathed at his side, both out of habit and to insure that it was near. If only they could reach the window, he thought, then he would surely have a chance at stopping their pursuer.

Midori was the first to see the approaching form in front of her along the wall. Her hand faltered along the wall, causing her to lose her balance and slip. Only the captain's agile hands were able to catch her, nearly pulling himself from the wall as he did so, but his grip held firm.

Lord Serant gasped, and called out, "Watch out! Behind you!" The sound of his voice brought alarm to Captain Brodst's ears at first because he had not realized anyone else was on the ledge with them, but as he registered the sounds, he placed the voice. The timing of Lord Serant's alarm couldn't have been more wrong, for as the captain's attention was distracted, his fingers slipped.

He pushed Midori against the wall as he fell. His eyes went wide with fear and desperation. Captain Brodst scrambled, clawing at the very air about him, attempting to grasp anything that lay near. Pain numbed his bloodied fingers as they tore into the lower ledge where his feet had been.

"Be gone!" cursed Lord Serant. "Death will be too good for you if you harm him!" Lord Serant shimmied as fast as he could, mustering all the strength and dexterity he could manage. "I warn you do not move!"

Lord Serant's heart dropped to the bottom of his feet as the figure approached Captain Brodst, leaning down to pry his fingers from the ledge. "Midori, get in the window! Hurry!" called out Lord Serant. He paused long enough to draw a thin blade. He reached back, taking careful aim, preparing to release only when he was confident he was direct on target.

For the first time as the figure leaned over to offer the captain aid, Lord Serant saw the man's face. "Geoffrey? Can it be?" he asked himself. Abashed, he dropped the blade. It fell tumbling, clinking against the stone as it plummeted downward.

"Oh, thanks be to the Father," he cried out, as he thought, with three you are free, and you are seven. Utterly amazed at the revelation, he did not move for a long time. He stood frozen in deep thought, contemplating the many things that had seemed foolish to him moments before. The words, he thought, the words were not gibberish; they held meaning.

The captain and his rescuer had already gone through the window and were calling back to him before Lord Serant regained his senses. Filled with emotion, he grabbed them both in a mighty bear hug and immediately afterward swept Midori off her feat. A heavy burden had been lifted from his heart.

He told them where the others waited, and they made a quick exit. A silence fell. Speech was not necessary as long as they had survived.

Calyin was filled with emotion as she and Midori met. The two sisters felt closer to each other now than they had since childhood. The exchange of emotions between them in these moments would bind them for life.

Fearing discovery, especially if anyone else had glimpsed their movements, they departed. Captain Brodst knew the obscure corridors of the palace as well as the two sisters, so he took charge. He conducted them to the far end of the upper level, coming upon a set of stairs that led to the rear armory.

As they descended the stairs reaching the final landing, Captain Brodst met a pair of cold, bitter eyes. The sword guarded in the hands spoke volumes to him as his life passed before his eyes. A single, monosyllabic word escaped his lips before he drew his sword. "Why?" he asked.

"I wanted to see the light leave your eyes as your world collapsed beneath you as it did from my mother's."

"But I loved your mother with all my heart. It was not my fault."

"Oh, yes it was."

"You are no son of mine."

"Then am I the bastard you fostered with the regal whore?"

"Step aside, for I could not kill you. To wallow in your charity would suffice my honor."

"You will not find escape!" cried Pyetr as his sword fell from his grasp.

The captain looked clear into Pyetr's eyes as he slumped, pained, against the wall. He lowered his eyes with shame and stepped passed him. The others behind him said nothing as they, too, passed by. Lord Serant stayed the call for blood that desired to move his trembling hand. He also understood that sometimes to live was a greater transgression than offering oneself to die. Pyetr would take his own life and pay his atonement in full.

Their retreat was short, for none knew where to go or what to do next; and as they reached a place they thought secure, at least for the moment, they began to argue and tempers flared. Calyin and Midori soon separated themselves from the other three, who ceaselessly debated without gaining ground.

"I will go nowhere; Imtal is where I belong," said Captain Brodst obstinately.

"You must! Can you not see that the city has fallen?"

"Lord Serant, something has clouded your wisdom. You cannot believe the words you are saying. The capital is far from doomed; if we fight, we will most assuredly win it back."

"Think, man! You know what has occurred. Do not let your pity blind your vision. We cannot wait here much longer."

"Lord Serant is correct," interrupted Geoffrey. "If we hope to escape, it must be soon. We do not have time to waste. I say we go to Solntse and return to Imtal with the garrison troops. My men cannot have deserted, nor can the garrison troops here from Imtal be very far off. They must have been sent somewhere. By my hand I will have the traitors swinging if I discover any—begging your pardon, of course, Captain Brodst. I shouldn't have said that."

"It was due me and I take no offense, but I could no more kill my own flesh and blood than I could kill a loyal servant. I believe time repays all those who are untrue. All the same, I still think we should stay here."

Calyin and Midori were conversing separately from the others. Calyin was telling Midori in great detail the words of their mystic visitors and Midori was listening with very earnest ears; something in the message caught her interest. Midori held her thoughts until Calyin had told her everything she could recall.

"I know the place," announced Midori as Calyin finished. She stopped and then mumbled something Calyin thought was, "Towards the rain. Interesting." Midori stepped between Lord Serant and Geoffrey to move towards the window. She had been listening also to the words of the three men behind her as she had been following Calyin's story. "Solntse, it is," she said, agreeing with Geoffrey.

Captain Brodst was quick to cut Midori off from further speech as he turned back to Geoffrey asking, "What are you saying?"

"Yes, what are you saying?" asked Lord Serant.

Geoffrey didn't respond; he liked the additional vote for Solntse and wasn't going to say anything either to add to or detract from Midori's statement. "Toward the rain," repeated Midori, and she pointed to the eastern sky, which was dark with heavy rains in the distance. "East is where we need to go. Solntse is east, so we will hopefully appease two of you. But what do you say, Captain Brodst?"

"Do you honestly wish to leave? I cannot believe what I am hearing from you, Midori."

"My good captain," returned Midori, "I believe what I have heard, and I think if we put our heads together we will find that the riddles are quite easily solved."

"She is right," said Calyin.

"We do waste time here, do we not?"

"Yes, but we must first find a way out of the city."

"We have only to try."

Chapter Ten

Valam, Seth, and Teren moved through the deserted camp wondering where everyone had gone. They searched through tent after tent only to find them empty, abandoned. Glumly they proceeded towards the center of the camp, reaching the command tent last.

Valam dismounted, he hoped, for the last time. As he cast the flap widely aside, it caught the wind and pushed back at him. He clipped it with his arm and entered. The tent was empty like all the others, save for a chest in the center.

He dropped to his knees and opened the chest. Its only content was a plainly bound book, a ledger of sorts, guessed Valam. Rapidly, he scanned the first two pages, gathering from this that it was a journal, Father Jacob's journal. He quickly turned through the pages of the chronicle, skipping to the last page.

Confused, he turned back several pages and started reading again. "What did he mean, 'Martin is gone and I am alone'," thought Valam. He read forward again, closing the book as his eyes fell upon the last word. Valam dropped the book on the ground, running from the tent, "Captain Mikhal, where are the ships? Are they near?"

"Just south," he replied distantly, "about a half hour's ride along the coa—" The captain stopped mid-sentence. "They didn't?"

"I am not sure. Come!" Valam shouted as he mounted, spurring his horse frantically, "Let's find out!"

Valam instructed most to wait in the camp until he and the captain returned, but a handful followed the two as they raced southward. Valam shouted to the wind, "No, Jacob, don't leave!" to which Seth returned, "I don't believe even my thoughts could reach him, my friend."

"Is he already gone then?"

"I don't know. We are too distant. As we draw closer, I will try."

Tsandra followed close behind Teren and the others; she was not going to be left behind. Captain Mikhal spurred his horse to the lead, as he knew the way best. Ahead of them lay low-lying hills, mostly a series of short inclines and declines that occurred only along the coast.

The shore they rode along reached out into the sea via an outcropping of rocky crags. As they rode, the shoreline changed, weaving back and forth from rocky outcroppings to straight-line earthen bluffs, which the water was slowly eroding away. In the distance, as the captain promised, lay a sandy-beached inlet, where the ships should be waiting.

Seth reached out with his thoughts, trying to reach a consciousness that could understand his words. At first he just called out with a name, and then a simple message, "Wait!" hoping the strength of his will could breach the distance. He retreated his will when he perceived that nothing lay ahead of them. He hoped it was just that he could not reach whoever was out there yet.

Teren veered right suddenly as if struck, coming to an abrupt halt. He thought he felt a tug of a consciousness upon his mind, but the voice he heard could not be here; it did not belong to the plains.

Teren turned back to the path and began again, casting off the thoughts.

Seth and Tsandra also felt the voice touch their farseeing minds, but only Seth returned the call. Nothing returned to him as he reached out, and he rode on in silence. Tsandra whispered to his mind that perhaps they had all been mistaken, which Seth accepted.

The snows had barely touched the coastal areas, but a thin layer of it still clung to the frosted ground, and not far away it lay in deep mounds. They rode as those possessed, knowing their travel-weary animals wished to rest. Other thoughts pervaded the riders' minds; they were also weary and did not have time to waste.

As they approached the inlet, which was still a good clip away, the tip of a mast seemed to protrude above the line where the shore appeared to join the sea. Seth reached out again with his mind and perceived a presence. "Wait! Do not go!" he yelled outward.

Valam released a sigh of hope. He hoped what he had read in the last pages of the book were not true. He did not understand everything he had read, but he hoped the closing was false. In his mind he pictured the last page, and slowly his eyes led him to the last paragraph, which he re-read again in his mind. "By the time you read this, we will have returned to the kingdom, our home; do not hold ill feelings toward us for we waited as long as we could endure, and this the last I write in honor of Prince Valam, who, among others, gave his life for your lands. Say a prayer for him so that he may rest in peace."

Father Jacob had always been long-winded, thought Valam as he returned from his reverie. As was Keeper Martin, he added a moment later. His thoughts soared as the white of a sail grew before his eyes. Indeed, it was only a small tip, but it was a sail, he was sure.

As they drew nearer to the curve of the coast which led into the inlet, it became readily apparent that many ships floated in the small harbor, not just one. In their thoughts, they sang for joy; it was a beautiful sight. Seth called out again, in thought, and told them who they were, and why they had come. He registered great surprise in many of the minds he touched, and one almost collapsed with shock upon hearing the sound of his voice.

Those on the flagship sent out a message to the other ships, which had also heard Seth's message, and were already commencing the orders to lower their sails and weigh anchors. A longboat launched from the lead and made for shore and was soon followed by a second one from a different ship.

"Brother Liyan, no, you must leave," directed a voice into Liyan's mind alone.

"We cannot."

"They must not see him."

"It is too late."

As the group was ferried out to the flagship, a single rider faded into the distance. Valam sighed as the waves sent a calm sweeping through him. He thought perhaps Cagan should have come with them; he would have enjoyed the ride immensely. Later, as an afterthought, a shudder ran down his spine as he watched in thought as a boat sank into dark churning waters.

The trek from shore to the ship was short, and soon the oarsmen were maneuvering the longboat gracefully along the port side of the waiting vessel. Valam accepted the outstretched hand as he stepped up to the deck, taking in with a single glance the whole of the ship from aft to stern as he did so. He was greeted with surprise and disbelief, and certain awe intermingled with relief and thanks.

"By the Father!" exclaimed Father Jacob. "We had given up hope of supplies ever reaching us and behold what they return with!"

Father Jacob hesitated as he reached out for Valam, a hint of doubt touching his lips. "I am real!" replied Valam. "Believe it!"

"I do, but for so long I have thought you had passed."

"No such luck, I am afraid."

Valam's reply brought a smile to the father's deeply worried face. "You must tell me everything! Don't forget anything! But wait—wait until later," said Jacob as Valam began to speak. "First things first. The supplies?"

"Yes, Father Jacob, the supplies are here although for a time we thought you weren't."

"I am sorry. I lost my faith, but it was only momentary," said Father Jacob. As he talked with Valam, the embedded lines in his face seemed to lighten and the weariness of his soul began to disappear. So much had been heavy on his mind lately. It was a great relief, a breath of fresh air, to see Valam's face flourishing with color, with life.

"How long will it take to unload these boats and return to camp?"

"Not very long at all," said Father Jacob, winking, "we have only men and horses aboard and few supplies. You will be surprised how fast they unload when the word is spread that Prince Valam, or should I say King Valam, has returned."

Father Jacob bit back any further words. His tongue had slipped; he had said too much. The fatigue had not so easily left him as he had thought; his mind was still not as sharp as it ought to be. Father Jacob hoped that perhaps Valam had not understood his words, but his looks gave everything away to Valam. Any sense of happiness left Valam's face as he realized the import of Father Jacob's words.

"When? How? How long have you known?" pleaded Valam, retaining his composure, but stuttering over his words.

"I do not know for sure," began Father Jacob, choosing his words very tactfully, "perhaps—no, not perhaps. Prince Valam, I am very sure. Come, we should withdraw to my cabin for a time."

Father Jacob was quick to note who was close at hand and could also have overheard their conversation. He was glad to note only Captain Mikhal, to whom he offered a glum smile as a greeting, and Brother Seth, whom he indicated should follow. They were the only ones close enough to have overheard his conversation. The others behind them, none of whom Father Jacob knew, were told politely to wait. Tsandra was the only one who was offended.

"Why did you not return to the kingdom at once!" demanded Valam.

Father Jacob looked hurt and did not reply. He was attempting to gather his wits before he opened his mouth and said anything further. Valam mistook the silence as another opening to lash out, which he did harshly.

Father Jacob quietly spoke the words that he would have preferred never to repeat. Quickly and precisely he brought Valam up-to-date. Father Jacob's account was very well spoken, which was a big surprise, mostly to himself, because of the confusion in his thoughts.

Valam was slow to respond as Jacob finished, and Jacob had not expected, nor wanted Valam to reply to his words. Nevertheless, Valam spoke. Sorrow overshadowed his words, which would hang heavy on all who were present for a long time to come. After he finished, Valam returned above decks; there was too much to be done to allow a delay to mull over past events.

Shortly after Valam left, Captain Mikhal knocked on the cabin door and entered. The captain remained very official as he walked in and announced that the flagman was already sending orders to the other ships. By his estimate, if they hurried, the camp, which included the new arrivals and many supplies, could be fully organized by nightfall.

Seth stopped Father Jacob, who was about to leave the room, after Captain Mikhal departed. Seth understood much more than Jacob did about Valam's current situation; a number of pressing matters were on Valam's shoulders already and Seth also knew enough about Jacob to say the right words to calm him. "It was not your fault, Father Jacob. You said the right things. He will accept it. Give him some time. I felt the things he did not say."

"You, Brother Seth, are a very wise man," said Father Jacob, as the despair began to leave his eyes.

"Yes, but I know another wiser," replied Seth. "Come, I have someone I would really like to introduce you to. I think you and he will have a lot in common."

Seth introduced Father Jacob to Teren, Tsandra, and lastly Liyan. He was right—Liyan and Father Jacob were very much alike. He could feel questions bubbling through the father's mind as the three talked. Momentarily, Seth's thoughts roamed to Valam, who had gone to the bow of the ship where only the wind in his face was a companion.

Valam stayed there for a long time watching the waves roll into the ship and feeling the swaying of the boat beneath his feet. He contemplated numerous things before he finally rejoined his friends, but most importantly he said a few long overdue words to someone who was gone. Afterwards he felt much the better for saying those words.

Chapter Eleven

High, fortified walls of stone rose before them, looming greater with each step. Even on their horses, the travelers looked minuscule compared to the heights of the peaks; the mighty oaks even paled in comparison. Their minds were filled with wonder, even though some had seen the guarded fortress before.

Noman reminded them that it was more an outcropping of rock, a mountain, than a man-made structure, but awe still marked their expressions as they passed within the city gates. The only requirement for passage was a token, an offering that spoke more even than gold to those who dwelled within the city's walls. All had readily given up their armaments without a word of protest. Most had heard rumors of the penalty for not doing so, and Noman ensured that they heard them again as fact, so when they were requested to relinquish their arms, they did so quickly out of fear more than anything else.

The horses and carriages were deposited at a livery that was tucked just inside the walls. No animals were allowed into the city streets, another rule that none challenged. The only good law they fell under was the hood drawn close to Adrina's face, and the cloak attached, which dropped to her ankles. A woman's flesh could beguile the eyes of the beholder, and that was an intolerable insult.

Concealment at this point was what they had planned for Adrina all along, and the cloak made it all the easier.

Noman carefully reminded them of the rules, begging them to insure that no one broke any of them. They quickly made for the closest inn. Noman also made sure that everyone knew why they were here, telling them that although the disadvantages seemed to outweigh the advantages, a great deal could be gained, chief among which was information.

The first inn they came upon was unremarkable in all respects from the outside, a fact that Xith highly approved. The inside was plain and clear, with a short staircase at either end of a long, almost oval-shaped hall. The atmosphere was dim but well aired, the kind of place they could feel right at home in, Xith especially.

As it was still very early in the day, the inn was mostly empty save for the inn-keeper and a single man servant, who was quick to show them to their respective rooms following the payment of a small retainer. The rooms were small and quite cramped with furniture, each having two beds, a washstand, standing closets, which were unusual. Most surprising was the table with four chairs, rarely seen in an inn in the kingdom.

The rooms had a stagnant odor of heavy smoke or possibly perfume that had been around for a long time. Since the innkeeper had only afforded them four rooms, several cots were brought in and crowded the tiny spaces, eliminating any hope of movement. This might have been deliberate. If they had no area to relax in they would probably use the inn's bar all the more. Strangers did not fare well in the eyes of the populace, but their money was never refused.

Xith wondered if they would have received better accommodations if he told the innkeeper that they planned to spend a goodly amount of time partaking of his ale. This was part of their plan, for there was no better place to gather information. Xith, Noman, and Nijal requested that Amir and Adrina wait upstairs and that Shchander and his men proceed to the tavern below while they went to have a look about the city.

Noman would have preferred Amir at his side, but he understood Xith's choice and accepted it as a fair one. The best place for Amir was beside Adrina. They need not fear for her safety while they were gone. Nijal was very quick to his feet and out the door, for he expected Amir to object.

The structures they passed along the city streets were in heavy contrast to the high stone walls surrounding them. Largely constructed of wood with little stone, they seemed an oddity. The levels spiraling up around them were also unusual and a masterful feat of architecture.

As the three strode deep into the city's center, the area over their heads began to look cramped. The upper levels of the buildings were connected by a series of interconnecting suspended bridges with some structures having as many as ten or more such bridges leading from their upper floors. Xith explained to Nijal that this was because the walls of the city had been constructed very long ago, and any room for expansion along the city's avenues had been used up centuries ago. The only direction that remained to build was up, an art the residents had perfected through the ages.

Noman looked for a shop that had long been on the second floor of the district they now wandered through. To get to the second level, they had to take a short cut through several stores connected at street level. This brought them to a staircase that opened to another shop on the second level, which finally carried them out to a bridge crossing.

Nijal took Noman's sudden halt midway across the bridge as a sign that it was okay to look about. He watched the people wander the streets below; most were tall and stout, even the women, or at least those he thought were women because of the cloaks wrapped tightly around them. He noticed that most of the people greeted each other with a bleak grimace on their faces, which changed to an expressionless mask afterwards.

Xith quickly pulled Nijal across the bridge and into an adjacent shop, which turned out to be a residence. They left hurriedly. "I thought you knew where you were going!" hissed Xith.

"It has been some time; give me a moment," said Noman.

They crisscrossed back and forth along the avenue, moving in and out of many different places, ending up several blocks from where they started, but Noman assured Xith that this was the corner he had been seeking. The new levels of the ever changing city had just thrown him off, that's all. Their confused actions brought much attention to their movements, and many shopkeepers and residents stared at them from their doorways.

The place they stood in front of looked more like someone's home than a shop of any sort. It was completely dark from the outside, and no sign hung above its door. It appeared rather deserted. Noman tried the door, which gingerly opened at his touch, and he urged Xith and Nijal to step inside speedily.

There was no light in the room save that which poured in from around the frame of the door. It took some time for their eyes to adjust to the darkness. As their eyes adjusted, they noticed that the room was completely empty, void of all furniture or sign of inhabitation.

"Nothing!" said Nijal, "Let's leave."

"Not just yet," said Noman, "this is the place we were looking for."

"But it's empty."

"Only by appearances."

Noman entered a corridor that Nijal had not seen until the other stepped into it. He then opened a door and deep amber light issued forth, for which Nijal was very thankful. Nijal turned to talk to Xith, but Xith was not there. "Come on, hurry!" whispered Noman to Nijal. Hesitantly, Nijal followed.

The room they walked into was extremely large but was as cluttered as their rooms at the inn. Nijal thought to himself that the owner would do well to move some of these things into the empty space he had been standing in moments before. At the end of a long, narrow table sat an old man bent with the weight of many years. The light came from a single lantern on a table beside him.

Noman pulled a long-handled dagger from his cloak, the likes of which Nijal had never seen. The blade was twisted from the tip to the hilt and inlaid with fine workmanship; an animal of sorts appeared on one side and a man on the other. Nijal saw this only because he now held the dagger in his own hand, as Noman handed it to him.

"Be true on your mark," whispered Noman, "you only have one chance."

"You mean, throw it?"

"Yes, but do not miss."

"Kill him?"

"Yes, of course."

Nijal was confused at best, but proceeded as Noman instructed.

The tip of the blade felt cold in his hands as he touched it. He drew his arm back straight and precise, taking in a deep breath, and holding it as he released. The blade fell end over end, directly on target, just as Nijal intended.

Nijal saw the dagger touch the man's head just between the eyes where he aimed it, but it went no further. The man raised his eyes from the tome he read as if impatient for having been disturbed. "Very peculiar way of greeting," rolled the words from the old man's tongue in a slow, drawn-out drawl.

"Yes, very peculiar indeed," replied Noman, adding after a short silence, "just returning the favor."

"Still holding on to that after such a long time, eh?"

"The past is often all we have."

"Yes, yes it is," said the man, indicating they should sit.

"Where is Xith?" asked Nijal quietly.

"He will return shortly."

"Has it come so quickly?"

"Nay, it has not been quick," said Noman, "I believe you still owe me one favor."

"Yes, the last," spoke the old man lightly.

"You know I would not ask if the need were not great."

"Old friend, you least of all need explain yourself. Talk, and I will listen."

Many words long and wise passed across Noman's lips in the hours that followed. Nijal mostly sat and listened, eyes wide with wonder at the re-telling. He also learned many things, and a great many things suddenly became clear to him.

Xith came back shortly after Noman came to the end and returned to the present. The old one's face lit up as Xith entered the room and crossed it to sit beside Noman. During his absence, Xith had acquired and filled a satchel. Something within had a heavy sweet aroma, which now rose and lingered just above the table, seemingly within reach of their watering tongues.

"Is it clear now?" asked the old one of Xith.

"I did not see it until it was beneath my nose, but as we came inside, I knew it could only be your house. You said one day I would meet him, and until a short while ago I did not believe you. And here you sit as if waiting."

"I was. Now, for me it is complete," said the man, adding after a lengthy break, "with the last, of course." He spread his lips to form a toothless smile. "You were always the obstinate one, weren't you?"

"That I was, but I remembered my promise," said Xith, drawing a small package from his satchel. Nijal passed it on, and the old man snatched it up, setting it on the corner of the table beside him as if it were gold, where it lay unopened.

He cleared his voice, deep and harsh, vibrating the air in the room. And then there was silence while he stopped, apparently engrossed in thought. "The time approaches although you see it not. Its shadows are far reaching and some already think it has arrived, but alas it has not. You will mark the time beyond it, when your eyes are once again filled with sight." The last sentence had been directed entirely at Noman, which was very clear to those who watched. His eyes grew distant and unfocused, and his face grew pale.

Nijal could no longer comprehend the words. As he strained to hear them, only bits and pieces carried through to his consciousness. Puzzled and frustrated, he mulled over each sound he perceived, but soon all understanding was beyond him. Only a single fragment of all that followed remained in his mind as the sound of words came to a halt. "The dragons are with her."

"Until the next, Y'sat," called out Xith as he, Nijal, and Noman departed.

"Are we returning to the inn?" asked Nijal.

"No, we have one more stop. Stay close," chided Xith.

After returning through the maze of shops, bridges, and buildings, they found themselves back on the ground level and a short time later they left the center of the city behind. The wall now loomed overhead, and it blocked out the last of the late-day sun, so now they wandered through the shadows, which for Nijal was not a comforting fact.

The dwellings they passed along and sometimes through, up and around, were newer; and construction, almost entirely upward, was ongoing. It was apparent to Nijal that both Xith and Noman were looking for a place he suspected they had never been to before. As far as he could tell, they probably only knew it by name, or even face, if it were a person they sought.

They walked until only a single street stood between them and the northernmost part of the wall. The narrow byroad ran east to west and was obviously losing the fight to maintain a distance between the buildings and the wall, both of which appeared to be closing in on it. At the far easterly corner, a thin tapering stair circled its way up the wall, the only stair they had seen in the whole of the wall.

Xith smiled as he saw the stair and turned almost mid-step, taking a bearing on it and the wall. Directly in front of him was a small alleyway. Two shops down, out of the darkness, shone a lantern. Below it, hung a little wooden sign with a picture of a clenched fist.

Unlike the cramped alleyways that led to the alehouse, the Clenched-Fist was quite spacious and resounded with laughter and song, which took Nijal completely by surprise. Xith pushed Nijal to the fore, and so he entered first, followed by Xith and then Noman.

The bar was crowded with people drinking and singing, but Xith steered Nijal to a dark, dingy back room, where amidst the gloom sat a group of men who did not appear to notice them. Their eyes were fixed on the wall at the far end of the room and a man who stood with a set of knives in his hand. On the wall was a target of sorts, where after much deliberation and calculation, the man directed his blades.

Nijal snickered and whispered to Xith, "I could do better than that," words that he would soon regret as Xith replied, "That is what we hoped."

"Why me?" asked Nijal.

"We, my friend, are in need of a little pocket money, and you need the practice."

"This is for money?"

"What else would it be for?"

Nijal knew right then that he was in for a long evening. "But I don't even know the rules."

"All the better," retorted Xith, "all the better."

"But, but—"

"Listen closely. Here are the rules; they are quite simple. There are three marks, the hands, left and right, and the head. If you lead, you pick the mark; if you follow, you must make the same marks as the opponent. You have three blades. Aim for the center of each mark; beware the outstretched fingers; how hard can that be?"

Xith left out most of the details in the rules, but Nijal soon caught on as he watched. "Are you ready?" asked Xith and before Nijal could answer, Xith raised his wager to the board. A murmur rose as he placed the gold piece down beside the one who stood thus far undefeated.

"You little man?" boomed a loud voice.

Xith wavered his head, and pointed to Nijal. Nijal sank in his chair under the stern gaze he quickly received. The man smiled and said, "Watch, and Pilio will show you how it's done."

Pilio stood stiffly, meticulously aligning himself with the target. After much deliberation, he delivered his first knife nicely, center right hand. He followed through with a second to the head, and the last to the left hand. His blades were all directly centered in their respective places.

Nijal still had to hold back a laugh as he watched Pilio. He looked as if he were under severe strain as he took aim, and his relief came only when all three knives had left his hand. He weighed each dagger in his hand before he started. He found it odd that all three were of different weights, another fact that Xith had obviously neglected to tell him. The differences in weight made it more difficult to follow through with aim and delivery.

To some degree, Nijal now understood Pilio's hesitation. He also considered that now it would be more difficult for him to be centered on target, as the blades were still in the target. He calculated his first choice. He considered a long time before he released the first, but it held true to its destination. After a quick adjustment for weight and positioning, he threw the last two. His shots, although nice and clean within the target, were not as centered as his competitor, and Pilio quickly claimed his prize.

"Again," said Xith, this time putting two gold coins on the table.

Pilio accepted the offer without thought; he would take a fool's money any time. His next three shots, to the surprise of the onlookers, were all to the right hand, and were nicely packed around the center point of the palm. Nijal tossed a stern look to Xith; there was no way he could match or even win. He was left with little space in which to place his blades, but he tried. Two to the center, and one to the outside, which cost Xith his gold.

Pilio's grin broadened as he plucked up the gold and tucked it away into his purse, a small leather satchel tucked into his belt at his side. Noman said nothing so far, but he watched intensely. Xith again placed two gold coins for a bet.

Nijal watched Pilio with grave concern as he, with great care, placed his marks on the target, center, left, and right. "Relax," soothed Noman as Nijal paced the floor. Nijal's first knife, although slightly off center was placed well. He hesitated on the second, considering the blade in his hand. The second glided from his hand, landing fair, but the third fell dead center, and to his surprise he won, which he only knew because of the dejected look on Pilio's face.

With a slightly red face, Pilio gave up the gold coins, and Xith readily accepted. Nijal paused, as he had never been first and had to think about where to begin. Pilio stopped Nijal a moment and traded sets of knives with him. Although confused, Nijal accepted, giving his blades back to Pilio.

The balance of the new daggers was completely different from those that Nijal previously used, causing him to delay as he considered each separately. Satisfied, Nijal began again. The wins and losses shifted back and forth for a long while with neither side clearly claiming victory, although Pilio's purse was visibly shrunken.

Xith tossed in a "Good, good!" now and again, but he, like Noman, was mostly quiet.

Nijal was growing quite pleased with his performance as the night drew on. His lack of common sense and his vanity cost him the next two matches, but he won the third quite skillfully with three neatly thrown scores. He winked at Pilio as he exchanged blades with him, taking careful pace from the target. He also cast a wink towards Xith and Noman as he cast his first knife.

The wink cost him dearly, for he twitched just as the blade released from his fingers. Pilio's eyes went wide as the tip struck one of the outstretched fingers of the left hand. Suddenly the room filled with the noise of people shifting heavily in their chairs or coughing. Nijal smiled at Xith and turned to Pilio and shrugged his shoulders. Xith was clearly worried and angry, but he walked over to where Nijal stood and calmly said to him in a low tone, "You must get two more fingers of the left hand. Do not miss."

"Or what?" whispered Nijal in jest.

"Just do it!" snapped Xith, greatly displeased.

Nijal stared at Xith as he walked away and retook his place beside Noman. The many eyes fixed upon him, quietly watching, bore heavily upon him. He didn't understand what he had done, but he knew when to listen to Xith. For a very long time, he stood contemplating the dagger in his hand and the target before him. Xith took in a deep breath as the second dagger struck the middle finger.

As Nijal stood poised with the third dagger, he could feel the room stop with him as if everyone waited to draw in a breath. He closed his eyes; the air was charged about him as he heavily breathed it in. He opened his eyes and fixed on the target, drawing his hand back slowly, releasing only after he calculated the balance of the blade in his hand. "Yes!" he cried as it hit. Xith shook his head at Nijal, who still did not understand the gravity of his situation.

Pilio was more tedious and cautious than ever as he stood at the ready. He insured the placement of his feet just behind the line, but then he had to insure the validity of the line again, so he paced it off and then repositioned himself. The whole process was long and very meticulous. The joyful expression had long since left Pilio's face. He closed his eyes in relief as the first took the index finger of the right hand cleanly on mark.

Pilio paced back and forth as he concentrated on his next mark. He even went so far as to measure the balance of the dagger on the tip of his finger and to check the movement of the air within the room. All of a sudden, he stopped and placed the two remaining daggers he held onto the table, rubbing his sweaty palms until they were dry. Then, after flexing his fingers and cracking each knuckle, he picked up only one of the daggers, moving slowly and methodically back into his stance.

His face showed displeasure as the knife tumbled from his fingertips, but it hit its mark, and he sighed deeply in relief. He was growing visibly nervous as he placed the last blade carefully in his hand, also insuring its balance before he drew his arm back and released it. The entire process took the better part of a quarter of an hour.

Astonished as it struck, Pilio rushed to the board to check, as did several onlookers. The tip of the knife had struck directly on the line of the third finger. Being an honest man, the only virtue he held to, Pilio accepted his loss.

Pilio pulled the blade from the target and handed it to Nijal, saying, "I didn't mean to offend. Take whichever one you like." Pilio placed his hands outstretched onto the table. Xith jumped up from his chair and ran towards the two, afraid of what Nijal would do. "We will be quite satisfied with quadruple our original wager."

"Quadruple?" asked Pilio, raising his quivering voice high.

"Quadruple," replied Xith.

Pilio sighed, hurriedly pulled from his purse a handful of gold, and passed it to Nijal. He thought the sum was a very fair amount, given the circumstances. "Good match, master," said Pilio. Xith immediately took Nijal away. The three of them hurriedly left the Clenched-Fist.

A little confused and slightly hurt, Nijal turned to Xith and said, "I didn't know."

"Never mind," returned Xith.

Noman's response was somewhat gentler than Xith's and he made a valid point. Xith had not told Nijal all the rules of the game. "I think he did well, quite well, all things considered."

Chapter Twelve

Chancellor Volnej detached himself from the other six. He was alone, pacing heavily across the floor. Many thoughts weighed on his mind: the kingdom was without council, without an heir, and soon to be without a capital. He had watched the keepers fall, the council fall, the priests of the Father fall, noble hearted men fall. His heart could not endure all the pain, nor could his mind.

He was too weary and old to have the will to go on a prolonged journey of any sort, let alone try to escape. He would only slow the others down and surely cause their capture. His mind was resolved; he would stay in Imtal. In his own way he could not stand to leave it nor could he abide to see it fall, but he was sure that he must stay.

The venerable chancellor thought of a way to insure that the others would leave him. He thought about it as he listened to them. He had served king and prince and long-ago queen while on the high council. He considered his life to have been very fulfilled and fruitful, but now he saw only an ending before him. As he approached the others, it was Calyin who understood the message upon his face first and she begged him to come with them, but his mind was sternly set.

"With three, we are seven," whispered Calyin as she held his hand firmly.

"No, that is not true. I do not believe I was included in those words. In fact, I am almost positive."

"I think the chancellor is correct," said Swordmaster Timmer. "I also believe my place is here."

"As do I. We stay!" said Captain Brodst.

"No, Captain Brodst, your fate is with them; of this I am also sure. Listen to an old man, who is many years your elder speak to you with wisdom."

"Do not worry," said Timmer, moving towards the chancellor. Timmer also understood the reasons Volnej thought it best to stay. His sword arm was not what it used to be, and if a real fight came, they would not survive it. They needed speed, and on foot they did not need old men to slow them down. "I will take care of Chancellor Volnej. We will find a way through this, but you, my friends, must go. I think together we can get you past the city gates, but beyond it there will just be the five of you, as it was meant to be."

Lord Serant's voice turned icy cold as he stared at Captain Brodst; he could tell that the captain still was not convinced that he should go. "I have never fully accounted what occurred in the square after the struggle and the mysterious two who appeared before us wearing faces very dear to our hearts. I have not even spoken fully of this to Calyin, my beloved wife, for he bade me speak to none until the time had come when the truth could be prolonged no more. But in fact, few ever saw the face of the stranger. Of those they were mostly Geoffrey and his men, who are now twice indebted to the one, if I am correct."

Geoffrey lowered his head and then raised it.

"The remainder who saw him are gone save a few of us here at this very moment. I know questions lie in your minds as they do in mine, and I am also afraid that in truth I know little more than Lord Geoffrey, but I believed then and I wholly and firmly believe now the words that the one called Noman spoke to me. He said, 'Our paths are coming to an end and a meeting, and our time is at an end and a beginning.' He spoke of many things quickly and carefully, for he wanted me to remember in full detail when the time came, if it came; but he had little time to tarry. He told me that none would question what they had seen on the square that day beyond what I offered, and no one has. He told me the names of the three I would journey away from the darkness with, and of that I had my doubts, for how could anyone hold the future so well in their hands and still not know it in its entirety? But now the faces stand before me in an hour of grave peril. Geoffrey, Midori, and Captain Brodst."

Calyin raised her eyes as if wondering if she had been mentioned.

"Yes, my dear, he also said he saw a hand clasped in mine, but not a face and that is you. So you see, Captain Brodst, you must come. Your fate lies with us."

"What of the seven the others spoke of?"

"Of this, I am sure. It will be revealed to us all in good time. Come, we have delayed far too long."

Turmoil, the thing they counted on to make their escape possible, was decreasing. The ebbing of the sounds of battle and the emptiness of the halls and courtyards told them this. Although they were still using obscure corridors and rooms, they still expected to meet some resistance as they made their way; however, up to now they found none. They hid themselves some 200 feet from the rear wall of the palace, staring in disbelief at the open, unoccupied gate.

"There is some trick about. There must be," whispered Lord

Serant.

"I do not believe so," replied Volnej.

"I side with Lord Serant. I do not trust it, but we have no choice but to move forward and soon," added Geoffrey.

"Let's go!" said Midori moving from their guarded spot. Lord Serant put out his arm to halt her. "Wait," bade Serant. He squinted to the far corner tower. "There, do you see it," he said pointing.

"I'll be," said Geoffrey as he also caught a glimpse of the forms hiding in the shadows.

"How do we get past?" asked Captain Brodst, considering the options himself as he asked the question.

"I see two options: run or take them out."

"I'll vote on running," quickly stated Timmer, even though he had the least chance of success for such a measure.

"Surely there are more in waiting. I say we find another way."

"I do not believe we have the time. Timmer, Volnej, and Geoffrey, you take the right, and we three will take the left. Captain Brodst, your job is to get their attention."

"And then what?" whispered Captain Brodst.

"Don't worry; I trust your judgment. We'll follow."

"Thanks, thanks a lot!" muttered Brodst as he crept carefully away from the wall. The others behind him split into two groups as Lord Serant had requested, one moving left and the other right. The captain counted his blessings; at least he knew the back wall better than the others. Stairs stood in each of the towers at either end of the wall with two more narrow staircases on either side of the gates within the guardhouses.

Captain Brodst was very careful of the sound of his footfalls on the hard-surfaced stairs, but even so the rock carried an echo upward. He was fortunate to know exactly what lay around each turn, and as he passed the last stair, he stopped. He shrank down to all fours and peered around the corner, looking in both directions. He noted two sentries to the left and several more far to the right.

He watched them for a time, hoping the others were doing likewise before they swept forward. One of the guards, a tall, lanky-looking fellow clad in a loosely fitting robe with a heavy mailed suit beneath, was signaling to someone in the square opposite the palace walls. "Damn it," cursed Brodst. The man fell as he was clubbed from behind. His companion was quick to follow him.

Captain Brodst ran forward, still bent over, coming up behind one of those to the right. Before he reached him, Geoffrey had already waylaid his companion and the man was about to scream, but Brodst clipped his tongue just in time. Captain Brodst pulled Geoffrey down behind the wall, signaling for the other two to do likewise.

"What is it?" asked Geoffrey.

"In the square there are more. Pray that they did not see your foolishness."

"We had to act," said Geoffrey, but as he turned back, the captain was gone. He had already crept back towards Lord Serant. Fortunately, Lord Serant had the good sense to crouch down after the successful attack. Captain Brodst whispered the news to him, "There are others in the square."

"Yes, I know," replied Lord Serant.

"Fool, then why did you stand and take him."

"The sentry below had turned his back to us."

Captain Brodst swallowed any further words. He knew Serant wasn't a fool, so he should have known better than to think he would be careless in so grave a matter. He thought to offer an apology, but Lord Serant had already turned to other matters.

"We were not seen, I am sure," spoke Geoffrey as he reached the place where Captain Brodst perched, peering over the wall ever so slightly.

"Good, good. Timmer, Volnej?"

"They watch the stairs at the tower and the guardhouse."

"Come, we must be swift. Two more approach," said Lord Serant, springing to action. He carried everyone with him as he made for the place Timmer watched. Serant issued hurried orders; he supposed that two men were positioned on either side of the gate. Geoffrey and Timmer would take them out. He would go straight for the one who stood in the center of the square. He assumed that that one was the leader, and was the one he had seen signaling the others. Volnej was to make certain that Calyin and Midori reached the far side of the square and the alleyway beyond. And Captain Brodst had the two who approached from the palace proper; he was to take them out as he saw fit, only doing so if it became necessary.

As Serant reached the bottom landing, he stopped firm, waiting for Geoffrey and Timmer to pass him before he began to move again, meanwhile drawing his sword and a small blade. He touched the two on the shoulder as they passed, so instructing them to halt. He waited for the one to turn his back to him and as he did, Lord Serant whispered, "Go!"

Lord Serant sprinted across the square, his feet softly striking the stones. His boots lay discarded some distance away. His blade was swift and true as he released it from his hand, dropping the man where he stood. His sword soon followed up to insure that the man was dead. He whispered in his mind as he did so, "Fool, soft leather does little to protect you in battle. Death has found you."

Lord Serant carefully scanned the area around the square in a wide circle. He saw Calyin and the other two reach the safety of the dark alley. Timmer and Geoffrey had felled their opponents and were also on their way to hiding. Only Captain Brodst was absent. "Come on," whispered Serant under his breath. He turned nervously, pausing only to take in the surrounding shadows again. "Come on," he thought again.

"Yes," struck his mind as he saw the captain's form racing towards him. He retrieved his dagger and relieved the dead one of his blade while he waited for Captain Brodst to catch up to him; then the two crept off across the square.

From the shadows of many alleys, byways, and small paths the seven stole from the city center toward the postern gates on the lower east side, a direction that Lord Serant hoped would not be as closely watched as the others, since it was not an obvious exit. It had been sealed for decades; furthermore, it lay just off the lower market square in plain view.

Lord Serant was pleased to see that Calyin and Midori had wisely collected several blades for their own use, so he stashed at his own side the short sword he had obtained; an extra blade would always come in handy. The streets were mostly empty, which did not surprise Lord Serant. His heart sorrowed for the citizens of Imtal, whom he could not protect from King Jarom's greedy hands, but he vowed to return and amend the situation at the first opportunity. Under other circumstances, he would have thought his deeds cowardly, and cowardice did not sit well with him. But for now, in view of what he had seen, he considered his actions a tactical, necessary retreat.

Sore bodies carried them and weary legs moved tired feet, but their minds pushed them on beyond their limits. Soon they found themselves on the edge of a small deserted marketplace. Lord Serant marked the progress of the sun as he planned their movements. They would move just after dusk; the wait would not be long. All things considered, he thought this day was the longest of his life. It seemed to him that the sun fought to linger in the skies overhead to prevent darkness from arriving.

The minutes, or hours, of waiting seemed to go on forever, but darkness eventually began to fall. The air around them had a peaceful silence as it had since their arrival. The beating of their hearts seemed to echo around them. Their breaths became great bellows and the shifting of their feet a blade on a grindstone. Eyes flickered nervously back and forth, up and down, ever watching.

"Are you sure you know how to open this?" whispered Brodst to Serant.

"I am sure," replied Calyin, speaking before Lord Serant could reply. "A certain boy I knew long ago had taken a fancy to this very exit, or entrance rather—" Her voice died on the last words, and no one heard them save for Serant who was directly beside her.

"Yes, he did show me," he softly whispered into Calyin's ear; his voice was also saddened. "With luck he will return, though I hope not soon. The goings-on would shrivel his heart and pluck out his eyes."

The sound of horses' hooves froze his heart and his lips. Everyone drew tight against the wall, withdrawing into the gray shadows as best they could. Two horsemen broke into the square directly across from their position, coming straight for them. Serant edged back along the shadows, but he held firm for a time, hoping the riders would not come near.

The clatter of several pairs of hooves against hard rock carried loudly to their listening ears. The two riders seemed to circle the square two or three times as if searching. Once or twice Brodst and Serant perceived eyes on them, but then as swiftly as the two appeared, they were gone. The sound of their retreat echoed for a long time before it faded away. Lord Serant slumped against the wall and sank to his knees in relief; they would wait for a short time before they would go for the wall and escape beyond it. He hoped the night would be very dark.

In a tiny cleft hidden three bricks high and two bricks in along the high stone wall, lay the gate key, where it had lain now for many years. Lord Serant breathed deeply and flashed its form back to the others who yet waited in the shadows. The night was as dark as he would have hoped; stars peeked in and out of light cloud cover and a twinkle of brass caught Captain Brodst's eye. He bade the others to follow his lead into the square.

One by one they crossed the square to the dark recesses by the wall. Geoffrey was the last to leave the alley, his methodical gait, though scarcely audible, grew closer. Five waited patiently for his arrival. Timmer remained where he was; this was the end of his journey this day. The chancellor had only left his side to insure that the gate was secured before the two made their retreat, which would be separate from the others. The chancellor and Timmer had business elsewhere within the city, and not beyond it. Lord Serant fiddled with the key in his hand, waiting to release the latch when all was clear.

A shrill noise brought cold shivers. Geoffrey slumped flat against cool stone, lying motionless, waiting to insure that movement was safe. The noise passed, as sounds in the dark often do, and Geoffrey rose to his knees and crept away. He did not relax until Serant touched his shoulder reassuringly. "All is well," he whispered.

Lord Serant touched key to keyhole and turned it; after a slight hesitation and a little resistance, the old lock released and with a creak the gate opened. He did not dare to push it open more than a foot, fearing that the noise of the old hinges would surely rouse someone's attention. Serant was the first to slip beyond the city's walls and into the breezes of the night. Here Volnej parted with the others. Good-byes were hurried and speechless, as there was nothing more to be said, and their voices need not be heard.

Chapter Thirteen

Hours before the sun rose, the camp was a jumble of activity. Renewed hope and faith filled the thoughts of many. Prince Valam had returned at long last. They had enough supplies to carry them through the cold that lay ahead, and now they were ready to train for the coming challenge with all their hearts, more than ever before.

Seth regarded Liyan with inquiring eyes. There was something bothering Liyan, but he could not tell what. As he watched Liyan, he paced back and forth, and every now and again, he would glance out the small opening at the front of the tent to note the weather.

Several hours past first light, a messenger arrived with a summons for them. They were to meet the others in the command tent. The messenger said that Prince Valam was already anxiously awaiting their arrival. The two followed the messenger back towards the center of the camp and then circled off towards the command tent.

By the time Seth and Liyan arrived, almost everyone was already present and seated around the conference table, which was strewn with scrolls and maps, and even the remnants of several breakfasts, which were being cleared away as they entered. Seth wasn't surprised to find that Teren had already returned to the plains and his watch. He could tell that Teren had longed to be alone and away from past memories.

Tsandra sat smugly beside Cagan, and the two were engrossed in conversation. Evgej, Valam, and Father Jacob had withdrawn to a quiet corner away from the confusion at the center table. Captain Mikhal and several other men that Seth did not know were seated around the center table although Seth did not see the one called Danyel'.

Valam quickly returned when he noticed that Seth was present. He had been awaiting Seth and Liyan's arrival. Just as they were about to begin and the room grew quiet, several men hurried in and took their seats, apologizing for their tardiness. Valam did an account of who was present and who was still unaccounted for. Only Danyel' was still missing. He dispatched another runner to find him.

The room began to grow restless after a ten minute wait with no sign of Danyel'. Captain Mikhal grew visibly flushed as the lieutenant was his responsibility, so it became his fault that Danyel' was absent. After waiting several more minutes, Valam decided to begin without him even though he had counted on the other's presence.

Introductions were first, which Valam carried out at length, hoping Danyel' would arrive before he finished, but Danyel' did not. Valam went through a long list of names, titles and positions, adhering to the elaborate way Seth's people formally announced themselves. He started off with Liyan, and ended with Cagan. Tsandra was annoyed, for he had saved her for second to last, and she thought he was going to rank her last. Afterwards, he similarly announced those from the kingdom, saving the six lieutenants for last, and with side consultation from Captain Mikhal he made it through their names without error.

He finished and took his place at the table, marking each of the names in his mind, associating each with something that would stick in his memory and help him recall the name. Lieutenant Willam had piercing eyes of coal that held a hint of sparkle, perhaps a touch of blue or maybe it was just the reflection of the light. Pavil had a long wispy mustache and a stunted goatee. He stopped at Eran for a time, listening to what Father Jacob was saying and accidentally skipped to Tae, whose auburn locks were immediately distinctive, and then he backed up to Eran. He didn't really note anything that he could mark in his thoughts, so he went on. His eyes fell on Tae again. He stumbled once more over the face, which he had seen often at Quashan', but the name did not jump out at him, and he wondered why. S'tryil was another easy one, for he was the bladesmen to whom the prince and the entire kingdom was deeply indebted. Plus if he recalled correctly he had known a Lord S'tryil in his youth, perhaps the lieutenant's father. He would have to talk with S'tryil about that later.

Valam smiled as Father Jacob's words sparked his memory. Redcliff, that's the name, he thought, and he cast a sidelong glance at Tae although he couldn't quite recall how the nickname had come about. The last one Valam knew well; he did not need anything to recall the name. Ylsa had served directly under Captain Evgej when he had been a mere swordmaster third-class, and she had helped him, in fact, to attain the rank of swordmaster first-class. The rank of captain had come much later, of course, and only recently, but she was also a mystery to him, as Evgej had been until a short time ago. "Was it a short time?" thought Valam to himself. In all actuality it seemed so very long ago that the two of them and Seth had been together in the Belyj forest.

The weather outside turned severe as if on cue as Father Jacob raised the topic, discussing Liyan's concerns at length. Jacob cast a dreary sidelong stare at the flakes of snow falling just beyond his touch. Brother Liyan was correct—this odd season was full upon them, as was readily apparent.

Father Jacob paused only shortly, and then returned to full eloquent speech, laden with elaborate words, trying firmly to make his point, which he had considered thoroughly during many long and empty nights. He had been all set for a return trip to the kingdom and was rather disappointed at the turn of events. At long last, Jacob concluded and offered the floor to Valam, who was slow to draw on the cue offered him.

Valam had only briefly returned from his reverie and stood, as a commotion outside caused him to stop cold on his first word. He was the first to go to the door and first to hear the excited runner's message. "Riders from the north." Valam came to attention quickly. "How many?"

"Lieutenant Danyel' did not say, sire."

"Danyel'—where are Lieutenant Danyel' and his men?"

The runner pointed to the North, "Just beyond the first hill; they wait."

"Is he mad?" asked Valam aloud, although he had meant only to think it.

The runner nodded courteously and begged graciously to be dismissed, which Valam did without second thought. Valam's face grew pale as he retreated back into the tent and spread the news. He did not delay to run toward the far northerly side of the camp, clutching his sword. As he approached, he saw nothing but a rather large commotion spreading like wildfire around Danyel', who was mounted.

His eyes scanned the distance, but he saw nothing. He called out to the lieutenant, but his words were drowned amidst many voices. He waited until he was at the lieutenant's side to gain his attention. He did not have to speak, for the men quickly made a path for him to Danyel'; it was done without words and without hesitation. The men held him in extreme reverence since his return, even beyond that which his office normally rendered him.

"My prince, you have come. I give thanks," spoke Danyel', echoing his men's respect for Valam.

"What is it?"

"Listen."

Danyel' did not have to ask for silence. It followed as if Valam had ordered it. Valam listened, but he could hear nothing. "Wait," offered Danyel', "put your ear to the ground; it will tell."

Valam put his ear against the hard ground and listened. At first he heard nothing, but soon afterwards a faint rumbling sound rose to his ears. "How far away are they?"

"A good ten miles, but they come, sire."

"Can you tell how many?"

"My prince, it is a large group or the thunder would not carry such a distance. I would guess hundreds or more."

"Please part with the niceties," spoke Valam, "I am no king," and responding with the humbleness of Seth's people, a way which he had grown accustomed to and now preferred, he said, "I am the governor of South Province, son of Andrew, King of the Great Kingdom, this is true, which does make me a prince, but no more. I am very honored by your words and your reverence, but if such a tribute is to be paid to me, let it be earned in the field of battle and nowhere else."

In so saying, he endeared himself even more to those who listened. His voice became silent as he put all his attention on a distant point. Seth, Cagan and Evgej soon arrived, and after a short explanation, they waited, poised. Behind them the camp roused, as if to battle.

Seth considered the possibility that those approaching did not yet know of their presence, and his thoughts could possibly give that away to them if he reached out, so he would be silent until the force was close at hand.

Liyan was troubled; he watched quietly, whispering his thoughts only to Seth's mind. Behind him, Tsandra stood poised defiantly beside her mount, and forming behind her were those of her order, who gathered at her summons. Cagan and Evgej, who now stood to Valam's left and Seth's right, waited also.

Evgej, who had been afraid of the seas and very often seasick on their journey to the Eastern Reaches, missed the water and the craft of his forefathers whom he had long ago forsaken. He had never told Cagan that his father was a shipbuilder and that his father had been the one to build the ship for him, the one the rocks and sea had lain to rest. Evgej cut off the memories, thinking them odd for a time when his hand played along the hilt of his sword in waiting.

The uncomfortable waiting ended as a herald rose to their thoughts and to their hearts like the sound of a bugle in triumph. The will of Teren entered the minds of all who stood waiting. He told them he carried with him a band of mountaineers or so he named them, those he considered to be of his order, which was not that of the brown.

Teren's companions, all strongly built for elves, looked to be worthy adversaries in the trials that lay ahead. They, like Teren, lived on the Great Plains and roamed its vast span, changing their place of dwelling like the wind and with the seasons. Most often, or so Teren explained to Valam, they were to be found in the mountains that were the border between east and west, and it was their true home. They had come at Teren's bidding and because they believed it was time to let their presence be known.

Chapter Fourteen

Noman, Xith, and the others departed Zashchita just as the darkness of night waned. Shchander discussed the news he and his men had learned while at the inn. Noman was very pleased to note that word of the princess' disappearance was heard on no one's lips. Xith was also pleased; however, Y'sat's words still weighed heavily on his conscious, as he assumed they did on Noman, but Noman carried them better. Xith considered it good fortune, though, that most of the news was pleasant.

The next two days passed relatively slowly as they forgot the enchantment of the city. The dark specters that seemed to be with them before they had reached Zashchita returned and it was with heavy hearts that Noman and Xith kept on. Their thoughts often went to Ayrian and to Vilmos—the two that seemed to be lost to them—and to Adrina—the one who they seemed to be losing.

They held to the main roads through brief stretches of open prairie, yet mostly they moved through thick, lush forest greens. Growth in this area was very different from the heavy pine, tall oak, ash, elm and even a few cedars and walnut. An abundant mixture grew in the old forest, but the great forest now lay far to their west. Here the trees tended to be thick groves. Those they rode through now were beautiful, deep, and green, and the pungent smell of pine assaulted their nostrils. Ahead lay a large stand of thick, dark-wood trees that stretched out far beyond their view, which was apparent only because of the high, fir-covered hills they rode along now. Each time they mounted a new hill, a different piece of the land ahead was revealed to them as they peered out through the branches.

Adrina was bored as she sat in the carriage with the sun lightly playing across her face. She rubbed the mark glumly; she could feel life within very often now. She stared openly at the one who sat directly across from her, hoping her eyes would stir his tongue although it had not yet in many hours of riding.

When they entered the thick, dark wood, it became quickly apparent to Adrina, for the sun vanished. She did not have the advantage of looking out over the horizon to see what lay ahead. She moved close to the wall of the carriage, hugging it close, feeling comfort in its presence beside her.

"Do you ever speak?" questioned Adrina, driving away the darkness she perceived with her words. "Do you have a name?" she further asked before a response could be rendered. "Are you always this tight-lipped?" queried Adrina.

"Seldom, and yes on both accounts, Princess Adrina."

"What is it?"

"What is what?"

"Your name?"

"Shalimar," quietly whispered the man, as if his name were an evil thing.

"That is a nice name," returned Adrina, attempting to stir his tongue.

Shalimar's only response was a slight smile, which was quick to fade as his eyes resumed their far-away stare. He longed to be elsewhere although he was also happy to be right here. His feelings were very mixed.

Afternoon shadows soon came; and shortly afterward, night fell around them. They made camp not far from the road, far enough so they were out of sight but close enough so it would be easy to leave if the need arose. The coach was their primary concern; it could not travel over rough terrain and needed a clear path. It also cast a large shadow, one passers-by might see if they looked closely.

Another day arrived and went, then two more passed. The country they were in was very different from that which they were accustomed to, but the changes were very subtle. The land had a feel of wildness to it, and a sense that most of it laid untouched by the hands of man. The road narrowed to a wide path, but tracks were deep along it although they had met no one since they had departed Zashchita, a fact that did not seem significant to them.

Xith was quietly brooding; he and Noman had just had a very lengthy argument, which Xith felt that he had lost. After thinking about it, he decided he would not let the questions sit. He clipped his mount and raced up alongside Noman. "I still do not like it. I tell you, I feel an absence. At least let me try, just a little test, a mere spark."

"Xith, I do not think it is wise; perhaps we are free of any who would follow, but afterwards, who would know?"

"Do you not believe the words of Y'sat?"

"Yes, I do, but we must wait."

Xith couldn't help the smile that lit his lips and cheeks. He liked to see the fire revive in Noman's eyes. He turned to respond, but as he did the happiness left his face and the group came to a sudden halt. Amir's sword danced in his hands as he reined in his mount alongside Noman.

"The forest has eyes," called out Amir.

"Yes, I know," said Noman, turning to smile at Xith. "Put away your weapon. They will do us no harm this day."

Without question, Amir lowered his sword and sheathed it. He then spurred his mount towards Nijal, to the forward watch. Shchander and a few of his men still claimed the rear watch, and they trotted along at a good pace behind the coach. Adrina still sat discontented in the carriage with the tightlipped Shalimar to watch over her. Although she was thankful that the face remained the same before her, she wished Shalimar would say something more than a morning and nightly greeting, which was nothing more than courteous speech.

Night found them as their path came to a small tributary of the great river, the Krasnyj, which was flowing very well in these eastern lands that they rode through. Morning came, bright and cheerful, with late afternoon catching them looping down a gently sloping hill into a vast, high-rimmed vale with a lake sweeping across most of its midsection. The last sounds of birds and day creatures left them as night arrived, and the sounds of night appeared in their place with the gentle croaking of frogs, the song of crickets, and a soft northerly wind.

Xith cast off the dark shadows that had hung over him for days, and all found time to bathe in the lake before retiring under the starlit sky. Noman knew the lake and the surrounding valley; it was a near halfway point on their journey and a pleasant place to relax and forget the worries of travel and all else that lay behind for a time. He also recalled a name for it, though he would not say if someone had asked him. He preferred the ways of old, when naught had name except that given to it by the Mother. A tree was a tree and a valley was a valley. He remembered a people of long ago, which he knew were now scattered far across the seas; and staring out over the gray waters before him, he wondered how they fared. He did not know what suddenly brought on the peculiar thoughts, but they came; perhaps it was the stranger that he had touched in Adrina's mind some time ago, or perhaps a distant thought had triggered his recollection.

It was late morning before they could draw themselves away from the pleasant shore, find the strength to move around it to the far side, and take the road up and out of the valley. Laughter had found and lightened many a heavy heart. Adrina had finally been able to carry on a conversation with someone other than herself. She had felt that everyone had been shunning her as if they feared her or she had a disease. Now she was happy, and a smile touched her lips and brightened her cheeks.

As they mounted the steep hills, they looked back over their shoulders down into the pleasant lake; only Noman searched beyond to the edges of the forest, seeking something that was not there. The eagerness of morning was quick to fade as a light drizzle found them late in the day, continuing until the night. A deep chill loomed in the air of the camp that night, and very skilled hands worked long and hard to build a fire to warm cold bodies.

The wet weather stayed with them for three more days, rutting the roads and slowing their movement to a crawl. They again found themselves amidst the green and brown of forests; in fact, this had been true since they completed their uphill ascent of several days ago. Here the land was mostly flat although it held a slight downhill slope much of the time. The air seemed to be growing colder each day as the weather grew more and more foul. The sight of snow would not have surprised them.

Now they lunched in a small clearing just off the road, stopping to wait out a hard downpour and using the time to rest weary animals and to bring nourishment to their own tired souls. Long into the afternoon they waited for the storm to pass or let up from its long torment, but it did not. So here they were forced to make their camp for the night. Neither spark from skilled hands nor flint rock brought fire to the wet wood they gathered, and still fearing their use of magic, this night passed by cold and wet, without the benefits of a fire.

Scattered shouts in the night roused the sentry, and soon everyone was awake or mostly awake, returning to sleep only when weapons were close at hand and the shadows in the woods had long since passed. Amir was last on watch and first to greet the early rays of a dawning day, a day that he sensed would be clear and cloudless. He was also the first to discover that Adrina was missing.

Chapter Fifteen

Clouds moving across the night sky brought shadows, dark and odd to the land. Calyin and Midori followed Lord Serant and Geoffrey. Captain Brodst kept to the rear. They used the darkness as their blanket, pulling it with them, carrying it along beside and around them, pausing momentarily when it slipped back from on top of them, and moving again when it returned. Lord Serant moved his feet with great determination and much perseverance. He wondered at the strength of those with him; he had heard no complaints since they had made their escape from Imtal even when his own body felt like a weight pulling him into the ground.

On the backside of a low, sloping hill, amidst a small stand of tightly packed oak, they stopped for what remained of the night. They could go no farther. It was here that Calyin finally broke into tears, great heavy sobs that were muffled within her lord husband's strong embrace. "Oh Edwar," she whispered to him. "So many lost and for what?"

Lord Edwar Serant stood firm. He moved Midori and the others back with his eyes as he put Calyin at arm's length. "If there are any who must hold strong, it is us," he told her. "We must hold strong and remain true to each other and Great Kingdom. There will be a time for retribution."

Calyin sucked at the air and forced her mind to calm. She was an Alder and the strength of her family ran in her veins. For a fleeting moment her eyes turned accusingly to her sister. The unspoken words that passed between the two were clear to each. Calyin at first blamed the other and then forgave. Midori, who had once considered herself an Alder but was no more, accepted her share of blame but patently refused forgiveness. If there was to be forgiveness, it would come from the Mother.

In two-hour shifts, they switched the watch; though tired and weary of body and mind, none slept soundly, and morning found them in much the same state they had been the night before—drained. Travel by day was a poor choice but a necessity. They were still in the kingdom and to their knowledge only Imtal had fallen, so they pressed on cautiously.

The bright warmth of the sun brought no cheer. In the distance in the east, storm clouds loomed, as if they were a sign, and towards the east they continued. For a time that morning, they followed a shallow stream that afforded them water cool and soothing until mid-day, for which they were very thankful for they had no water skins with them. The water sustained their empty bellies, yet it did not satisfy the rumblings of hunger within.

Lord Serant promised that Kauj lay just ahead, and if they maintained a good pace, taking adequate breaks; they would reach it late in the evening. The others well knew where the city of Kauj lay, but with Serant's words the promise became real to them, and they strove for it. They stayed well away from the road, following the gullies and ditches in and around the hill country they walked through.

Midori perceived a hint of the Mother with her this day, for which she was very thankful. She had been so empty without another presence in her consciousness. Late in the afternoon, she dared to touch the will of the land with hers, and was pleased when it flowed back to her. The domain of the Mother was hers again, and she was ecstatic. Guidance flowed to her mind as if she had regained her sight although she still perceived an absence around her.

As they stopped just before dusk to insure that they were not off course, a call came to her crisply from the wood a short distance away. It bade her to hurry to its confines until the darkness approached. Midori quickly led her companions to the shadows of the wood and they followed her unquestioningly.

They had no more than reached the trees and found cover when they heard the clatter of hooves. They did not move again until long after the silence returned. From then on, they moved even farther away from the road. Movement this night became difficult as the stars of the previous night were completely blocked by clouded skies. Later, the road was very difficult to find in the darkness.

A distant sound of music coming from the north reached their ears. Puzzled, they continued swiftly, pausing only briefly. Those that wore hooded cloaks, pulled them close around themselves, and those that didn't raised their collars high. The sight of buildings in the distance brought relief to their heavy hearts.

Unfortunately, Kauj only had a single inn. Tiny as it was, they still hoped to take a brief respite before they continued on their way. With luck, they would not have to remain the entire night, and they would hopefully be able to purchase horses. Their minds were consumed with thoughts of food and warmth.

Geoffrey went alone into Kauj while the others waited at a safe distance. He visited the inn first; then he sought out the stables. The inn was very quiet. He saw only two customers, solemnly sipping their draught, and the innkeeper. He stepped just into the doorway but did not inquire about rooms. He went back to the street.

He knew of two stables in Kauj, or at least there used to be two stables. He walked to the nearest one, which appeared to be in business although it was secured for the night, as he had thought it would be at this hour. Upon cursory inspection, he counted several horses in the corral to the rear, but they appeared to be mostly nags. He could not see within the stable stalls, but any horse was better than walking, so he was not completely discouraged.

Afterward he rejoined the others and led the way to the inn. Once inside, they were quick to inquire about rooms. The innkeeper had three empty but one was already promised. They would have to share the two, which suited them; they would have taken only one. They also ordered food to be brought to their rooms, but the innkeeper could only promise them gruel and hard bread at this hour. They did not refuse this either.

They were quick to retire to their rooms but not before Lord Serant and Captain Brodst eyed the two who sat in the far corner drinking. Something about them caught their interest. Cautiously, the captain queried about the two, pretending to have an interest in peddling his wares to them. The innkeeper told him that he hadn't seen the two before and that they were not very friendly, so he recommended staying clear of them. Captain Brodst smiled and said thanks and then went upstairs.

The gruel, which they would normally have considered tasteless, was very welcome and satisfying. After eating their fill and washing up, they slept, and it was morning before any of them awoke. Calyin was the first to awaken, and startled by how high the sun was, woke the others.

All took turns cursing themselves for their error, but it could not be denied that the sleep had done them good. As long as they were already here past morning, they would eat and gather provisions for the journey ahead. Brodst was the one chosen to venture downstairs, which he did.

The inn was fairly busy this morning, mostly with travelers stopping only for a quick meal as they passed through, or so it appeared. The captain did not delay in making arrangements for supplies and horses and soon returned to where the others waited, gathered all in one room. Captain Brodst admitted that he did not like the feel of the inn this morning; he perceived something amiss though he knew not what.

The rattle of trays startled them as several were placed on the hall floor. Directly afterwards came a knock on the door, a soft rapping.

Captain Brodst answered the door, pulling it open only partially. He recognized the servant as the one from last night, and sighed, accepting the food graciously. Sometime later, the servant returned to retrieve the trays and dishes. He also informed the captain that the foodstuffs he had wanted were ready, and that he had sent a message to the stable master. Captain Brodst thanked the boy and gave him a small coin as a token of thanks.

"What do we do now?" asked Calyin of Serant. "Do you still think it is safe to journey to Solntse this day?"

"If that is still our course, I say yes."

"If?" asked Geoffrey. "I thought we were set."

"I am not so sure now. I think—I'm not sure what I think, but I sense something."

"Yes, the Mother speaks to me this morning from afar; this does not bode well. I also think a change of course would be better."

"I would still rather be in Imtal; at least there I would know the specters."

"A change of words, I believe, is in order. It is not good to mention things of darkness, lest they come."

"I am sorry, Sister. I regress," the captain spoke the words with a grin on his face, as he stared at Midori, who stared back at him with an equally knowing smile.

"If we change our course, what of the warning? Have you pondered the meaning of the things they said to us?" spoke Calyin, her eyes mostly falling on Midori, who understood best of all, she thought.

"The words were not meant to confuse us, as was already said, but merely to make us think, to make us give deep consideration to our path, and yes to give us a direction to begin and end in. The in-between, I think, is mostly up to us."

"Let's delay no further. I want to put a great distance between us and Kauj."

"Lord Serant is right; we should be off."

Geoffrey went to collect and pay for the horses, which he purchased without trouble, while Captain Brodst saw to their provisions and Serant retrieved some water skins and other miscellaneous items from a nearby merchant. Midori and Calyin remained at the inn, passing the time by talking as only two sisters do. Thoughts of Adrina and Andrew carried over into their conversation; they missed them both.

Fortunately, the nags they rode upon proved to have good stamina; and by late afternoon, the shadows they perceived in Kauj seemed to be far behind them. The sense of nature surrounding them put Midori at ease. As they rode, she turned her thoughts inward for a time of reflection. She was the first of the Mother, yet she observed certain reservations she knew others before her had not. Her thoughts flowed to a figure. The face of an old man came before her and she wondered how he fared. He had not returned as he said he would, and she needed his support, his guidance.

She thought about time and wondered where she would be during the vernal equinox, when the time of her calling came. She did not know whom she would choose, but surely, as the first, she must choose. She thought about the other priestesses at sanctuary, and how they fared without her guidance. They knew that the first, second and third were gone, and perhaps, she thought, they may be lost. As she dwelled on this, she knew this to be false. Her mouth fell agape and now she understood the emptiness. They had crossed the rights and transcended without her. "Why, Mother?" cried Midori in her thoughts. "Why did you sanction this?"

"Midori?" called Brodst. "Are you all right? You look so pale."

"Yes—yes, I am fine," softly responded Midori, sadness evident in her voice. "Fine, fine, fine," laughed Midori, sarcastically. She bit her lip and thus stopped further words from issuing from her mouth. She pulled her hood tight about her face and withdrew into its recesses and cried heavy mournful sobs.

Chapter Sixteen

The words of the mountaineers were odd to Valam's ears; somehow, they were in the same tongue as Seth yet different. He was glad they were quick to adapt to his own language, which greatly enhanced their ability to communicate. He decided that they were a strong bunch, and the power was not only in their hands and minds, but also in their hearts. They were free spirits. He also found that they were quick to sudden anger, and quick to turn from it and laugh. They played with emotions sending it as the most prevalent item in all their thoughts, using it to their own advantage.

Their skin and eyes were a deep, burnt tan in contrast to Seth's paler skin. The plains had been harsh on them, and these were the first of Seth's kind. Valam wondered whether the signs of wear and tear on their features were the result of great age or simply evidence of the harshness of their lives on the plains. Ekharn was their leader although they claimed to have no leader. They counted all of their kind as equals.

A small group gathered in the center of the camp, preparing to depart. This day they would journey back to the mountains with Teren as their guide. With hesitation, Father Jacob gave his blessing for Prince Valam to accompany the party as Ekharn wished and with a very heavy heart he watched the band leave the confines of the camp. He hoped Valam would never leave his sight again, and he was torn with lament as if he was losing what he had only recently found.

Valam smiled courteously in response to Yulorien's words floating through his mind, but momentarily he cast his attentions back to Jacob, whose countenance spoke many things. It wasn't until much, much later, as they plodded through the rocky coastline north, that he realized what was said to him. He repeated the words in his thoughts, "No, my friend, the Queen-Mother holds no dominion over the mountain folk, although we do count her blessings."

The journey along the coast to Ekharn's camp took only one full day. This time of year often found them encamped on steep bluffs jutting out into the sea, the mountains rising high behind them, and in front of them the plains. As they mounted the bluff, Valam caught sight of a white snowcap on the mountains as far as he could see. The places he was led into seemed at first gloomy and foreboding, but soon they were streaming with light and cheer.

Passageways that began with great canyons became narrower and shallower, tunnels that were made by skilled hands with chisel and hammer. They wove together a series of interconnecting rooms, halls, dwellings and much more that were all natural and would have been otherwise inaccessible. Valam felt empty without Evgej, Seth, and the others who had been his constant companions for a very long time. They had been forbidden to accompany the mountaineers although exception had been made in the case of Mikhal and Danyel' and the two were in the party today.

The three and Teren now sat in an enormous hollow awaiting Ekharn's return. Yulorien sat with them although he did not speak.

Valam regarded the rock-hewn benches they were seated upon, set in a semi-circle around the chamber. In the center of the room an earthen hearth spewed warmth, its smoke drifting into an unseen chimney.

A lengthy hour later, Ekharn returned, and as he did Yulorien stood and bowed his head. As a polite gesture, Valam did the same and the others except Teren, who did not move, followed his lead. Behind Ekharn walked a woman in a white flowing gown. Once she was seated, Yulorien raised his head, and after momentarily regarding her, he took his place.

"You need not pay homage to me," whispered a voice, powerful, yet feminine, casting with it an expression of warmth and also a feeling of welcome. "I have no persuasion over you or any of your kind, though I am the Mother of my people."

"The Queen-Mother," flashed through Valam's thoughts before he considered that his mind was open.

"I am no queen, I have no kingdom nor any domain, unless you count the lands you place your feet upon now, but they are not mine to offer, even to myself."

"I am sorry," said Valam. "I did not mean to—"

"There is no need for apology; no offense was taken or given. I brought you here so I could speak openly with you without fear of reprisal. There are those who would not look favorably upon my presence, and there are those who do not know that I exist. I wish it to be kept so at least for now. Do you know that the Mother of the Eastern Reaches attempted to send your people away before your arrival?"

Valam's eyes and thoughts gave evidence of the direction he thought the conversation flowed. Teren jumped to his feet almost immediately. "I am no traitor to my people, Prince Valam, of this I assure you."

"Please, Brother Teren, seat yourself. He will see the truth of it; give him time. You are no traitor." Her words flowed, mixed with truth and understanding to all present. A suppressed message of "wait, and you will see," was also sent with it simultaneously. "I want you to know the facts; this is why I have brought you here. You are being played like an errant pawn. The fool is one step away from obtaining the swordmasterless king."

"King?"

"Do you not think that I know? I see all, but little do I question until it is time. Once there were two queens and two kings in the lands beyond the seas, the lands that now lie in desolation, so the balance was held in check, but no more. We are here, and yours are there. Valam, a prince, an heir, a king, a pauper."

"Do you mock me?"

"No, I praise you. Do you not understand? Regard what I have said, and in time you will come to know."

"I am at a loss," said Valam.

"You are at no loss and understand me well. The words I have spoken are not beyond your minds, but beyond your ears. You hear but do not listen."

Valam returned to the first words spoken to him and asked, "Why would the Queen-Mother send away those she needs."

"You know the answer. She told you herself. Think!"

A flood of remembrance came upon Valam and carried him away. The world about him became gray and shadowy, and if Teren had not protected his head from the stone, he would have slammed against it when he collapsed forward. He saw the paths in his thoughts, a vision that played out two-fold for him, overwhelming him and sending his body into shock as the vision came to the end, as he saw his life come to an end. Now he understood Tsandra's words, but it was too late; the moment had passed.

As light returned to his eyes, Valam was unsure how long he had been lost or if he had been lost at all. He opened his eyes, and he was still seated where he had been; Teren, Mikhal, Danyel', and the others were all still there. "How long have I been gone?"

"The length is not the key, it is the knowledge. Now, do you understand?"

"Yes, I remember, but why did I forget, and how did I—I was dead."

"You were and you weren't. As is this, that was but a crossing, a possibility that is now passed, but now you have the answers, and what will you do with them?"

"I, I—do not know."

"I will give you time. In your heart, you will know what to do, and you will do it, but heed this. That which you think is occurring usually is not, and that which you do not expect probably is. Do not regard her falsely, for she does not hold you thus. She did only what she considered just, and perhaps it was. Now that you have seen the many lines, you know what your fate would have been at each turning. But now you are beyond the turnings, and I can show you no more."

"I saw myself die more than once. How can this be?"

"As I have stated, this was your past. Yes, you would have perished if you had stayed in the kingdom, and—"

"Then what I saw is real."

"Perhaps, but possibly it is only what could have been if you had been there. I cannot say, but you must consider it in your heart of hearts and act accordingly."

"And the second time?"

"Yes, another possibility, but do not dwell thus on the past. Move forward and decide; this is why we have returned. Why I have given you counsel. You must know all paths and decide for yourself which to take."

"Why do you help me? And why, Teren, did you allow me to come here? I still do not understand."

Teren paused and let the other speak first. "I help you because I must; there is no other reason."

"You must?"

"Prince Valam, I also do what I feel is right and just for my people."

"It is all right, Brother Teren, you do not need to justify yourself in his eyes; he does understand if he will only consider. I wish not to say more, but I will add this: a gift is not always free; it often has its costs, and now the balance is brought back in check."

Valam began to speak, but he was cut short and bade to be silent. "'Why are Danyel' and Mikhal here, you think. Consider your own thoughts. Your path is with them, not the others. Alas, I have said too much; you must go."

"Go?"

"Yes, but only from this chamber. Return with all haste to Leklorall and ask of the queen your questions. Ask her of the sword as well. Awaken now and remember." Her last words carried much more than simple litany. As with everything she had said to him, mingled with it were a mixture a feelings and deep emotion that would take Valam some time to sort out if he could do it at all.

Valam watched her as she walked away, and just before she entered an adjacent corridor to disappear from sight, she glanced back at him and said again stronger and with more urgency, "Awaken now and remember."

Chapter Seventeen

Adrina was missing. The camp spun with excited activity. Shchander and his men were sent to search the woods in the immediate vicinity while Nijal and Amir set to finding Adrina's tracks. Noman and Xith were quick to collapse into sudden but friendly argument. They didn't discover until much later that one of Shchander's men was also missing.

By afternoon, troubled eyes stared desperately to Xith and Noman who were still arguing. Xith soon turned to Shchander with many questions, to which Shchander could respond honestly. Shalimar was a man to be trusted, and he held no ill in his heart. Xith turned to Nijal, regarding his nervousness and asked, "Did she say anything to you, anything at all that you counted odd?"

Nijal was slow to speak, but he did. "That night, I had an odd—no, it was nothing."

"Speak, man," said Noman commanding Nijal to bring words to his lips. "All things have significance."

"The night Adrina woke screaming, when I coaxed her to return to the carriage. I watched her. I saw her eyes as she lay there. She was afraid, very afraid. For hours I kept watch, hoping she would drift off to sleep, but she never did. I am not sure, but sometime during the time I was there I had a dream. I may have closed my eyes for five minutes or for several hours, I am not sure. When I awoke, her eyes were upon me as if she knew the dream I dreamt. She asked me again if we could go outside, and this time I did so without hesitation."

"The dream, what was it?" asked Xith intrigued.

"A voice," replied Nijal.

"A voice?"

As Nijal began, his voice quivered and his hands twitched nervously. "After that, I did not want to be near her. It was a very strange thing. It is my fault. I should have been with her, not Shalimar."

"Nijal, stop babbling. Go back to the dream. Tell me about the voice."

"The voice?"

"Yes, the voice, tell me about it. Nothing can hurt you. Close your eyes and tell us about the dream and the voice."

Nijal closed his eyes, and all became silent around him as the others waited for him to speak. Nijal still was hesitant; he thought it best to let his dream be lost. "I was surrounded by darkness, so much darkness, and he was there. He came out of the darkness, which seemed to follow him, and after a time, I could see, as if my eyes focused. Black flames licked the air, streaming from dark coffers. He was seated on an ebony throne. He bade Adrina to give him the child, but she would not—" Nijal's voice faded off, and he broke down into sudden sobs.

Xith looked to Noman, who returned his concern. "Nijal, listen closely, who are they that Adrina spoke of?"

"The shadows, they spoke to her—and the dragons, they spoke to her."

"When?" demanded Noman, looming over Nijal.

Nijal cowered down to his knees, "Once out of the blackness, they asked her to follow them."

"And you did not tell us? What were you thinking, Nijal, son of Geoffrey?" yelled Shchander angrily, cursing Nijal the only way he knew how.

"Wait, do not be harsh with him. I can see it on his face; he only now remembers. He did not know himself until he spoke the words. Is that not so?" stated Noman, his tone now very kind and understanding.

"Yes," replied Nijal honestly. He said nothing of Tnavres, the tiny dragon Adrina harbored, though later he would be unable to explain what held his tongue.

Noman began to speak again, but he stopped, and then turned, his eyes wild with surprise and relief. "Amir, Shalimar—Adrina?"

"I found them," said Amir, "and you won't believe this, only about a half hour walk from here. Gathering flowers, the truth be known."

"White flowers growing along a peaceful stream; it was so serene there," said Adrina.

"Flowers?" demanded Xith, losing his temper briefly.

"Yes, beautiful white flowers. I picked some for you," said Adrina, offering Xith a bouquet, and as he accepted them, staring into her eyes of pure innocence, he forgave her and said nothing further on the subject. Noman started to object, but as she handed him a grouping of flowers, he held back, only chastising softly, telling her never to go off alone again, to which she responded that she hadn't gone off alone.

All thoughts of dark shadows were cast aside, and soon they

were moving rapidly along the trail, trying to make up some of the lost time. Only one significant change had occurred, and it was that now only Amir and Nijal would ride with Adrina and keep watch over her. No one chastised Shalimar, as he had already punished himself and repented wholly for his mistake, which had been an honest one.

Noman saw Adrina in a new light from then on. She had the gift of persuasion, there could be no doubt. She knew how to get what she wanted. Shalimar was no fool. He had been led astray and by what Noman suspected could only be the guiles of the Voice—a thing that would be most troubling if it were true.

Chapter Eighteen

Gray skies hovered overhead as night came, and the group stopped. Midori counted her blessings, for they had made good progress this day, and it had passed without incident. She cheered up but not until long after she lay down to sleep and well after her shift at watch. Sleep finally came to her just as she considered the possibility that maybe, just maybe, she was at a crossing, a time when there could be two who were first to the Mother. She recalled despondently the fact that not long ago she had been only the fourth to the Mother; and even with Jasmine and Catrin's demise there was another who by all accounts should have progressed to the highest position before her.

It was Calyin who awoke Midori some hours later by shaking her softly. Calyin had held the final watch and she awoke her sister before waking the others. "We must talk," Calyin said quietly, pointing to a place away from the others.

Midori nodded and followed Calyin into the darkness.

"The men are divided," Calyin whispered when they were a safe distance away from the camp. "My lord husband wishes to escape to the north. Geoffrey and the captain wish to rouse the garrisons of High Road and Solntse, then return to Imtal. They say Great Kingdom has not fallen, that only Imtal has fallen. What does the Mother tell you?"

Midori wanted to tell Calyin that the Mother told her she was not the true first and that the Mother was so distant from her that it seemed she was alone. Those things were not exactly the truth, however, and she held her tongue saying instead what was safest. "Imtal has fallen, the Kingdom lives on."

"What of the Great Houses? What of the garrisons? Can you sense anything?"

"She senses," said Lord Serant approaching out of the darkness, "the great change is upon us."

"My lord husband," Calyin said formerly turning to face Edwar Serant.

"You speak now behind my back?" he asked her.

Calyin lowered her eyes momentarily, then looked directly at him. "She is my sister. We are Alders, despite what she thinks. We do not run and hide."

Lord Serant spat openly. "You think I run willingly? You are my wife. You who should know me better than any."

"My lord husband, I never met to imply cowardice. I seek only answers. The Delinna I once knew was strong and resolute. Even in the face of our father, she stood to her convictions."

Lord Serant beaded his eyes and said louder than the previous whispers, "Are you saying I lack conviction?"

Midori thrust herself between the two. "I am right here," she said. "Don't speak of me as if I am lost. I made my choices and I have no regrets."

Calyin whirled around to face Midori. "Shall we then get it all out in the open?" Her voice was full of venom as she spoke. "I hated you for what you did. I hated you for your choices. But I respected you for your choices as well. You had only to speak his name and father would have had him swinging from the rope. It would have satisfied all, would it not have?"

"No," said Midori emphatically, tears in her eyes. "It would not have satisfied anything. Don't you see that it was about power? He couldn't have cared less about honor and the word bond of our father."

"He?" cut in Lord Serant.

The strong words had by now roused Geoffrey Solntse and Captain Ansh Brodst. Both were standing not far off. "They speak of King Jarom," said Captain Brodst knowingly.

"Stay out of this," said Midori and Calyin at the same time. Calyin added, "You've done quite enough already."

"Just what's that supposed to mean?" asked Midori. "Ansh could no more have held back than I could have."

Afraid the two sisters were about to come to blows, Lord Serant gripped Calyin's wrists. "We must return to the road."

Calyin held firm. "No, not until we've said what must be said."

"Agreed," Midori said, returning her sister's glare.

"Say it," demanded Calyin. "Say that father was wrong. Say that you were wrong. Say that you are an Alder by blood and by blood you hold."

"I will say no such thing, Calyin. You will never know how hard it was for me to walk away. To leave Imtal. To leave all that I knew. To leave him. You may think the Priestesses of the Mother are beyond the affairs of the Kingdoms and hold true to none, but this is not so. Our duty, our first duty, is to the peoples of Ruin Mist. I did what I must because the Mother showed me the paths. Marrying Jarom Tyr'anth would have only hastened the path of destruction. Surely you know this—you must know this."

Calyin was trembling. Serant released his grip on her wrists and embraced her. "Enough," he said. "You are sisters by blood, and by blood you hold. I can see it if you do not. We must return to the road now or all will be lost."

Like thieves in the night, they began anew. Lord Serant assumed the lead and Geoffrey took the rear. Captain Brodst rode beside Midori and Calyin. Several hours of veiled sky remained before dawn and they were going to put this time to good use. Until just before first light, they maintained the road, and shortly afterwards they moved far to its outskirts.

The land had gentle, gradual slopes going downhill. In the distance they could now see the ridges that marked the Borderlands, and beyond them the snow-capped mountains of the north. Geoffrey knew this region the best as it was within the area patrolled by his fellows. In his youth, he had been on many patrols in this area himself. The closest garrison of the kingdom lay where the borders of the Barrens, the Borderlands, and the Great Kingdom met; and now they had just moved beyond its grasp.

They still thought it queer that they should attempt to avoid the very ones who should by all means be their confederates, but they would still follow caution and hope it was folly when they reached Solntse. As afternoon came upon them, they saw several patrols pass along the road at a distance, and an ever-increasing amount of traffic. This was not odd at all. They saw groups of wagons, riders, and even people on foot. Sometimes the passersby traveled in mixed groups but always they had some sort of armed company with them, usually an escort of two to three men heavily equipped, who probably required higher fees than would the rogues who could have found them.

An attack by outlaws was now Lord Serant's primary concern

also, for they had not much to offer in the way of monetary gain. They stayed close together with eyes constantly on guard and hands always at the ready. Serant gave heavy consideration to moving beyond the kingdom borders and into the borderlands. He didn't believe all the tales he had heard about the place; but if so many believed them, it would surely be a good place to be. The rain that had held off in previous days found them at first morning light as a drizzle but it quickly turned into a downpour. They sought cover or, possibly, to outrun it. Unbeknownst to them as they raced to escape the storm, their course turned northerly; and before they knew it, the land had turned to rock and crag. However, they did not stop, nor did they heed their own instincts.

Lightning crackled in the air around them, sending sparks of energy through the air, and growing ever nearer. Their steeds turned of their own accord as the brilliant bolts struck within a few feet of horse and rider, and all the riders could do was to hold on and pray they could maintain their mounts. The sound of thunder suddenly swallowed all sound, and a split second later a flash lit the sky to their immediate left. Midori fell on the hard rock as her horse reared.

As she fell to the ground, she rolled away from the horse's feet, which were seeking unintentionally to stomp her life away. Both Lord Serant and Captain Brodst saw her fall, but only the captain could turn his mount around to offer her a quick hand. The reins stung as they bit into his hand, but he did not release his right grip. He grasped her arm at the elbow and was able to pull her to safety.

Midori rubbed the sore spot on her head only for a moment before she locked both arms around Brodst's waist. She wasn't going to fall again if she could help it. She searched for her horse, but it was now long gone, lost among the ridges and the many turns in the path. A spot of white caught her eye; it almost looked as if a clear area lay in front of them, but she wasn't quite sure.

Suddenly, they broke past the clouds, the rain stopped, the lightning receded, and the setting sun filled their field of vision. Captain Brodst reined his horse to a sudden halt. Directly in front of him, the path fell away into a very steep downward slope. As he gazed, he saw that they were on the very edge of an enormous valley—more a ravine than a valley. As he looked, he changed his mind. It was definitely a canyon, narrow and deep, winding like a great serpent through the rock.

"Downward—" whispered Midori.

Geoffrey didn't like the looks of the place; his choice was to wait until the storms passed and turn back toward Solntse. "We must go to the garrison; only then will we know."

Captain Brodst had heard Midori's faint murmur. She had whispered almost directly into his ear. He gave weight to both Geoffrey's and Midori's words. "I say we follow Geoffrey to Solntse," stated Brodst.

"I say," started Serant, "that we continue along our current path and see where it takes us."

Calyin was the only one who had not spoken her mind, and the other four turned toward her to hear her opinion. She wasn't as quick to make a judgment as the others and she returned Midori's wry look to her. Midori thanked Captain Brodst and dismounted.

"I believe we should continue; there is much at hand that we do not understand, and it is best to follow when led, to see where the path takes us."

"Three to two," spoke Geoffrey sadly. He shrugged his shoulders, shedding the sense of foreboding he perceived, and urged his mount onward at a cautious pace. After Midori mounted behind Calyin, the rest followed his lead; and as they journeyed down into the depths of the canyon, the darkness of night seemed to come immediately over them or at least its shadows did. The sky overhead was still a washed-out blue.

The descent was extremely drawn-out since they had to follow a staggered path crisscrossing the wall of the canyon many times. By the time they found the canyon floor, it was too dark to continue. The rush of water led them on for a time until they came to the edge of a river, where they made camp. They did manage to find enough scrub brush in the immediate area to get a blazing fire burning, giving no heed to precaution.

Lord Serant clapped a hand to Geoffrey's back in response to his far-off stare during their evening meal. "It isn't that bad, my friend. Soon you will be home with nothing but time on your hands, and all this will be far behind you, behind all of us."

"I hope so," responded Geoffrey weakly, "I hope so."

The captain, who had wandered off in search of more wood, returned. His eyes were almost as distant as Geoffrey's as he sat next to Serant. He looked to Midori and Calyin who quietly watched the flames, and then to Geoffrey and Serant. "Do you really think so?" asked Brodst.

"It is the desire of my heart, yes."

"Lord Serant, I mean no disrespect when I say, this—I have been thinking very carefully—"

"Don't—" whispered Midori.

"I must go to Solntse. We are only a full day's ride away—we cannot turn away. What of the garrison troops there in full company? Tomorrow, I will go alone if need be, but to Solntse, I will go."

Captain Brodst spoke the words that had been on the tip of Geoffrey's tongue, and Geoffrey was quick to add his opinion, which was to go to Solntse. "We'll take the capital back by force. We'll round the garrisons from the whole of the kingdom! And we'll march on Imtal and drive Jarom back to his lands as we would a mad dog!" Two pairs of eyes fell to Lord Serant, and wondered why he held his thoughts in check, and why he would continue along this path, which was completely against his nature.

"Do not say your thoughts!" announced Serant. "Or I'll cut out your tongues myself. I thought we gave this great consideration before we began this journey. Our path is fated—" As Lord Serant continued to speak at length, Geoffrey understood Lord Serant's reasoning even though the captain did not, for he understood the superstitious nature of those of the Territories and the captain did not. Honor took second place to beliefs, which were very strongly based. Geoffrey also saw the hatred Lord Serant held for Midori, not because he disliked her personally but because she had the power to hold his fears over him and show them to him.

The night was calm with the gentle sound of the river lulling their thoughts for a time. Lord Serant opted for the first watch, and he remained on guard all through the night, waking no one to replace him. The stars appeared so very far off as he stared at them; they did not bring answers to his questions, for he did not seek the answers. The blackness of night slowly dissipated replaced by morning light, but no sun.

Geoffrey and Captain Brodst parted from the others as morning came; the three who sat around the fire watched them retreat without saying a word. Lord Serant, Calyin and Midori would continue on their own. The canyon floor proved to be very rough and strewn with boulders, making it extremely difficult to traverse. With only two horses to bear the burden of three, they would walk this day.

Their thoughts were with the two who went to Solntse. They did not fear for their own safety. Three could survive as easily as could five and three could possibly remain more invisible than five. Before, they would have retreated from any force and that had not changed. A fight was not what they sought, so they would not confront a hostile force. They continued on through the rains and sleet, downward, inward, outward, upward, wherever their feet led them.

Chapter Nineteen

"Valam? Valam?" asked Jacob. "I am finished." Jacob nudged Valam a second time with no response. He quickly began to speak again, "I am sorry, gentlemen, for taking up so much of your time, but now I conclude and give you to Prince Valam."

"Valam? Valam?" said Jacob, louder than he wished. He smiled graciously and then apologized. He shook Valam, who was slow to open his eyes. "My prince, I am most sorry. Perhaps we should delay this meeting until tomorrow."

Valam opened his eyes, blinked once, then blinked again. "Captain Mikhal?" asked Valam.

"He has not yet arrived, I am sorry."

Valam sat up straight and looked around the tent. His eyes opened wide. "Ekharn? Where did Ekharn go?"

Sensing something was wrong, Father Jacob dismissed all present saying, "Let us adjourn until this evening, or better still, tomorrow morning. I apologize again most graciously."

Valam stood, excused himself, and walked out, but just before the entry, he turned back to look at those seated around the table, and he smiled and said, "Eran, brother of Ylsa. I should have caught the resemblance." Valam fled to the middle of the encampment, waiting for a thing that did not come. Puzzled, he waited, quickly walking away as Father Jacob approached.

He sought refuge not in his own tent, but in another on the far side of camp. He did not seek out Evgej, or Seth, or even Liyan. His search led him directly to another. He did not pause at her door or announce his arrival. Actually, he did not even think anyone would be there. He was shocked to find someone was indeed in the tent.

"You need not lower your eyes," spoke Tsandra, whispering to his thoughts. "I have no secrets."

"I am sorry. I did not think—"

"Yes, I know. Just wait one moment. No need to leave. I shall only be a moment," said Tsandra without even a trace of embarrassment in her words. She stepped into her woolen robe, and then slipped on her boots. She smiled at Valam's wide eyes and bade him to sit. "Your thoughts read like an open book. I thought the time before last when we spoke that we discussed that problem of yours."

"I—I—guess we did," answered Valam. "Wait, wait a minute. This is not what I came here to talk about, so don't lead me astray."

"Well—"

"I understand now what you said to me as our journey began; though, to be honest with you, at the time I did not."

"I thought you would come to understand it, but isn't your timing a little off? Is this why you walked out of council?"

Valam glared back at her and asked, "You can't read what I am thinking right now. Can you?"

"Yes, you are still embarrassed, but I think it will pass."

"That's precisely it," replied Valam, confused.

Tsandra sensed the falseness of his words but did not know what made them false. She wondered what he was hiding from her.

Carefully, she prodded his mind while she smiled at him, and she grinned even wider as he smiled back. She found no hidden walls in his center, yet there was something she could not see.

"Why did you do it?" asked Valam.

"Do what?"

"Why did you gather your forces? Was it really for the queen? Or was it over me?"

Now Tsandra comprehended where he was going with his interrogation. "It was for the Queen-Mother; I feared for her safety. I am a warrior; mine is to protect."

"No. The order of the Red are the protectors. Is this not so?"

"It is the right of the Brown to protect also."

"But you protect your people, do you not? You hold the Queen-Mother in check. Is this not so?"

"Where do you get the audacity to speak of such things to me?"

"Is this not so?"

"I think you should leave."

"I will go nowhere!"

"Leave, or I will kill you, myself."

Valam removed his sword from its sheath, and stood eyeing her intent. He considered her words, her tone of voice, and her stance. She did not stand at the ready like one who was willing or wanting to fight. He turned his blade around and handed her the hilt end. "Do me in if you will," said Valam kneeling down on one knee and bowing his head, an act he knew would infuriate the heart of any warrior, no matter their origin.

"I would not strike you down in such a way. Do you think me so treacherous?"

"No, I do not think there is treachery in you, but perhaps you could find the truth and share it with me."

Tsandra was stumped. Where had the questions come from so suddenly, and why now? She had not meant it to come to this. She had merely done what needed to be done, nothing more, so why did it now smite her in the face. She did not make it secret this time that she wished to enter his thoughts. She burst into his mind, seeking to tear it apart and search his every thought but was repelled from the emptiness she found. Again, angrily, she forced her will into his mind. Her eyes went wide with fury.

"It wasn't any of those things, was it?" asked Valam, oblivious to her will upon him.

"Get out!" she yelled, reaching out with all her wrath, again forgetting to enclose its reaches.

"I will not, not until I hear the truth. Tell me, Tsandra of the Brown. Find the words in your heart of hearts and speak them to me."

"I don't know what you are saying."

"The time for playing games with me is over. I remember. I remember it all."

"Oh, really. You remember what?"

"Do not be coy with me! I am asking you in all honesty. I believe you want to tell me the truth, but what keeps your tongue in check?"

"That would be me," spoke Liyan stepping into the tent.

"How long have you been standing out there?" asked Tsandra.

"Only a few moments, but I know of what you speak. I heard the name you spoke, though I think others did not catch it. I don't even think Tsandra heard it."

"What name are you referring to?"

"Why the name of Ekharn the old, of course?"

"Where did you learn it?" asked Tsandra, confusion showing on her face.

"In a dream of sorts."

"A dream, or was it Seth?" asked Liyan, searching Valam's thoughts as he asked it.

Valam stood there staring at Liyan for a time before he responded, but his words were cut short by another. "No, it was not I, brother. You should know I would not speak of such."

"Tell us of this dream, if you may," asked Liyan, yet speaking aloud.

"I don't think I may, Brother Liyan."

Liyan furrowed his brow, but did not reply to Valam; in thought, he told the others what he knew about Valam's words and about Brother Ontyv's visit. Tsandra's response was only a passing complaint, but Seth's was anger, anger so strong it turned his face livid. "Please sit, sit all," begged Tsandra. "Let us talk as friends, as we are all friends in this room."

Tsandra continued to speak, but not aloud; now she carefully thought to enclose her words only to those around her. "Ours is a tale best left untold, but I will say you are correct in your words, Prince Valam Alder."

"Yes," added Liyan, "the Brown began from tragedy and necessity, and so you see, not all our past is bright and glorious either. We, like your kind, also came upon many turnings during the dark times, times that are possibly upon us once more, but now I think we have a correct balance."

"She said there were two queens and two kings," said Valam, slipping, moving his thoughts into words.

"She?" asked Seth, and lagging only moments behind him, Liyan stated the same thing.

"The past is best left to remain in the past. Let us progress not regress. I will be honest with you and say Brother Ontyv did come to send your people home, for this is what the Queen-Mother wished. She did not want you to go home to your lands, and to your fate, for she had altered your fate already in bringing you here at the first. She did not want it to return at the last. I am afraid in so doing, she has upset the balance, and many dark things have come to pass in your lands. For this we are forever sorrowful, Prince Valam."

"No," said Valam, his voice full of wisdom as he spoke, "the balance is brought back in check. Our past is also catching up to us."

"You, my friend, have learned much."

"Yes, and no."

"What will you do now? Will you return to your home? Or will you stay?"

"I do not know, to tell you the truth. I must think, and there are several I must confer with before I decide."

"Father Jacob is a wise man. He will know what is right for you where we may not. Go and talk to him."

"I was not referring to Jacob. Do you know where I can find Teren?"

"Teren?" asked Tsandra, "Why, whatever for?"

"I know where Teren is," said Seth. "He arrived in camp only a short time ago and he asked for you, but at that time I did not know where you were, and I only now recalled his inquiry to mind."

"Yes, I would. Seth, thank you," said Valam rushing out without even saying good-bye. His exodus led him back to his own tent, where he hoped to find Teren waiting. He wasn't surprised to find another there. Valam closely inspected Jacob's demeanor before he said a word. What followed was largely an apology and a subtle explanation, neither of which actually said anything.

Luckily, Father Jacob was clever enough to see through it all to find understanding, the only thing he had hoped to attain. The two sat regarding each other for a time and then Jacob left, departing just as Teren found his way to Valam's quarters. Teren entered without announcement and without offering greetings to Jacob. Neither was surprised to hear an alarm sound throughout the camp moments later. Riders had been spotted approaching from the north, a large group by all accounts.

Chapter Twenty

One day passed without concern, and a second; now thoughts switched to their arrival at Krepost', which would be soon. Xith considered the time lost as a whole, and he figured that they were now several days behind schedule, perhaps more. He took into consideration the rains of the previous days and their directions. They would have to push hard, very hard, for he knew that soon the storms would arrive, and with them passage to the north would come to an end until the seasons changed.

Strangely, they met their first travelers along the road this day, which was not entirely coincidence. Casually, nonchalantly, they greeted each other as they passed. The caravan consisted of many wagons. Xith counted twelve in all as the last one creaked on by. Adrina was unusually excited as she watched them cross alongside the carriage through her small peephole. Nijal was still halfway between sleep and consciousness despite Adrina's nudging and did not wake fully until much later.

Adrina rested her hands on her stomach. She thought back, trying to remember how much time had passed, how long it had been since she'd met the Dragon King. There were many things she did not know, but the one thing she did know was that Tnavres's presence was both a curse and a blessing. When she took the tiny dragon, she thought her move bold until the Dragon King mocked her saying, "As if you had a choice."

The Dragon King also told her that one of them would be his regardless of what they did. Matched doors of black and white were the final test. White was supposed to bring the hope of life; black death. She chose black; Vilmos chose white. The dragon's milk later saved Valam from the deadly poison and perhaps cursed him. The dragon's milk later saved her and perhaps cursed her as well.

Feeling overwhelmed by all these thoughts, she snuggled tightly into the corner, drinking in the warmth against her hands, sending back feelings of joy and happiness. She dozed off to a light sleep, which did not come without dreams. When she awoke, Nijal's eyes upon her seemed to delve into her very soul and as she looked up with sleep still in her eyes, she was startled. She shrank back as he reached out his hand to her until her wits were fully gathered. "Nijal, I am sorry. I thought it was—oh, never mind. I'm starving. When will we stop for lunch?"

"We already did. I am sorry I did not wake you. You looked so peaceful sleeping, I did not want to disturb you."

Adrina frowned and rubbed her belly. Nijal was hesitant, but eventually produced a small basket, which had been tucked beneath his discarded cloak. Adrina was quick to snatch it up and devour most of its contents, saving only two apples. She gave one to Nijal as her way of saying thanks, and because he was looking hungrily at them in her hands. "Apples, I love apples!" exclaimed Adrina. "Where did you get them?"

"On a little sojourn through the wilderness three days ago."

"Late apples are the best, sweet and tangy, with a coat thick and crunchy!"

೫ಆ Mark of the Dragon ೫ಆ

The great road took a turn to the north as evening fell upon them at a crossroads of sorts. Many paths seemed to sprout not far from the point where they had chosen to camp for the night. Some were old and largely overgrown. Others were apparently very well traveled; neither weed nor bush could be seen, at least as far as they could see or as far as they dared to venture. They were sure, though, that they were on the right path, for the great road had many characteristics that marked it, and they had been waiting now for several days for it to take its gradual turn to the north.

Neither Xith nor Noman liked the feel of the place they were in, and so they set a double watch this night. With so many to choose from, it had been two nights since Nijal last sat the watch. He took first watch, weary as he was, without complaint. He had only wanted to rest and to close his eyes, but he would have to hold off for two more hours.

Time dragged on slowly for him, but at least he was able to carry on a fragmented conversation with Shchander. Before he knew it, he was lying down to rest. Shalimar and another relieved the two, and after them Amir and Trailer took over. Trailer was a nickname for one of Shchander's men, who was most often found as the last man in the group; thus he had gained the name Trailer.

For the most part Shchander's men were very tight lipped. They held to the code of the warrior and the free man, and they took their responsibilities very seriously. Shchander, as their leader, was their voice and acted as such. The only person who appeared to be put off by their silence, and quite visibly so, was Adrina. She had taken a liking to Shalimar in an odd sort of way, and he had taken much abuse for his previous thoughtlessness. Amir smiled as he thought of Adrina, and soon he pictured another in his thoughts. The last two on watch were Xith and Noman, against the wishes of all present, who contended there was no need.

Xith was cheerful as morning came but withdrawn to his thoughts. After a meager breakfast, Amir and several others went for a short hunt, which they should have done the previous night but had delayed. Soon, after cleaning their catch this day, they were putting distance between themselves and the place where they had camped.

The air was cool and as they now moved through an area populated largely of oak, the rustle of crunching leaves beneath them was the predominant sound. For the most part, the trees were bare now, with few leaves that sought to hang on against the wishes of Mother-Earth. Some grew thankful for the sight of pine, which never lost its color. Its green appeared brighter amidst the brown.

Noman watched Amir very carefully this day. He saw the tension in his muscles, which Amir sought to ease by flexing and massaging. Noman watched Amir play as if he held a blade in his hand, sweeping slowly about his body. Noman knew this was more than just practice or unease. Amir's senses were very keen, and when he was agitated, the waiting preyed heavily upon him. Noman kept fully alert this day.

Just before mid-day, they happened upon a traveler who journeyed alone. The man turned out to be a minstrel of sorts, and he passed a short while with them playing songs: songs of the sea beyond the forest and the city in the mountain, of green sky and blue lands. He was a pleasant fellow, and they paid him no heed, which was odd in itself. The singer never offered his name, nor did they ask. Neither did he ask for theirs, although in passing he did mention the name of Krepost', the aerie on high.

Xith turned cheerful thoughts now to the path that lay ahead of them. He had not been in the fair city in such a long time that he had forgotten the laughter and mirth it held, which was in strong contrast to its sister city deep within the forest. Even Noman recalled the place with fondness. Although he had not been there in a long time, he did not think it had changed much.

Their camp this evening stood light, with only a single watchman. A low fire burned in a small hearth throughout the night. High overhead even the stars came out in force with a near-perfect moon in their midst. Amir passed the guard off to Shalimar who in turn gave it to Trailer, and then to Nijal; and if Nijal had known better, he would have counted the hours of his watch.

The day arrived with a bit of rain. Although it was mostly a fine mist, it held a hint of ice. After a sluggish start and a short hunt, they returned to their path. They soon found themselves near the edges of the Krasnyj in a place where it raged in full fury, a sign that they were close to the fabled city. They took a much-needed reprieve alongside the cool, actually icy, waters, but they bathed and filled containers just the same.

Adrina also seized the opportunity to rid herself of the filth of travel, and bathed in a secluded pool with only Amir to watch over her. He promised he wouldn't look. Adrina bade him to turn his back nonetheless. The cold water took mental coaxing to enter, but she did, and once she was within it, it did not seem so uncomfortable.

She leaned back, rinsing her hair. Pleasant, peaceful thoughts flowed through her mind. When she opened her eyes moments later she was shocked to see Tnavres withdrawn from her and in the water beside her. She wasn't sure if the tiny dragon was swimming or floundering, but she stood and plucked him from the water all the same, chastising him with her finger.

"Return," she commanded in a harsh whisper. Tnavres glared at her, then locked his jaws around her hand. As his teeth plunged inward, the flesh of her hand turned to stone. She gripped her forearm and squeezed with all her might, trying to stop the progression.

"No, no, no," she whispered as tears streaked down her cheeks.

"You don't listen," came the voice.

"But I have listened. I gave you all I could. What more can I give?"

"Tnavres will tell you when it is time. Do as you've been told."

"No," she whispered.

Tnavres entered her angrily, letting her know the force of his will. He sank into the flesh of her upturned palm, swept up within her arm and crossed her innards to his resting place in her belly. His mark was upon her right palm now where she could look upon it and remember.

Adrina found that getting out of the water was even more difficult than entering. The air was colder against her skin than the water, and she did not wish to leave it, as much as she tried. "Amir," she called out softly, but when he did not turn, she said it again louder, "Amir!"

"Yes," he said turning around.

"Turn back around!"

"My dear, what is it you wish of me?" asked Amir, knowing exactly what Adrina wanted.

"Please hand me my wraps and without looking."

"I told you I won't look."

"Just give them to me," said Adrina standing up, reaching out to get the cloak Amir had in his hands. Amir made her walk a few steps to get them before he finally gave them to her. A smile lit his face as he turned away. Adrina's face was flushed with both embarrassment and anger. He thought it suited her nicely.

Adrina glared at him, and stomped back to where the others waited for her and Amir. "A little bit of privacy!" shouted Adrina as she retreated into the coach, throwing down its shades and locking the doors. Amir approached Xith. With a grin still on his lips, he went up to the carriage door and knocked on it two times.

"What! What?" shouted Adrina, not opening the door.

"You'll want these," said Amir.

Adrina peeked out the window to see what he held, and then threw the door open. She was quick to grab the remainder of her belongings and then in anger, she touched her right hand to his shoulder. Amir chuckled, a deep, rolling laugh. The sound began as a trickle, and just as it rose, it stopped. Amir flexed his shoulders, and rolled his head to ease the stiffness.

He dropped to one knee as he fought to draw his sword. "Noman!" he strained to scream, but nothing issued forth. An icy hand dealt him another blow, this time to the left shoulder. He turned his head to look at the creature he perceived behind him just as it stepped forward.

Pain shot through his legs, then his back, and finally his arms. Wildly, he flailed the air using the last of his strength to lash out. He fell backwards to the ground with a thud, striking his head against the coach as he went down. As his world faded to darkness, Adrina closed the door to the coach.

Chapter Twenty One

Stone walls rose high and sheer about them. Calyin, Midori, and Edwar Serant wound their way among the many turns, delving deep into the shadows. A soft tapping sound followed their path, high above, though none below knew it. They walked in a single column with Midori to the fore and Serant to the rear, each leading one of the horses. They held to a slow, steady pace, carefully picking their way among the rocks and crevices. Frequently, they thought of Geoffrey and Captain Brodst.

Ahead the canyon appeared to end in a solid rock wall, but still they made their way toward it, seemingly inch by inch. Lord Serant followed the lee of the river, not paying heed to the wall's proximity to them. The churning of the water spoke volumes to him. Somewhere in front of them, the river's path turned downward.

The river gradually cut a deep course into the rock and a distance of only a few feet separated them from the waters. As the depth gradually increased, Lord Serant began to move away from the river's edge, and it was here that he first noticed the etchings into the rock. A shallow path of sorts had been carved out of the rocks through years of wear. The path ran smooth and straight. He regarded it as a roadway of sorts and supposed that long ago this path had been heavily traveled.

Some hours later they stopped to gather their bearings and to provide tired bodies with a bit of nourishment. The sheer wall looming immediately before them, jagged, tall and insurmountable, was perhaps an additional reason they had decided to stop. Here the trail ended, but they did not acknowledge its presence.

A high, shrill sound from high above startled them, and all conversation stopped. The three drew their blades and watched, waiting as many figures slithered down ropes in front of them and to either side. Those across the river they did not fear, for they saw no way for them to traverse it, so they turned toward the others. Slowly, they sought to retreat.

Serant flailed out with his foot, only to come upon empty air. He cocked his head back, and half turned to look. He saw the river swirling with white waters well below him. He turned quickly back to face those approaching with his eyes continually darting to the two at his side. A gleam, a glitter, he caught in Midori's eyes, and anger was upon her face. She held her long dagger before her without wavering. Calyin gripped her blade with nervous hands, but she did not lower it as those that came closer demanded.

Lord Serant looked again to Calyin and then to Midori. He quietly told them that should all else fail, the river was their safest route, no matter their thoughts on the subject. He touched Calyin's hand one last time, and then moved forward two steps. Calyin moved towards him, but he pushed her back. "And just where will you be?" said Calyin into Serant's ear.

"Lower your blades; we mean you no harm. We only wish to separate you from your purse, and then we will leave you."

"Do as I say!" said Serant, hurriedly.

"I will not go," returned Calyin.

"Tsk tsk!" shouted the man who now stood directly in front of Lord Serant; only their blades separated them.

"Just what is it you want?" asked Serant, in a haughty deep bass.

"Only your gold, nothing more, nothing less!"

"You may have all the gold we carry if you leave us now."

"Give it to me, and we shall leave. You have my word."

"A word is a bond, is it not?" asked Serant, moving back a short pace.

"Why, of course, of course. If a man cannot keep a promise, he is not a man."

Lord Serant fumbled through his cloak and retrieved a small leather pouch, which he tossed to the man. The man sheathed his sword, untied the small purse, and emptied the coins into his hand, counting each in turn, and shaking his head at each. "Surely you have more than this?"

"That is all the gold I have."

"What of the ring on your finger and the gem on the crown of the hilt of your sword?"

"They are not gold."

"Ah yes, but are they not worth their weight in gold?" questioned the man, raising his blade again.

"Midori, I trust Calyin's life in your hands. Do what you must!" called Serant pushing Calyin into Midori. He lowered his eyes to the waters of the river only for an instant, and then whispered, "I am sorry," as he pushed them both over the edge, and into the waiting waters.

"Bad, very bad. I do not like that, and when I do not like something, I usually kill the offender."

"Just as well. Today is a good day to die!" shouted Serant

charging the man.

"Not likely—" spoke the man as he called to his confederates.

Lord Serant struggled under the weight of a heavy blow, and for an instant he stared through crossed blades into his opponent's eyes. Only then did it become obvious to him that the man he faced was oblivious to his lineage, and perhaps he truly only wished his valuables, but Serant would not part with them. There were only a few tangible things he valued above all, and one was the ring that had been passed down through generations from father to son, and the other the sword of his forefathers.

"One against dozens!" shouted a voice, yet a good distance away, "Not very fair at all!" Captain Brodst and Geoffrey wasted no time in their charge, sending men scrambling to avoid being trampled by horses' hooves. Geoffrey raised his mount on its hind-legs just to the right of the one Serant fought, while Brodst offered a hand to Lord Serant. "We could not leave you, my friend. The farther we drew away from you, the heavier our hearts grew. Come, let us be off!"

The two horsemen made a quick, decisive retreat. Lord Serant looked back, fixing upon the upturned face. "Another day!" called out Serant, "Another day!" The man sheathed his weapon and then turned his back to them. He did not order his men to pursue because he knew the time of their next meeting would be sooner than the other thought. Serant watched as the attackers withdrew, climbing back up their ropes.

"Your timing couldn't have been better!" exclaimed Serant patting Brodst on the back.

"Where are Calyin and Midori?"

Lord Serant brought a hand to his chin, "Oh my—" he thought.

"The water—they are in the river."

"The river?"

"Yes, the river. I didn't see any other way."

Geoffrey and Brodst began to laugh because for a moment it seemed funny; but the feeling passed, and it suddenly was not humorous any more. Lord Serant scoured his thoughts, searching for a quick solution, which did not come. At the time, it had seemed his only choice, but now he knew it was a brash act. He did not like to think that he was a fool.

"What in the name of the Father is that?" exclaimed Captain Brodst reining in his mount suddenly, so suddenly that Lord Serant almost lost his grip.

"That is not of the Father, of this I can assure you," replied Geoffrey. Even though he could not clearly see those that readily approached, he recognized them. He knew nothing good would come of their meeting. The hunter beasts had only one thought on their minds, and that was their prey. Geoffrey and Brodst began to turn their mounts around, back in the direction they had come; midway, they realized their dilemma.

Neither Captain Brodst nor Lord Serant had seen anything like these before, but immediately they sensed danger and instinctively they reacted. Geoffrey bade them to return their weapons to their sheaths; as much as he hated to admit it, he knew this was an encounter they would lose, and he knew this as surely as he lived and breathed. A tiny voice in his mind hoped that perhaps they were not the objects of the beasts' hunt, in which case they had nothing to fear.

As the creatures drew closer, their distinctive features became quite noticeable. They had the appearance of men, but a thick, fur-covered hide enshrouded their forms. Their faces were long with an elongated snout, and white upturned fangs sprouted from their mouths. Even at a distance, Geoffrey could see crystalline droplets ooze from the nearest creature's mouth, a sign that he was looking for.

Geoffrey yelled for the captain to follow him and then retreated back down the canyon, the way they had come. Very soon they found themselves approaching the high canyon walls. Those waiting above rejoiced at the sighting, and one in particular had a broad grimace on his face. "Welcome back!" called out a now familiar voice.

"What do we do?" asked Brodst.

"This is not good, definitely not good."

"No, it is not."

As they turned their mounts around to face those that came up from behind them, the ravine, wherein lay the river, caught their eye, and more importantly the sound of rushing water caught their ear. Geoffrey did a mental calculation. He approximated the bandits' numbers to be around twenty or perhaps a little more. He also knew their kind well enough to know a small reserve was probably waiting. It was at least a two-to-one ratio.

He turned back toward the leader of the bandits. He wanted to get close enough to recognize the clan, but this was also his gravest mistake. As he staggered forward, the distances closed between the two forces. They found themselves in the middle of a stand-off, and he knew they were the prize.

The pack leader of the hunters, who identified himself to the bandit chief as Ermog, dismounted at a careful distance and approached singly. He called the bandit chief to a council of words, and though he spoke in the tongue of man, his speech was slurred and did not carry well. Only the other's words carried fully to their ears, and it was these words that sparked Geoffrey's interest.

In the interim, he conversed with Serant and Brodst, speaking quietly, stopping as the two spoke, and starting again in low whispers, passing his concerns on to them. The bandit leader had recognized Geoffrey and thus discovered the identities of those that accompanied him. He was playing with Ermog for the price of the bounty. Geoffrey knew the teachings of the histories and the passing down of the sons of the fathers and the realms, but the Borderlands were a realm outside all else. Nowhere did the histories speak of the Bandit Kingdoms or the Hunter Clan, societies that were older than that of the Great Kingdom but had never gained recognition in civilized circles.

Geoffrey understood the references to blood and sword, coin and fist, and as the two leaders returned to their ranks, he knew what he must do. He dismounted slowly, signaling for Serant and Brodst to do the same. He made sure they made no sudden movements, and he maintained his speech in low whispers. After a close but limited survey of the ledge and the waters below, they jumped, hoping and believing the river would carry them away to safety.

Chapter Twenty Two

Valam waited patiently for Mikhal and Danyel' to return with the scouting party. The group of riders, anticipated to be large, turned out to be only the small band that had been dispatched earlier and a large group of strayed horses. His eyes lit as he saw Mikhal and Danyel' race their mounts toward the place where he waited. He did not waste any time with pleasantries and quickly invited the two to accompany him.

The three went to Valam's quarters, where Teren yet waited without saying a word to anyone else. Teren listened intently as Valam spoke to the others, waiting for the correct time to speak his mind also.

"Prince Valam, if I may interrupt for a moment. You are missing the most important point. The four of us were given the gift of sight for a reason, a very specific reason. We merely saw you move through the steps. You must decide for yourself, but remember this in your decision. Choose your path with great care and follow it through to its completion."

"I wish I knew for sure," quietly whispered Valam. "I always pictured Captain Evgej and Seth at my side, no offense—"

"The future has many turnings. Perhaps it will be so. Perhaps we play a part in the paths of your future, or maybe we are your turning points in the path."

"That is a curious statement, Brother Teren," said Danyel'.

Two days passed and still Valam struggled with the choices in his mind. He knew not which direction to take. Thoughts of home appealed to him even though he knew the dangers that awaited him if he returned. This day weighed heavily on him. Teren returned to the plains, which were now completely buried beneath a very thick blanket of snow. Even the coastal areas received a fair amount.

The sky overhead promised that today would be clear and cloudless, and it was with a heavy heart that Valam returned to the affairs of the camp. The cold spell had left its mark on the camp, and supplies of wood for their fires were now depleted once again. They also had to face the fact that many months of cold might lay ahead, and the tents would not make this hardship any easier. They needed to find adequate shelter.

The small villages of the plains now lay deep in snow also, but the heart of the plain was not where they wished to go. The cold was just tolerable here; there it would be more than unbearable. They needed to find a better solution and soon. The cove where their ships were moored was suggested by Father Jacob, and Liyan also seemed to think this would be a good choice as it was partially sheltered from the winds and close enough that the move would not be excessively taxing.

The move began slowly and for a brief period it kept everyone occupied. Teren returned during the interim and took Danyel' and Mikhal away with him. When the change of camps was completed, Valam came to the hard decision to use their remaining wagons as the source for their fires. He vowed even if they had to start burning the longboats they would always have a fire in each hearth through the cold nights.

Valam stood still, oblivious to the light drizzle falling around him. His thoughts were heavy and his mood decidedly stern. He muddled over words he must speak when he returned to where the others waited. Jacob called a second meeting to solve their current problems and to find insight on the direction they were moving. Inside, all sat waiting; even the seven lieutenants were present. Seth ventured out into the elements, finding Valam gazing fixedly at some distant point that was probably only known to Valam. Seth knew and understood Valam's situation. He had discussed this at length with Liyan over the past several days, and he knew Valam actually didn't have a choice to make but rather to accept.

Valam hadn't even turned to acknowledge the presence beside him although he had noticed. His voice began softly, gaining volume only as it reached the final syllable. "—I must return to Leklorall and from there, perhaps home—"

"Yes, I know."

"I wanted to tell you before I told the others."

"You need not explain. I understand. I will miss you heartily."

The two stood silent for a long time before they joined the others in the meeting. Father Jacob was pleased to see the two enter together. As Jacob took his place at the table, Valam looked to each face around the room, recalling the names of each as he did so. Brother Liyan had donned the gray of his office; Tsandra was arrayed in brown; even Seth, Valam noted for the first time, wore the red of his order; and Teren wore black.

Cagan was not in attendance, but Valam had not expected to see him here, with ships so close by. Stretched out in a line to the right of Captain Mikhal sat the seven lieutenants. Valam looked puzzled for a moment upon seeing two empty chairs in the far corner before he recalled who was not present.

He crossed to the head position without further delay. His mind stumbled and stuttered, as did his tongue, as he began to speak. "Father Jacob, Brother Liyan, Brother Seth—as all of you know, I have been quite pensive as of late. It is very difficult to hide the discontent of your heart. Oftentimes the facts speak for themselves, and as I have considered the many things that are ahead for all of us here, I have stumbled over a host of obstacles, which were mostly phantoms of my own creation. I soon realized I really only had one choice to make, and this did not come without the help of a very close friend—and just a few, short moments ago—"

"Storm approaching!" interrupted the page as he burst into the tent.

"Will we never get this meeting completed?" asked Jacob, raising his eyes, and speaking upward.

"Storm?"

"Yes, sir, a storm—"

"Shoo, shoo, go back to where you came from. Go on, Prince Valam, please finish. Wait, wait, wait, one minute there—pass the word to raise stocks high in case the snows are severe and to prepare for the cold—"

"Yes, sir—but begging your pardon, of course, you don't understand."

"And just what don't I understand?" asked Jacob with more vehemence than he intended.

"Nothing, Father. May I return to my duties?"

"Yes, go!"

The page departed with an appearance of defeat on his face.

Father Jacob shook his head and then reclaimed his seat. Valam hesitantly began again although he paused long to recall where he had left off. Now the import of what he had been carefully building up to seemed trivial, so he just came out and said what he intended to do.

"I must return to Leklorall, for only there, I believe, will I find the answers I seek. From there, I may perhaps find that I need to return to Great Kingdom."

Surprised gasps issued from many, quickly followed by a loud murmuring. A few, like Father Jacob, had been expecting it, and the anxiety of waiting to actually hear it was finally released. Valam was most surprised by Teren's response, which was disbelief. He had received a similar response from Mikhal, which he counted as disappointment.

"I will select a small group to accompany me, but I will only take those who willingly choose to return with me."

"I do not think that will be a problem, your highness," said Redcliff. Danyel' immediately responded with a wide grimace and a sharp glare, forcing silence upon those around him. Valam started to speak again but stopped abruptly as Evgej entered.

"Didn't the page reach you?"

"Yes, he did, and as a matter of fact, he just left. Don't worry, captain, we are well prepared for the snow. We have already made provisions."

"Snow? No, Prince Valam, the storm comes from the sea. Cagan is extremely worried."

"This cove should harbor us from the worst. We will be safe."

"I am not so sure. Perhaps you had better accompany me."

Father Jacob stood with a pained look stretched across his

features and approached. He spoke in low whispers to the two, carrying them off a short distance to the corner. When he finished, he excused himself from the meeting and accompanied Evgej outside, leaving Valam behind, very confused.

As Valam walked to the front of the table and stared into the eyes of those about him, worry and fear touched him. Jacob's words played in his mind, "You must decide now," he had said, "you must decide now or it will be too late." Jacob already knew what the winds carried toward them.

"I think the time has come, the time when I must leave. I must return to Leklorall before the sun sets this day. There are powerful forces at work here both for and against us. Brother Teren, Brother Tsandra, I would have you accompany me if you would."

Valam ignored the pointed remarks that jumped into his thoughts mid-stream and continued. "Brother Seth and Brother Liyan, I regret that I think your place is here for now. Lieutenant Eran, you think I don't remember your name, but I do. Willam the Black, Pavil the Bearded, S'tryil, Son of Lord S'tryil of High Province, Ylsa, sister to Eran, and Tae, Master of Redcliff, your places are here, save you, S'tryil."

Valam regarded S'tryil for a moment. "I shall need a new captain, and you shall be the one. Captain Mikhal and Lieutenant Danyel' shall accompany me. Father Jacob and Evgej shall remain."

S'tryil waited until it appeared that Valam was finished speaking before he responded. "I cannot accept the honor bestowed upon me. I request that you pass the rank of captain to Ylsa. She has already earned it."

"Lieutenant Ylsa's time will be soon; your time is now, Captain S'tryil. Take command of your men and follow Father Jacob's instructions."

Valam continued to ignore Teren and Tsandra's remarks, which hit him full, even as he walked away. The wind outside, a strong breeze, immediately assaulted his senses, carrying with it sand and debris from around the camp. Valam had to shield his eyes with his arm to see clearly. He was amazed at the speed with which the storm raged towards them.

"Prince Valam, wait!" came the plea into his thoughts, even as he fought to seal them.

"I do not have time to waste! Tell the others to meet the long boat crew and go out to the flagship. She is Cagan's favorite, or so I have heard."

"They spoke nothing of Tsandra. Why is she—"

"Perhaps I have my own reasons. Now please hurry!" shouted Valam.

"Valam wait!"

The voice aloud caught Valam by surprise for an instant until he recognized it. "Yes, Captain Mikhal, take the lieutenant's detachment to the flag ship. Cagan is already there."

"But they are not—"

"Yes, I know," replied Valam as he walked away.

"Yes," returned Valam in thought as yet another voice disturbed him. Tsandra was quick to pick the thought from his center. "How many?" she asked. "The choice is yours," he replied.

Valam was interrupted one more time on the way to his tent, but this intrusion did not bother him. He and Seth had been through a lot together and to part now when they had come so far seemed ironic. But sometimes, thought Valam, "Irony was truth." And so when all preparations were made, he watched Cagan's steady hand lead the ship into the tack, turning back only after great hesitation.

"Goodbye," he whispered in his thoughts to Seth, Liyan and the others. "I have faith we will see each other again soon."

Chapter Twenty Three

"Amir, Amir? Can you hear me? Answer me."

"Noman?"

"No, I am Xith. Welcome back; you just sit there. You have been under too much strain lately. You will ride in the coach today and rest."

"Xith?"

"Yes, you just rest now, everything will be fine."

"Where is Noman?"

"Never mind, you just rest there a moment more."

Xith indicated that Shchander and Nijal should help Amir into the carriage now. The two did as they were bid, but it took a third to bear such an enormous burden. Nijal grabbed Amir on the left, Shchander on the right, and Trailer took the feet, stepping into the coach first and then carefully turning with the others to carry Amir inside.

The pace was lethargic this day as anticipation grew to a new high. The road joined with the great river and now ran along its course. Krepost' lay a day away at best and soon the sea would separate them from the lands of East and West. Noman turned to thoughts of supplies they would need for the north, and while the others turned to thoughts of Krepost', a song sprang to their lips.

Adrina stared fixedly at Amir with open concern upon her face. She watched him for a time, growing restless, and finally turning her attentions to the scenery around her. She could hear the churning of water even over the rolling of the wagon's wheels and the clippety-clop of the horses' hooves. A voice startled her, and though she knew better, she stuck her head out the window, looking for the speaker.

"You would do best to turn around, friends," rang the lofty voice.

"Turn around?" asked Xith. "Why whatever for?"

"And what makes us your friends?" asked Nijal.

"Whoa, hold on there. You be talking to old Kelar. I can see clearly you are from the west and have traveled far, so I will tell you this: 'tis not a good time to be happening upon our fair city."

Noman smiled and considered the words before responding. "We will watch our path, friend Kelar, thanks." Kelar just waved and continued on his way. The others in his party passed without saying a word. Xith turned to Noman and raised an eyebrow. He was glad to know some things didn't change. The people of Krepost' were still as odd and unpredictable as he recalled them.

Hours later, after several stops, the descending sun on the horizon lighted a most magnificent sight. High upon a steep bluff with cliff walls cascading down to meet the bay sat the city of Krepost', coming into view at long last. The only road that cut its way to the top of the aerie lay just across the river. The distance they needed to traverse and the climb would unfortunately cost them several hours of toil before this day was over, but they would gladly pay the price.

A cool breeze came in across the bay on a direct westerly course, bringing with it an odor of salt that assaulted the senses. Travel-weary bodies gained a new surge of energy that swept them onward; even the horses seemed to sense a long-deserved rest ahead. Shchander raced Nijal to the river, charging his mount to the very edge of the water.

The two stood there, waiting for the others to catch up. Nijal considered the promise he had made to himself some weeks ago when the nine men had joined their company. Once they reached the coast, their journey together would end. As he watched Shchander's lighthearted mood, he let the thoughts slip away. He would consider them at another time, perhaps after several days of rest.

Xith reined the horses to a halt, stepped down from the coach, and then walked over to a lantern hanging from a small post. For a moment, he thought about lighting it with a spark of magic, but the idea was short-lived. He retrieved flint and steel and set a spark to the lamp, raising it high above his head, and rotating it from right to left.

In the falling light, he waited for the signal to return, thinking that perhaps the brightness of the setting sun obscured the response. He waited until the sun sank from sight, and then repeated his signal. He paused, waiting patiently, and then handed the lantern to Nijal. Hearts sank after minutes passed with still no response; nonetheless, they waited.

Discouraged, they set up camp without much discussion. The lights of the city pointing the distance canceled any feelings of merriment. This stage of their journey would last one more day, and there was nothing they could do about it although Xith did work up a long list of harsh words to launch at the barge-master.

Amir awoke from a long day's sleep just as the sky was shrouded in darkness. He was still quite groggy as he approached the fire where most were seated. The smell of fish surprised his nostrils. Nijal and Shchander muttered something about idle hands when he inquired where the meal had come from. Stiffly, Amir sat down on the ground. The raging hunger in his belly was quenched, but only after his third helping.

As the time for the first watch arrived and the men began to retire for the evening, Amir offered to take the first watch, claiming he wasn't tired in the least. Shchander, who was supposed to have the first watch anyway, said he would hold the watch with Amir. The sounds around them began to die out, the crackle of the fire was replaced by the swirl of the water, and later the sound of laughter drifted into their ears and into their thoughts.

Shchander turned cold eyes to the glow in the distance. Before the last embers from the fire were extinguished, he stocked and restored it. Soon it was a cheerful blaze once more. A sudden crackling sound from behind him startled Shchander. He stood and walked toward it.

"Don't worry, Shchander. It was nothing."

"But, I thought—"

"Only an animal passing by, come back to the fire."

Shchander sat back down, casting away the dark thoughts in his mind. As the last hour of their watch wore on, the day's travel caught up to Shchander and his eyes grew heavy. He could scarcely hold them open. "Go get some rest. Shalimar will take over in a few minutes—I can sit out the rest by myself," offered Amir, and Shchander accepted. Sleep found him as soon as he put his head down to rest.

Amir never roused Shalimar or anyone else. He sat the guard throughout the hours of darkness. The first shards of morning light found him sitting beside a low fire. His attention was turned toward the black waters where the river joined the bay. He was careful to wake Noman and Xith last.

Breakfast was quick, and most did not eat at all. The ferry came into view just as they broke camp. Xith waited, lantern in hand, closely eyeing the old one who guided those who pushed the barge along its course. As it landed on the shore, Xith blew out the lamp and set it back on its post. He organized the words that gnawed at his thoughts all night. "Hello—" he greeted the barge-master coldly, stopping only to work out his remaining words.

"Well, a good day to you, and such a beautiful day it is. Well, well, what are you waiting for? Come aboard, and I will take you across the river for a pittance."

The warm salutation caused Xith to stumble in venting his wrath and what came out was not what he intended. "And just how much is that going to cost us?"

"Less than you would think, my friend. Come, step aboard, and we'll carry you off to the northern shore. The fair city of Krepost' waits. The market is just awakening. You can catch a fair amount of goods for a goodly sum if you are quick. So you must hurry!"

"Do you wish payment now or later?"

"We'll have time on the river for petty things. Come and listen to the words of an old river man. I'll tell you things you've never heard, and I'll charge you a meager fare, but only for the river's crossing. You need not pay for the words unless you've a mind."

Xith cursed low under his breath and boarded with the others. The barge-master caught the malice in his eyes and was quick to burst into a story and to set the barge on its return course. Thankfully, everyone was able to get onto the ferry without trouble. The river here was quite swift although in this section it was also shallow and was normally turbulent. The raft was of generous proportions.

Four men guided the barge toward the other shore, one in each of its corners, as the master explained its workings, among the many tales he spun in the short time. He explained how the ferry had two landings on the opposite shore and that the easterly one was the one they should wait at on their return route, for the other was just the landing for the return from the southerly shore. He told them how two asses bore the barge back to the departure landing against the river's current and he even worked the sum of their payment into a song.

Feeling sorry for his wry demeanor, Xith dropped twice the necessary coinage into the old man's hands as they disembarked. As he rode away, he glanced back with a hint of laughter yet in his eyes. He watched the two mules pull the ferry along the river's edge. The road to Krepost' was the only path they could follow, and as it was where they were bound for, they took it with great eagerness, following as it slowly wound its way to the top of the bluff.

The answers Xith and Noman sought were beyond Krepost', but for now the small company was safe. The city would house and keep them until they were ready for the next, more dangerous, part of the journey.

Chapter Twenty Four

Lord Geoffrey of Solntse awoke in darkness. "Calyin? Midori? Brodst?"

"No, they are not among us."

"Lord Serant?"

"No, it is only us."

Geoffrey's thoughts spun. The last thing he remembered was the encounter with the bandits and the hunter clan. "Dead? Are they all dead?" he asked, fearful of the answer.

"Perhaps. I do not know."

"Where—where am I? Why is it dark?"

"They like to keep us in the dark."

"Who are they? Wait a minute—who are you?"

"Don't fret so much. You should relax; you have been unconscious for days."

"Days?"

"Yes, I am afraid so."

"Do you know where the others are? The ones who were with me."

"I am afraid that I only saw you—well, actually I didn't really see you. I heard them carry you in."

"It is cold in here. Where is that wind coming from?"

"There is a blanket there, beside you."

"Thank you."

"No need to thank me. I have done nothing."

"What is that sound? Who is that?"

"Oh, him. Don't pay any attention to him; he goes on like that all the time. Here, try to drink some of this."

Geoffrey was thirsty; he drank deep. An instant later, he was spitting out what he hadn't already swallowed. "Oh, that's awful; what is this?"

"Would you believe water, or so I am told. It is horrible, but wait till you try the food."

"—Oh—I don't feel so good."

"You should rest. Find sleep, and find solace in it."

"What an odd word! Makes me almost want to laugh."

"Odd times—odd times."

"What do you mean?"

"Shh—they come. Just sit quietly."

"Who?"

"Shh—" The other shuffled in the darkness. "It is okay; they only brought food. Here, eat some of this."

"Your hands—what is wrong? Oh, I am sorry. I didn't mean to—"

"No offense taken, and I am sure if there were a spark of light in this hole, you would understand."

"What do you mean? Oh, I am sorry. I shouldn't pry. You are right; this is awful."

"It is all right."

"How long have you been here?"

"A long time—too long."

Geoffrey eased back, pulled the blanket around him, slipping quickly into a deep sleep. When he awoke what could have been hours or days later, he ate the leftovers in the bowl beside him, choking down whatever his stomach sought to spit back up. The other did not stir. In the darkness, Geoffrey could not tell if the other were sleeping or dead. He hoped the former and not only because the latter would mean that he was alone in this forsaken place.

Some time later, the guards brought food and water. Geoffrey ate and drank, perhaps more than his fair share. What followed was a seemingly ceaseless cycle of sleeping, waking, and eating. His strength returned. The other in his cell remained strangely quiet, withdrawn perhaps by something Geoffrey had said.

Feeling stronger made him bolder. When the guards returned, he shouted at them, "I demand that you release me at once!"

"You make no demands here!"

"Release me and my companion at once!"

"Hardy, har, har—you make me laugh. Hey, he wants to go home!"

"Set me free, or I'll cut your heart out myself."

"Cut my heart out, free?"

"I am a free man. You have no right to hold me."

"So you are. Sprout wings and fly away, but even those will not help you here."

"Take me to see your leader at once!"

"Our king is a very busy man, but I will tell him you wish an audience. You are such an important person that I am sure he will jump to his feet and come running at once."

"Do you mock me?"

"Why, yes, of course!"

"I will hold you in contempt for this!"

"Contempt of what? What are you going to do to me? If you do not shut your mouth, I will not even bring you your food."

"I would much rather starve!"

"Then so be it. The other one with a big mouth will not eat today!"

"Do you think I care?"

"We shall see—we shall see."

Geoffrey said no more, his thoughts going first to those he thought lost: Prince Calyin Alder, Captain Ansh Brodst, Lord Edwar Serant, Sister Midori—she who had once been a favored daughter and princess of the realm. *Were they all dead now like the Alder king? Had the enemies of old broken the heart of the kingdom? Did Solntse yet stand and were her people yet free?*

He whispered the free man's creed, "I am a free man, and I will die as such." He begged the Lord of the Heavens to spare his son, Nijal, if no other. "Please, oh lord," he whispered. "Has madness beset the lands?"

As he despaired, his hand longed to find the hilt of his sword and do what any righteous man would do in an hour of need. "A free man," he said, mocking himself as he paced in the darkness. He shouted to the heavens, "Oh lord, help me find my way, bring light to end the darkness."

"You want light?" said a voice from the hall. "What else is it you long for, old man? Perhaps you seek a blade? Perhaps you seek a way out?"

"I want only light so that I may see. Please, I beg of you."

"Light, eh? You'll regret it. Soon you'll long to return to

darkness, trust me."

Geoffrey heard a bolt being moved aside. A moment later a thin line of blinding white light poured into the room from a small window cut into the heavy wooden door. Geoffrey shielded his eyes; the pain caused by the light was so intense that he fell to the floor writhing.

"Still want light?" the guard asked, laughing as he fully opened the shielding window.

Geoffrey put his hands over his eyes to stop the pain. "How many days and weeks in darkness?" he asked, his voice trembling.

The guard offered no response save for the retreating echo of his footsteps as he moved down the hall.

Time passed. The long minutes blended together one after the other. The light became almost bearable. The guard returned. "I've been told to give you this." Geoffrey heard the clank of metal as something was thrown into his cell.

Geoffrey tried to open his eyes. His vision was blurred; all he could see were white points of light and a narrow path of what was around him. He groped with his hands in the darkness, found what the guard had thrown into the room. "A blade—you give me a blade?"

"When your vision returns, you'll know what to do with it."

"Do you think I will take my own life?"

The guard laughed, a deep mocking cackle, as he walked off.

"The blade is for me," said the other.

Geoffrey could see only a blurred outline of someone sitting up in the bed across the room. "For you?"

"For you to use to kill me. They like to pair us with our enemies. What satisfaction it gives them, I do not know."

"Our enemies? Wait—you know who they are? Where we are?"

"I do," said the other. "Before I tell you what you want to know, you must agree to put down the blade."

"You think I would kill you?"

"You are bred to this purpose, as I am."

"So it is true that we are enemies?"

"It is. But cannot enemies of enemies also be friends if there is need?"

"Perhaps it can be so if the need is great."

"And the blade?"

Geoffrey dropped the blade, saying to the other, "I am listening."

"Good," said the other, "then I will tell you what it is you want to know."

Geoffrey thought to himself that what he wanted to know was much more than any one man could tell him. He wanted to know the fate of the kingdom, whether the garrisons had liberated Imtal, whether the treachery had spread to Solntse, where he had gone wrong. He also wanted to know the fate of the crown prince, for surely if there was one who could bring unity to the lands and restore order it was Prince Valam Alder.

Chapter Twenty Five

As Prince Valam Alder surveyed the ship from the high deck, the sky growing darker by the moment, he saw a glowing shimmer shoot up the main mast. The soft golden glow lasted only a moment; but the way the light moved reminded him of Eldrick, the tree spirit, and a time beneath the Sentinel tree that seemed so long ago. Tree spirits, he had been told, were as ancient as the winds and the lands. The teller had also told him of the Fourth, an ancient power that could move through the world unseen by all save the Watchers and those few who could see into the land of shadow. It was said that the Fourth clashed against the very winds of Ruin Mist and could blow across the mountaintops.

What was meant by the saying Valam could only guess at; but Ekharn of the mountaineers, the elves who in ancient times dwelled in the Silver Mountains of East Reach, had told him so many things in the moments between dream and waking that his mind was still reeling these many days past. Ekharn's queen was the one who had told him to return with all haste to Leklorall and to look to the Queen-Mother for answers. She had told him to ask of the sword as well just before she told him to awaken and remember.

The time between the end of the dream and waking seemed an eternity. He was only now piecing together everything Ekharn had told him, and he only now understood that Ekharn had told him many things that he perhaps should not have. "Our times are but echoes. Find the dream when life's need is at its greatest," Ekharn had told him at the last. And now at the behest of a long-dead queen, he was returning to Leklorall to seek answers to questions he wasn't sure he understood.

Cagan, the elven sailmaster, stood at the wheel of the fleet's flagship, directing the ship through the tack. Beside Cagan stood Tsandra and Teren of the Brown, two elves Valam had grown to trust, as well as Seth. Captain Mikhal was on the main deck, making his way to the high deck, as Valam watched. The captain's return meant that the men were prepared for the heavy seas and that all was secure below decks—or as secure as was possible.

Sullen gray skies spread out across the distance. Cagan fought to meet the waves, but with each change of direction the boat faltered heavily in the turbulent waters. Prince Valam keenly focused his attention on the deepening black of the sky overhead. He sensed something that spoke ill to him; in these thoughts, he was not alone.

Tsandra and Teren were also concentrating on the energies of the storm. As before, they sensed more at work here than the hand of the Mother. A presence or a great force of will touched their thoughts lightly, though they did not sense it. It followed the thoughts in their minds and then fell away from them.

Cagan stood stoutly with his legs firmly planted on the deck. He strained under the weight of the helm as it tried to thrash about. Defiantly, he again turned the ship into the wind, directing the sails into the tack. His voice rose above the rasping of the waves and the moaning of the vessel. The bosun repeated his orders in seemingly ceaseless chords of shrill notes; all about the ship men moved to the sounds, tightening or loosening a sail or line here or there, as Cagan commanded.

Safety lines sprouted and stretched to the far corners of the deck. A rope found its way to the captain and lashed him about the helm. All the while, those that were now forced to move below deck were unaware of the proceedings above though in their minds they held images that were close to the truth. Danyel', who had retired below after they set sail, lounged back as if nothing were going on. He chewed absently on a bit of bark he had saved in a small pouch. The bitter, sweet taste in his mouth carried his thoughts away.

Captain Mikhal fidgeted with a small worn coin in his hand. He rolled it in and out of his fingers, playing it from one side of his hand to the other. Out of the corners of his eyes, he maintained a watch on the others. He did not adapt to the idleness as well as everyone else seemed to although he did note concern upon Valam's face.

The sound of water pouring down to the lower deck sent an alarm running through the thoughts of all. Startled minds brought feet scrambling to the mid-section hatch only to find more water, which drenched those close to the opening. Valam was the first to the ladder, and he was quick to secure the latch. He counted his blessings as the lock clicked, and he immediately heard the rushing of water above.

Valam waved the others back to where they had come from. He grinned broadly but not harshly at the concerned faces. This was not his first storm at sea; he had endured worse, or so he thought. He found his way back to the place he had occupied earlier and sat down. His thoughts began to reflect inward, and he turned to images of home, most especially what lay ahead for him.

A great creaking moan sent a shudder throughout the ship as if it bore an enormous weight. The bow and then the stern tumbled with a crash and then quickly rose on high. With the third crash came a cry and fear spread instantly. A rushing sound followed, like wind rustling through trees. Bodies swept with the water floundered helplessly, scrambling to catch anything available. Those that were able made for the hatches and safety.

The center hatch was the most congested as many began to flee the rising waters. For a moment the panic stopped and a cheer rang out. The shouts died out as the water continued once more on its course.

✳ ✳ ✳

City walls that had seemed so large in the distance appeared to shrink as the small band approached. Slowly the walls blended in with the raised cliffs and rocky crags. Krepost' had no immense protective wall as did its sister city though in its own way it was protected. As they rode, Xith cast long glances to the heavens, wondering if it was a fool's folly to try to breach the heart of darkness. Had they outwitted Sathar the Dark and the Fourth himself? Or did the darkness want them to believe they had? Was the trap set and were they already in its throws?

No guard marked the entrance to the city, nor was there a watch raised in the forward or postern towers. Here they tethered their mounts and parked the coach. Several reluctantly elected to remain behind until the others returned. Inside the carriage, both Adrina and Amir had gone back to sleep, which none remarked about, which was just as well. Adrina had been wide-eyed since the river crossing thinking about the gatekeeper of Krepost', who legend said might or might not chase them over the cliffs into Statter's Bay and to their deaths. However, as the hours passed and the company slowly made their way to the city high in the mountains, her enthusiasm and fear had waned.

The streets were deserted, and silence prevailed. Nijal squinted at the orange ball looming in the distance. The clouds above were just beginning to break up. The one thing about the city that was not disappointing was its size. Nijal compared it to that of Solntse, which was the greatest city of the West.

As they trod through street and alleyway on a course that only Xith knew, they came upon the market that the ferryman had mentioned. The sight and sound of so much activity suddenly springing to life took them by surprise. They had just circled around a squat, long, one-story building, and the market had suddenly appeared before them. They stood at its edge, staring in wonder.

Xith did a cursory inspection of his belongings and then led them into the square. He was quick to recommend that they keep a hand on anything valuable, adding that things had a way of disappearing though no one would admit to their theft. He also mentioned that accusing someone of thievery was not the brightest thing to do. Noman laughed as he added his agreement with that statement.

All manner of beast, fowl, food, and aromas assaulted the senses as they wandered among the stalls. Xith greedily snapped up bits of herbs and spices, mumbling to Noman as he made each purchase. The market at Krepost' was unrivaled for the variety of its goods and services. It was the last stop, or the first, on the East-West road, and almost anything could be bought here if the price were right.

Xith had forgotten how excited bartering made him. A youthful spirit overcame him as he frantically dashed about, searching for all the things that were on an imaginary list that he appeared to be recording his purchases on. The satchels, which had been his first purchase, were now filled to capacity, forcing him to slow his pace.

"I don't understand—" whispered Nijal, "Where did all these merchants come from? Where do they get all the goods?"

"That is the wonder of Krepost'!" replied Noman.

"No, really?" pleaded Nijal.

"Another time, another time, my friend."

Noman moved back to assist Xith without further regard to Nijal's insistence. Nijal sought out someone else to turn his questions on and found Shchander; but he did not know, either. He, like Nijal, had rarely been beyond Solntse; and while the markets in Solntse were grand, they were small compared to this.

Xith continued through the myriad of small tents and open stalls. He still had not found the one place he actually had sought, although he imagined it still lay somewhere near the center if he could reach the center. Hesitantly, he began to pass by things that he would otherwise have jumped at the opportunity to buy; yet as always the list of things he would later discover he had neglected would be enormous. He winked to Noman as he snaked through a twisted course that brought him at long last to his destination: a place where shipwrights and ship's mates gathered in the market.

"Where can I find the day's Master of Records?" he asked the sailors seated within the high-ceilinged tent. Soon after finding the master and making an inquiry about passage to the northlands, his voice was booming over the noise of the market. "What do you mean, there are no ships bound for the North?"

"Just that, I am afraid," said the acting Master of Records. "There are no ships bound for the North."

"The season is yet weeks from its end. Lead me to a captain that has an eye for gold."

"I am afraid I cannot. Now, if you'll excuse me, the day is long and I must retire."

"It is only mid-day!"

"Mid-day is closing time in the market."

"I know, I know," muttered Xith.

Noman held back an urge to do something vile to the Master of Records. "Where can I find one of the shipwrights?"

"At this hour?"

"Yes, at this hour?"

"Most likely at an inn, taking a bit of lunch."

"And which inn would that be?"

"Take your pick. Now, if you'll please excuse me, I must be off, or I'll miss my own lunch."

"Would this change your mind or delay your retreat?" asked Nijal, waving a small bag weighted with coin.

"No," replied the man flatly.

"Come," spoke Noman, "the others will have missed us by now."

"Wait," offered Xith, "I have something that will slow your retreat." Xith shuffled through one of the satchels and procured a small, blue bottle. "Last one in the market, my friend, and it's yours if you just help us on our way."

The man stopped and looked, eyeing Xith carefully. "I take it you have been here before?"

"Many, many times," returned Xith.

"You must forgive me; I thought otherwise."

"No offense given, none taken."

The man smiled and nodded. "Two Hands is the place you seek."

"Still the same," replied Xith.

"Yes. But if you knew that already, then why did you trouble me?"

"I see now that you do not understand. This is good."

"Wait—do I know you?"

"Probably so, for I know you. The most curt officer of them all."

"Obviously you have not met my company's captain."

"I am not sure."

"Come and I'll take you to the Two Hands, but once there you are on your own. And I still cannot guarantee you will find what you seek."

"I seek no guarantees, my friend."

"Good, good. As I said, I offered none, even with your gift."

"No problem. We will wait and see."

"Come quickly and follow at a goodly step or you'll most likely find you've lost your way and your guide."

Xith cast a glum stare at Noman, his dark thoughts from earlier in the day returning. Surely the trap was set and they were within its throes. But who were the conspirators in the dark plot against them? Did they dare trust anyone at all?

※ ※ ※

Father Jacob paced nervously back and forth, cautiously eyeing the threatening sky. He was not pleased with the turn of events. The timing just was not right; too much seemed beyond his control. The will of the Father had been barely perceivable for some time now. It was as if he were alone. He marked this as the third time this had occurred, and the growing number of occurrences frightened him.

Both Liyan and Seth sat quietly watching Jacob, reading his every thought unbeknownst to the good father. Their intent was not to intrude on Jacob's privacy, but to clarify their own muddled thoughts with another viewpoint. They could sense a portent drawing near though they didn't know what it was. Perhaps, they thought, it was the storm that carried the ill tidings to them.

Liyan slowly turned his consciousness inward for a time of reflection, wavering from the link he held with Seth and unintentionally severing that link. In his mind, he pictured the paths, and he began to piece them together, beginning at the time when Seth had left for the kingdoms of men and methodically moving forward towards the present.

Beyond the relative safety of the confines of the small tent the three occupied, the camp was teeming with frenzied activity. S'tryil, the newly appointed captain, moved about the camp, striving to maintain order. He still disliked the new authority given to him. It felt like a great weight. He was neither great nor proud like his father although he did inherit his father's values, which were simple and true.

Extra stakes were being driven into the ground around each tent with ropes being attached and anchored. The hope was to give better support against the coming high winds. Stores of food and supplies were being moved under cover. Small bands of sailors were returning to their ships to ready them for rough seas. The harbor would give some protection from the winds and high seas, but it would not shield everything. The elements of wind and rain would still find them. The sea would most likely claim a boat with a heavy anchor.

S'tryil eventually found his way back to Jacob as did the five lieutenants. Their work was now complete; very soon they would know whether they had erred or had been successful. For a time, they moved to a warm spot near the small hearth that was erected at one end of the tent, but they soon found themselves surrounding Jacob as he stared beyond the table, beyond the doorway, into the festering sky.

Chapter Twenty Six

Cagan fought a losing battle to gain control of the sinking ship in the vile storm. He had turned her about and aimed her at the shore. Though the course never held true as they were tossed about, they still would hopefully reach safety before the ship was claimed by the seas, which would devastate him.

Teren played with the voices in his head that called to him. "Why do you leave us?" they asked. He shied away from all save one—the one that was just at the furthest reaches of his will. A large wave swept over the deck and nearly toppled him and several others. Thankfully, his grip was strong, and the rope between his fingers burned into his hands only slightly.

All had moved topside to escape the rushing waters below deck. With each new crest and trough, the wind changed direction in the sails. Some were only slight course deviations but others nearly overcame the masts, causing them to bend and bow beneath the heavy strain. Rains came first as a light mist but immediately turned thick and heavy as the storm descended upon them.

The deck of the ship became slick as did the safety ropes. A second set of hands toiled at the helm. Valam had made his way slowly and carefully to the forward deck. He took a stout rope and lashed himself to the wheel as Cagan had. A voice from within the ship called out the depth of the rising waters.

Already, Cagan noticed the sluggishness of the response from the wheel. The ship would soon flounder beyond his control if the masts did not yield first. He cursed loudly in a steady stream of words, which were his commands to his bosun. The calls still sent able-bodied men to action though the response time was slow.

The first spark of lightning to strike close at hand sent a shiver through Cagan. As if rain, wind, and wave were not bad enough, now the storm lashed out at them with yet another of its treacheries. Each new bolt echoed both in his eyes and in his ears. He laughed at his folly, mocking his own thoughts. The lightning gave him a new source of light in the darkness of the storm, and whether it was good fortune or misfortune to see the line of the coast highlighted in the distance he did not know.

Cagan saw only the shadows of rock and crag ahead. He noted a shift in the balance of the ship as it sought to settle to one side. Quickly he called out to correct the sails. The bosun's alarm rang, and the men responded when the top deck first encountered the crest of the gigantic wave. Screams of despair rose. Several were swept into the seas and readily claimed. Their screams of panic did not last long.

The ship surprisingly did not give in. As it was whirled about at the bottom of the wave, it righted itself though it was still heavy in the water. Cagan gazed through the flashes, searching the shadows. Cautious thoughts carried his mind to the two longboats they carried. He marked them as their last resort and had them readied, even though he knew they would be of little use in this storm.

A sound almost like a clap of thunder stifled his senses. Cagan held his breath deadly still. He closed his eyes and bowed his head. As the center mast crashed to the deck, the rigging and sails went with it, draping the onlookers. Mercilessly the waves turned the ship and overcame her, even as she flopped from side to side.

Many hands went to the longboats and launched them into churning waters. Those that were close enough scrambled inside, and the sea claimed even a few of those. Neither Cagan nor Valam had left the wheel; there they remained. They watched the small boats being brutally battered by the rough waters. They chose not to die in that manner. They would rather come to an honorable end, dying the way they had lived.

The dull glow of a light suddenly came into sight. The storm played among the shadows around them, offering them no clues to its origin. As if in anger, the rain increased in velocity, pelting them with an ever-thickening volley. A shimmer in the distance caught their eye. A murmur resounded in their ears as yet another clap of thunder fell upon them. The bolt struck dead in front of them, lighting the area in a great circle, and for the first time, a glimmer of hope was revealed.

❊ ❊ ❊

Midori woke from a dream. Frightened, she shivered alone in the dank corner in which she slept. A tear marked the outline of her face, and just as it dripped to the floor, a smile, a mocking smile touched her lips. Her enemy knew her soul well, she thought for a moment. She found little comfort in the knowing, and quickly turned away from it.

A voice pierced the silence and the darkness about her. Though she heard it, she did not listen. She still grasped the images from the dream in her mind and would not turn away from them. The Mother had called out to her, or perhaps it was only a wish in her dream; she did not know, but the voice could not be mistaken. She did not know if the message was one of her own creation or of reality, but she held to it.

"Today," she thought, "today is the day when I will know the truth of it." She groped for her blanket in the darkness and pulled it snug around her. The cold stone beneath her negated the little warmth it offered. She closed her eyes in an attempt to find peace in sleep and her dreams again.

"Outside the sun is already high in the sky," spoke a voice in close proximity to her.

"I do not care. I only know that it is dark in here and cold, and I am tired. My soul is weary and wants to rest. So please leave me in peace this day, or night."

"My dear Midori, princess so fair, first daughter of the Mother, heir to all."

"Don't start with that today. Please let me rest. I—I—" began Midori, "I am so tired."

"Your mind is awake, and your body grows weary but not from lack of sleep. You have slept too long; it is time you woke up. Move about. Move your feet. Do not sit and stagnate this day."

"You were the one who told me to sleep. What do you wish me to do?"

"Yet that was some time ago. That is long since past. We have much to discuss and times grows short. So listen to my words, and regard them for a time. Then when you are ready, respond to them in any manner you see fit."

"I think we will have plenty of time for as many discussions as you please. I don't think we are going anywhere soon."

"Maybe, maybe not. Have you not returned to your senses yet? Are you a princess, or are you the first to the Mother? Well, a response would expedite matters."

"I'm thinking; give me a moment."

"There should be nothing to consider. Has your mind grown that clouded? Is your judgment impaired beyond even my grasp? First consider this: is the darkness all that bad? Is this the only thought in your mind? If it is, you need to seriously reconsider your woes."

"I do not think I can. I fear the dark, to be truthful with you. You cannot see in the dark, and without sight, you are lost."

"On the contrary, there is much one can see in the dark if you only have the will to look. Did not your teacher pass on to you the lessons of your senses? Your eyes are but one of many."

"This is the second time you have spoken of my teacher. Which do you speak of, as I have had many?"

"Your first of course, for in truth there were no others before or since."

"You knew the shaman?"

"Yes, for as long as the wind has blown across the northern mountains."

"Then you are—"

"But of course I am."

"Am I dreaming, or am I awake?"

"You are very much awake. Now, will you listen?"

"Yes. Please forgive me."

※ ※ ※

Xith and Noman pressed on, following their guide. The others returned with the heavy bags of goods Xith had procured to the place where the remainder of the party waited. Nijal was hesitant to part from the two but did as he was told. Xith grinned ear to ear, and Noman knew at once why. Xith had not known the name of the man who was now their guide; in fact he had probably never seen him before this day, but that did not matter. The man wholly believed that Xith had. Just as importantly, this belief would be relayed, discussed by those who watched.

The pace did prove to proceed at a very fast pace. Their guide turned corners, crossed street and alley, detoured around obstacles, both animate and inanimate, without a moment's warning. His demeanor did improve greatly though as they walked a ceaseless string of words issued from his lips, which most often was heard as an unintelligible mumble.

He did offer his name, which was Vajlar Kapriz. Xith had managed to salvage that much from the man's unbroken soliloquy. Xith took it in the old tongue, and it did indeed fit one of Vajlar's demeanor. Xith wondered at the confidence the man had in them, or perhaps he thought Xith already knew his name in full, which was not often given to friend or stranger.

At length, they finally arrived at a place where a somewhat odd sign hung, on which was scrawled, not printed, the words "Two Hands." Vajlar paused for a time outside the door and caught his breath, pulling himself up to his full height as he did so. His stride was no longer quick and sloppy but crisp as he entered and crossed to a table.

He bade the others to join him and ordered three draughts, for which Xith paid at Noman's insistence as Vajlar never reached for coin or purse. Their guide drank two full tankards before anything passed his lips other than ale. As he began to speak, it was clear that his mood had changed; and, although he was not rude, he made it clear that they were outsiders here and should watch their step at all times.

Vajlar drank two more draughts, still at Xith's expense. His cheeks grew bright red and his eyes began to gloss over. It seemed that he was in a talking mood once more as words spewed from him endlessly again; and though they were now slow, they were slurred with the liquor. Xith smiled politely, knowingly. The guild was the true gatekeeper of Krepost' and indeed, as myth and legend implied, there was great danger for unwelcome travelers.

The story that Vajlar embarked on was in no way related to what they wanted to hear. As it drew to a close, the hour was growing late. The sun outside, if they had been able to see it, would have been past afternoon and leaning toward dusk; but this afternoon the two were saints of patience, or at least Noman was. They offered no complaints, bent only on listening intently. After a few too many tankards of ale had passed their lips even though there were lengthy pauses in between, they began again only at Vajlar's insistence. They began to lose sight of their objective, and they even started to understand the story they listened to. Xith acted extremely nervous, as was expected, and especially since the table was littered with a line of tankards, all of which he had paid for.

After the table had been cleared and then filled, Xith, who seemed to be the only one with his wits attached, lost his will to wait. "Vajlar, my friend—" Xith paused for a lengthy burp, playing the part a bit too over-the-top as far as Noman was concerned, "Are you ever going to tell us—point out to us—the one we seek?"

Vajlar pretended not to notice that Xith had spoken and continued on with his conversation, which was now completely one-sided. He had, after all, still one willing listener. Noman, who had one hand pressed against his face with his elbow resting on the table, was indeed listening. Noman turned his attention to Xith, only after it became clear that Xith was not going to let his words pass.

"He doesn't know," responded Noman, nodding his head slightly to let Xith know everything was proceeding as expected. There was also a much more subtle message in the gesture: don't worry so.

"What do you mean, he doesn't know? Then what are we doing here wasting time?"

"Listening to the story of course."

"You are following that?"

"Yes. Now if you'll be silent, I can return to it. Please continue, Master Vajlar. Pay him no heed."

✳ ✳ ✳

A sharp shift in the wind raised the flap of the tent and threw it back. Mist from the rain reached the table in short spurts. Jacob moved to close the flap, but Ylsa had already done so. She pulled the flap taut, and secured it tightly this time. Father Jacob offered her a wink as a gesture of thanks.

The atmosphere in the room had been gloomy for hours. Some wandered next to the hearth, warming their feet and hands, while some just sat at the table looking forlorn. Jacob absently scratched words onto bits of parchment. His thoughts were elsewhere, floating beyond the waters of the sea.

A sudden shaft of light shining into the chamber startled him. He lifted his eyes to see a hand groping at the knots tied about the doorway, and a figure entered. It was drenched from head to toe, and perhaps the only dry thing it possessed was the lamp it held, which was shining fiercely.

Jacob noted the rain striking the ground in thick pellets. It was turning to sleet. None moved as the hooded man walked to the table, set the lantern down, and began to remove his saturated cloak. Jacob nodded as the man shook the water from his hair and walked to the fire without uttering a sound save for the chattering of his teeth.

"Cursed storm," Captain S'tryil muttered under his breath, removing his boots and setting them upon the warm stones. "Water is rising in the camp; the rain is no longer sinking into the earth. It is just settling on the surface. If I did not know better, I would say that a great flood is at hand. The cliffs along the far walls are running with heavy cascades of water. Even the sea is in extreme turmoil. We have had to draw the farthest line of tents back, or they would have been lost. The waves are coming in greater than I have ever seen. Our scouts to the north and south report that the trails are being washed away. In short, the only way out of this hole will be by rope."

"The ships, captain, are they all right in the bay?"

"As far as I can tell. Captain Evgej has not returned yet, so I am not positive. The darkness has completely enshrouded us; the storm is full upon us. I think it best if we all just stay indoors until it passes. I have passed the word to report all matters here as expediently as possible."

Jacob mulled over the words for some time. The absence of Evgej suddenly touched a chord in his mind. There were two others who were also absent. He continued with the parchment, writing until he considered it complete, and then he pressed it flat and placed it in a large book amongst many others. The rain flailing the roof of the tent had stifled most of the thoughts he would have logged this day. For the most part, words had crossed from hand to pen only after long, pensive pauses. He sensed something ill afoot though he could not place it.

* * *

Lord Edwar Serant waited for the guard to return. "Very well, I will just sit here and do nothing, as you wish, but I will say this, I do not like it. You could at the very least offer me something to eat. A little food, maybe. I am growing very hungry. Do you have any food? Yes, I am talking to you, who do you think I was talking to? I wasn't talking to myself now, was I? Well? Are you just going to sit there or are you going to get up off your lazy ass and get over here and open this door? Wait, wait! I was just kidding. Come back—yeah, that's it. Just sit back down. Don't trouble yourself with paltry thoughts or simple facts, like I have not eaten in days and have no water, nor any place to go to the bathroom."

"Use the corner; that is what they were made for."

"The corner? Please, spare me. Are you ever going to move from that spot, you lazy oaf?"

"That's it! This one gets a muzzle. Fetch me the straps!"

"Wait, wait, I just want something to eat. I promise I'll shut up then."

"Really?"

"I swear."

"Listen here, any more trouble out of you and I'll chain you upside down for the rest of your miserable life. I chained the bird man upside down and he nearly died. You, I'd leave you there until death. Is that what you want?"

"You know, friend, you really should tone it down a little."

Edwar Serant turned about. Before he could answer, the other in his cell said, "Oh, you're awake, finally."

"How long have I been asleep?"

"You were not sleeping, my friend, you took a nasty blow to the head. You are lucky to be alive."

"Well, with all the noise the loudmouth was making, he could have waked the dead."

"Poor choice of words, I assure you. Let me take a look at you. Sit up—Oh—Oh, my—"

"Is it bad?"

"No. It is healing nicely."

"Where am I?"

"I wish I knew myself—wish I knew myself."

"Do I know you?"

"Perhaps. Don't worry about that right now. You just lean back and take it easy."

The guard returned, "Hey, you there, here's your grub. Eat it all, or you'll not see another bite."

Edwar Serant glared at the guard through the small window in the cell's door. "Do you think I really care? I'll—mmm, not bad. My compliments to the cook; this stuff is almost good enough for sows."

"I'm warning you—"

"I would be quiet if I were you," said the other.

"It's a game. He really loves it. I don't think he'd ever really put me in a muzzle." Serant gave the bowl of food to the one who had just awoken. "Here, eat this."

"This is really bad. How can you eat this?"

"It is all we will get, so eat up. What about you? Here, take some of this."

"I'll pass."

"Me, too."

"No, you both need your strength. Eat or I will spoon-feed you."

"Your voice—it sounds so familiar to me."

"Most probably, my friend."

"No, really."

"That's probably because it is. Now you just eat and then close your eyes and return to sleep. The strength will return to you in a few days."

Lord Serant waited for the guard to approach and then began, "All dressed up and no place to go, no feed in hand, nor tree nor bush, nor blade of grass in sight. I long for the sun to shine upon my face, and a cool northerly breeze to blow upon my brow."

"Give it a rest! Do you want me to deny you food and water? How long do you think you can last without food and water? A week at most, I'll wager."

"Once I see your captain and he sees how you have treated me, then you'll be the one whistling a tale."

"If you were a king of some great land, I might be afraid, but for all I know you are a tired, worn mercenary that lost his way while guiding a couple of ladies. At least they are worth their weight measure."

"What if I am a king? What will you do then? Will you run and hide like the mongrel that you are?"

"That is it. I will waste no more breath on you this day. Go sulk in the darkness."

Lord Serant heard a grate slide into place, and all light left his cell. He did not care if they denied him food and water for a time, for he knew that they would be forced to feed him again in due time. Damaged merchandise would not fetch a fair price.

He had gleaned much more from the guard than the other knew. His conversations, though seemingly muddled, were pointed and led to the solutions to the riddles that roamed his mind through the many hours of silence that followed each such conversation. He knew where he was being held, and by whom. He knew where the others were being held, and he now knew that Calyin and Midori were amongst the prisoners their captors had taken. More importantly, he knew the sisters were alive.

One question that had weighed heavily upon him, though, still lay unanswered. He still did not know how or by what route he had come here. A fog lay over patches of his mind. He recalled everything up to the encounter with the bandits, yet he was not among their kind. It was also obvious that his captors did not know who he was, which was most definitely to his advantage.

In the dark, Serant surveyed his domain. The cell in which he was kept was small. He measured it at three paces by four. The walls were worn smooth. The ceiling was beyond his reach. Though he never caught a fair glimpse of it, he knew no shafts led into it. The sole source of air was from the door, where a faint breeze always blew.

In one corner, many marks were scratched, single lines drawn carefully. Though he had never seen these in the light, he knew their count: three hundred and ninety-seven. Counting them was a ritual that occupied part of his daily routine. They served as a reminder to him to remember, or approximate, his own days of captivity. Thus far he had made seven marks in his own corner. He guessed that he had been held longer, but these were the seven that he could note for sure.

This day he etched his eighth mark into the wall with a small piece of steel. The origin of the bit of metal he could not guess though he did think that it had been lying on the floor precisely where the former occupant had left it. Time had rusted its edges and dulled its point, but he had sharpened it and worked it in his hands until the last vestiges of the rust were gone.

* * *

Nijal's path led him, Shchander, and the others on an indirect roundabout course through the city but not immediately back to its entrance. Xith had, after all, told him to find the first inn at the edge of the city and take rooms there. Xith had not said which edge of the city, so he needed to explore all avenues.

In all, Nijal summed up the city as less than he had imagined it to be. It did not have the grandeur of Solntse or the complexity of Zashchita. The streets were arranged in a simple series of avenues and byways that spread out from a central point, which was the market. The market was the one redeeming quality he found here. The city was otherwise unremarkable.

Disappointment settled immediately in his thoughts. The song the minstrel had spun for him had led him to believe that the city was enormous and spread out across the horizon; in reality, it was compacted onto a simple highland plateau. His search ended at the foremost gates, his former energy depleted.

Trailer sat upon the carriage in the coachman's seat with two others at his side. Shalimar stood near the rear of coach, head tucked down inside his hood and eyes closed. The first order of business was to rouse Adrina and Amir who were apparently still sleeping inside the coach and ready them for quick travel.

Nijal made the mistake of choosing the door where Shalimar stood, and he quickly found a sharp blade at his throat as he attempted to open the door. Even with the edge of a knife pressed to his neck, Nijal managed a laugh. He clasped Shalimar on the shoulder, praising him for his speed.

"I still wouldn't do that, friend," whispered the man.

It was then that Nijal realized that there was an extra person in his count. He drew back warily, eyeing the hooded man. "Who are you?" demanded Nijal, reaching for his sword.

"Whoa, whoa, slow down there. I mean you no harm. If I meant to harm you, I could have done that long ago. These fools would never have noticed."

"Just who are you calling fools!" shouted Trailer, jumping down from the seat.

"Why you, of course, but I did not mean to spark anger. I meant it only as a statement of truth. It was obvious to me that this coach was missing a master, and I just waited until he returned. You are he, are you not?" said the man pointing to Nijal.

Nijal nodded his head in agreement. "Good, good, then all is in order," began the man, throwing back his hood as he spoke and stepped forward. "And if I guess the situation correctly, you seek passage somewhere. Am I right? Why of course I am. Why else would you have journeyed here? Let me get an eyeful of you. I would say you're not from anywhere near. I would guess, the Kingdom. Am I right? Why of course I am. I am never wrong. I see your situation this way. You need passage on a ship, and I can get it for you. If the price is right, of course. You have money, don't you, my friend? Nice coach, I might add."

"You are rather quick to speak about things you know nothing about. If I had a mind to be angry, I would be enraged at your pompousness."

"Whoa, whoa, I am not pompous, please. I did not mean to offend. Here, take this. I am Awn of the Guild. That coin will lead you to me if you ever have a mind. I know where you can get a fine ship—for the right sum of gold, of course. Bring it with you, and we will talk. I will leave now. Good day!"

Confused, Nijal turned wide eyes to Shchander, who returned the gaze. Nijal considered the words, but then, giving up hope at understanding, he shrugged his shoulders and returned to more immediate matters. The horses were left at a stable that was close at hand. The stable master was quick to barter for their keep and their shoeing. He was also quick to chastise them for the condition of the mounts. "A good shoe and a good horse will take you a good distance, but a bad one with poor shoeing will only get you a lame horse."

Nijal understood the practice but endured the lesson. As the man continued on with his story, a journeyman began work on the first horse's shoes, shaking his head with the same flicker of anger in his eyes towards Nijal as the stable master had. He muttered something low under his breath about those who should be saddled and ridden for a time to see how they liked to proceed in ill-fitting shoes. Nijal persevered, hoping still to get a fair price for the carriage as Xith had instructed him to do.

He left the stable pleased with the sum he had obtained even after the charges had been deducted for shoe and keep. An inn lay just down the adjacent street and as Nijal was sure it was the one Xith had spoken of, he appropriated several rooms in it. He played with the small coin, obviously not made of gold or anything else of worth, which the stranger called Awn had given him, contented to wait until Xith and Noman returned.

Chapter Twenty Seven

A solitary hand clawed its way up onto the beach and soon a figure followed, struggling to stand upright, moving awkwardly through the swirling water about its knees and bearing a heavy load upon its shoulders. Pulling, holding on, the figure struggled against the forces of nature, dragging behind it a small craft and though wind, rain, and surf claimed the last of its strength, it stood gallant.

Behind, yet a good distance off, a second craft made its way toward shore. The oarsmen grunted and groaned defiantly. It was not by chance or fate that they came upon the shore but by sheer determination and perseverance. In time, twelve stood where a full thirty should have, but thankfully not all were lost. Some had elected to remain at sea, and a few others would come after the return trip.

Of the twelve, one stood out almost regally in her defiance of the storm. A curse sprang from her lips, and she meant it to be heard aloud. The group did not delay long upon the shore, quickly turning away from the sea, heading immediately into the midst of the camp, scarcely separated from the raging water.

Jacob's face went deadly pale as the faces appeared out of the shadows of the night. He could not find words to speak, and his eyes expressed the fear he was feeling. The twelve went first to the fire, removing water-soaked garments, warming frigid, swollen toes and hands. The fire was stoked and the chill swept from the air before any one of them turned to speak.

"Cursed be this day! This storm is wholly unnatural. The water is rising upon the shore, almost reaching the first line of our camp. The ground is saturated, water flows across it as if we were sitting upon a great river. A curse on its creator."

"The Great-Father would not appreciate your curses upon the Mother, though I still welcome your return, my prince, and I think your curses are pardonable. Why have you returned? Where is Cagan?"

"I am here, good father," quietly murmured the elf, "but there are many others, many who are not—"

"What happened? The ship?"

"Yes, lost. You would not believe the strength of the storm. If it had not been for Captain Mikhal and Tsandra, we would have gone down with the ship."

"How many were lost?"

"The count is not sure, but I believe we must turn to other matters before we grieve properly. However, a moment of silence is in order," Valam reverently whispered the words into the thoughts of those present. It was with a heavy heart that he spoke the words of passing. He did not rejoice this day for those who had journeyed to the Father, only sorrow.

Liyan was the first to break the quiet and return to the present. "Prince Valam is correct in his summation of this day's occurrences. Brother Seth and I have debated long over this subject. We have felt this power before. The first time it came to us, we counted it as a work in the natural order of things, but facts have changed. This storm was created, not born of the Mother. A strong will is in opposition here. We are sure of it. You can be sure this storm was long in the creation. It did not happen by chance or suddenly. We are witnessing perhaps the toil of one's life or many lives.

"The forces could have been guided for many weeks or even months until they came to this point, gradually working up to the raging torrent we now endure. One thing you can be sure of is that the enemy is aware of your presence, has known, or has most probably seen us. Perhaps this is his way of acknowledging it. Our enemy knows many things, including the paths in the future. He has survived the dark path, and nothing holds secrets against him though we strive to."

"Brother Liyan, can we not fight the storm and send it back upon its master? Send those that created it scampering for cover, running back into the holes they emerged from!"

"That is my wish, but first we must consider this. Prince Valam, you spoke well about the rising waters in the camp. We may find our own deaths here in this sinkhole. Water circles all around us, the earth shifts beneath it, perhaps the trap is already set. I can only hope that it is not."

Captain S'tryil stepped forward. "We have already tightened the circle of tents, moving them away from the water's edge and the walls of the cliffs. The scouts to the north and south last reported that they can no longer make the journey along the paths leading from these shallows, even with rope and toil."

"This is not good. We must think clearly and act quickly."

※ ※ ※

Princess Calyin Alder glared at the barred door before her. She paced slowly in close circles around the tiny cell. She waited for a sound that she knew would begin far off and then grow closer. Time for her had stood still these last days. She knew not whether it was night or day, only that after a long wait a tray of food and water would be brought to her.

Today, however, was different. She woke to find more than the necessities of food and water, and she had found a beautiful silk dress. A basin of water, clear and uncontaminated, had also been placed in the room. The food held a wonderful aroma and taste.

She bathed in the basin, which, although small, had met her needs. The water was cool and caused her to shiver, but as she placed the dress across her shoulders, she warmed up. She wondered at the sudden change in her captors—or tormentors rather, as she thought of them.

The hours passed slowly after she had bathed and eaten, and now she waited, growing increasingly agitated. "Were they playing another game with her for some pleasure unbeknownst to her?" she wondered. If so, it was a cruel game with evil intentions. Nevertheless, she waited, still pacing back and forth, waiting to hear a sound, the click of a key in a door that she knew was just at the end of a long hall though she could not see it, or the shuffle of feet against the hard stone floor.

The sounds were all she had left, tiny shuffles and tiny clicks, for she never heard voices, not even when she was served. Not a word broke the guard's lips, and after some time she had given up hope of it ever happening and had stopped speaking as well. Momentarily her eyes fell to the sole source of light, a lamp that burned ceaselessly just out of her reach. She had never seen anyone filling it though it was always full.

Her thoughts wandered for a time to Midori, who had been with her when she was taken. She recalled her capture through shadows and unclear images, but she could not recall why. A tender spot high on her forehead still attested to her struggle though soon it would be gone, healed with time, much time.

A faint echo far down the hall caused her to freeze. She strained her ears against the silence, but only silence returned. She passed the sound off as yet another phantom of her imagination. She hesitantly returned to her methodical pacing, content for the moment with only the thoughts flowing through her mind for a companion.

Heavy on her mind was the whereabouts of her lord husband, Edwar Serant. She didn't know how but she sensed that he was not dead, that he was near. She longed to feel his touch, to touch him in return—the warmth of his hand in hers, the feel of his lips on hers. She longed to see that rare smile, to know again a few private moments when the steel in his veins slipped away. It was in those moments that she knew the truth of life, love, and laughter.

"Oh Edwar," she whispered just to hear a voice spoken aloud and to know something other than silence. "What game do they play with us? Will we be together when it is done?"

❄ ❄ ❄

It was nighttime before Xith and Noman found their way beyond the Two Hands. Nijal offered his story of Awn and the ship he promised to acquire for their use, but at the time neither Xith nor Noman was in a mood to listen to it. Xith was clearly the more irritable of the two. As he not only told Nijal to shut up, but he snatched the coin from Nijal and retired without a word, muttering something to the effect of, "No-good thieves and heartless beggars."

Nijal considered Xith's rash act long before he took the coin back from the shaman's hands as he slept. He had plans of his own for this evening; it was too early to retire. With Shchander as his accomplice, he ventured out into the city, finding little comfort in the gray shadows the night brought.

Torches around the perimeter of the cliffs cast an eerie glow and cast odd shadows about, but they did not let it dampen their determination. Nijal stopped beneath a lamp in a doorway and took a close inspection of the coin on both sides. The front bore the outline of some figure; the face was worn, its outlines indecipherable. The back was a weapon perhaps, maybe a sickle, or so Nijal thought.

The streets were not lively at night, which was not odd. They had been mostly deserted in the day although there were lit lanterns in many of the doors. The sound of laughter ahead drove them on, around a corner, across a street, and into an alleyway. They stopped, however, for no lamp or sign graced the door the sound carried them to. They waited in the dark of the alley, listening to singing and cheerful shouts.

A pleasant memory held Nijal there lingering for a time, but Shchander was agitated and tapped his foot nervously. Dim areas brought him little joy and much discomfort. "Let us be off," he whispered to Nijal, who did not listen to him, "let us be off quickly."

"Okay, okay," replied Nijal moving back into the street. For a long time afterward, the only noise they heard was the soft pounding of their own feet, broken only by the sight and sound of a night guard passing by. The guards had only slowed to scrutinize them but did not slacken their pace for long as they did so.

Abruptly, they heard singing again. A group of three approached cheering loudly, obviously prompted by an evening of drinking. Nijal joined in the merriment of the mood, shifting into their chorus, a common song in many places. He took a chance, using the spontaneity of the moment, and took the small coin from his pocket, asking the three to look at it.

One man stopped cold in his song, the one who had been in the middle, and walked up to Nijal, blowing his foul breath in his face. "You, friend, would do best to put that back into your pocket and be on your way."

Shchander quickly pulled Nijal away from the man, fearing that a brawl might take place at any moment. He continued to drag Nijal by the arm until the two were well away from the others. He didn't know what the sudden shift in moods was over, but he wasn't about to delay and find out. It was only as he stopped that he noticed Nijal tucking the coin back into his pants.

"Did you have to go and do that?" Shchander yelled, "We're not looking for a fight."

"I wasn't looking for a fight, only information."

"Well, it seems you picked the wrong group to ask. We have to be more careful; remember we are the strangers."

"You are right about that, but we are not the strange ones."

❋ ❋ ❋

Teren discarded the calls at the periphery of his consciousness, turning his attentions back to the words of Prince Valam and Brother Liyan. "Nothing but darkness," he told himself, "nothing but darkness." Valam clenched his fist until nails bit into his palms. He was openly angry, which didn't happen often. "We must fight!" whispered in the hollows of his thoughts. His words wore the shape of his mood; if there were those who should pay for their deeds this day, he would make them pay.

"Some very dear fellows passed this day to rest in the house of the Father, as it is said in your words. I grieve in my heart though I know I should not. They died as they lived, struggling to the last."

Valam could speak no more. He paused long before his rage led him on. "The storm, is there a way to fight it? Can we send it back upon its masters?"

Liyan, Seth, and Tsandra considered Valam's words in earnest. They did not know for sure whether they could or not. After a time of reflection, they vowed to try. Liyan was the first to journey to the center if his soul and reach out with his will. For now the others waited.

The sky was dark and sad about Liyan as he touched his will to the air about him, bringing it in gentle circles up to a lofty height. Darkness was the immediate response to his center, but he moved through it as his spirit shifted through the very billows of the clouds overhead. A sudden sense overcame him, perhaps a taste, a taste sour and vile, causing him to withdraw.

Awaiting Liyan's return and his approval, Seth began his own journey of will. He proceeded with caution as Liyan instructed. Weather, clouds, and rain were mostly outside the things Seth had learned, though he alone perhaps knew more about its control than did anyone else present, having undergone each of the seven teachings.

Seth did not take the same route that Liyan had, which had been a direct route to the center of the storm. No, the eye was a dangerous place to linger. Seth chose the most indirect path to the storm, sweeping his will lazily inward from a great distance upon a slow easterly breeze. An image flowed to him of clouds, huge puffs of black and deep shades of gray. The sky above was mostly clear, save for a light haze much higher up.

Seth adopted the haze as his vantage point; it was a form of nature that he understood, and it was completely separate from the fury spinning below it. Yet even at a distance, the pervading omens of evil were gnawing upon him. He delayed no longer than he thought he should before he quickly drew his will inward.

Tsandra followed Seth's cue and reclaimed the search for her own. As an initiate of the Brown, she held a slight advantage over her counterparts; she knew well how to find the heart of the enemy. She was quick to pursue it across the distance, finding it almost at once. A quiver befell her chin, a tremor flowed from her head to her feet, and a black cloud caved in her will and sent her in anguish to the floor.

She was still and cold and her breath was scarcely perceptible as the cloud took on the form of an eye, a great, grave, ebony eye in the window of her mind. It held her paralyzed in its grasp, mocking her as it drew life from her veins. Tsandra's face paled and her eyes closed.

"Sever the link!" thrashed Seth into her mind with a tidal wave of force, "Break it now!"

Tsandra did not respond. Liyan joined in, tugging the darkness away from her thoughts. Seth screamed again, this time both aloud and in thought, "For the love of the Mother! Be gone! Crawl back to your dank recesses!"

The darkness gradually faded, and a tiny flutter of a breeze began to blow in the room, rustling the scrolls spread across the table. Jacob clamped his hands over them, spilling pen and ink as he did so. A lull came over the chamber but not before another victim was claimed. Seth joined Tsandra on the damp floor, wheeling about and smashing the back of his head against the table as he went down.

A voice again reached out for Teren's mind. Tiny and weak though it was, he heard it but did not recognize it until long after it and the disquiet faded from his thoughts. Seth stirred, and all seemed right. He knew life yet flowed through Tsandra. She would not be so easily felled. He knew this well.

The three suddenly realized a thing that had been a haze in their minds, and though they revealed it to a fourth, they told no one else. Teren left immediately after the telling, parting with few words. He alone knew more than the others, not because of any special powers he was endowed with, but rather because he was privy to a small piece of knowledge the others knew nothing about. He would reveal nothing until his return; though he dreaded enduring the elements, he did so without hesitation.

"My compliments to the chef, once again. Was the buzzard finished or was he still licking the bones of this carcass when he found it. A man cannot live on dried bones and water. And another thing, the feces in the corner is growing a little stale. Would you mind disposing of it?"

"The bones are from a friend of yours; I thought you would like the claws."

"Really, these are a bit small. Perhaps you could bring me a bit of water. My friend in here does not look well. You really should show some compassion. I promise—if you bring me a bucket of water so I can wash my face and hands, I will seal my lips for an entire day. I will speak no curses. I will bite my tongue. I swear."

The guard scoffed but seemed to approve of the idea. His gait was still slow as he moved to retrieve a bucket of water. He thought it ironic that something he was going to do anyway could get him some hours of abatement. Bucket in hand, he returned, removing the grin upon his face as he approached the cell door.

"Now, you promise to speak not a word for the remainder of this day. Right? Swear it on the great book."

"I swear I will not speak a word that will fall upon your ears this day, and I swear it upon the great book. Would that I had it with me now for knowledge and comfort."

"I take that as a yes?"

"Yes."

"Move back, back away from the door, or you will get this water across your face!" shouted the guard, as he unlocked the cell door.

Geoffrey had been listening to the chatter shifting through his thoughts, but the queasiness had not fully left him. A recent beating had done him no good, and while he sought to blame it on his companion's rashness, he could not. He had also been enjoying the heckling—well at the time, anyway.

Using his elbow as a brace and a lever, he pushed himself up against the wall, taking extra care not to let his head touch the wall although the cold of the stone did feel soothing. He marveled as a second bucket of water was placed in the room. He took it as a sign that the bulwarks were repenting for their cruelty.

He wondered just how many days it had been since he had seen the sun upon his face or tasted the sweet smell of fresh air upon his nostrils. He did not envision food, for none was in his belly nor had any been in his belly in the immediate past. A hollow gurgling reminded him of that without his having to think about it.

"You have a gift with words, my good friend," spoke Geoffrey as the other placed a bucket of water before him. He splashed the cool water, not noticing its lack of foulness, across the back of his neck and up onto his brow. Afterwards, he drank it in hearty gulps, filling the cavity in his gut.

"I am truly sorrowful for what they did to you. I did not know they would do that."

"I know, I know. I am all right; the worst has passed. Is it day or night?"

"I would say it is day. I can see the sun high over a calm and pleasant scene. Not a whisper of cloud to mar its beauty."

"Yes, but that is only in your mind."

"It is all I have left. Remember, they can never take that from you."

"No, they can't," said Geoffrey, laughing, retreating into his own thoughts. It was a pleasant place he found. For a time his vision faded in and out, and he just relaxed, leaning firmly against the wall, feeling its coolness run through him.

✳ ✳ ✳

Noman was the first to awaken to the fullness of a new day. His mood was cheerful, and he woke Xith without a second thought. Xith, continuing to play the game for the watchers, awoke in a frightful mood, but it was quick to pass.

"Well what is it? What is the terribly important reason you detained us all through the day and almost into the night?"

"None whatsoever. Just a whim, I guess."

"A whim?" demanded Xith.

Noman worked his cheeks into a grand grimace, "The story was good, don't you think?"

Xith returned the smile and gave in, adding a hurried apology for his earlier shortsightedness. "I deserved it, wholly and completely. Yes, I did."

"Yes, you did."

"You don't have to agree with me."

"A quick breakfast, and off we go."

Noman gestured ever so slightly; Xith took in the opening of the peephole in the wall with a panning glance. His chuckle was low and hearty, building up all the way from his diaphragm to the tip of his tongue. "What was I thinking?" thought Xith, as he scratched his forehead absently. Puzzled, he looked about the room. Amir lay in a cot near the sole window in the room; across the room two cots were empty, but that was not what he had been thinking about. He walked into the hall and knocked on the door of an adjacent room and entered.

Xith surveyed the room all in one glance. Content, he walked back out and closed the door, nodding to Shalimar, who had opened the door for him. Adrina was still asleep, so he had not wished to disturb her though she seemed to be having a fitful dream, turning over twice in the short time he had been in the room. Nijal and Shchander weren't present, as expected.

As he stood back in the hall, he had to think hard before he recalled which room he had come from; but before he opened the door, Noman came out and led him downstairs, where they ate a light but wonderful breakfast of fresh baked bread and thick, meaty soup.

Leaving the inn, Xith and Noman by-passed the market, circumventing it by a wide berth. The walk seemed to ease the haze from Xith's thoughts. He noted for the second time a faint thought wandering by, but he was not able to grasp it. Soon they stood beneath a now-familiar sign that swayed slightly in a light breeze, pausing, hesitant for an instant, before they entered the small wooden door.

The tavern was mostly deserted at this time of day; only the stalwart of stomach could partake of ale or mead first thing in the morning. Neither was surprised to find Vajlar. It was, after all, the seventh day, a day of rest, the fourth since they had crossed into the territories. This day was the only day the market opened late.

Vajlar sat, mug in hand, cheerfully preoccupied with matters of his own. Noman nodded pleasantly but did not join him. His gaze moved to two who sat in the shadows in a far corner, almost out of sight. Only as he approached did he see the third. The last man was larger than most, built broad at the shoulders, yet squat. A black hat, round and flat, sat just above his brow.

"I seek Two Hands!" called out Noman. "I heard a tale that he has the best ships in the east and is fairer than most with his fees."

"You heard right," retorted a thin, pale man.

Noman eyed the man up and down, crossing the last bit of distance to the group's table. "You do not look like the one I envisioned."

"That is because he is not he. What is your business? And I do not mean to be rude when I say be quick about it, for we have some rather pressing matters to discuss."

Xith watched the man who sat in the middle, the large one. He had seen many of the shipwrights though he did not know most of their names or their affairs. He had never seen this one before. He thought about the market yesterday and for the first time, he was aware of an absence, but he did not know what.

"I seek passage north for myself and a fair number of companions."

"You look like a man who knows a great many things; surely you know the storms are upon us. I will venture none of my ships, no matter the sum."

"Our journey will not go as far as Taliltan."

"But where else would you go, my friend? Stay here in Krepost' until the spring and then I will give you passage. I could even arrange a bargain fare. Now if you please, we must be alone."

"Would a price in gold equal to twenty times our number be worth your trouble?"

"That, sir, would depend entirely on the number of your company."

Following the shipwright's gesture, Xith and Noman pulled chairs beside the table and sat down. Noman tossed Xith a wink; they now had the others' ears. Greed was always a quick sell.

"What if I said the number of our company was also twenty?"

"It would tweak my interest, and the hunger in my heart, and the glitter in my eye, but to lose a ship on the return trek would cost me twice that sum in the long run."

"How long does the journey to Taliltan take?"

"A fortnight at best just in the going. The storms are too close."

"We seek passage only beyond the Stone Peaks, nothing more."

"There is nothing there; you will find only snow and desolation. Your company would be lost in such a foolish endeavor."

Noman seemed to grow anxious, perhaps faltering in his resolve to exercise patience. "Would you make the trip?"

The three shook their head no. The mountains would perhaps cut off three days of the trip, but they knew the seas better than most. The length of the trip made no difference. In younger days, they might have risked it. Gold in hand was better than idle ships. But the years had taught them when it was time to stay in port, and now was that time.

"Name your price. I will buy ship, crew and captain."

"You are too quick to buy. What is your urgency?"

"We all have secrets, do we not, Master Two Hands?"

"Double your original amount, giving me one quarter the balance now whether we go or not, and I will consider your words."

Noman weighed the options in his mind, of which there were few. He would have agreed to any sum whether or not he actually had the full amount. With Xith's agreement, he plucked several sizable stacks of gold from his purse and spread them onto the table. Nimble hands snapped the coins up after only a moment's scrutiny. They were told to return on the morrow.

Chapter Twenty Eight

A tiny figure, a horse and rider, passed along a shrouded background, unseen by most, laboring long. After coming to a sharp incline, and finally overcoming it, it pressed on. After the relative shelter the coastline offered and the ocean waters afforded, the rain felt icy and permeated the rider's clothing. He dared not draw the strength of the land into himself, nor had he for a significant amount of time now.

He knew things the others did not know, and now it all became clearer—the voice, the storm, the vision, and many other things. They all fit together now, and he understood, or at least he dared to hope that he did. As his eyes sought to pierce the gloom, he held no fear in his heart, for he knew well the place he traveled through. He knew its ins and outs, its hiding places, its glens and dales although to most it appeared a featureless, flat, obscure place.

As he rode deeper into the lands, the thick mud turned hard, slush at first, and then it became unforgiving miles of snow and ice. He moved beneath the encompassing veil, then suddenly vaulted into a pale, lucid pool. He stopped, staring in wonder, remaining fixed for some time, before he continued on.

His thoughts scattered almost as surely as the wind drew him on. He did not think of much but the voice and finding its source. It clawed at the edges of his consciousness. As it gnawed, growing ever more persistent, he turned away from it. Another stood at the corners of his thoughts now, searching for him as readily as he sought to retreat.

Angrily, he spurred his mount on, at a pace faster than he knew he should. The echoes along the paths of his mind rasped and whined, demanding acknowledgment. He returned nothing to their master. His mind was closed, protected by his will. The other bent to subtle tricks and played for senses that were not so easily dulled; all it wanted was a sound, a direction. Even a single sigh would suffice.

Hands fell to ears, though it was to no avail. The noise was only meant as an irritation, but it also nullified secondary thought and saddened. To see the forces of nature wrested so fully could sicken even the stalwart of heart. No reply was offered, for to do so would reveal much more than the sender wished. A shudder of relief passed as the shadow regained its search, confident that nothing remained unseen.

The figure of horse and rider paused a second time. A flicker of elation came as a soft word carried forth, and now the rider dismounted, turning a discerning eye outward. A dim outline, a trace of a shadow within a shadow, scarcely perceptible, revealed itself, and only an astute observer could have known what it was. It was toward this form that the rider proceeded.

Teren did not know how many long hours had preceded his discovery, or how many followed, only that all lay in obscurity behind him. For now, he stood at the foot of a great and vast embankment. He turned back to face the trail, footfalls in deep mounds of snow that ran in a fairly straight line to this point, following it, until it faded into obscurity. In so doing, he seemed to come full circle as the path behind him had. He waited patiently now, no longer in a rush for that which must come.

✳ ✳ ✳

Captain Brodst shivered unconsciously as he huddled in a shallow recess. He had not eaten for days and the hunger in his belly was growing ravenous. Water, fresh or stale, was one thing he did not lack. It ran in plentiful trickles all around him, coming from the great stream that lay ahead beyond an outcropping of rock, just out of his sight. He waited for death that would not come and in the disarray of his mind, he thought he would welcome it more than the task that was ahead for him.

He was caught in a perpetual cycle of concealment and pursuit. The shadows of night were his favorite companion. In it, he had no difficulty distinguishing his surroundings. He knew them well. A door, solid, belted, and barred, was just beyond the great pool, which was filled by a constant flow from the stream above. Rope ladders reached up to the sky from either side of the falls. A small door of stone lay perpendicular to his hole, near the second ladder. Nothing had passed through or along since his arrival.

Captain Brodst noted the rapid approach of night, and he welcomed it. His back and legs were stiff and cramped. He needed to stretch the agony from them. From his tiny hollow, he watched the second sign of night pass. A contingent of guards changed places, making their way up and down the rope ladder in pairs. He watched those passing until he counted a full twenty-four, twelve shifting in either direction. His eyes fell upon the door, watching as it swung open, knowing it would only do so when the entire company stood at the ready.

He began to stir and uncoil, blending the sound of his movements in with the sound of heavy boots upon rigid stone.

Afterwards, he waited, marking the time with the footfalls. Three more came and went singly; this he knew even though he couldn't see them because of a jutting of stone that blocked his sight. Evening was now here.

The captain slipped into the pool, closely timing it with the slam of the door as it shut the final time until morning, and though water had been his nemesis throughout the day, that was no longer true. The water in the pool was deep and vast, and most importantly, warm. He wondered why the water was warm, since the stream it fell from was so cold, but he welcomed it without complaint.

Although the warmth felt good to him, he did not delay long. He rinsed the grime and the smell from his clothes and his body, taking great care not to delay. He had seen moving shapes down below, and he did not want to find out what they were. He quickly rinsed the water from his clothes, twisting and turning them until they were as dry as he could make them.

He waited for a shift of feet at the door, and then emerged from the pool, quickly dressing. The air was cool but his skin still held the warmth. He would not shiver until much later, at least not uncontrollably. A scratching noise mixed with a heavy rasping caught his ear, and he stood still, stiff and wary. He leaned into a crevice in the rock and waited. Time passed, and the night drew on. He knew a moon was out although he could not see it. Later, his internal alarm quieted, and he became calm, waiting once more for the day.

✳ ✳ ✳

A day spent in waiting did not sit well with any members of the group. Xith had bags of trinkets to sort through and organize, but he was the exception. Many discouraged eyes and hearts sat idle, whiling away the time with meaningless chatter. Adrina had waked at long last, but with an irritable temperament that made most around her wish she would return to slumber. Amir was the only one who listened to her though he knew not why. Even the city as a whole was quiet this day, which was not unusual. It was a day of leisure but not for merriment.

Noman grinned as he watched Xith lose his count for the second time and begin again. He busied himself watching those passing by on the street below the window even though they were few. His mind had not stopped, but it had slowed. There was something gnawing at his consciousness, but he didn't know what it was.

Outside, the sun reached the high point in the sky; inside, a silence fell. Dinner was being served. Xith moved to the hall to relieve himself and to take a short walk, but something called for him to linger, and not to go, and so he was quick to return. He ate the food absently and then he joined Noman by the window.

Adrina did not let eating interrupt her storytelling, and as Amir still listened intently, she continued. Her dream had been frightful and all too real. She spoke of faces and voices, but most vivid was the image of a boy who spoke to her and bade her to follow him through his dreams. She had not wanted to follow, but at his insistence she had.

Hours passed, and towards evening most joined the innkeeper in his hall for the seventh-day feast, which was a very gracious one. Roasted fowl, goose, hen, and wild meat, were served, along with an abundance of fruits and vegetables that were taken from the inn's storm stock. The inn was full, so the innkeeper did not mind, for there was still time to replenish them before the snows set in.

After the meal, singing followed, and spirits were raised. The innkeeper was delighted as the newcomers joined in the festivities, singing a simple chorus that they knew the words to well. As it turned out, it was a very popular song in these parts. It wasn't until much later that they discovered that they had only recently met the songwriter: the wandering minstrel named Kelar.

Upstairs, Xith gave Noman a puzzled look, still not comprehending why Noman had allowed Adrina to go downstairs with the others. Noman let Xith wonder. He would, perhaps, offer him an explanation later; for now he would let him sulk. The meal they consumed was not as grand as the one the others had, but it sufficed.

A door closing behind them startled them, but they relaxed when they saw it was only Amir. He had returned early. His heart was not in singing this night, but he could still hear the voices from below. Amir joined Xith and Noman by the window, which Noman had returned to despite the darkness. Noman nodded to Amir; he had expected him to return before the others.

"Dark, isn't it?" whispered Noman.

Xith didn't reply. He didn't think the question had been directed at him. Amir was slow to respond but a "yes" did pass his lips.

"It is as veiled as the window to your soul, perhaps," added Noman. Noman closed his mind for a moment and with a flicker of thought, made easy by many long years of practice, he created a shadow, loosing it upon Amir. Amir did not react at all and the first blow caught him numbly, sending rage through his mind.

His sword was not close at hand and he had to struggle and tumble his way across the room, dodging blow after blow that only narrowly missed him. He took refuge beside a bed in the far corner of the room, searching frantically for the sheath that held his blade. He could not find it.

Amir was forced to face the creature that was formed in his own image, a shadow of himself. Many long days had passed since he had last practiced, and he had not been stretching his muscles properly. He fixed his blank eyes upon Noman, knowing a grin lay upon his face. With clenched fists he faced his opponent, who was not restricted in the way that he was.

The air shifted and Amir lunged low to the floor, just as the swish of a long blade sought to reach him. Caught in an unfair situation, Amir freed his only weapon, his mind. He still had speed and skill unmatched by most though his shadow also had these. His one true advantage was that it did not know what he thought now, and if he turned to the irrational solution, he might find victory.

Rage had been his first thought, and so he let it lead him on. It built and burned within him. He brought foot and fist to play, dodging, jabbing, and punching. The shadow's blade was almost always only a heartbeat away. He followed the patterns of its movement, shifting in and out of its path. He heard each exhaling and inhaling of breath, his and those around him. The image in the center of his mind was himself, and this was what he must defeat.

He was shocked as the vision took on another form. He saw two. He had never fought two before. How could he win? He did not even have a sword to defend himself with. Amir stumbled over a chair, immediately kicking it out of his way. Pain stung him as he ducked and smashed into a table. His rage carried him on, and he picked it up and cast it across the room, where it fell to the floor in tattered shards.

"Out!" he bellowed at Xith and Noman, who stood silently

watching, "Out!" Amir warily circled the room. He picked up a leg from the table only after a long pause. He sized up the foes on either side of him now. The shape of one was obscured and hazy in the window of his mind. While one had sword and shield, the other wielded razor sharp talons.

Noman waited at the door, watching intently, and he only offered Amir his sword after much consideration. "Go!" yelled Amir as the blade touched his palm. In that instant, he became a new man. His oafish blundering subsided, and his thoughts cleared. The wavering at the edges of his mind was now gone also. He stalked with skill, and guarded with expertise.

He turned to face the two, who were himself, and just before he launched himself at them, he smiled. The smile would have been short-lived if he had understood the true gravity of the situation. Because he did not, it lingered long upon his countenance. He successfully repelled a combined assault—a claw barely fingering the outline of his brow, and a trickle of blood beginning to flow.

Amir cast it off as sweat, which also poured down his face. He moved the hilt of his sword into his other palm, wiping the sweat from the former before switching it back. He defended with both hands upon the handle, cutting left before sweeping upward right. He watched the images shift in his mind, feeling the movements of feet and hands.

He played upon the weaker, the first, sending wave after wave of assault against it, only blocking against the second. He had decided that he must defeat one before the other, or else he would fail. He had never before failed a lesson. He did not think Noman would have unleashed two against him if he did not have a chance, and so he struggled on.

Frenzied attacks followed as he was pressed into the corner. A second blow caught him and its sting was icy cold upon him. He felt a shiver run up and down his spine, and the pain was real. A clawed hand lifted from his back as he sank to the floor, but it would take more than that to wrest the sword from his hand.

He lashed out wildly, laboring to move, and as he did so his edge connected. His heart jumped with glee. One was down, and now only one remained. He spun from the corner, bringing his blade full around. He was again too late in his reaction. A sting touched his shoulder, and his left arm fell limp at his side.

Pain woke his numbed senses, and it was then he realized that there were yet two shapes moving against him. A cry sought to come from his lips, but he stifled it. Again and again he tried to scream, but in vain. He turned his concentration on the image that was blurred in his thoughts. He launched full against it, neglecting the other, and oddly the other attacked no more.

Amir clenched his teeth against the turmoil building within. With only one arm, his weapon was still poised, and yet moved swiftly. His determination was such that it overpowered the numbness of his senses, and finally the creature's true form was revealed to him. Its grip on him was gone. The spell was lifted.

He bargained for a close attack and pushed it this time to the corner, just as the door flew open. Xith and Noman entered, their faces ashen. "Out!" growled Amir, "This fight is mine!" He sliced out with his blade, catching its tip in the wall. It marked a deep two-foot long gouge. The creature turned and sought to flee from the corner, racing quickly towards Xith and Noman.

Amir chased it with his blade, sinking it in repeatedly. The anger within him was hungry and it drove him on. He noticed for the first time a shimmer of light fall with each blow that he dealt the creature, and now it turned to greet him, licking its fangs and hissing evilly as it groped out with its talons.

Reluctantly, Noman and Xith did as they were bidden and backed out the door, leaving Amir alone to the fight. In the hall behind them, others now joined. Adrina was the most visibly shaken. She tried to make her way into the room to stop the fight. "You don't know what you do!" she cried.

Amir marked her words with a series of desperate attacks. He had been the one to entice her to its darkness, and though he had only seen the world these last few days through dreams, he still blamed himself. He had let his guard down and had failed in the watch, but he was not the only one upon whom the spell played.

He feinted back from a blow that would have struck him clean in the face. His blade met the outstretched arm well, and he severed it. Although it was a creature of magic, he still saw the image in his mind as he felled it. Holding his blade deftly, he swung, striking cleanly. He cleft the creature in half as it floundered in anguish. In a flash of searing white light, it blinked from existence, back to its master.

Amir was tired and nearly spent, but he did not stop. He stood his ground firmly as he pointed the tip of his sword towards those in the hall. "There is one more among us. Step forth, and I will send you quickly back to your hole. But if you delay, I will make your pain great and make you linger while I destroy you piece by piece, this I promise you!"

Only after Trailer lay dead on the floor by his own hand did Amir set aside his sword and succumb to fatigue. All his energy was spent. He was so tired that he wanted to close his eyes and drift off to a pleasant slumber. He wouldn't let himself drift off though. Something told him not to, for he would not return from the place he went to. Noman turned to Amir with a heavy heart, tending his wounds with deep care.

Xith procured an ointment from his bags and applied it to the wounds. He hoped it would slow the festering of the creature's touch and perhaps even prevent it. The commotion had stirred all the residents of the inn and even the innkeeper himself. A body upon the floor was a very disquieting sight and was a sign of ill fortune on this special day.

Newcomers to the scene assumed the fight had been between the two. The one lay still upon the floor, the color drained from his face, and the other cringed against the wall as his wounds were being mended. No one offered an explanation. They were all left to guess. A small sum of gold exchanged hands before the inn returned to normal.

"Our plans are known," Xith whispered to Noman.

Noman nodded grimly.

❋ ❋ ❋

"We can wait no more for Brother Teren's return. We gave him until morning, no more. The storm still has not faded in its ferocity. We must try to fight it ourselves." Father Jacob said those words in his mind yet not aloud. Others around him were thinking similar thoughts, but some understood better than most the need for speedy action.

They had sought out the center of the storm once and had been cast back. They all understood that the eye was upon them now. The nighttime hours had not been wasted in idleness; many plans had been drawn, discussed, worked, and re-worked. Morning had found them without the warmth of a fire. No new logs were sent for. They had decided, and though the decision had come after a long strenuous debate, they were going to stick to it.

Liyan explained in loose terms some of what he knew, but he did not reveal all. The key factor was that the enemy knew of their presence and that now they were prepared to resist, and nothing more. The members of the Brown were assembled beside Tsandra, and they were no longer afraid to free their will upon the land at its full.

During the hours of twilight and first light, the struggle was born. The will of the masses was gathering, sending back a force of its own. It was vigorous in the manner in which it gained speed and strength, but it was steadfast in one point: it must remain unseen, growing from a distance, just as the rage they were enduring had. Their opponents had had time, where they had little; however, nothing would hold them back now.

They still had one of two paths to follow. They could attack either the creators or the storm itself. They had not decided, and for now the simple fact that the choice lay ahead was enough. Seth acted best as the watcher. He moved and shifted his will across the sky in spurts, never delaying long in one place, but always watching and in this he proved to have abundant talent.

Liyan was the mediator, the voice between Seth and Tsandra. His was a consciously chosen tedious task, for in this capacity he could also keep Valam, Jacob and the others informed. The waiting was the most difficult thing he had to endure. He abided well for a time, but he eventually grew impatient and shuttled between conscious thought and the link. He was mostly concerned about the possibility of failure, and if they failed, what their next choice was.

Neither Captain Mikhal nor Danyel' had delayed in their return to duties. Captain Mikhal returned to the affairs of the camp. As he was the leader, he had many things to attend to, chief among which was flood control and keeping the paths on the ridges open. The Seventh returned to his own, commanding a small detachment of scouts as they ventured north.

Most were unaware that morning arrived because the light in the sky remained the same. The strain of exhaustion from the many hours of work began to show. In the interim, between the still of night and the fullness of day, a counterforce was constructed, and now they moved it across the sky. It gained force as it ran, flowing fluidly upon the winds.

Seth guarded it as it moved, seeking out its course. His head swayed and bobbed. His eyes were tightly closed, but they saw many things. He floated beyond the clouds at the very edges of the air. Soaring upon the rivers and streams of the currents, Seth ran before their storm. He was its watchdog. And he waited.

Tsandra guided the forces around her as they flowed from her followers. She channeled it upward, and the power nearly carried away her soul. Her center was at its very peak, but still they needed to give more, much, much more. She linked outward, moving her thoughts to those around her, allowing them to channel the power with her. She formed a link that became an interconnecting network spreading out from her in a great spiral, and the strength of will began to flow greater than ever before.

❄ ❄ ❄

With wonder in her eyes, Calyin followed her escorts, two large figures outfitted in thick mail and heavy weaponry, down the long corridor. She had often considered what it looked like, what avenues or halls lay past the small stretch she knew. As she walked, she counted the footfalls, knowing each turn in advance without looking.

As they drew away from the area she had been detained in, she began to note the crossings of the halls, always keeping a careful count in her mind. They walked at length without pausing until they came to a set of double doors where they halted. Only one of the guards proceeded through the door while the other remained with Calyin. There was a long wait before the other returned. When he did, it was clear that he was not pleased.

The march continued on, and just when it seemed they would never stop again, they did. Since their last pause, they had climbed four flights of steep, narrow stairs and walked down many halls that seemed almost to be without end, weaving in an ever upward, and perhaps inward, direction. Calyin wasn't exactly sure of her whereabouts although the air did seem fresher, not acrid, as it had been before.

She was taken by surprise when the doors were opened before her to reveal a great chamber. Heels striking the polished floor sent vibrations resounding throughout the room. Calyin counted a full forty steps from door to center. During the time they crossed the room, her eyes had been busy. The sun shone in through high windows along the center of the ceiling. She thought it was beauty incarnate, an exhilarating sight after so long in a dimly lit place.

The hall was plain and simple in comparison to the iridescence of the sun falling through thick prismatic panels. The only thing of note was the granite throne, chiseled from the rock of the room and placed midway just off their present path. The throne was empty. They stood before it, waiting.

A door opened on the far side of the hall opposite the one they had entered. A woman with long, flowing ebony hair was ushered in without escort. A spark of hope caught Calyin for a moment, but it was soon to fade as the woman approached closer. Her hair was pulled up tight on one side, and her dress was of cloth conservatively designed. She crossed to the great chair but did not sit upon it.

Almost immediately after the woman touched her hand upon the stone, a trumpet sounded and a large group began filing in. They were arraigned in shining mail with bronze over-plates formed at the joints. While they were equipped with no manner of weapon, they appeared a very effective defensive force. They held feathered helmets in gloved hands, slightly shifting them from side to side as they walked.

A figure followed. He was without adornment, but Calyin knew in a glance that he was royalty. His gait was bold and led him straightforwardly to the chair although he did not sit. He waited.

A second figure emerged from the door at the rear of the hall. He wore a gray robe. His entourage was large and did not seem altogether friendly. This group stopped at a mark a few paces to the right of Calyin. She counted eleven of them.

Calyin watched as the minutes passed and new groups appeared and formed around her as if she watched some dance where she alone did not know the steps. Four lines now stood to her left, and the group to her right changed to five as she looked on. After a time she lost count of the footsteps and the number of persons present. And after a time, the room was full, save for a single seat, which was not yet unoccupied.

The dance had ended; however, Calyin still waited. The air that had until a short time ago been fresh and pleasant now reeked from the mass of bodies; there were too many for the room despite its size. Calyin soon grew weary of delays and her attention drifted back to the sunlight filtering from above.

Her gaze and her attention were fixed elsewhere when the final figure entered and took his seat. She had not seen or noticed the soldiers come to attention upon his arrival. She did not notice the cushion placed upon his seat or the drink poured from a golden vessel into a jeweled goblet. A man approached her with the drink and kneeled before her, but she had not seen that either.

"It is customary for the guest to drink. You must drink," said the man in low tones. Calyin was slow to respond to the words, and she did not take the glass that was offered. She waved it away. "I wish nothing from a servant."

"I am no servant, my lady. I am Prince Sy'dan Entreatte, second son of the lost kingdom. Please do not affront me in front of my people."

"You call me a lady, yet you treated me no better than a common slave. What kind of a people are you? A simple gesture and all is forgotten? I do not think so."

"Please keep your voice down. Do not despoil my honor. Drink, it is customary. Please, I beg of you, and I must make pardons for your ill treatment. I did not know. I will see that the rogue that treated harshly one so fair will pay."

Calyin accepted the drink even though she knew the tongue that spoke softly to her was forked. She found no pleasure in its refreshment. Calyin looked contemptuously at the seated one. A chair was procured for her to sit upon though she refused. She bided her time. "What have you given me?" she asked, her voice weak.

Prince Sy'dan took the goblet from her hand before it could fall to the stones of the floor. When the drink began to take hold, she staggered backwards, uneasy on her feet, but still refusing to sit.

"I see you do not agree that we are gracious hosts. Have you ever been in the cells of your garrisons? They are not pleasant places, I can assure you. You were treated far better than I, far better than the High Lord of Shost. Yet now I welcome you to my hall and promise you that your lesson is learned. All things have a price and a penance."

Calyin started to speak her mind but held her tongue. Prince Sy'dan indicated his gratitude with a small bow and a smile. Ashwar did not let the silence hold in the room long before he broke it. "I welcome you, Princess Adrina Alder, into my home. I am Belajl Entreatte, High Lord of Shost, returned from the Dark Fire. In a moment the potion you drank will let you see true."

The name startled Calyin, causing her to look befuddled. She almost stated that she was Calyin Alder but again said nothing, turning her confused look to a smile. "What of my companion, where is she?"

"The others are quite safe for now, I promise you. No harm will come to them if you cooperate."

"Others?" thought Calyin. She immediately wanted to ask to whom he referred. "What is it you wish of me?"

"Your secret of course."

"Secret? I have no secrets."

"Do you know the bounty that rests on your head? Which is wholly redeemable whether you are alive or dead, I might add."

Calyin understood the "play your cards well" that was inferred. "Perhaps you should explain to me who it is that wants me and then I can tell you."

The High Lord considered her sincerity for a time before

responding. "I honestly do not know it in full, save that it is a king from a far off place and he wants you. For the sum, I do not care what he does to you."

"If it is gold you want, I can offer you plenty."

"My dear, it is more than mere coins, I assure you. Do you not know the full of it yet?"

Calyin puzzled on the word full; he had spoken it twice. Her head started to spin and suddenly she was dizzy. She was pushed into the chair beside her. She tried to focus but couldn't. Everything was muddled. "I don't feel well. May I rest?"

"Soon, very soon. You will rest. Yes, I can promise you lots of rest. I did not cooperate for nothing. Tell me, princess, what do you know of this stranger and why did he journey to Imtal?"

"I—I—don't feel well. I must sleep—"

"Walk her around, you fool! You have given her too much! Hurry, or it will be you that takes her place!"

A soft voice whispered into Calyin's ear. It sang pretty songs in a melodic tone, and its questions she answered. The sun was so beautiful coming through the window, so beautiful, thought Calyin. The voice promised to take her away if she would just pay attention and answer. She tried her best. She wanted to rest so very much. Darkness did eventually find and carry her off.

Chapter Twenty Nine

Nijal's search had carried the two through the night and now in the hour between day and night, his gait at last slowed. As luck or other fates would have it, he had found Awn and now they followed him. Awn and his companions led Nijal and Shchander to a place they did not know and unfortunately could not see, for they were blindfolded.

They had gone a great distance before they stopped and in the silence the two heard the echo of water falling, but it sounded odd and unlike the fall of raindrops against a rooftop. They were told to remove the blindfolds and for the first time they looked upon their surroundings. The questions that had been roaming through their thoughts were almost immediately answered.

They knew that at some point others had joined them. The faces were only now revealed. For several minutes they strained to hear a whispered conversation, and then they continued on. Shchander marked the corridors they crossed and moved along in his mind. The walls were odd-shaped, rough-hewn, perhaps carved from solid rock, or so he thought.

Nijal was troubling over completely different matters. He stayed close to Awn, trying to follow the flow of the conversation Awn was having with one of the newcomers. He couldn't discern much from the muddled tones except that the other was unhappy with the current situation. Nijal thought he heard a name mentioned, or perhaps it was the name of the man Awn was speaking to, he wasn't quite sure. It soon became very clear to him that Awn was very angry over something this man had done.

"We will be there soon, my friend. Do not worry," said Awn becoming aware of Nijal's closeness.

"Where are we? Are we still in the city?" asked Nijal.

"Of course we are in the city—quite so—indeed," replied Awn, but Awn didn't listen long enough for Nijal to ask him another question. Awn turned back to the man beside him, quickly returning to their discussion. Shchander pulled Nijal's shirtsleeve to gain his attention and waved for Nijal to come closer to him.

Shchander whispered quietly into Nijal's ear, "Well, what do you think?"

"What do I think about what?" replied Nijal

"Shh! Not so loud. What do you think about these tunnels?"

"Tunnels? I hadn't noticed really," Nijal said, and he hadn't until just now. Torches lit the path before and behind them, bracketed into the walls by thick iron spikes that were rusted with age. Dust swirled about their feet as they stepped, and the ceiling was hung with cobwebs. Nijal ran his right hand along the wall. Although its appearance was rough, it was smooth but riddled with pockmarks.

"What time do you think it is?" asked Nijal, whispering again.

"Growing well into a new day, I would imagine," said Awn, "you needn't whisper."

Both Nijal and Shchander grew silent, feeling like children who had just been scolded for doing something they were not supposed to. "Relax," added Awn, "you are with us now. No harm will befall you." Shchander was still silent, but Nijal admitted he was more worried about his whereabouts than anything else at present.

"You are with us now—and as I said before, there is nothing for you to worry about."

"How far have we walked? Where are we? The air is rather cool and damp. "

"The air from the sea is always a mixed blessing. It is cool and soothing most of the time, but often it is very damp."

They came to a long gallery and here the group was forced to walk single-file. A long, hard look in the direction they had come revealed nothing. Their only source of illumination was the torches they now carried. The walls in this section were unadorned. The smell of sulfur permeated the air. Lofty glances to the ceiling only revealed darkness, as it was beyond the reach of the torchlight.

Oddly, Nijal had kept track of his steps here, losing the count at around five hundred strides, but the hall still stretched out before them and then was lost in the shadows. Just when Nijal thought their path would never end, light flowed through the tunnel from its terminus. It was like bursting into the bright sunshine of a new day, which it was, in fact.

Delicate rays poured into a room or chamber, as Nijal considered it for a moment. Then he decided that it was a grotto, a grand, tremendous grotto, for no other word seemed to capture what he saw. He couldn't contain himself and he let out a cry. Its echo alarmed Shchander and the other, which they did not easily recover from.

The whole of the hollow was suddenly alive with people running about. Men charged the entrance with spears and swords, children scurried into hiding places, and careful, discerning eyes could notice sentries along the high places in the walls readying bows and arrows.

And then all went blank, as if a hand had suddenly passed over the sun. Total darkness enshrouded all.

For an instant, Awn cast Nijal an angry glare. Then he announced his arrival and that of his companions. The gloom quickly lifted and most returned to what they were doing before the scare. Others turned to welcome the visitors without rebuke. The party was led swiftly through the maze of structures set about the place toward the farthest reaches of the far wall. The tempo was such that the two observers were not able to see much of what they passed, nor did they dare try for fear they would lose the way or their step. The site they came to was cramped and profusely crowded. Many long bench-style tables were crammed into the small space, filling it to capacity. It appeared to be a meeting area of sorts, also serving perhaps as the dining hall as food smells hung in the air.

The hosts wasted little time explaining their plans to their guests, speaking of nothing else, even when pushed in other directions. They did not care to speak of themselves or their people. This was not the business of outsiders. Both Nijal and Shchander were quick to understand that it was not luck that had brought the two groups together but a result of deliberate planning.

The two were introduced to many new faces, most of whose names they quickly forgot as face after face began to run together. They were alone now, save for Awn, after a very trying debate and discussion. They had found that the glint of gold was the primary objective of their new friends, which was not surprising considering the impoverished state in which the people lived. Nijal soon understood why his fellows reverently referred to Awn as the Prince of Tongues and the Grandmaster of Thieves.

"You are in grave danger," Awn told them. "Any ship you

manage to hire will be full of cutthroats, brigands, and—"

"Thieves?" interrupted Nijal.

"You speak of things you do not understand, friend Nijal. The guild serves the people. Were there no need, there would be no guild." Nijal tried to speak. Awn cut him off. "Listen and listen well, my friend. There are no honorable sea captains left in Krepost'. The honorable few and their crews set sail from here many long months past."

"Why should I trust you?" Nijal asked. It was a thing that had been on the tip of his tongue for some time.

Awn stood, removed his leather jerkin and then his long-sleeved shirt. Nijal's eyes lit up. A single massive tattoo flowed across Awn's biceps, shoulders, and back. It was the kind of tattoo he had seen on many of the older men in his father's service. The kind of tattoo that marked Awn as a blademaster for hire and told the story of his battles. "I am a free man and will die as such," Awn said, his voice strong and his eyes directed at Nijal. Nijal and Shchander both returned the words, speaking the free man's code proudly.

"The Bandit War, you were there?" asked Nijal.

Awn nodded. "At the start of it, I was but a boy in my father's service. By the end of it, I was sure I wanted no part of it. You are the spitting image of your father, you know."

"My father? Then this isn't—"

"No, it isn't." Awn gestured to four men who stood suddenly closer than Nijal and Shchander were comfortable with. The four grabbed and held the two. "Don't struggle. They mean you no harm. I do only what I must to protect you."

Nijal was pushed from behind and held down. He screamed as something white hot was pressed into the small space behind his left ear. When the strong hands relaxed, he came out swinging wildly only to find empty air as the men who had held him stepped away into the shadows. Awn's hand on his shoulder calmed him somewhat. "What have you done to me?"

"When next you see your father, tell his lordship that Feghan of the Wall has repaid the debt owed," so saying, Awn snapped his fingers and blindfolds were returned to Nijal and Shchander's eyes. "We will return you now to yours. When the time comes, show the coin and the mark, and you will be spared."

❋ ❋ ❋

At once, Teren perceived the somber mood; it mirrored his own. His own heart was heavy, though not with failure. He knew why the plan had fizzled and the reason was moving ever closer. An enormous host, a vast and powerful horde, swept towards them. Teren alone knew their hopes and desires, which he did not have to look into their hearts to find. Despite the rain's torment, the slickness of the ground, and the improbability of the move, the forum came to the hard decision to evacuate the camp before they were swept into the sea and before the enemy came to their door.

If a battle were to find them, they wanted to have the upper hand and not the reverse. They had endured too much and trained too long to fail so miserably. The snow on the plains, though thick, would not be altogether inhospitable. Tents were left where they stood. Only stores that could be readily carried out by hand or packed onto horses were taken. Even the ships were left in the harbor and those on board were to remain there until the waters calmed.

Stakes and poles were driven deeply and firmly into the ground along the paths leading out of the low areas. Ropes were strung along them to ease the way and provide extra support. Men waited with teams of horses to pull burdened animals along the inclines. Those leaving the camp may have appeared disgruntled, wet and muddied, but they were not disheartened. They would endure. It took a considerable feat of stamina and endurance to command the movement of thousands, but Valam shouldered the burden. Thick columns spread out in row after row, forming many different groups. Some walked, others rode, but all moved onward.

✳ ✳ ✳

Ansh Brodst trembled with joy as he undressed. He did not waste any time in putting on the new pants, overshirt and fine leather boots. The boots were several sizes too big for him, but after he had removed and stuffed them, they felt very good. Footsteps startled him and he stopped, pulling the body that lay on the ground near him further into the recesses.

He snatched up the helmet and placed it on his head, running awkwardly in the mailed shirt, but he made it to his destination before the other approached. He bade the other to proceed before him, and he followed at a close distance. The harsh clank of a door behind him calmed his nerves, but then a sudden voice behind him sent shivers through him again. He stopped as ordered and waited.

"You two off to the armory. That uniform will not do, and you, captain, are late!" The last part had not been directed at Brodst, but for an instant he almost responded. Without calling undue attention to himself, Brodst carefully scanned each crossing they came to, listening intently if the moment allowed. Thankfully, the one before him was in a hurry and wasn't paying close attention.

Captain Brodst considered ducking into one of the crossing passageways and disappearing along it, but he discarded the thought.

Something told him to continue. He was sure the armory lay somewhere just ahead.

A commotion down one of the hallways caused him to slow down. He turned and peered down the hall but found nothing. The voices came from a room or path he could not see, and he did not waste any time checking it further before he continued on. The armory had been just ahead behind the sleeping quarters, but Brodst did not make it that far before he was called out.

"You, there, halt at once!" bellowed a high-pitched voice.

Captain Brodst froze solid. He turned around wearing the expression of one caught, and it was very fortunate that his face was hidden beneath the helmet. His expression would have given him away. Instinct told him to stand at attention, and he did this quickly without a second thought. He did not speak, but rather he waited.

"Just where do you think you are going? I bet I know, you sniveling worm," barked the other as Captain Brodst's heart pumped wildly, and the veins along his neck and temples pulsed. "You are a lazy good-for-nothing oaf! A laggard. Several hours of standing at attention will cure you of the wish to sleep when duties are at hand."

Captain Brodst thought about pleading otherwise, but he dared not speak a word. Standing at attention would not be as severe a punishment as getting caught. He flexed his arms, bringing his hand tighter against his legs. Over and over in his mind he repeated a little prayer, a simple plea.

"That is right; do not move until I tell you to move," roared the voice. Brodst eyed the man, but not too closely. He was scrawny from head to toe, thin and pale, and very young. "Get this man a cloak. You are lucky you—I do not have time to chastise you properly, but I will mark you in my mind. Do not think I have forgotten you and do not leave my sight until I dismiss you, because I will find you again. Quickly, now, tie this cloak about your neck! I need a tenth man! Move, move, move!"

Brodst heard the man laughing at him as he took his place in the file. His body shook convulsively, but not from fear of reprisal. "Thank you," he whispered in his thoughts, as relief spread over him. As the squad began to move, he unfortunately closed his eyes to take a deep breath. He ground his teeth together as he was kicked into movement, vowing he would repay this little wretch if he ever got the chance.

Soon he found himself one of many in an enormous hall filled from end to end. He was all the way in the rear against the wall, but he still had a clear view. He could almost see the entire gathering; only the center was blocked from his view. The air was hot and stuffy around him. He was sweating profusely, but he still did not remove his helmet. He looked about, calmed by the fact that others also wore theirs.

The shuffling of feet died out, and a firm voice took its place. He listened to the message, not understanding at first, but a name sparked his interest and nearly caused him to fall. He had locked his knees and as he shifted backwards, he lost his balance. He attempted to relax. He knew better than to lock his knees when at attention. A different voice, soft and fair, took him by complete surprise, and he did fall.

"Remove your helmet, you fool!" whispered several voices to him. Many others just called him a fool, and pushed him back up to his feet. He shed the helmet as he was advised. Streams of sweat ran down his face, which was beet red. He searched to the left and right of him to see if anyone took particular interest in him. It did not seem that anyone did, but a voice saying, "Eyes front" told him that someone was, indeed, watching him.

"This is it," he told himself, as he waited and listened. He began to look for a way out, any way out. He cursed himself for being foolish. He could have ducked down any of a handful of corridors, but he had not. He was stuck in a no-win situation. He heard the yelling and screams. He wanted to run forward with all his heart and be with her to comfort her. "Damn it!" he cursed as he sprang forward.

His eyes were wide with terror as he came to stand in the midst of the host. He had Calyin by the hand and didn't know what to do. Many frenzied thoughts swam through his mind, any one of which he could have taken and would have if the voice had not commanded him to do otherwise. "Walk her around you fool!" it had said, and he did.

He walked her around in small, close circles, whispering into her ear. Her words made him sink his head low, as she was coerced to tell all the other wanted to hear. Tears mixed in with the sweat pouring from his face, and fortunately mingled with them unseen. His heart was pounding so loud that he thought everyone around him could hear it, and then suddenly it was over. She was being taken from him, and he followed.

✳ ✳ ✳

A small group of three talked long into the night and when morning arrived, they were fully awake. Their minds had been asleep for so long that it was wondrous suddenly to find full cognizant thought. Amir's face still flowed with anger. Xith and Noman were calmer but were also unsettled. They had been caught unaware and did not know how long the shadows had walked among them. They wondered what secrets the shadows had told their masters and what damage had been done to them that could not be repaired.

As daylight came, they turned to other thoughts. Breakfast came first, and then the three walked to the small inn where Two Hands should be waiting for them. The city was peculiar to Amir's perceptions; he knew he had walked its streets in the recent past from the hazy images in his mind. Although he recalled some of its avenues and turnings from the past, he still found himself noting with remark some of its structures.

The market was open and in full operation already, and as it was an alternate, though rather circuitous, route to their destination, they opted to pass through it. Xith purchased a few baubles at Noman's recommendation and a rough hide pouch, which he filled with his purchases. Amir drew the attention of many passers-by due to his size. Noman had brought him along specifically for this purpose. This day he wanted to be marked.

The three reached the inn shortly before lunch as Noman had deliberately slackened their pace. They ordered a full lunch from the innkeeper and ale for all. They ate, savoring each bite and sip, waiting for a robust figure to approach them. After a time it did, accompanied by two others. Without a word or nod of acknowledgment, Xith untied a small purse from his belt and tossed it. It fell with a hefty clank onto the table beside them.

As Two Hands reached for the bag, Noman raised his hand, warning him away from it, saying, "We would have your decision first, Master Two Hands. What is it?" Noman smiled when he saw the other nervously rubbing his fingers together as he began to talk.

"We have, or rather I, have decided that it is not in our best interest to undertake this endeavor—"

"Then why did you wish this?" asked Amir snatching the bag from the table.

Two Hands seemed to shrivel as he hunched over, smiling. Amir undid the drawstrings of the pouch and spilled its contents. Ten many-faceted jewels rolled across the table. Even the dim light in the hall marvelously reflected their fiery red. Noman picked one of the gems up, holding it up to the light between his thumb and forefinger. He shook his head back and forth as he returned them to the bag.

Noman held onto the last one, still waving his head. "Such a pity," he said offering it into a waiting sweaty palm, "Do not hold it long lest its weight corrupt your desires."

"This alone is worth the sum I asked for. Would you give them all to me?"

"You would require a king's ransom for a few days' work. Don't be hasty. For the sum, I would require your personal services, but there is, of course, a catch, and it is not that I do not trust you, but I will give you the remainder only at our destination, nowhere else."

"How can I be sure you won't play any tricks on me?"

"The same could be asked of you, my friend. Do we have a deal?"

The shipwright rose up to his full height, perhaps considering the words or perhaps considering the weight of the gem still tucked in his palm. For a lengthy span his eyes were withdrawn and unfocused, and in his hand he played with the new trinket. "I have been out of the winds for some time; you could do better with a different lot, but I think you have made a fair choice in choosing me. My ships are strong and true as are my captains. I warn you now, the seas will be rough and there can be no turning back or all is lost. We must make haste; we shall leave with the first allowable tides. Do not delay in gathering your company and return at once! I shall take you all the way to Taliltan. Passing the storm season there will be refreshing! Krepost' must await me until the seasons change!"

Noman carried the biggest smile of the three as they departed the inn and as an afterthought he returned the pouch to Xith. He almost felt bad for what he had done, but he was also thankful. Two Hands had not snatched up a different gem from the table before he had offered him the one. He even whistled a short, sweet tune as they walked back, moving through its notes several times.

✳ ✳ ✳

Thick tufts of snow were thrown high into the air as two files of horsemen trotted across the plains. Dampness made the snow cling to all it touched. Danyel', who normally rode at the fore, was now at the rear of the group. His eyes were cast upward and searching.

Radiant shafts of light pierced the outer boundaries of the dark cloud cover overhead. The group stopped for a time to brush bunches of ice from their clothing and from the horses' hides. Danyel' split the group into two, sending one section to the immediate north and directing the other to the west. It was during this time that a figure making directly for the gray of the storm slipped past them unseen.

Danyel' knew this section of the plains very well, as he had scoured it for its every hidden recess down to the last. He mentally marked the stretch of land; the boundaries of it formed a line along the route the others had taken west, where their excursion carried them. They now held to a gently sloping northwesterly route, going toward the foot of the mountains.

A river flowed here, cutting a wide vein into the heart of the mighty range of stone. Danyel' paused again, waiting for the first party to catch up. As he disliked idleness, he set to work rubbing his horse's legs down. He did not want the mixture of cold and wet to bite into the beast's muscles. It also kept him busy and gave him time to think, as mundane chores often do.

When the force became whole again, they began to follow the river's path inward. As commander, Danyel' was at the front. His eyes were downcast now, searching for different clues this time; however, the gust of winds against the snow revealed little.

Once inside the canopy of the rock, the air became warmer and the snow's depth lessened. All along their path, narrow canyons reached back into hidden recesses, but they held to the river. There was a clear path cut along it beneath the snow, which was obvious to their experienced eyes.

The file had become single now and stretched out a fair distance. A sense of foreboding told Danyel' to proceed warily, and he did. Every now and then, he sent one or two of the men to search any small tracks he found, but so far no fresh trails had been spotted. His eyes began to probe among the rocks almost as often as they turned toward the ground or the path ahead.

His exploration carried him deeper than he had dared to venture before. He brought everyone to a halt for a time, but after a short wait they continued on. The day was young, he told himself, or wanted to believe. The file was narrowed again as they began. Danyel' found himself in the middle as the path narrowed, running tight between a steep cliff wall and the river's edge.

The water ran swiftly here and was capped with white swirls in many places. As an afterthought, after seeing a shallow recess in the rock, he instructed two riders to remain there until his return.

Although his mind was troubled, he proceeded. The sun was out and its warmth touched his face, driving away his earlier dark thoughts. It was deep among the shadows of a grotto, and also deep along their path, that a discerning eye noted the remnants of what perhaps was once a footpath that was now overgrown due to disuse.

The captain set additional sentries at the fore of the overhanging rock wall and proceeded on foot with several of his fellows into the recesses of the hollow. They walked through the shadows of the rock and a short space later emerged into the fullness of day. The river ran quietly just out of sight, funneling down a cavity in the stones. The waters had split, turning both northeast and northwest.

Captain Mikhal's curiosity was not satisfied as he continued on, this time along the river's edge. But for now he turned his thoughts away from it to more pressing concerns. The day was half gone; a time for decision was upon him and afterwards Mikhal commanded his men to return east. The ride out was not as slow as the careful, watchful pace they had taken inward, and quickly they found themselves looking upon the plains from the foot of the mountains.

A short respite and light meal did little to erase the captain's concerns. He had been quite sure this would be the pass the others used. The river forged a profound trail and it was mostly level, providing a firm surface for sure footing. He knew of two other passes along the range, but they were narrow, steep, and treacherous. He knew of another far to the north, where the mountains shifted east. Teren had taken him there once, and if he recalled correctly it was many days' travel away. They had no time for such a journey, so he decided to continue towards the coast.

He was sure that evening would find them back in camp with nothing special to report. His fears were finally put to rest. He had promised Valam his riders would return this day, and he meant to keep the oath. The afternoon air held a chill as it swept across the frozen lands, and cloaks that had been worn loosely with hoods tossed back were now drawn tight.

Reins were pulled tight, hearts were pounding, and thoughts were suddenly churning as riders appeared from the north. They were pushing their mounts hard, racing them with all the speed the animals could manage. Their numbers were such that even across the snow-covered ground, the muffled sound of hooves rolled across the plains.

Captain Mikhal turned a complete circle as he watched, unsure which way to go or whether to flee. Should they wait in the safety of the pass until the others passed hoping they had not already been discovered, or did they run east, or did they face-off and charge? He made a rough estimate of the numbers against his own and without delay he dispatched two of the fastest riders east.

His face turned stoic and poised as he circled a second time. He was very sure they had been spotted and were the object of the charge. He would give them something to concern themselves over other than the two that fled. He did not have to speak a word or break the patient silence for his fellows also to react. Many of them had served under the captain long enough to read the signs upon his face. They charged, spreading out in a single wide column, and while Captain Mikhal led them, they followed not because they had to, but because they wanted to.

Chapter Thirty

The gentle baying of the ship soothed Adrina in her dreams and carried her through them. She awoke clutching her feather pillow with both hands. It was her constant companion in her sleep, accompanying her to the world of her dreams. The place where he lived and breathed and talked to her. In her eyes he was yet a hatchling, though she knew he was not. A loud noise caused her to stir, though only momentarily. She was quick to roll over, touching a hand to her belly. She whispered quietly to herself, telling Tnavres, the dragon that slept within her, to calm himself.

Nijal watched her sleeping form as he had been instructed, with contempt for her in his thoughts. He was losing sight of the urgency and the purpose of the endeavor towards which they charged. He was also still sulking and had been sulking for a considerable amount of time. He had been thoroughly berated by both Xith and Noman, and not only once. Xith still brooded over the matter himself.

Nijal turned a glum stare at Shchander, who had also been sentenced to maintain the watch over Adrina. Shchander returned a wry look, saying he was enjoying the idleness just as much as Nijal was. Although being confined below deck to remain with Adrina during the day had not been meant as a punishment, the two saw it as such. Shchander was also upset because he had parted with the last of his gold on Nijal's advice, as had Nijal. The two were quite penniless now, having even advanced the few bits of wealth they normally maintained on their persons at all times, a golden belt buckle which had been a gift, a silver blade which, although it had no edge, was somewhat of a family heirloom, a polished stone that Nijal had kept for luck, and a small gem fixed within a locket.

Shchander was also troubled and saddened over Trailer's death. He had been a good man and a valuable companion. The dark tidings could not be ignored. Noman had explained many things about the happenings, which Noman himself said he had also only begun to comprehend. How much did those that sought them out know now, he wondered, and how much would it cost them in the end?

Nijal couldn't take the silence anymore and the bottled-up energy within him was about to burst. He had to do something. For a time, pacing back and forth in long strides appeased him, but the pleasure was short-lived. "All right! All right!" he exclaimed "I am sorry about the damned pendant! I promise I will buy it back for you, no matter the cost!"

His bellowing was so vocal that it woke Adrina, and she opened sleep-filled eyes to the dim light of the cabin. She listened to the two argue for a time, thinking it was quite comical. Thoughts of her dreams were far behind her. She was hungry. The galley was fairly well stocked and so her meal was hearty.

Nijal was delighted when Adrina wanted to take a stroll above decks. Pleasant seas would not last long; very soon they would be beyond the safety of Statter's Bay, and rough waters lay ahead. The night drew in as they watched with the wind in their hair. The sun cast golden hues along the waters and in the sky. Xith had also been above decks. He marked the skies in his mind, for he feared he would not see them again for some time.

The early hours of the second day did, indeed, find them in open waters. They appeared unruly at first after the calm of the Statter, but the captain promised that they were nothing compared to what was ahead. By the third day, seasickness abounded even in the strong of stomach. The winds they met were powerful and direct from the north.

Amidst the torment of the seas, Xith felt safer than he should. He even touched a wisp of energy to the tips of his fingers. It seemed so long since he had been in the dark city, Tsitadel na Magiyu, the fortress of magic, home of the Priests of the Dark Flame. He procured a wooden walking stick that had been carefully wrapped in thick cloths. He remembered the fellow he had taken it from, the small flame emblazoned just above the heart. He loosened his tunic and scratched his right shoulder, fingering the outline of an old scar.

The eve of the fifth day found them in gale-force winds. The ship was almost floundering, but it held above the water line. Two Hands had been below decks with them for two days. Only the captain and his sailors dared to venture above decks now. Xith had been coaxed into a game of King's Mate, which had been the main object of intrigue for the better part of the day.

Adrina stayed tucked away in her small cabin, though now Amir sat with her. She yearned to run the halls of the palace in her bare feet as she had done not long ago. A feeling of joy flowed to her, and she returned it. Reluctantly she stretched out onto the bed and fell asleep as she tried to fight her weariness.

A squall blew in and the wildness of the sea became unsettling even to Two Hands. His face was ashen, and perspiration streamed from his forehead. The ship bobbed to and fro in sweeping arcs, sending everything not nailed down crashing about. By morning, water had found its way into the bowels of the ship, standing several inches deep in most places, and whether it was from leaks in the hull or from the overhead seals no one knew, but either way it was a matter for grave concern. Taliltan seemed farther and farther away, even as it theoretically drew nearer.

Eight days out, lookouts spotted the Stone Mountains. This was grim news, as it meant they were days behind schedule. The seas ahead appeared even worse than those behind. Two Hands knew these waters well. He had been a captain for years before he had purchased his own ships. And he was the most frightened of all. The storms were undeniably upon them, and they were too far out to turn back for Krepost'. High cliffs and scarce inlets prohibited them from finding a landing place within many days of their position. Continuing north was their only choice, and they opted for it.

All free hands turned to bailing water, basically a futile effort since the water quickly returned, but it occupied time and prevented a complete flooding. Their supplies were the first tragedy of the flooding. Food was despoiled and water became contaminated by the salt. The end of the second week found them without rations of any kind. Rainwater was gathered to sustain them, although it provided no real nourishment.

Noxious odors of mold, mildew, and decay began to overcome them. Sleep was difficult and managed only when one reached the very edge of exhaustion. There was no way to get rid of the dampness. Clothes constantly wet against the skin began chafing and causing sores. Beds were wet and soggy, as were blankets. The only source of warmth was the press of bodies into a small space.

Above decks things were worse. High seas and strong winds prevailed. Waves continually washed over the decks. If the rain was not a heavy, unrelenting downpour, then it was a light, irritating drizzle. The mainsail had torn twice now and been repaired at a high cost. One man had lost his life saving the sail, and another had been injured. The rear mast was cracked and most of the forward jib sails were damaged beyond repair.

As seas permitted, the captain fought to keep the sails raised, but the weather was not as gracious as he would have hoped for. Squalls blew in suddenly and were slow to dissipate. The demise of two more sailors prompted him to ask for volunteers to replace those lost. The crew had been light to begin with. Now with three gone and several injured, there was little hope without additional manpower.

Two Hands had not ventured above deck since the storms had hit, as Noman had surmised. He had grown too fond of wealth and too fat. Although Noman believed that Two Hands had at one time been strong and fearless, this was not the case now. Noman was glad the others were not cowards. Shchander had proven the bravest of them all. He had elected to act as the lookout when seas permitted. Four times he had climbed to the precipice on top of the center mast with little to show for his bravado save that he was still alive.

Mutiny was avoided only by the graces of the Great Father and perhaps due in large part to a certain mark upon two fellows of the strange company. The hope of reaching Taliltan safely faded, so the ship turned toward the coast. The intention was to find an inlet where the ship could be moored safely. A high rock wall along a serpentine coast was all they found. Unsure how far they had come or an approximate distance back to a safe point, they pressed on, still keeping a close but lengthy distance from the rock line, as was necessary to maneuver in the changing gales.

A miracle happened the eve of the next day when the rear mast snapped in heavy seas. In a desperate attempt to turn the ship about before it capsized, the captain mistakenly turned inland instead towards open waters. A rock prominence leaped out at them like a great tongue. Settled atop its summit was a white tower, and while its light was extinguished, it was distinct enough against the black backdrop to be discerned. An elongated channel led to the mouth of a canal leading into a small harbor, which was nestled amidst a set of rolling, lowland hills. In a westerly course cutting through the tallest of them was a road. The city of Taliltan was tucked just out of reach beyond the crest and trough of those two hills.

Their stay lasted only long enough for recuperation. The road north was an arduous one, so they didn't delay. All felt the sense of urgency now—the destination seemed so close but just out of their grasp. They also had to make a quick escape before Two Hands discovered their ploy. Noman took hefty pains to stall payment until they were almost ready to leave the city, making sure he had a full complement of horses ready to go at any hour.

The time came quickly enough on its own. Noman only hoped he could maintain the illusion long enough to slip out of town. Now that he had had plenty of time to consider his deed, he honestly felt bad for swindling the old shipwright. The bargain had been kept, after all. They made a hasty departure after payment, nonetheless, without giving it much further thought. It had been a necessity.

Chapter Thirty One

Two frantic riders raced southward, paying little heed to the sky overhead as they approached the coast; and when they came upon the army amassed there, they did not stop. They drove on until they came to Prince Valam, who rode proud and tall even though his clothes were soaked and his snarled hair still dripping. The two conveyed their message just short of the onslaught, but fortunately the chase had staggered the wave of attackers with the fastest riders reeling in, hovering just short of advancing, waiting for their comrades to catch up. The men and those of Seth's kind had waited too long for a contest and even the weariness of their spirits did not slow their retaliation as King Mark's army swept in from the distance.

The chill was cast off as the kingdomers and East Reach elves advanced in column formation. Their only advantage was the fact that they had formed up just a short time ago and were preparing to move out again when the two scouts had returned. Those with swords were quick to ready them. They made the first push, and they cut a deep gouge into the midst of the oncomers. Spears were raised in the wave following the swordsmen. Bows were rapidly notched with arrows as the archers spread out in a wide circle and fell to the rear.

Chaos spread as spirits soared. The columns were all mixed;

soldiers charged en masse. Many were toppled by their eagerness and then trampled by their own mounts. The first voice raised above the confusion of the field was Ylsa's. Her words were commanding and dominated. Her section rallied around her. Pavil was next to gain control of his men as the two sides faced off, seeming to pause for a moment while both adjusted.

Willam would gain the name Willam the Black this day, both for the color of his eyes and for the scowl upon his lips as he charged his lancers and pikemen into the heart of King Mark's riders. His charge ended the lull and it would not return for a long time to come. The first thoughtless advance had cost them dearly. As a whole they had far fewer on horseback than the others. Willam sent his lancers forth wisely, advising them not to get mixed too deeply in the midst of the enemy, but pikemen on foot were also of great use against riders and he sent them to form a shield wall against an enemy push.

Valam surveyed the field of battle from a distance, careful not to be in range of enemy arrows, which dropped in great barrages. Seth rode beside him. Together they studied the turmoil, searching for the weak points in defenses and bolstering them as the need arose. They looked for the enemy commanders, who, unlike their counterparts, were maintaining a great distance from the melee. For the most part, Valam's lieutenants were acting on their own.

Tsandra waited beside Liyan. Her riders offered their mounts to others who needed them more desperately than they did. Their fight would be much different from the others. It would not be fought with blades or arrows or hands. It would be carried upon the wind, pulled from the forces of nature around them, and unleashed upon their opponents, who, like them, gathered, waiting.

The bows of Ylsa's forces were raised, waiting. She followed with precise timing, slowing the advance down, then ordering the archers to drop back and cover the flanks. She was also waiting on arrows, which were spread out amongst the supplies. She ensured that the volleys were directed only at thick clumps along the front and rear lines, trapping the forces in the middle.

The only one who watched without action or contemplation was Teren. Anger marked his face; this was the exact scenario he had wanted to avoid, and they had almost made a clean escape. Evgej was beside him, his sword drawn and his horse prancing eagerly to join the fray; and so he did, joining a charge of Eran's long swordsmen.

Dark shadows spread across the land. Many thought the rains were returning, but it was the night arriving. The day was coming to an end. A shield barrier was finally raised in front of the pikemen. The siege was full at hand from both sides. The enemy seemed to stream toward the battle in ceaseless droves drifting down from the North.

S'tryil guided the only force that was entirely on horseback and his men were seemingly tireless in their assaults. He managed to keep a large portion of his men out of the direct melee, dancing in and out of a tower shield wall erected especially for them by Eran. The barrier proved an extremely efficient defense against the enemy's retaliatory attacks.

Only one group had not engaged in the combat yet, and they were beginning to thirst for a taste of the struggle. Redcliff had to remind them quite often that they were affording a defense for now and must wait. In truth, they were doing much more than just waiting, they were also creating order among the soaring numbers of injured, the jumble of bodies, and the supplies.

The full depths of night found them under a starless, moonless, overcast sky. The fighting broke off and a shield wall encircled the forces as best as could be managed. The lash of arrows shooting into the darkness, however, did not stop. Small raids were led against the other camp regularly, which proved to be a good countermeasure to the enemy's sporadic attacks.

A death toll was taken, and it along with the injured and the missing was high. Valam thought it eerie to see the Brown slink off into the shadows of the night one by one, never to return. Distant cries from the enemy camp told of their effectiveness. Tsandra felt his watchful eyes peering towards her and whispered carefully only to his mind her thoughts. "It is neither odd nor unusual. If your Lieutenant Danyel' were here, his men would have done the same, except our measures are much more effective."

She moved closer to him, touching his hand to reassure herself it was him she perceived in the darkness. Valam whispered back to her quietly, but she told him not to use words, only thoughts. "Will they not do the same?"

"Yes, they will. All the more need for ours to move faster. These clouds are not here by chance but rather by mutual agreement."

"Mutual agreement, what do you mean?"

"This is not your concern. Set your thoughts on different goals."

"Can you tell how many of them there are?"

"Yes, I can, as can they."

"Why have they come so soon?" he thought to himself, whispering after a moment, "too soon." His thoughts drifted back to the first time he had listened to Tsandra tell him to think thoughts to himself. For an instant, his mood became light as the thought of her asking if he could eat and think at the same time crossed his mind. The moment was, however, fleeting, and for another hurried moment another's face came to the window of his thoughts. The face was fair and beautiful, the image crystalline.

"She would want to see you too," confided Tsandra. She sadly turned away from him back to her own concerns, disappearing from his side. Valam felt a sudden coldness next to him as her warmth left his side. The night proceeded, with no one actually sleeping or resting.

A large push caused a sudden panic and anyone who had been sleeping or near to it was fully awake now. Liyan, Seth and Valam had come together to muddle over plans. The lieutenants also joined them, telling of their losses, supplies needed, questions about the care of the wounded, and also offering good insight toward plans of attack and defense. The night would not find day without several silent assaults.

In the confusion of battle no one had noted Captain Mikhal's absence, but now the search was on about the camp for his whereabouts. A few shielded lanterns were also raised to aid the search. The first and most obvious place to begin was among the jumble of dead, but his body was not there, nor was it among the injured. Quiet probes went out to the field but had no luck.

With the dead of night came the chilling cold of the winds across the plains. Spirits fell to a new low for a time after a large raiding party went out and none returned; gentle cries in the night were all that were heard of the last moments of their fellows' lives. Later rumors from scouts that the enemy was withdrawing proved to be false, but hopes were renewed.

Seth carried his thoughts across the winds into King Mark's

camp. He had been carefully guiding it and allowing it to build up momentum for hours now. As it returned, he could hear their whispers and see their movements. Scattered as if ants across the plains he saw shadows moving and he knew their sources. He knew Tsandra was now out there someplace among those shadows.

✳ ✳ ✳

Captain Brodst saw Lord Serant being brought before the king just as he exited the chamber, but he could do nothing to help the other. He was caught in his own dilemma, from which he saw no apparent escape. He walked beside Calyin, calming her with murmured whispers. On the other side of her stood another and the two walked to a place the captain had not seen before.

Brodst was thinking quickly and wildly. He had only made it past the king by sheer luck and nothing else. The way he figured it, he had already strained the limits of his luck for a good, long time. Soon, though, they were alone; but before Brodst could think of a plan of action, they came to a sealed door. Two guards stood on either side of it, and one held the key.

A hand sign of sorts was passed back and forth before the door was unlocked. The barred door clanged closed behind them as they walked down a darkened corridor with a series of open doors. As they stopped in front of a second closed door with no others in sight, Captain Brodst began to make his move. He let Calyin fall to the ground and swung around behind the other, reaching up for the throat.

He stopped only an instant before he connected. The other had pushed open the door, and it revealed an empty cell. The other captives were nowhere to be found. "Damn!" cursed Brodst. Moments later, he was lying face first against the cold floor. He remained there still and quiet.

After depositing Calyin into the cell, the other turned around, chuckling at Brodst. "You fool, get up," he laughed. "That'll cost you. Ale on you this evening. Wait a second. What sector are you from? I've never seen you before."

Captain Brodst stammered a reply, settling for a shrug of the shoulders as he stood. His mind grew crazed now as the man stared at him trying to attach a name to the face. Brodst clenched his fist tightly, an instant away from lunging, watching the other's eyes closely.

The man started to shout, "You are—" but Brodst snuffed the words from his lips with a hefty blow to the face, "Kyail—."

Desperately, Brodst dragged the man into the cell with Calyin. He sat down between the two still forms, glaring at the door at the far end of the hall. It was just out of his line of sight, but he knew it was there, and he waited for it to open, praying hard that it wouldn't. Hand to face, gnawing on the inside of his palm, he sat engrossed in thought. Agitation was etched into his countenance as minute after minute slipped by.

He searched the man, stripping him of his blade and his belt. As he waited, to his dismay, he found a full bucket of water and a plate of bread. He bit his lip twice devouring the food, gulping down the water as quietly as he could. When he had finished, by his judgment at least, it was time to act before suspicions arose.

Calyin began to giggle. At first it was low, scarcely audible, but then it began to rise to a howling scream. Brodst quickly covered her mouth. "Shh! Quiet down!" he cried. A call from the opposite end of the hall frightened him.

"I—we're alright, just delayed."

"We have orders that she is not to be molested. Come out at once!"

"Molested?" Captain Brodst was repulsed by the idea, "Um, she fell down. I thought she was unconscious."

"Okay, just hurry up, you two."

"Shh!" intoned Brodst again. "You are going to get us in trouble." He slapped her face harshly several times. "Snap out of it, Calyin. I need you. Come on now. Stand up! Damn it."

Brodst was back to his wild, rambling thoughts. He began walking Calyin around, forcing her to move. "Calyin, listen close. Have you seen the others? Have you seen Midori? Where are they keeping them?"

"Calyin, Calyin, listen to me," he pleaded again and again. She wanted to, but she couldn't shake the dizziness from her mind. The world was still spinning round and round. She heard his words as if through a tunnel. He stood at the opposite end of it, far, far away, yet she could see his face beside her. He was pushing her down to the cold floor now, and calling something, "Was he telling her to go to sleep and sit quietly," she wondered.

The cell door opened abruptly and she saw a shadow pass before her eyes, moving behind the door. She saw the glint of steel and a figure fell. There was a cry of pain, or at least she thought she heard someone cry out. "Maybe it was a plea," she thought. "Someone was begging for mercy." She saw a second figure fall and then the room became quiet and still.

"No! Don't get up!" yelled an angry voice as she tried to stand, "You just sit there."

She thought she heard fighting again; perhaps one of the forms had risen from the floor. She was sure of it now. She heard the clanging of blades and a fight. "Are you there?" she cried. A whimper, perhaps a moan, drifted to her ears and then she heard a thud. The room became quiet. "Hello?" she said, or thought she said, "Hello?" No response came. "Oh—" she cried out; the room was spinning again. Her head felt queasy and heavy.

She heard the click of a key in a lock and then footsteps that seemed to be fading away. Everything started spinning again. The world turned gray as the footsteps became inaudible. She closed her eyes and fell into a wakeful sleep in which odd images moved in and out and then stopped. The world was still, and she fell into a deep catatonic state.

Chapter Thirty Two

The route out of Taliltan had taken them along the northern road, which ran next to the coast, but at the first crossing they turned westward. To an observer, the thirteen black horses could have been an omen of ill fate, though none in the group paid attention to the count. The roads in the Lost Lands were much like the land itself—rough and haphazardly hewn.

Xith and Noman spoke quietly but tersely, their voices barely carrying above the plodding of hooves. "You know what will happen when we reach Tsitadel?" Xith asked.

"I have no doubt. He's known all along."

"And the wards revealed the mark?"

"Yes, yes," hissed Noman. "We were but fools to hope otherwise."

"May the Father keep us," Xith said quietly, reverently, as he urged his mount on, ending the conversation.

Mountains carved the land into awkward sections, running straight from the beginnings of the Stone Mountains in the South. Spiraling arms led inland at first and then jutted north. Further north they split in two, dissecting the country into thirds. The seat of the broken land lay far to the north, and the hand of the regent rarely reached the sleepy villages that dotted the eastern coast.

Trading was the most important thing in these parts, where in the storm season your wealth mattered not so much as the usefulness of your possessions. Only a few towns lay inland away from the sea, and the small borough they would pass through come nightfall was one of them. A piece of gold there was as useless as the edge of a blade would be against the frozen rock they traveled across.

Thoughts of Tsitadel were prevalent on most everyone's minds. It had once been a catalyst of might, and its home tucked away in the snowy north had proven to be its bane and its greatest blessing. Xith knew the battlements it sported better than most although Amir was the only one of the company who could attest to their strength. Beyond its portcullises and gatehouses, and within its barbicans, bastions, parapets and long, sleek, lofty walls, was the very thing they sought.

A fine mist of tightly compact snow flurries fell upon them as the sun mounted in the sky, only partially blocked by a modest cloud cover. Noman shifted his attentions to Xith and Amir and brooded. Seeing clouds looming about the mountains in the distance sparked sad memories. He wondered about the children and what would become of them in the end. His turn as the guardian was coming to a close and he wondered if Amir could tell that his days were also numbered.

He hadn't told Xith that on the last day in Krepost' his vision of the paths had returned; he had kept that to himself. He watched Amir for a time and saw his agitation, understanding it. He meandered with his mount among all his companions as the hours of afternoon swept by, looking to each of their faces and speaking quietly to them. He came lastly to Adrina, not knowing if she would have the strength it would take. He told himself she would, or rather hoped she would. Then he told her a thing that perhaps he should not have. He told her of the hidden dreamers and the mystics who walked the paths. "Remember," he told her, "The thrall can only hold the willing."

As they had all hoped, a small village nestled on the lee side of a rounded hollow came into view as the day waned. Xith bartered with the innkeeper over the worth of the baubles he had collected in the market of Krepost', and they were given rooms for the evening. The small inn only had two sleeping rooms barely large enough for four apiece and two chambers that held nothing but a single cot. The party required them all, and still three would go without a place to lie down this night.

Xith, Noman, and Amir took up residence downstairs while the others retired upstairs. Later, the three found comfort in a private room which was normally reserved for special occasions. It was divided from the main hall with doors that could be secured from the inside. They also found sleep, but not too quickly for they had much to discuss before the start of the day.

For the most part, the conversation had not led anywhere until Xith properly cleared the air. He understood all too well the coming events. He was frank when he asked, "Will you tell them before we reach Tsitadel or will you just let them discover it on their own?" Amir started to respond, not because he thought the question had been directed at him, but rather because he had just realized the issue himself.

"Is it true?" he asked, savoring the words.

"Yes, perhaps," replied Noman, "but not the way you would hope. It is too long a road to know for sure."

"How else could it be?" questioned Amir.

"It would be best if I said nothing, but I think that you are wise enough to make your own decision when the time comes," began Noman, as if only he and Amir were in the room. He continued, still ignoring Xith's presence, but not meaning to offend the shaman either. "Old friend, the time of choice is ahead. You must choose one of two ways." His voice trailed off to a whisper as he said the next few words, "It is as before." And then he became very articulate and earnestly forthright as he finished, "He will offer you peace eternal. Will you take it?"

Noman did not wait for Amir to respond; he promptly turned to Xith and said, "No, I will not tell them. It is not for me to tell. Yet be that as it may, you are free to do as you will. But in so saying, I have one thing to ask of you also. It is simple. Just remember your time of servitude, what brought you to the path you have embarked upon."

Xith considered Noman's words at length before he offered his response, a gentle smile, as he touched his head against his rolled up cloak and closed his eyes. A heavy rap on the closed doors startled everyone, and caused Xith, who was nearly asleep, to jump up. They relaxed when a recognizable voice asked them if they required anything before the other retired and as they didn't, the innkeeper walked away.

Before the group left the inn the following day, they gathered some food stuffs they had not had time to purchase in Taliltan and with fresh breads and dried meats tucked into their satchels alongside newly acquired water bottles they departed. Adrina was feeling rather groggy this morning. Her stomach was upset and it was all she could do to keep her breakfast down. She told no one that the dragon mark upon her was growing—had been growing the further north they went. A stint on horseback did not improve her feelings either, and she was growing irritable; however, as afternoon came on, her sickness passed.

The small town would be the last remnant of civilization they would see for days and the farther inland they went, the deeper the snows became and the narrower the trail they followed. They continued west despite the obvious lack of a path, bending to a slightly northerly course from time to time. As if two nights of sleeping on cold ground with little fuel for fires had not been bad enough, the third day, a storm front nestled itself along the foot of the mountains in front of them.

The night ahead promised to be snow-filled and cold. Against the general consensus, Xith drove them to continue on well after darkness fell. The winds had picked up and thick snow flurries cascaded downward, whipped about by the gales. Xith had no intention of freezing to death on an open trail and continued to lead them, despite numerous requests to stop. At first, Nijal had spoken mostly on Adrina's behalf and upon her request, but now he also wanted to stop and try to set up camp somewhere. They had passed through many good hollows, as he saw it.

Amir chuckled as he listened to Xith swear under his breath. "Ahead to the right," he whispered. Not paying attention to the voice, Xith started to answer, "But how can you see?" But he cut himself short and instead returned to his mutterings. Needless to say, he turned to a strong northerly course. The shadows in the stand of trees he searched for loomed a short distance away.

The trees afforded shelter from the storm and its snow and also provided them with an abundant supply of wood for their campfire. All grumbling, including Xith's, ceased as sparks were touched to the first timbers. A few hours were passed with warm and cheerful talk. Shchander even found a song within him, borrowing a few words from the first song that sprang into his mind. Its nonsensical words seemed to make sense under the canopy of trees with the fire reflecting upon the boughs, and he came to understand the song's meaning.

After an early morning start under dreary skies, the sun appeared and at first the mountains seemed so close that they might be able to reach out and touch them; nevertheless, they were still hours away. A squat series of swells leading to the base of the rocky peaks needed to be traversed first, but once the companions reached the hills, Xith promised that they would be able to see the outer walls of Tsitadel.

* * *

Only a few hours of the darkness remained. In all, the night would not be counted as a complete loss. They had accomplished much this night, and the enemy had been forced to withdraw to a different position. Horror came with the first shafts of light; the invaders had withdrawn, but their numbers had doubled. Machines of war and of siege loomed across the horizon, waiting to move and to strike.

At the vanguard of the first assault came the machines of war; they did not roll or creak with the turnings of wheels, but instead they moved across the plain with ease and in silence. Valam wondered at their size and configuration; only a devious mind could have constructed such tools. Spiked walls with slits for arrows attached to rams preceded mobile catapults and ballistae at staggered intervals, allowing clear shots for the engines of devastation.

The speed with which the machines swept across the land was incredible and unfathomable and they were upon the defenders before they could properly react. Walls of spikes met the shield wall in a fit of tumultuous rage. Screams of panic and despair arose as man-size projectiles careened through the air, meeting many a target and more often than not piercing two or three through before their velocity slowed. The struggle began again.

Valam no longer had time to ponder the origins of the enemy's devices of terror and destruction—he was face to face with them. He looked first to Seth for advice, but just as he did so a shaft of bright sunlight fell upon him. He shielded his eyes from its sting with his hand before he adjusted to the new light. He blinked wildly several times as the white haze cleared.

The enemy stood facing them; they had not advanced. Neither side had attacked yet. The survey did not last long before the first cries to arms rang loudly. Valam rubbed his tired eyes and then, still puzzled, he poured water from his water bag into a cupped palm and splashed it onto his face. Many others were mounted and scrambling, or just scrambling, as Valam finally got onto the back of his horse.

The battle strategy they had conceived during the night began to unfold, but it was clear that the invaders had been making plans of their own. A large toll of dead at the place where the enemy camp had been set up the previous night told of the deeds of the Brown. A trail of bodies led all the way back to the enemy's current location. There was no sign of those who had delivered the deed, and it was assumed that they lay somewhere among the casualties in the field.

Valam wished he could be elsewhere right now. His heart was not in fighting this day. Doubt filled his thoughts. He no longer knew if he had the prowess necessary to prevail. He desperately needed to find strength and resolve.

A voice called to Valam, "Your dreams can carry you far in an instant. You can walk the paths of an entire lifetime in a single beat of your heart. Open your mind to me for an instant. My will is straining—act quickly." The voice was warm and compelling. It held compassion and perhaps love. Valam could not resist it, so he did as it bade and opened his mind.

Images of the thousands around him faded as he followed the voice. "I have seen you in my dreams many times. Here take my hand. It was not time before. We must try again." Valam went where the beautiful voice bade him to go. A vision, only an outline at first formed. Her hands felt warm in his as they began to go up a long winding staircase.

His heart was pounding so wildly he could hear its clamor. He had wanted this very thing to happen to him so desperately that he completely freed his mind. The two climbed for what seemed hours until they finally reached the summit. "Am I dreaming?" asked Valam of himself with a last moment of resolve. "You are dreaming the living dream," came the response into his mind as the other pressed tightly against him.

Valam moved forward to kiss her. As he did so, a sudden bright light filled the chamber and everything became clear. The sunlight bathed the thin dress she wore and highlighted the outline of her body beneath. She undressed and then began to undress him, and he let her. Her eyes were serene as she watched him and a gentle smile touched her lips. The smile grew to laughter as she pulled him to a nearby bed. Valam began to ask a question, but she forced him into silence with her lips. He held her tightly now, recalling fond memories from an earlier time.

She moved back suddenly and her smile turned to a laugh as she drew him in. Her face blurred and then returned. Valam scrambled back to the wall. A gasp fell from his lips as he did so. The laughter turned to a shrill cackle. A voice lifted mockingly to his ears, "The mightiest of the western lands falls to the simple guiles of a female. I have searched throughout the night for you and now at last I have found you. And I can also see that I have your attention. Do I not? Valam, Prince of Fools."

Anger raged through Valam as he glared at the creature that sat before him. The thing reached out its hands and touched his legs. His body began to tremble as a chill overcame him. Distraught, Valam clenched his hands around the creature's neck and began strangling it. The roar of the voice rose as it sneered at him with new fervor. "Squeeze harder, go ahead. Kill the messenger. Its will was already spent in the delivery. I command you—kill, feel the blood upon your hands as you extinguish life.

"Do not fear for your life, my sweet prince, I have not come for you this day. Oh no, your suffering will not be so quickly over. Your death will be long and drawn out. You will die only when I am finished with you. Go ahead, kill her. Try harder. I know you are stronger than that. I have come only to give you a warning and a possible way out. If you turn back now, you may return to your own lands and in time you may save them. If you stay, you will find death, but not your own, until I have had my fill. Which will it be?"

Valam's reasoning became warped and twisted as his grip clasped increasingly tighter. He was beginning to enjoy killing and his face lit up. "I will not go. You will have to kill me first!" shouted Valam. As he spoke, his hands crushed the hideous creature's windpipe, and then he heard the neck snap. He was happy, and he cast it away without remorse.

"I leave you with only one image to contemplate—reality," laughed the voice wickedly as it faded away. The glowing of yellow eyes loomed in front of him as he returned. He found himself kneeling in the snow. His hands were still clenched. He gasped as he saw a pair of eyes looking up at him. In them he saw pity and no fear. He began to cry as he recognized the face. "What have I done?" he wailed, "What have I done?"

"You will pay for this!" said Valam through tears, "We will destroy your army in the field of battle, where there is honor. And I will do it again and again relentlessly until I have avenged your trickery! I will chase you to the ends of time!" He stopped, for he could no longer continue. He picked Tsandra up tenderly from the snow, brushing it off her face. Endless tears rolled down his cheeks. "I will get you!" he vowed.

❄ ❄ ❄

Brodst stood perplexed at the crossing of two corridors. He could only guess which he should take. The weight on his shoulder was heavy, and he desperately needed a reprieve from its burden. He did not delay at the corner much longer; instead, he turned right, marking the characteristics of the adjacent hall into his memory. He finally came to a halt in a secluded alcove.

Although he tried to put Calyin down onto the floor as gently as possible, she still fell rather unceremoniously and immediately afterwards he slumped against the wall and slid down to the floor. He was exhausted and his body ached. The sudden intake of nourishment had done him more harm than good. He had eaten more than he should have after going without food for so long.

He grabbed Calyin's chin and swung her eyes up to look into his. He could see that they were beginning to focus again, and the color was returning to her face; but he still was determined not to remove the restraint from her mouth. She had already aroused enough attention for one day. He sat idle for as long as he dared before he continued on.

For the most part, the halls were empty and he assumed that a meeting still ensued in the central chamber though he did not know how much longer he could count on the quiet continuing. Most of the corridors off the hall where Calyin had been held led to private chambers, which confused him more than helped him in his search. He couldn't understand the reason a single cell would stand by itself with such an elaborate control system leading to it. Locked doors, guard houses, and check points that led to only one place, and after a time his puzzlement brought him back to the hallways he had come down.

He jingled the ring of keys around in his hand, contemplating each, a ring of nine keys in all, and he tried to recall the number of doors he had passed. One key stood out as odd, perhaps older than the others, and more finely crafted. He remembered that that was the key that belonged to the innermost door. He walked back along the chamber, depositing Calyin behind the second door, which he locked.

He fit all the keys to doors along the chamber save two. He held the two up and inspected them closely beneath the light of a torch. A stirring sound startled him and he broke away from what he was doing, quickly running back to that innermost door. One of the guards within was beginning to arouse. He cursed himself for not killing them all and went back in and finished the job he should have done earlier. He also took the time to properly and thoroughly search each of them; he had been in too much of a rush before to do so. He didn't find much of use.

A rasping sound from far off forced him to stop and at first he thought it was Calyin groaning. He claimed one helmet for his own and another blade and ran back up the corridor. He bent down and checked Calyin, but she was still incoherent. He heard the sound again. After he began to look around, he looked up to the barred window. A face pressed close to it startled him. His heart jumped, and his breath was heavy and shallow.

"Um, yes?" he said dumbly as he stood. A small hand raised a bucket up to the window, and Brodst almost broke into laughter. His mind began working quickly; the smile left his face and his eyes turned angry. "You, errand—" began the captain. All the while he spoke he squeezed his palms together, "You are in the wrong area! This one has already been fed."

The figure staggered back under his apparent wrath, "But, but."

"Don't interrupt me. Do I need to accompany you personally? Is that what you need? Do you need someone to hold your hand to ensure you do the job right the first time?"

"No sir, no sir. I'll be off straightaway."

"Wait, wait, hold on there," stated Brodst, again thinking quickly. "I still think I had better accompany you."

"No need, I promise you."

"No need indeed. Halt where you are!"

Not knowing what to do as the boy disappeared, Captain Brodst unlocked the door and went to chase him. Unfortunately, the boy was still standing in the hall; he had only been out of eyesight. He saw the body of Calyin on the ground and began to scream. It was all Brodst could do to catch the boy before he scrambled away. He had one hand tight around the boy's mouth and the other attached to the scruff of the boy's shirt as he dragged him back down the hall kicking. The boy's hollow screams were only loud enough to reach the captain's ears.

Brodst saw the fear in the boy's eyes and used it to his advantage. He brought the tip of his knife up close to the boy's neck and pressed it tight until it pierced the skin. After a long one-sided conversation the two came to terms. The boy was scared to death; that was very clear. "What is your name?" asked the captain, seeking to calm the boy's nerves.

"J-J-J-Ja-cob," whispered the boy, barely audibly.

"Jacob is it? I knew a Jacob once and he was a fine man. Now you listen close and listen well." Brodst paused and continued slowly, "I will not hurt you unless you try to run. I do not wish to kill you, but I will in the blink of an eye if you try to run. Do you understand?"

Jacob nodded that he did and his shivers calmed a little. Brodst picked up Calyin and then ushered the boy on, taking great care to return the blade to his free hand and then put his arm around the boy's neck. "Take me down no central corridors, you hear. I do not want to see another living thing. Now, move slowly, and remember—if you act wisely, I will not harm you. I promise."

Brodst moved through the long corridors, maintaining a prudent step. He tried not to delay much, but in his weakened state the burden upon his shoulder seemed to grow, until he was finally forced to stop. He had rested three times now, and the restlessness of his companion was increasing with each such stop. He stood eyeing the boy; he could read the other's thoughts well. Any moment now, Jacob would try to make his escape.

The time arrived sooner than Brodst expected, and almost

immediately after he had bent down to raise Calyin to his shoulder. "Smart, very smart," thought Brodst as he snagged the boy by the scruff of his collar. Captain Brodst reiterated his earlier promise, ensuring that Jacob understood the benefits of obeying him. "How far from here?"

"Not very far, I promise," whispered Jacob in a soft voice.

"How many guards will there be?" asked the captain. Jacob shrugged his shoulders feigning that he did not know. "How many guards will there be?" spoke Brodst repeating the question.

"Yo-o-u-u're, no-o-t go-go-ing to-to k-k-k-ill him are yo-o-u?"

"Not if you help me. If you help me, I will kill no one unless it becomes necessary. I promise. Do you know the guard on duty?"

"Y-y-ye-e-s, I th-th-th-ink so-o—"

"Jacob, listen to me closely, I am a man of honor. We hold to our word. I hold to the warrior's oath. And if I make a promise by my own code I must keep it. Do your people have an oath of truth?"

"Y-y-e-s."

"Would you like to be a warrior someday? Yes, I think you would make a fine one. If you help me, I and my friends will leave, and we will not come back. This I promise."

"But you are spies, and spies should die," said Jacob, suddenly filled with bravado.

"Spies? Spies," said Brodst. "We are nothing of the sort."

"Your friends are devils and demons with the wings of bats and they eat people."

"Eat people? Do I look like I could eat another man?" chuckled Brodst, "Who has been filling your mind with this nonsense?"

"No one. I have eyes. I can see."

The captain put his hand on the boy's shoulder, and while

looking him straight in the eye, said, "That is nonsense. Do you see this woman here? Is she not fair and beautiful? How could you say such a thing about one so pure? Does she look evil to you?"

"N-n-no—" replied Jacob returning to his stammering.

"What if I told you that she is a princess of a fair and wonderful land and all we are trying to do is find peace, to bring our land to peace. If you help us, we can continue on our quest; and if we are lucky we will find a way to return peace to our land. Will you help us, Jacob?"

Jacob had listened intently to each word; his eyes seemed to perk up at the mention of a quest, and he envisioned it a grand a wondrous thing. This man called Brodst did seem to speak the truth. "I will try, but you must cast away your blade." Captain Brodst threw it away without a second thought; he did, after all, have several backups.

The walk to the place that Jacob promised that Brodst's other companions were held was short and went without mishap. A barred, closed door stood at the end of the hall before them. The plan was unfolding well. Brodst smiled as he slid Calyin, still unconscious, to the floor. As he did so, he looked to the movement of the shadows cast upon the floor by a light in the interior of the other hall. Mixed with the lines of the bars mounted in the door, they had an odd shape, but he thought he could discern only one distinct figure. The other shadows were perhaps reflections off an adjacent light.

The captain motioned for Jacob to proceed down the hall as planned. "Go on," he whispered, while waving a second time. He turned to look behind him hesitantly, knowing what he would find; and as he turned, he also muttered a curse under his breath. Jacob was gone. He looked around the corner, both left and right, but the boy was nowhere in sight. Despite his situation, he saw the humor in the situation. He had been outwitted hands down.

He sat there, engrossed in thought, contemplating how long it would be before the boy sounded an alarm that would cause his end. The longer he remained idle, the more foolish his resolve seemed; but in the end, he found no recourse but to continue. He sorted through the new possibilities, and thought it best to continue with his original idea. He slipped his hand into the inside pocket of his cloak to retrieve the keys and for an instant his eyes grew wide with dismay and horror until he remembered which pocket he had placed the keys in. The bulge was quite obvious, so he did not search for long.

He quietly walked toward the door, guarding each footfall, waiting until the shadow grew short before he tried to put a key to the lock. He cringed with each clank or jingle the keys made on the ring as he turned through them, holding his breath and closing his eyes in a hurried petition. As his palms began to grow moist, his hands began to shake and his fingers started fumbling against the lock.

The quivering spread to his body; trembling, he collapsed against the wall. He paused, fearing to move, and he heard footsteps growing closer. He waited, afraid to even breathe, until the footfalls faded away again. To his amazement, the next key he raised to the hole caused a resonant click, more similar to a dull thud. As he had his ear pressed against the door, it sounded loud as he turned it.

He did not open the door or attempt to open it. He waited, unsure of the sound of the footsteps from within. He sat motionless until they began to fade away, but he did not make his move quite yet. He pulled himself together first, mentally coaxing the fatigue away. He paused until he heard the sounds again, but still he waited until they turned away. As they did so, he slid the door open, ever so cautiously.

He regarded the back of the figure moving down the hall through a narrow slit until he was confident he could make his move. After he had removed his boots, he slithered through the opening noiselessly, returning the door to its original position. As it clicked close again, he crawled on his haunches down the hall, moving slowly at first and then gaining momentum, until he half stood and half crawled. He was standing hunched over as the figure turned back towards him, drawing his weapon as he did so; but by that time Brodst was upon him at full force. His initial blow knocked the guard sprawling to the floor; his sword slipped down the hall one way and his body slammed half into the wall and half against the ground the other way.

Brodst hadn't intended to kill the man, but the other did not move again. He wondered if Jacob had been here now what the boy would have thought. Would the boy have accepted it as an accident? Brodst didn't have time for regrets and he pushed the thoughts out of his mind. He retrieved Calyin, placing the door's lock back in place. After he put back on his boots, he carried her down to the far end of the corridor.

He fumbled through all the keys in his ring until he discovered the one that fit the lock. The detention area was set up in a series of circling cells that split off to the left, right, and straight ahead. Not knowing which way to go, he turned right first. It seemed a logical place to begin. His face lit with joy; after several disappointments, he came to an occupied cell. Strangely, the cell was unlocked, and its occupant sat in a dazed stupor.

Brodst immediately smelled the stench of liquor and vomit in the room. He stared for a long time at the face, but since he didn't recognize the other, he began to turn away. Confused and angry, he stomped off, swearing loudly. He hoped he would never find Jacob again, or he just might strangle the boy.

Chapter Thirty Three

"Father, is she dead?" begged Valam of Jacob, "Is she dead?"

"Hold on, hold on, give me a minute. I think you have only choked the air from her lungs. Back off, please, give me some room, I beg of you." Father Jacob bent his head low to listen to Tsandra's heart. He loosened up her tunic and pressed his ear against her flesh; the faint sound of a beat joyously found him. At the present, he could do nothing for her except ensure that she was comfortable and kept warm. He mixed some medicinal herbs into a hot, thin broth and forced her to drink of it, but time would have to heal her. He had so many others who needed him just as desperately, and they did not have the possibility of life without his aid. While Jacob turned back to his mending, Valam, with the help of Seth, turned back to face the field of battle.

The remnants of the first wave were returning, and a second sweep was close at hand. For those caught in the heart of the melee there was no reprieve, but a few fortunate ones managed to return and muster with their compatriots for the next charge. The shield still held firm, and behind it streams of arrows arced up into the sky, screaming angrily as they were released from long bows largely constructed of yew.

Tae's forces no longer held back but pushed forth as Prince Valam wished, striking out together with riders of S'tryil in a large flanking maneuver that led them in from both the left and the right. While the pikemen had carried the first charge, so now the task was passed on to Lieutenant Pavil's men. Their long swords were brandished high as they issued forth.

Valam and Seth came, responding to Ylsa's call, and together the three orchestrated missile attacks into the enemy weak points, which did not occur without counter strikes. Ylsa was urgently concerned about the new breaches in the shield wall, which even one of Eran's skills could not repair. At first the avalanche of single riders crashing against the high shields was slow, but the tempo was picking up considerably. Short blades did little against horse and rider.

Seth's mind was wandering elsewhere; his concerns were lost on the two around him, but Valam's thoughts were quick and his actions were decisive. The circle of the camp was at first tightened and then immediately reinforced. Evgej drew up close to them on horseback, and his impatience to join the heat of the fight was clear. Without saying a word, his expression asked them to join him. Valam's mount was brought to him, and he drew up regally onto it, outfitted in heavy mail, bright and thick, garnished with double bucklers, and his own double-handed blade.

Seth nodded, responding to Valam's inquiry of him, "Yes, it is time," he thought, but he quickly returned to the depths of his own deliberations. He counted it odd that he looked up to catch Valam's eyes just as the other rode off. He watched the two figures merge with the few remaining riders centered on S'tryil, turning away as they plunged into the fray. He looked to Ylsa momentarily before he walked away to find Father Jacob.

An enormous herald rang as Prince Valam launched his mount into the fight, wielding Truth Bringer before him. Evgej rode to his left, wielding a finely crafted long sword, of the bastard type. His shield was long and obtuse, having a blunt top and a rounded bottom with a central spike, also bearing numerous dents from the previous day's activities. S'tryil's outfitting was more conventional, more akin to that of his company. His sword was of the two-edged variety, but it was notched and marred with much use. His shield was simple and round.

The variety of their outfitting had little impact on the morale of their fellows, and their standing added only slightly to the sudden edge they held over the others in the field at their arrival. It was their straightforward charge into the very heart of the fracas and the fierceness of their blows that brought the cries of their names. Where true leaders led, others willingly followed.

Seth found Jacob and Tsandra after a slow search through the camp, during which he surveyed the number of wounded and the totals of the dead. He did not speak long with Jacob before he turned to Tsandra, and soon afterward Jacob left to tend to other matters. "Did you find him?" he called into Tsandra's mind again, pushing his will upon her to stir her to a conscious stream of thought. "Will he listen?"

Tsandra's response was weak and shallow, but her will still had a flickering of strength. The search through the night had carried her far, and she had found him, and he had repaid her as he said he would; however, she had also repaid him in turn. "They are all gone—" she whispered, "—save him. He will move for the prince." She had meant Valam, but for some reason she could not bring herself to utter his name.

"Come quick!" yelled a page, running towards Seth, "Brother Teren found the captain." Seth was slow to believe the page's words, but the thoughts could not be denied. He ran across the field to the place the boy indicated. Teren had only just dismounted and the captain lay on the ground, his head cradled in Jacob's lap. Captain Mikhal's eyes were almost shut and his face was pale, almost unaware of the life that he sought to cling to. Death was sure and slow upon him.

Seth and Jacob together did what they could to aid the captain and ease the pain, yet his wounds were deep and many. A fire lingered within Mikhal that yearned to burn bright though it was only a spark. The two watching saw the same tiny spark, and it gave them hope. With a wave of his hand, Brother Seth carried Mikhal off to a world of dreams, where the pain would momentarily not find him while they tended to his injuries.

On the field, the story was different—the hurt and agonies were now being inflicted upon the opposition, who massed around their encampment. The bodies of thousands littered a path that led west and south, the line of the enemies' retreat, but the fall had not been without its recourse. Prince Valam halted his advance at the crest of a small mound on the plain, created primarily by the shifting of the snow amidst the smothered, dying grasses. The enemy warriors also waited in a defensive line, their will to fight and to win hardly tainted by their losses, and they had no remorse for the fallen.

Behind, the archers drew up closer and spread out to a broader semi-circle. Each was assigned a bearer of the shield to protect his point, and the fanning-out ever increased in a wide arc that aimed to smother the thick, central cluster before them. A few, the most skilled of their group, were assigned to eliminate the remnants of the bowmen across the field.

The fighting continued, though with a brief lull; for a time, it had seemed to halt. Seth returned to his thoughts after he had tended to Mikhal. His work as a guide this day was not over; two were yet to be found. He returned his will to the air, beginning it once again on the simple hint of a soft breeze, spiraling it upward and floating it lazily along the currents.

The other lieutenants of the field momentarily joined Valam as he surveyed the host, together with the counsel of Evgej and S'tryil. Despite the growing turmoil around them, they formulated a new plan. The more mobile riders drew back, and the ranks of the pikemen were redefined and ordered. The bladesmen were switched into as many positions as could be afforded. The ranks that could be spared, along with all of Redcliff's forces that remained, were moved back to secondary ranks.

Valam followed through with the ideals his honor dictated to him. He did not entirely know the customs of the peoples of these eastern lands, but he knew those of his own. He wished Seth, or perhaps Liyan were with him now, but his own camp looked so far away from where he sat. Nonetheless, he ordered the flag of truth and parley raised, not fully knowing if the others would accept it and momentarily forgo their call to arms. In his mind, he saw the outcome of the battle only one way; and while his honor might have been his undoing, he adhered to it, for it was at the basis of who he was.

"Valam, no!" shouted a voice into the prince's thoughts, but it was too late. The call to parley was accepted, and six riders from either side rode across a short span into a hostile ring with weapons sheathed though guarded. Valam stopped short of the one who greeted him, not dismounting, waiting for the other to speak first. He was not surprised when the words of the enemy leader sought to enter his mind. Valam pushed them away, saying boldly, "We speak with words, aloud, and ask that you would do the same."

"Do you surrender then?"

"No," replied Valam, beginning the proper introductions as Seth had taught him.

"I am Arakthel second family, first heir of the western faction of Ayuil. I mix no words easily with my enemy. Speak quickly or die."

Valam breathed heavily, studying the other's countenance before he spoke further. In truth, more than anything, he had wanted a face to go with his hatred, but he gained nothing. The voice did not match that which he sought, or the other disguised it well. The face was not an unkind one. Valam's testament was simple; he asked the other to withdraw and in so doing spare the lives that were being wasted.

"It is you who does not understand," returned Arakthel. "We are but the greeters; behind us comes a host ten fold as great. You will be the one to perish."

Arakthel began to laugh, a sound Valam quickly recalled. Valam's face became stoic and his eyes flamed as he rose up true in his saddle. His cry, as an arrow struck him while he was drawing his blade, brought thousands upon thousands to his beck and call, in line upon line of rich unyielding formations. There would be no holding back anymore, no more fear of the unknown. The six riders spurred their mounts, attempting to flee the compressed ring of the enemy, but escape would not come so readily.

Long, pointed blades held in stalwart hands severed rider from horse, followed by ones that now bore short blades in either hand. Behind them flowed a steady stream of assorted blades, long and short, single-handed and double-handed. Those on horseback circled around to north and south, coming in from the back side with a tremendous, energetic force. Ylsa and her archers were not left out; they, too, advanced, shooting on the run, in a wild frenzy.

Willam was the first of the kingdom lieutenants to fall, though his demise did not come with his slip from the saddle, but while he was attempting to wrest his blade from its sheath only moments after his long pole had skewered two of the enemy. The others maintained their mounts and for a time their lives in the swirling chaos around them. They swept the great circle from the inside while others worked at it gallantly from the outside.

Valam, unfortunately, lost Arakthel in the frenzy. The blow to his shoulder was numbing as his lifeblood poured away. He held the great sword in one hand, still shifting it agilely, stroking it with skills quite akin to that of a sculptor's. Two forelegs mauled one who was bold enough to stand before him as he looked for his enemy. Arakthel was nowhere to be found.

In the name of glory and for the sake of their prince, hundreds were brought begging to their knees only to lose their lives. Valam's own anguish and hatred ran among his own kind and drove them as nothing else before had. They did not only kill, but they maimed, crushed and desolated. For a time they surged on images which were around them yet weren't, images of fields on fire and homes being ravaged; and always in the background amidst the soft purr of the wind was the crying of many, and mostly of children.

The enemy was routed and on the run, scampering away in desperate retreat. Those that could began a hearty pursuit while those that couldn't watched. Some could only observe with amazement; the end had been swift and vile. Pristine edges of crisp lines and columns moving to bannered engagements were distant, blurred thoughts, meaningless in the face of truth.

When only the dead, the dying, and the victors remained, the sudden fever ended. Calm came and even the air became still and silent. Valam sat tall in his saddle, but not as regally as he had earlier, amidst a littered field. A black riderless horse stood nearby, and though five others were closer, Valam only saw the one, and he mourned the loss. Death had a face, and it was the last vestiges of Willam, Willam the Black, that Valam envisioned.

Momentarily Seth transfixed his eyes to Valam's, looking where the other looked, and then he turned away. His deeds this day were done. A few paces behind him, Liyan regarded Seth, nodding with approval. The day was spent, save for one last thing, which Seth had already set in motion. Far away to the north a figure staggered, sword languishing in weary hands. He fell to his knees and slipped from consciousness though not towards darkness.

Driven by forces beyond his grasp, the figure rose again only minutes after it had fallen and though still staggering deliriously, persisted until it came to kneel before its prince. The mounted one did not look down for the longest time, for his gaze was held elsewhere, but in time Valam did come to look upon the face of Danyel' with dismay and admiration.

Chapter Thirty Four

"Oh my," gasped Brodst as he sank to one knee, "what have they done to you?" The boy, Jacob, had not misled him after all; his face was full of emotion as he looked upon the figure he knew to be Lord Serant. Serant seemed to be suffering from the same potion that Calyin was. Brodst knew he would have to find the others first, and since he had gone to the left and the right already, he went to the farthest reaches of the detention area, which turned both right and left. He opted for the left, and moved forward in that direction.

The path ended in darkness and Captain Brodst stopped cold. He hesitantly retraced his steps the other way. He almost thought he could hear voices and perhaps he did. He kept walking, crossing the place where one hall merged with another, veered left, and then stopped. "It is about time, you old fool!" yelled a vaguely familiar voice as Brodst approached a closed door. He craned his neck, facing his ear towards the barred viewing area in the door while he was also attempting to peer into the partially shadowed cell.

"I could smell you coming down the hall. Pig snouts again?"

"Move from the shadows so that I may see your face," retorted Brodst. A long pause followed, and then almost at once two faces turned towards the light of the entrance. "In the name of the Father," sighed one of the occupants. The two would have moved closer to the door except that they were shackled about the hands and feet.

Brodst sorted through keys, searching until he found one that worked. His jaw dropped as he entered the room and took a closer look at the two faces. "Lord Geoffrey, who is this man?" From down the hall another voice cried out. "Keeper, is that you?" Brodst asked almost in a whisper.

"Questions, questions, get us out of these cuffs first. My hands ache, my feet hurt—"

"It is you, isn't it, but how? How and why?" questioned Brodst, his voice rising and then faltering. He tried all the keys on his ring, gasping as each did not fit, coming at last to the final one, which also failed. "The guard, the guard—" spoke a little voice in his mind. He had never searched the guard. He ran out of the cell without explaining anything, running until he came to the fallen figure. He quickly stripped the boots and pants off the guard, finding in the process a short dagger and a leather pouch. A search of the shirt and outer robe revealed a tiny black bottle and, thankfully, a set of keys.

On his way back, just before he turned left, a voice came to him, full and beautiful, causing him to lurch to a halt in mid-gait, and it drew him towards it. The darkness would not stop him this time. He turned back to retrieve a lamp only to find that it was fixed to the wall. A quick investigation of it showed that it burned oil, quite cleanly overall. He ripped the pants he had just acquired into two large pieces, wrapping one piece around the top of a short knife and then dousing it in the oil as best he could, using the flame to light it.

"Hello?" he called out as he wandered through the empty corridor, "Hello?" He came to a door similar to the one he had stood by earlier. As he stared beyond the path of his makeshift light, he caught the reflection of two eyes looking at him. He moved closer and saw the outline of a face in the pale, orange-red light. He saw traces of dark, flowing hair and high, pale cheekbones.

Again he couldn't open the cell quickly enough to satisfy himself, and he cursed under his breath until he found the right key. He was half way to the one with eyes with a soft glitter in them, arms spread wide for an embrace, when he realized there was another present.

"You may proceed. We are old friends, she and I," spoke a soft, raspy voice. In the odd light of the torch, the speaker appeared to be bathed in luminescent gold. Brodst looked on in bewilderment. "I will not harm you. You needn't think that—"

And then Brodst recalled the others who were still awaiting his return. He bade the two to follow him quickly. The keys to the manacles were among the set he had found on the guard. They did not waste words or time now, moving first to retrieve Lord Serant and Calyin. The captain wasn't the only one taking notice of their two new companions. Geoffrey's face turned ashen and Midori's went wide with wonder.

Serant was still groggy, shifting in and out of consciousness, yet he was still faring better than Calyin. Before they could discuss a plan of action, everyone began talking at once. It was obvious they would not be able to proceed without clearing the air. The loud noise was having a deep effect on the two unconscious ones as well. In their heads, the clamor sounded like the roar of immense beasts. It was all they could do to keep the noises out.

"I think we should first discuss our escape," spoke the Keeper, being of more precise mind than his fellows. "We will have plenty of time later, I hope. My good captain, can you lead us out of this wretched place?"

"I believe I can, Keeper, but I, too, am curious now. The more I dwell on your face and that of, of—"

"I am, Ayrian, Lord of the Gray Clan."

"You need say no more, my friend," interrupted Midori, "he is a friend and that is all you need to know. He is an old and very dear friend."

"Thank you, but as long as we shall proceed with a telling, then it is time that I spoke the thoughts and deeds of my heart. Once there was a powerful clan. We dwelled among the hills and dales, gliding over pleasant valleys, drinking of golden waters in the high places among the mountains. I could soar and circle the skies in that place lazily for the remainder of my years. But alas, it is gone, and I, I alone am the last of my race, once proud and true of heart." Ayrian spoke so eloquently that they were able to envision the place and the people that he spoke of. In a softer light, his feathers, talons and beak, though still odd, did not appear so out of place. And the more he spoke, the further the listeners were drawn into his plight, a plight that had carried through times ancient and distant, but they now understood. He continued to speak richly in a flowing, exuberant manner. Much later, those present would reflect that perhaps it was a song that Ayrian sang to them, rather than speaking. Time seemed to flow on the edge of his words. In reality, when he finished only a few precious minutes had slipped by. "Alas, I am the last. I am Ayrian, Eagle Lord of the Gray Clan, when once there were tens of such clans. But our reign was supreme and revered. It is all gone now, faded from the most distant memories."

"Not entirely so," replied the Keeper with tears in his eyes. "I am Keeper Martin, head of the council of the Keepers of the Lore. Your tales, though remote, still lie among the histories in the Great Book though in truth they occupy but a few paragraphs of a single page. Perhaps with your help we can build upon it and make the lesson whole."

"Alas, dear Keeper, the tale is old and spent. The timing is not right."

"I would still like very much to hear your tales at length at a further date," Keeper Martin said.

"Yours is the tale we would wish to hear, Keeper Martin. How in the name of the Great-Father did you come to be here? Here, of all the forsaken corners—"

Geoffrey interrupted before Keeper Martin spoke, and the keeper nodded his approval at Geoffrey's intent. "He and Father Jacob sensed the changes occurring in the kingdom. Our messages had been conveyed to them, but it had been too late to return. The journey had already begun—"

"Yes," began Martin stepping into the conversation, "we were desperate. We saw the images in the dream messages. We knew King Andrew had passed though we did not want to accept it. Strange storms were upon us, the lands were growing cold and icy, our stocks were almost depleted—I had no choice but to attempt what had seemed a fool's gambit. Father Jacob did not want to let me go, but as days passed, we had little else we could do. And now I have been here so long that I cannot even recount the days—weeks, days, or months, I am not entirely sure, but I am sure that if those that I left behind did not get food and supplies, they have all perished."

"Perished? Surely they cannot all have died?" begged Brodst, "What of Prince Valam? You have said nothing of him. With all those ships, could you not return?"

"I do not know. During the journey some ships were lost. I am afraid that Prince Valam's was one of them."

A shocked silence came over them, but it was Midori who spoke first. "Are you certain?" she asked quizzically "I feel no sense of loss." If it had been another that spoke those words, those present would have thought them shallow or ill witted, but Midori was different. She was of the Mother, and the Mother knew all.

Everyone let the conjecture fall away, switching at once to other thoughts. "Keeper, how did you come to be here? You still have not told us," asked Captain Brodst.

"I attempted to use the device that rests in the council chambers of the keepers. My resolve was fixed, and in my desperation I saw no other solution. If I could have just managed to teleport back, all would have proven to my benefit, but something went wrong. I do not know what; I can only surmise. But to be truthful, I will need to ponder this more fully. The last thing I know completely is that I prepared my thoughts, cleansing my mind for a dream message. Instead of directing them as I normally would, I focused on the council—more specifically, the device."

Keeper Martin paused hesitantly, surveying the faces around him, "Imagine my elation when it worked. Even in my dreams I could feel the sense of intense cold and sudden darkness around me. I awoke hours later only to find myself here, already in chains, and with the End Man's whip upon me. I can only offer a calculation as to where here is. Perhaps Geoffrey knows better than I?"

Geoffrey shrugged his shoulders, but he was not alone in not knowing exactly where they had been taken. The memory of their arrival to this place was fogged over. As they all considered it, this seemed strange. Midori turned to check on Calyin and Serant. They still needed more time for their bodies and minds to cleanse themselves.

"You, friend, still have not told us how you came to be here," asked Captain Brodst pointedly of Ayrian.

"Not unlike Keeper Martin or any of you, I do not fully know how I came upon this place. It seems to draw you, though, doesn't it? Its power is almost beautiful it is so pure."

"What do you know? You speak as though this were a great spectacle, while I see nothing of the kind. What do you know? Tell me!"

"Captain, you needn't speak harshly. We are all friends here; the enemy is out there," said Midori, pointing her finger. She glared at him until he lowered his eyes and his temperament calmed.

"More often than not, those seeking find and those that don't learn. Perhaps if you had the mind, you would guess, but then again, maybe not."

"Why are you being cryptic?" bluntly asked Brodst again.

"Captain—"

"No, it is all right, but if I must do the telling, then it will be away from here and under circumstances fairer than these." Ayrian spoke slowly and plucked a ring of keys from Captain Brodst's pocket. He held each up for examination and while he did so, he began mumbling. "Seven could not bind him, though they tried, behind door and key. The last had been consorted and fashioned with powers as old as the winds; still they could not stay time. Its slow gentle creep was upon them. Extra restraints kept his confederates. Even near the end, they leashed his most beloved for at least a short span. The course has run full again, yet it is a different tale, is it not? That he would be she, and she with he, would still be free."

"Ayrian? Ayrian?" called out Midori at first gently and then harshly, "Ayrian?"

Ayrian continued on for a short time, "—that that of the end should now try to be that of the beginning. The wonder of it, even if it had been wrong."

Brodst was as slow to turn away from Ayrian's words as Ayrian had been. Lord Serant was somewhat coherent and could walk with some assistance under his own power although Calyin would still have to be carried. Geoffrey shouldered the burden of Calyin, while Martin and Brodst helped Lord Serant, but it was Ayrian who led the way from the detention area with much confidence.

Chapter Thirty Five

The morning air was still and fresh. With it, there was a certain liveliness in the camp, an eagerness to be off, to find what was ahead. Adrina, though she had been the last to awake, was the first to rise to the saddle. She shook off the shadowy images that had been invading her sleep and pondered pleasant thoughts. Among the trees she could hear the scampering of small animals and the gallant trumpet call of a few tiny birds whose name she did not know.

A light cloud cover at first obscured an otherwise pristine morning, but in the first hours of the new day it burned away, revealing a clear cloudless sky. The hills they galloped through shifted from a gradual rolling grade to a steep vaulted pitch as they neared the mountains, and they leveled off to what was perhaps a plateau or mountain plains. Tall peaks loomed up, screaming their presence into the very air. From the slopes at the bottom, the view was dazzling.

They rode smoothly, coming to an abrupt halt almost too soon. The winds had just picked up, bringing in the scents of the highlands, a mixture of aromas. Simple stands of trees dotted the mountainsides, mostly of pine or evergreen. Waters of a stream that flowed from an unseen lake down across the plateau now ran swiftly, thanks to the previous night's precipitation. There was also a hint of grasses that had once been tall and proud hidden now beneath this season's early snows. Guarded walls stood before them; the journey was at an end.

Underneath the parapets the gatehouse stood, its outer portcullis raised and unhindering. A line of thirteen horses forming two columns rode into its confines, reaching the inner gate, which sat low. The gatehouse stretched a full sixty feet between the thick avenues of the wall. A set of malignant chains hung lifeless, attached to a wheel on the far side of the house.

They looked up to the small cavities set into the floor of the roof, which in truth formed the floor of the second level. Then they looked beyond the gate into the heart of a city that most would never see or know. The spires of a great palace, perhaps a castle, dominated the village. Around it in many clusters were domiciles small and large—inns; bars and keeps; shops of various assortments, some with small signs suspended over their doors; and many others, too numerous to be named.

Access was made possible by a winding of the heavy chains round the wheel. There were no heralds to greet them this day, and for the most part the city appeared to be silent. Still, the day was young, but not altogether so. Amir was the most agitated by the lull. He flexed and huffed, mostly to himself, yet also with Noman's watchful eye upon him. Nijal and Shchander talked in sullen tones between themselves.

Xith searched through his bags for something he couldn't quite find, touching his hands at long last to a silver flask and retrieving it happily. Before they continued, he gave it to Adrina.

Most noticeably befuddled over the absence of life in the city was Noman. He did not know how he could have been wrong. He had seen the path's end so vividly. It was time, and this was definitely the place. A gnawing emptiness drew him. Step by step and almost in a daze, he went across the city that was spread out before him like a hearty feast, moving toward a central place where he knew a square lay.

The market was empty and mostly cleared. A few vacant stalls pockmarked its otherwise clean face. The group stopped here and dismounted. Dust swirled around their feet as they did so. Noman conferred with Xith and Amir before continuing on, leading their horses across the square to a long, winding stair. This new section of the city was perhaps more ancient than that surrounding it, more elegant than the latter.

As they crossed, a parapet with merlons kept them from the innermost area. They passed easily through gate-like breaches at the ground level. Beyond stood a palisade. Its walks showed its age, but all in all it was preserved well.

The inner keep, a fortress with numerous lofty spires, had no outer moat, which Amir counted odd since he vividly recalled one. All things change with time, he thought. Its stones were weathered and scarred, but this marring in no way detracted from the sudden impact of its grandeur. Remnants of a path followed towards the immense prominence, which was the outer door, two great timbers of dark wood with iron bands.

Their horses were left on their own; within the set of walls, they could not wander far. The company proceeded up the path by foot. The walk across broken bridges made them uneasy, and hands edged toward sword hilts, but none took note of it. They tugged on the rope on the entry to the right, but nothing happened. A second attempt on the left, followed by sending a strong rapping with the metal knocker set into the doors also brought no results. It was a small push that caused the doors to open, and they swung easily inward on vast, silent hinges.

Adrina controlled the smile upon her lips and stepped aside so Noman could go in first, followed by Amir. Noman quickly opened the doors wide to let in some fresh air, for the air inside was thick and stale. A long hall was revealed and though lines of torches adorned its walls, none were lit.

With several torches in hand, they entered. The corridors they came upon, turning neither left nor right, were quiet and clean but unoccupied. A faint clicking noise began, rumbling low from beneath their feet, growing in volume the deeper they delved. As the noise became more audible, it sounded like the tapping of a long wooden shaft against the hard stone, and it was almost precisely timed with their footsteps.

As they chanced upon and crossed an open courtyard, they looked upward toward the walks set into the outer walls. The tapping sound was louder here and seemed to emanate from above or around them rather than beneath them. A large fountain sat silently brooding in the middle of the courtyard. A greenish quagmire now rested where crystalline waters had once run and every now and again something within the slime gurgled and churned. The group steered wide of the fountain.

Amir turned mid-stride on his heels, whirling his eyes upward, glaring. He had almost expected to hear trumpets blazing forth in herald from atop the cornermost tower. As he turned and stopped, he smacked into Adrina, who was suddenly shaken from her thoughts. He rested his hand upon her shoulder as he whispered his apology. Still, though, he had felt a presence from the tower.

He stood poised for a time regarding the edifice, a leering tower of dark stone. Puzzled, he gawked at it for an extra few seconds before he turned away. Noman followed Amir's line of sight, moving from blackened window to blackened window until he reached the summit, and then suddenly his eyes came to rest on a window three rows down and one to the right. He wasn't sure if it were the sunlight playing tricks through the open tower or if he actually saw the shadow of a figure standing there watching them. A sudden shiver came over Noman, bringing a line of goose bumps up his back, rising from the tip of his spine to the back of his neck. He forced himself to look away. Xith smiled.

The shadow was gone when Noman turned to look back; only the light of the sun's rays remained to play along the face of the tower. They continued on, stopping and starting, not realizing that a veil of silence had come over them. After a deliberate pause at the top of a stair opposite their entrance, they returned indoors.

Adrina watched the others pass through the doorway, but she lingered a moment in the sunlight, bathing in its warmth. She sighed deeply and then followed the others. A hand reaching out grabbing hers, startling her. Her heart raced and then slowed, a sudden glow touched her face, falling as her chin dropped down. She met a pair of eyes, liquid blue, and shining like newborn stars. The face that swathed the eyes was equally as warm and inviting.

Xith watched Adrina go, fading into the realm of dreams and shadows, saddened like a father losing his little girl, though no one else knew. He was now the last one, walking along a hall that stretched out in front of him, seemingly without conclusion. He perceived movement behind him and spun about.

At first he greeted those behind him with warmth even though he knew of their treachery. The one he fixed on stood with head poised proudly, leaning his weight upon a thick staff. His face was badly beaten on the right side, causing that entire side to hang listlessly. He stared at Xith through eyes that were scarcely open.

"He will no longer let you in, and you cannot hope to find the door. That is a pity," spoke Xith coldly.

"I no longer require permission to enter. I come and go as I please."

"Then why do you walk these halls without purpose?"

"I was waiting for you, dear friend, and now I shall have everything I ever wanted."

"You are keeping the secret from even him, aren't you? That is heroic, but you are still a subversive fool. He will find a way into your mind. You cannot hope to trick him."

"It is not heroism, I assure you. It is the one thing he wants, even more than your knowledge of the arcane arts. And do you know what is so exquisitely simple about all this? He doesn't even know that I could give him the key if he would only ask."

"And just what do you seek in return? Will you stand at his side and act as his right hand?"

"I want nothing so basic. I want to be both his hands."

"You, Talem, are the naive one. He will use you until you are spent and then he will cast you away. You are nothing—do not forget that."

"No, I will give him the two things he wants most, and I will give him you also."

Xith stepped away angrily, casting aside the bag he carried. A quick glance to the rear showed him that the others still walked the path without end. He wondered how far they would go before they realized the truth of the illusion. Surely, he thought, Noman would guess it.

"We shall end this here and now—you and me. I shall let you corrupt all that you touch no more."

"They will not allow it," said Talem, indicating the robed figures around him.

"You were once the most promising. I should have known the truth of your ways, but I would not believe them. They told me the same about him, but I still have hope."

Talem roared with laughter, "You are spent. Give up now, and I promise that when the time comes, your pain will be swift."

Xith raised a warning hand, "Do not make promises you cannot keep." Xith spun his hand before his face, preparing to release the energies he had been drawing within him over the past few minutes.

"Don't!"

"Don't what? This?" replied Xith spinning a ball of fire from his hands, "I know you, Talem; your magic is not real. Mine, on the other hand, is. We will end this now! You shall not leave this sanctuary with life yet coursing through your veins. I promise you."

Talem cringed as flames sparked around his shield wall. The heat of the fire brought tiny bursts of perspiration to his brow. Talem's followers rebuked with fires of their own, bombarding Xith time after time. Even under the strain, Xith didn't wipe the smile from his lips. He wore it broadly, proving his strength.

"I have been savoring this spell for some time. I think you will like it," Xith said menacingly. He crossed his hand before him in a line and then formed a fist. Talem mocked him as nothing happened; the magic just seemed to fade away. Xith returned his scorn with equal generosity.

The stones beneath Talem's feet began to bow and warp. A din filled the air, a rasping, popping, cracking sound. A crack appeared, minute at first, and then the floor rent and broke. Talem fell clawing and grasping at the wall behind him, clutching to the edge just before he was swallowed by the hole. His eyes went wide as he watched his staff drop into the abyss.

Xith didn't have time for a second attack; he had to make an immediate counter. He gulped air as he restored the shield wall around him, wincing from the slight searing he had received. He looked away from Talem as he was scrambling to return to his feet, toward the source of his lament. He stared at each, trying to delve beyond their eyes and into their thoughts.

He knew Talem well enough to know his magicians were all frauds, having acquired their skills just as their master did. Which has the shield, he thought to himself, and would it be a ring, book, staff or maybe even a medallion? He knew the magicks of old better than most. He dreaded the thought of times he had assisted in their delivery to this place.

Seven, he considered to himself. Talem always had been superstitious. Xith eyed the second figure on the right evilly, glaring as he released a surge of energy. A blue-white ball streaked across the hall from his fingertip, enshrouding the other. He heard a barely audible whimper as the other was incinerated.

His assumption had been right. The barrier shield fell, and he began to take the others out one by one. They began running wildly about, trying to escape. Two fell into the hole that was still spreading about their feet, and the remainder Xith delivered quickly. Without a defense, they were felled easily. At the last, he felt compassion for them.

Xith's eyes crossed, and he groped for his back. A sharp pain had suddenly overcome him. He whirled around to see Talem standing behind him with a bloody dagger in his hand. Everything began spinning; and as he looked up, the ceiling was circling about him.

"The edge was poisoned—so sad, I had really wanted to have you as a prize. But before you go, I shall have your secrets. Tell me the place, Xith, and maybe I can save you. You can live. Isn't that what you want? Where is it?"

Xith bade Talem to draw closer as he began to whisper shallowly. Fixated on Xith and the desire for knowledge, Talem came closer and closer. "I will tell you," whispered Xith. "Come here." Xith edged backwards as he bade Talem to move forward, and as Talem hunched down to listen, Xith grabbed him about the collar and the throat, jerking him forward as hard as he could. Xith sidestepped and as Talem flailed at the air, trying to grab onto him, he kicked him in the face, and then both men fell. Talem's eyes were wild and staring. Xith saw huge balls of white with black pupils disappear into the emptiness below him. Talem's screams were also wild and horrible. He could not believe that he was about to die.

Xith, on the other hand, accepted it. He did not turn about or flail but instead counted the last moments of his life, knowing how precious each and every last breath was. He knew how important every last conscious thought was, and he was glad. He knew Adrina would be safe.

He waited, but he suddenly realized that he had not died. He was not even moving. He turned to look about, and his body was sprawled out on the floor at the very edge of the culvert. He began to wonder what the poison was doing to him. He was numb, but he did not appear to be dying, and he wondered if it were some trick of

Talem's, perhaps his last. Xith closed his eyes momentarily, clasping his hands together, and then, although he couldn't seem to bring his hands or feet to movement, he could still turn his head, and he did, turning his eyes outward, into the courtyard where he saw Adrina entering the path without end.

"Say nothing. Let them go," the voice told her. "They will not miss you, I am sure."

Adrina watched lips move, but she was drawn to the eyes, and the beckoning hand that told her to follow was just an image tucked far into the most obscure corner of her vision. She did so only because a hand returned to her own and coerced her decision.

"Do not fight it, let me in. I will do you no harm. I see he is in your dreams now. Do you have the strength to cast him away or will he sweep you away as he did the other? I wonder—would you allow me to follow?"

"Will he win?" asked Adrina.

"Only if you let him."

Adrina screwed her face up tight, as if she were just suddenly realizing a thing she had been trying hard to remember. "Where have they all gone?"

"Do not worry about them. They are gone so that you may be safe. You will rest here now till it is time. You are safe, my fair princess. Leave the world of cares behind and stay here as long as you like. You have made a wise and good choice."

As the other recommended, Adrina twirled around; and as the fading images of the outside world slowed, everything turned bright and luxurious. She shivered as a light spray of water touched her face. The fountain enclosure was in full bloom, as was the garden around her. A soft rapping noise filtered into her ears, coming from the four corners of the walls behind her, circling from west to east.

Adrina grew sad and listless. Her chin drooped again and emotions swelled up in her eyes. A gripping emptiness gnawed at her heart. She felt suddenly alone as if she had lost all that she cared for. Her lower lip began to tremble and she bit at it to get it to stop, but it wouldn't. At first only a solitary tear found its way down her cheek, rolling across her chin to her neck, but soon the anguish flourished. She wrapped her arms around herself to quell it, but that only caused the trembling to spread. She kneeled to the ground, lowering her head in heavy, almost mournful sobs.

"You have taken the first step and won; there is nothing to be sad about."

"But," began Adrina, "I think I will miss them." Her face was flushed deep red and her eyes were swollen and misty. She sniffled and pulled at her lip.

"Remember, I am here with you; I will not go, so you are not alone. We will walk together for a time, you and me. The next step will not be so easy, and progressively so, but we have time now, so rest, rest well."

Adrina's tears subsided, and although she still sat idle, she no longer felt alone. "Here, I think this is for you," she said, handing the other a small round object. Her thoughts began to wander back to happier, distant times and her mood lightened. After coming to her feet, she cupped her hands together and partook of the cool waters of the fountain. The water was sweet and satisfying as it passed her lips.

Overhead the sun was shifting from its apex, meandering west, and in time it came to touch the horizon, bringing with it an end to the day. Adrina watched it from time to time, sifting back and forth through her thoughts. Many faces crossed before the windows of her mind, some weathered and faded, some new and fresh. As the first shades of night arrived, Adrina found her happiness and a sense of peace. The future was no longer dark and uncertain. She was safe in this place. *Wasn't she?*

Chapter Thirty Six

With the help of the Ayrian's keen sense of direction, Captain Brodst, Calyin, and the others made their way out of the detention area. Ayrian and Captain Brodst quickly dispatched the few guards they encountered along the way. Soon they were all in the wide open chamber with the falls and warm pool where Captain Brodst had spent many long days and nights. They paused to plan their next steps and to examine the gear collected from the guards. Captain Brodst distributed helmets and armor. Geoffrey made sure each had a blade.

Keeper Martin took inventory of another type. He studied their wounds and maladies. Edwar Serant and Calyin Alder were recovering from the drink they'd been giving but were still groggy. Ayrian had deep gouges on his wrists and ankles where he had been shackled. He maintained a length of the shackle chains even now. Martin had seen its deadly effectiveness against the guards so he did not question the need for it; however, he did question the way Ayrian clung to it. He knew you chained a man to break his spirit and his will, but Ayrian did not seem broken, only angry.

Captain Brodst had scarcely taken his eyes off Midori since entering the pool room. For her part, she fussed over the wounds he had taken and the condition he was in. "What is it?" she whispered to him as he watched her work.

"Thinking of another life, another time," he replied. "If only—"

"If only what? I know what you are thinking. You had better think of the here and the now and not the could-have-beens."

Captain Brodst got a far-off look in his eyes. "I am a great fool," he whispered as he pulled away from her. He walked to where Geoffrey and Martin stood. Martin tended to Ayrian. Across the chamber, Calyin and Edwar Serant were enjoying a private moment. As he watched Calyin tend to her lord husband, he envied them.

It was a short while later as the group gathered at the basin of the pool that the one who had been in Geoffrey's cell approached them from out of the shadows. "Do you want to know the truth of your capture?" the other asked as he approached.

Recognizing the voice, Geoffrey stayed the captain's sword arm. "It is you," he said, "I had all but forgotten."

The other proffered the blade the guard had given the two so they could kill each other. Geoffrey did not take it.

"I do not hold you as an enemy," Geoffrey said.

"You should," the other said, "I am Ærühn, Dragon Man of the Stone Shields."

Geoffrey took in the full sight of Ærühn for the first time. Long black hair hung from the Dragon Man's head in dozens of thin braids. His forehead sloped back at a sharp angle and his flat nose made his thin-set eyes seem enormous round globes. The way the eyes bulged from their sockets reminded Geoffrey of the dragon lizards of the north whose eyes could follow you wherever you went without requiring the lizard to turn its head. "Ærühn, if you are the enemy of my enemy, can we not be friends?"

"It is no time to speak of such before you know the truth of where you are and why you are here."

Ayrian cocked his head a full half circle as only a bird or bird man could do. He probed the distance with his eyes, looking to the rope ladders that reached up to the sky from either side of the falls. He tightened his grip on the chain in his hands. "Find cover; they come. The door will open soon," he whispered, his beak clicking as he spoke.

"How many?" asked Brodst.

"Three, I hear three. There is another, but he does not come with the others."

"It's not the changing of the guards," Brodst said, "They send a full compliment of twelve at the change."

Lord Serant's eyes went to the rope ladders on either side of the falls. "Surely, there is another way out of this hole. I don't remember climbing when I was taken to the audience with the High Lord."

"Belajl Entreatte spoke to you?" Ærühn asked, looking as if he suddenly had a different opinion of Edwar Serant.

"Quickly, quickly," Ayrian said, interrupting.

Without a further word passing between them, Captain Brodst, Lord Serant and Geoffrey took up positions beside the ladders. Martin, Midori, and Calyin slipped away into a dark corner of the room. Ayrian took flight, delight reflected in his eyes as he stretched his wings and felt freedom for the first time in what seemed ages. He flew to a small recess in the wall beside a small door of stone, crawling into the hole and disappearing from sight. Using his bare hands and feet, Ærühn climbed the wall.

The way he moved reminded Captain Brodst of the way spiders crawled along a wall. His eyes fell upon the doors on high. He watched as both swung open, gesturing to Geoffrey and Lord Serant as he looked on. Be ready, he indicated wordlessly.

Two guards, one on each rope ladder, worked their way down to the pool room. As the guards reached the bottom of the rope, Captain Brodst, Lord Serant and Geoffrey set upon them. High above, Ayrian made his way through one of the open doors and Ærühn made his way through the other.

The melee was over quickly. Captain Brodst and Lord Serant gave no mercy. Above it was much the same: Ayrian and Ærühn found only fury in their hearts. Soon they were all up the rope ladders and running down the long hall to what they hoped was freedom. Freedom that seemed an eternity in the coming.

✼ ✼ ✼

Safe. Was she safe? The words echoed in her ears. As she questioned the world around her, the path split and reality sped inward.

As the images of the fountain enclosure and the garden faded, the voice called out to her. "You should have waited, Adrina Alder. We could have walked together until it was time."

"Time for what?"

No answer came as Adrina faced stark reality. She could see someone or something lying on the ground across the open courtyard. As she got closer, she saw it was Xith. He was on his back, his eyes open wide, staring up at the heavens. She shook him until he roused to conscious thought.

"Talem," Xith said, "The dark priest. Is he?"

"There is no one else," Adrina said.

Xith sat up. "Adrina? We must hurry; we must find the others."

Adrina helped the shaman to his feet. "This place—what is it?" she asked.

"It is the path without end." Xith turned his eyes away from her, surveying the courtyard. "A magical enchantment to protect the way.

It keeps out intruders, trapping them in a world between reality and dream. Only the chosen or the knowing can get past the path. Talem and his followers never got past the path though they learned to escape its grip and to navigate the between."

"Talem?"

Xith turned back to her. "What did you find in the path, Adrina?"

"The blue eyes, the voice. He told me I could walk with him. That I was safe. Would I have been safe?"

Xith gripped her forearms and looked directly at her. "No, Adrina. You were not safe in that place. Come, quickly now," he said leading her across the open courtyard into the tower of dark stone.

Xith and Adrina came upon Nijal and Shchander first. The two stood stock-still like statues. Both men's mouths were open as if they'd been talking between themselves when the path had taken them.

Xith called out to them, using the commanding power of voice, "Find the question in your mind. Ask it and you shall be free."

"But how can I?" Nijal was asking Shchander as he returned to the present.

Shchander started to reply but found himself at a loss for words as he stared past Xith to his men, still frozen.

"Quickly now," Xith said, "I'll explain everything as soon as I am able."

Xith helped Shalimar and the six remaining members of Shchander's men find their way beyond the path. Farther along the long central hall of the tower, Adrina found Amir and Noman. "Amir, Noman," she shouted, pointing to the two.

Within moments, Amir and Noman were free of the path as

well. Noman's eyes were wide with alarm as he turned to Xith. "Shadows," he gasped. "We've been battling shadows for what seems like days."

Noman took a step and nearly fell to his knees as fatigue overcame him. "Amir," he whispered. "Save him."

It was then that Adrina noted that Amir actually wasn't free. He will still frozen in place. Xith turned to Adrina and the others. "Take Noman from this place. Go to the courtyard. Wait there for my return. Do not return to the tower lest the path take you again."

Xith raised his hands over his head, spoke a word of power and entered the path. The realm he found was nothing like he expected. He knew instantly he was within the gates of the dark realm where the Fourth and his minions had been bound.

"I am here," Xith called out to the watchers in waiting. "Isn't this what you wanted?"

Movement ahead in the distance caught his eye. He ran. As he mounted a towering rock, he saw Amir. He closed his eyes, sucked at the air. "Great Father, give me strength," he implored.

Amir wielded two blades with deadly accuracy. He attacked and spun, around and around, countering and blocking the horde of shadow wraiths that surrounded and sought to overcome him. If Amir could see what Xith saw from atop the rocky precipice he would have closed his eyes, sucked at the air and begged the Great Father for strength as well. The mass of wraiths spread out in all directions as far as Xith could see, seemingly without end. Overhead floated ranks of wraiths whose arms did not end in hands but enormous rounded blades—scimitars—and who floated in the air as if with unseen wings.

Across the valley on a towering rock stood a figure who wore the bones of a ram as a headdress upon his cloaked head and whose armor was studded with the white and black ivory tusks of some great and mighty beasts. The figure turned now and Xith was sure the other saw him, also sure that the other was the Shadow Warrior King of old, a minion of the Dark Lord. He no longer had doubt in his heart that this was the place, that he was within the gates, that the Fourth himself was near.

He set into the battle, calling lightning to his hands as he did so. He used the lightning to clear a wide swath through the wraiths and reach Amir's side. "It is good to see you," grunted Amir as he fought. Xith answered by casting a blue white ball of fire from either hand as he sought to create a protective shield around them.

The shield failed almost as soon as he enacted it. There were simply too many enemies to hold at bay with the shield; so instead of trying to hold off all enemies, he directed the shield overhead and selectively behind them. His hope was to keep those overhead from descending and engaging, and to keep both of them from getting stabbed in the back.

As soon as he enacted the shield, he turned his attention to the wraiths, unleashing wave after wave of lightning and fire upon them, clearing paths long into the distance each time he did this. Amir fought gallantly beside him, his sword equally as deadly as Xith's magic. For every one of the wraiths they struck down, another took its place and there was no end in sight. The horde spread across the dark land as far as they could see.

"There is no hope in this," Xith cried out as he called forth the rock and stone of the land and rained it down upon the wraiths.

"There is hope," Amir shot back.

"There is indeed hope," Noman said, appearing suddenly next to

Amir. "Our presence is what caused this. The Dark Lord has many at his call. Quickly now, we must leave this place."

"No," Amir protested. "The gates are open and the keeper is gone."

"Not true," Noman said, lowering his cloak to reveal the form of the princess whose face was frozen in a wide-eyed expression, "I bring the key."

Xith angrily cast a wall of fire from his hands, sending back a sudden frenzied push from the wraiths. "We discussed this; there is another way. The boy. We agreed. The boy."

"The other is a boy no longer. You yourself said this." Noman turned around, swept his hands in a great circle, sending an arc of searing white light into the mass behind them. A swath of wraiths dozens wide and several dozen deep winked out of existence. He turned to Adrina. "Without fear," he told her as he touched her forehead. "Call him forth."

✳ ✳ ✳

Outside the command tent, Prince Valam walked the long line of captains and lieutenants. He stopped at the line of crossed swords symbolizing the leaders lost in the battle. The first marker was for Captain Eran of the long swordsmen. He cast a sidelong look at the mustered ranks, knowing in his heart the pomp and ceremony was necessary to restore faith and order.

Captain Vadan Evgej, who had walked silently at the prince's side, spoke quietly to the prince. The two then walked to where the long swordsmen were mustered. At the fore of the ranks were the masters of the sword, behind them the swordsmen, and further back those few of the sword apprentices that remained. He granted field promotions to three of the swordmasters, but it was Ylsa Heman, on behalf of her fallen brother Eran, who gave each their insignia of rank and office. Eddrick Reassae, Nobel Jrenn, and Seran Hindell stood proud and accepted the promotions graciously. As they were all from some of the kingdom's oldest Great Houses, Valam did not doubt that they would serve well in their new offices as lieutenants.

Before he turned away, Valam regarded Ylsa. He put his hand on her shoulder. Her archers had performed many a miracle on the field. "Captain of the Fourth Order Ylsa Heman," he told her as he directed her to the ranks of her bowmen. Several of the squires of the bow, ahorse at the back of her lines, let out a whoop. Valam grinned, saying nothing of the breaking of the attention order.

The mood was not as good among the decimated ranks of lancers and pikemen that had been led by Willam the Black. Willam was the first of the kingdom lieutenants to fall. While he had taken many of the enemy with him, his men had not fared well after the loss and had succumbed to a blood fury, charging relentlessly into the heart of the enemy until there were but few left of their original company.

Valam eyed the lone squire of the lance at the back of the ranks and called the young lad forth. The squire, no older than Valam himself, had a bold, wild look in his eye—a look that said he feared nothing and no one. "What is your name?" Valam asked the squire.

"I am Michal Klaive," the squire said.

Surprised to find a nobleman's son in the rank of squire, Valam asked, "Rudden Klaive?"

"I am my father's namesake," Michal returned boldly. "Rudden is my brother."

"And why are you a squire in my company when your house title gives you the rank of lancer by right?"

"My father says a man must work his way from nothing to something."

Captain Vadan Evgej's eyes showed his surprise at the bold tongue of the squire, but Prince Valam's face gave no hint of what he was thinking.

"Kneel," Valam commanded as he withdrew his sword from its sheath.

Michal looked to Vadan Evgej as if beseeching the other to intercede on his behalf. "Kneel," growled Vadan.

Michal knelt quickly. His eyes said he was wary of what Valam intended to do with the sword. As Valam raised his sword, Michal closed his eyes. Valam touched his sword to Michal's right and left shoulder.

"What is your preferred weapon?" Valam asked as he brought his sword to the top of Michal's head.

"The great lance," Michal called out, his eyes still closed.

"Then rise true, sir knight, and from this day henceforth be known as Knight of the Lance. You are a First Lance now and a knight, no more an apprentice. Do you understand?"

Michal nodded solemn understanding of everything that went with the title.

Valam turned his eyes to the short line of lancers who stood their mounts, asking "Who among you shall I name lancemaster?" Without waiting for a response he turned to the line of pikemen, asking "Who among you shall I name pikemaster?"

Not one of the lancers or pikemen said a word. Valam turned to Michal and asked the questions of the newly named knight. Michal offered no response. "Very well, then," Valam said turning on his heel to face the lines. "One and all, it shall be," and upon the saying a cheer went up from the ranks all around the lancers and pikemen. No few of the kingdomers knew of the deeds of Willam's men on the field, and no few held back their cheers.

"Captain Danyel'," Valam called out. The former lieutenant rushed to the prince's side from the fore of his lines, a new light in his eyes at the sudden appointment. "These men become part of your ranks now. Treat them as befits their great skill and courage; treat them as masters of the lance and pike. All save this one," he said turning to Michal.

"Captain S'tryil," Valam called out. The captain stepped out of the lines and joined the prince. "I trust you've a position of honor for a First Lance."

"I do indeed, my lord prince," Captain S'tryil said, bowing his head in formal fashion as the hour of ceremony required.

Valam addressed Danyel' and S'tryil's lines next, each in turn, before he announced the field promotions of Pavil and Redcliff to the rank of Captain of the Fourth Order. The new captains were then in turn given permission to promote within their lines.

New sergeants and lieutenants were appointed throughout the kingdom lines. Bow apprentices became bowmen. Horse apprentices became knights. Lance apprentices became lancers. Pike apprentices became pikemen. Shield apprentices became shieldbearers. Sword apprentices became swordsmen. Masters of the bow, horse, lance, pike, shield, and sword were appointed as well.

Before the ceremony concluded, Captain Evgej and Captain Mikhal were named to the rank of Field Commander, a rank that put them at the same level as commanders in garrison and the king's own Knight Captains.

Chapter Thirty Seven

Inside the command tent, Father Jacob kept the official record of the day's events. Runners moving between the ranks and the tent kept him informed. When the ceremony was over, Prince Valam dismissed the men and entered the tent. Upon seeing the prince enter, Father Jacob looked up from his work, said graciously, "The first battle ends in victory, my prince. You've done well these past days and this day as well."

"It is but the first of many," Valam said, just before gulping down the glass of wine offered to him.

"It is," Jacob agreed. "You've your father's touch with the men. You are a just leader and have their respect."

"Do I truly, Father Jacob?"

Father Jacob didn't say anything for a moment as he finalized the scroll before him. He stood and opened the flap of the tent wide so Valam could look out to the field where the lines were yet maintained. As the two stepped out of the tent, a cheer went up from the ranks. "To the High Prince!" came the cry and the words were repeated over and over across the field.

The commanders in company joined in the cheers for a moment before calling the ranks to attention. Valam watched, a broad smile that was almost a grin fell away as he saw riders racing toward the company at full speed.

One of the riders reined in alongside Prince Valam. "It is as foretold. They come."

"How many?" Valam asked.

The rider's dapple gray courser started prancing and the rider fought to get the restless animal under control. "A host of thousands, many thousands. They come from the mountains along both passes."

"How long before they are upon us?"

"It seems they march for the forests and not the plains. On Rivenwood. The city will surely fall before nightfall."

Seth rushed out of one of the nearby tents. Brother Liyan and Tsandra of the Brown were close behind him as were several of the outriders who had just arrived from the field. "From Rivenwood to Avenwood," he said.

"This can't be," Valam cried out. "We've been so careful in our watch. We took the field. The next fight should be at their door."

Seth felt something, a presence overhead trying to reach out to him. He was about to cast his will to the wind and soar up into the heavens when he found the link. For the briefest moment, he felt Queen Mother's every emotion. He knew her anguish, her pain. He was her protector and she was his queen as it once had been.

Cagan knew Seth's thoughts the instant the red brother emerged from the link. He spoke his fears before Seth could say anything, "King Mark's battle fleet took Maru. The city burns. The fleet sails up the Gildway to lay siege to Leklorall."

"That is nearly the truth of it," Seth confirmed.

"But how?" Valam asked.

"Queen Mother begs of us to break camp. Sail with as many men and elves as we can to the east and Maru, and then up the

Gildway to Leklorall. The rest to march on Rivenwood through the gorge to Avenwood and on to Leklorall."

"Is there any hope in such?" asked Vadan Evgej.

Valam withdrew Truth Bringer from its sheath and raised the sword high into the air. "We'll be at the heels of King Mark's army the entire way. We can harry their every step. They will come to fear us. That is the full truth of it."

They filled what few ships remained with supplies, men, and elves. The ships set sail for the east as they broke camp. The command tent became the last vestige of the enormous camp. Not long after, it too was taken down and carefully packed away.

As they rode away from the camp, an idea came to Valam. He remembered the narrow rocky valley between Avenwood and Rivenwood. He urged his surefooted charger along, racing to catch up with Seth at the front of the lines. Captain Evgej and Captain Mikhal sped along at his side, their mounts as eager as his to find the wind.

"Tsandra, Teren," he called out as he passed the brother elves on his way to Seth. The two unquestioningly turned their mounts in line behind Valam and followed where the prince led.

When he reached the lead riders, Valam ordered the lines on foot and ahorse to turn due east, calling for the brothers of the Brown to break ranks and join his conference with Seth, Tsandra and Teren. He also called out for Captain Danyel', Captain Redcliff, and others. Soon there was a company of fifty or more around him.

A wind swirled, tugging at Valam's cloak as he sat the saddle. He spoke to the Tae brothers first, addressing Redcliff before addressing Danyel'. "I once asked you to defend the House of Alder against our enemies, to die in service if need be. You have proven yourself many times over beyond the training field, and you have no more debt to me than to the wind. Do we understand each other?"

The mountain of a man who once had been one of his father's best training masters straightened in the saddle but said nothing.

"Danyel', you have proven yourself on the field as well. It saddens me that I must ask of you."

Danyel', like his brother, sat stoically in the saddle. He too was a tower of a man with a height and girth eclipsing that of most.

"I know you both to be mountain men, and I trust to you a task that I would trust to no others. Danyel', you once spoke of a sudden slide of rock that closed the entrance to your valley home. You told me of how your people dug through the rock the whole of spring to free themselves by summer.

"I would ask you to use your skill with great axe and hammer to create slides of rock in the gorge connecting Avenwood and Rivenwood. Tsandra, Teren, and much of the Brown will go with you to guide you on your way. Let them help you. Do this thing in such a way that it is for all time."

"It will be as you ask, my prince," Redcliff replied. Without a further word, he, his brother, and the others rode off to the north, to Rivenwood.

Tsandra was the last to turn into the file. "My oath to you: as I live and breathe so shall they."

"Be well," Valam told her, and then he watched her ride away.

❋ ❋ ❋

Ærühn stood over the fallen, dismay and perhaps confusion reflected in his eyes as he looked upon them. His long hair hung down, covering his face in a blanket of braids and beads. He had taken their weapons, a flask of ale, several bags of water, what armor he could salvage. It was the spell woven upon them that he could sense but not see that troubled him. He could feel the same spell in the air all around him now that he searched for it.

Geoffrey grabbed the dragon man's arm. This was the fourth in a long series of rooms that they had come to. All the rooms had been occupied and they had had to fight their way through each. "We must move on," he told the dragon man.

Ærühn looked up at him as if through a haze. Strange as it seemed to him, he could see Geoffrey but not see him—if such a thing were possible. "Yes, of course," he answered reflexively, only now realizing that he spoke in dragon speech and the other spoke in the language of men and yet they both understood each other.

Geoffrey hurried to catch up with Captain Brodst and the others. Captain Brodst stood next to Midori, Calyin next to Lord Serant. Ayrian waited impatiently near the door, acting as look out. Keeper Martin spoke quietly. "Nothing is what you think it is," he was telling the others as Ærühn and Geoffrey joined the group. "Isn't that so?" he asked the dragon man.

Ærühn nodded but didn't understand.

"We were all brought to this place for a reason. There is an ancient power here. It drew us in as surely as the scent of a flower draws a bee. What we must try to understand is why?"

"No," interrupted Lord Serant. "What we must know is where we are. Somewhere in the Rift Range I suspect, perhaps the Endless Ice."

"I was getting to that," Martin said. "But first you must understand the why of it. I think I have the answer." He looked to the dragon man. "Has the truth of it come to you yet?"

"This place makes us see what we want to see," Ærühn said. He pulled a blade from his belt, turned to Geoffrey. "This is the blade you were given. It was expected that you should kill me with it. I will ask you again, why didn't you?"

Geoffrey took the blade so as not to have to talk about it again. "With you I have no quarrel."

"Yet you left the blade for me to take. How did you know I wouldn't turn it against you?"

"If you were going to kill me, you could have done this while I was unconscious. Instead you put a blanket over me to keep away the chill. You gave me food and drink when you could have kept it for yourself. If I was truly your enemy, why would you have done such a thing?"

Ærühn snatched the blade from Geoffrey's hand and threw it across the room. "Do you know so little of my kind? I am a Dragon Man of the Stone Shields. There is no honor in killing the sick or the weak. My punishment was to nurse my enemy back to health so that I might see through his eyes before I battled him to victory or defeat. My punishment was to bring me low—to see as you because I did not see. Don't you understand this?"

Ayrian stepped between Geoffrey and Ærühn. "He does not know your law. How could he?"

"The Law is," said Ærühn. "It is known to all."

Keeper Martin touched a hand to Ærühn's shoulder. "It is what I was trying to explain. We do not see as you see. This place has a hold over us, as it has over you. It makes us see differently and only when we question do we start to see true. I suspect we are in a wayside of old. A place where all things seem familiar but unfamiliar."

"A wayside?" asked Captain Brodst.

"I've only heard tell of it in the most ancient of the texts. But I believe this is a place between the realm gates."

Calyin swept back her long black hair, looked at the keeper quizzically. "Keeper, the day is long. We must be moving along."

"We are caught in a wayside," Martin explained. "We are caught in the place between."

"The between? With the souls of the dead?" scoffed Geoffrey. "Surely you jest, Keeper. The between is for those passing beyond this life. It is where the Choice is made and the Wish."

"True, yes, but it is also used by realm travelers. Before any of you interrupt me, I would like Ærühn to tell you of the dark land of the hunt. I would like Ayrian to tell you of the Kingdoms of the Skies. I would like to tell you of Uver and a time when his gates connected all the lands. So Ærühn, will you tell us how your people move from the frozen land to the dark land of fire?"

"The Great Door. It is known."

"I'm afraid that it is not known. We know little of the Land of the Dark Fire or the Frozen Land of Ice and Snow." Martin swept his hand around the circle. "They know nothing. I know only what I've been able to piece together. The one thing I do not know is if it has begun. Has it, Ærühn? Is that why you are here? Are you the Hand on the Wall, Ærühn?"

Ærühn glared at Keeper Martin. His large round eyes suddenly wider than seemed possible. "He will know. He will be angry."

"Tell me of Prince Sy'dan Entreatte. Tell me of the High Lord. Tell me of the lost kingdom. What do the dark elves plan?"

"What would you have me say?"

"Will my telling do as well?" asked Belajl Entreatte, High Lord of Shost, as he and his people entered the room from hidden recesses.

"It would," Martin said, his expression betraying no hint of surprise, though he hurriedly hastened everyone to the doorway Ayrian was supposed to have been watching.

"It will not work for you," Belajl said.

"But of course it will." Martin unrolled the small piece of parchment he held in his hand. As he faced the high lord and his men, he spread his arms wide to keep the others back.

"You underestimate my resolve. You were brought here to change the path and so it has come to pass."

"Ah, but you forget that in the time before time, the lands were ruled by titans, dragons, and the great eagles. The Master Keeper knew, and so I know. I did not have to seek out the Hand on the Wall, the Hand sought me out. Is that not so, Ærühn?"

Ærühn nodded solemnly.

Keeper Martin spun around and pushed the others through the door. He ran down the long hall behind them, speaking the words of power from the parchment. The gate formed in front of them. Martin was the last to step through to the other side. As he did so, he could hear Belajl Entreatte scream, "May the two sisters carry you away! May you know the eternal sadness of Adrynne!"

In that moment, as he was swept from the world, Keeper Martin couldn't help thinking that he did know, and that there was one who knew the sadness and the longing better than any other.

❀ ❀ ❀

Thought and movement returned to Adrina. "Tnavres, come forth," she commanded. The tiny dragon exited her flesh snout first, dropping to the ground beside her. It extended its wings, looking up at her.

Adrina took in the sight around her: the dark creatures everywhere as far as the eye could see. Noman's steady hand on her shoulder. Amir and Xith battling the creatures with blade and magic.

"You are the key, Adrina," Noman told her. "You have the power to end this."

"What power? I have no power."

"Do not play with me, girl," Noman commanded. "Time is short. Do what you must."

"The mark," Xith called out from behind her as he unleashed a wave of flame into the ranks of the wraith. "You have the mark, Adrina. You are the servant. Did he not tell you the price?"

Across the field, the shadow warrior king looked on with sudden interest. The appearance of the girl was as foretold. The master would come now.

Adrina turned around to Xith, her mouth agape, tears in her eyes. She felt overwhelmed. It was all too much for her. As she turned, she extended her arms. Tnavres took this as a sign to sink his teeth into the flesh of her hand. His touch brought the mortification of her flesh.

"What is it you seek?" said a deep, powerful voice and as it boomed across the field, everything and everyone stopped as if frozen in time.

Noman knew at once the words were addressed to him and not to any of the others. "Show yourself."

"As you wish," said the other. The air over the field filled with a great clutter of tiny flying creatures. The creatures became one and that one creature was the Dragon King.

"You must restore order. That which has been released must be returned."

"I am but the keeper. This is but the game of the ages."

"Untrue, untrue, you are what you choose to be. The game is as you choose it to be."

The Dragon King roared his disapproval of Noman's words. "One truth. Choose well."

"No more games, Bæhmangarin."

The Dragon King called forth his queens as he spread out his enormous wings and together they blew fire down from the sky. The flames flew to the corners of the field, cleansing the earth in all directions. The flames enveloped the shadow warrior king and all his minions turning them to ash. The beat of the mighty wings blew the dark ash from the field; the flames continued to lick the earth.

"No more games," Noman repeated.

The Dragon King cast his head down, his flames bathing the earth. Try as he might, his flames did not reach Noman or the others. "This is my domain!" he called out. "Be gone!" He called to his queens and they joined him in raining fire down upon the outsiders.

"Bæhmangarin," Noman said. "Surely you've not forgotten the pledge. The faithful, those that serve are protected. Is it not so?"

"My princess," the Dragon King called out. "Step away from the others."

"No," Adrina said defiantly, "I will not."

"Do this or the prince dies."

Her eyes wide, Adrina looked to Noman and then to Xith. "You lie!"

"Show her!" the Dragon King commanded of the tiny dragon at Adrina's feet. Suddenly Adrina saw her brother. Valam was dressed in battle armor with his great sword strapped on his back. He stood on the balcony of a great tower, in a city that was foreign to her. Father Jacob was to his left. The queen of the elves was to his right. Lines of soldiers stood at the base of the tower. She heard shouts and cheers. "To the High Prince!" went the call. In the distance, beyond the walls of the city, she saw a large fleet of ships. Across the dark waters behind the ships, she saw the great black wave of an army tens of thousands strong sweeping in from the plains.

"Forgive me," Adrina said, her voice trembling as she stepped away from the others. The Dragon King roared his approval. In his upturned claw, he held a great sphere and he cast the sphere into the fading image of the prince and his men; then he and his queens set upon Xith, Noman, and Amir.

It was as before; the dragons could not reach the three with their flames so the dragons set upon them with fang and claw. Amir blocked the powerful jaws and terrible clawed hands of the Dragon King with his twin blades. Xith and Noman defended against the queen dragons as best as they could. Although their magic had little affect on dragon kind, it still stung as they unleashed it.

"It is time for truths," Noman told Amir.

"It is," the titan replied.

Noman turned to Xith. He looked directly at the shaman as he transformed into his true self.

"It cannot be," Xith muttered to himself as he watched Noman change form before his eyes. The figure before him was familiar but older, much older than he remembered.

"Aven, is that you?"

"It is I, old friend."

It was unlike Xith, the great shaman, the watcher of old, to be at a loss for words but he was, at least momentarily.

Bæhmangarin and his queens showed their great disapproval by blasting the group with fire. Aven stood defiantly within the flames, his outstretched hands keeping the flames away from the others. "My father, Dnyarr, Elf King of Greye, would disapprove."

"You betrayed him," roared the Dragon King. "You betrayed us all. You are the great betrayer."

Aven shook his head. "He betrayed his people. No single being was meant to rule over all the lands. There must always be balance. Surely you understand this. The balance must be restored."

Bæhmangarin and his queens bowed their heads. The Dragon King looked to Adrina. "You are the key, princess. The Fourth will listen and return. The balance will be restored."

Chapter Thirty Eight

The majestic spires of a palace grew before them. From a distance it appeared that a great serpent enveloped each, baring its head at each tower's summit. The company followed an ancient byway that unfolded toward the palace gates, which stood agape as they approached. Amir and Aven led the way, with Shchander and Shalimar close behind them. Adrina walked beside Xith with Tnavres perched on her shoulder.

The palace was oddly still as they entered. The eyes of most were fixed on the structure directly before them. Its six towers and one center spire with broad stairs circling their way to lofty pinnacles inspired their hearts. Here they paused, for the long race through the frozen wastes of the Lost Lands was now at an end. For a time they relished the moment. Eventually they did continue on, but the urgency was gone. The pace was slow and deliberate.

They marched up many stairs and came to stand before the doors of a grand hall. They did not hesitate or ask permission to enter; instead, they held their heads high, almost with regal airs, and passed within. The first signs that the palace was occupied arose before their eyes. Flames burned from huge urns placed along the corridor. A faint glow from a distant point told them where the end of the long hall lay, and as they walked its length their footsteps echoed, replacing the silence.

A set of double doors sat before them, but they did not have to touch a finger to them. The doors crept inward, as if on command, just after the travelers had paused. Adrina was visibly the most animated of all. She felt that here she would have her answers, and the past would be well behind her. She followed Amir and was the second one into the chamber beyond the great double doors.

The room was unexpectedly dark and shadowy, but its echoes gave its depth away as they slowly faded. Upon a raised dais low flames burned, casting eerie shadows about the chamber. Amir put a hand on Adrina's shoulder as she sought to move past him. He walked alongside her into the gloom. As their eyes adjusted, it became readily apparent that the shades of gray held shapes, and the images about the room called out to them.

Most visible of all the images was a figure standing on top of the dais, and as it lifted its arms up toward the ceiling the shadows were lifted. The hungry tongues of many flames sprang bright and crisp from their cisterns set along the walls. A handful surrounded the dais and swept out along a path toward the guests. The fires along the path seemed to writhe and move, dancing with the shadows cast upon the floor.

A herald of welcome issued forth and an enormous host swept from the recesses of the chamber. "We have waited long!" said a voice, pleasant and familiar. Amir and Adrina continued toward it. The others were more reluctant to follow. They held their places despite the warm invitation. Adrina turned to look back at Xith and Aven, waving for them to follow. "Do as you must," Aven whispered to her, but he made no move to catch up with her.

With her right hand, she scratched Tnavres under the chin absently as she walked, thinking how marvelous a place they had come to. Xith had promised her that here she would have all her answers. It was all she could do to keep words from springing from her lips. She wanted the questions answered and she no longer had the patience to wait.

At first she thought that the one on the raised dais was a woman, but as they drew closer she began to think otherwise. It was definitely the face of a man that she gazed upon, and she also remarked in her mind his fairness. She returned the gentle laughter in his voice as he spoke again.

Amir grabbed Adrina's hand and pulled her back, but she wanted to go forward. Her laughter fell hollow about the room as it died and she wondered what she had done in life to deserve such abasement. Further tepid words brought Adrina to her knees in deep, fitful sobs.

The eyes, Adrina remembered the eyes and the voice; it was so familiar, yet it, too, was changed. "Stand up, child," whispered Xith, coming up behind her and helping her to stand. His matter-of-factness sparked her anger. "Why have you done this to me?" she cried out.

"I have done nothing your destiny would not have brought to you."

"But, you were—" The remainder of Adrina's words were drowned out by her tears.

"I had no choice," returned Xith.

"You could have—"

"Silence!" screamed a loud and powerful voice. "I demand silence, and I will have it! I have not waited and watched for so long to hear your pitiful cries. Put them on their knees! I like them that way. And if they should stand, kill them all save the one. I want her to suffer until the last when I take that which is due me. Then when her suffering is at its worst and only then may you kill her."

The darkly robed figures swept off their cloaks to reveal raven-hued armor as they withdrew their blades. Adrina closed her eyes, expecting dispute, but none came. Her mind exploded. A white searing light swam through her mind, but she clung to the darkness. She rebuked with words of her own. "Would you kill your own flesh and blood?" she begged.

The other stammered through the next words. Adrina continued her verbal assault, sensing the dilemma. "That's right. I knew it when I first gazed upon your face against the light. You hold a likeness that I know well, though I can see you try to hide it, even now."

"I am He, and I shall have Silence! Speak not a word, or I'll separate you from your tongue!"

Even as Adrina attempted to stand, hands strong and true held her to her knees. "You cannot hide your past. You cannot deny your heritage. I heard the words Keeper Martin spoke the night you were birthed, and he cursed your name!"

"You lie! Foul treachery spews from your lips. Cut out this creature's tongue and bring it to me upon a plate so that I may relish it."

Many hands held Adrina's head firm. She bit at the hand that probed her mouth. Tnavres clawed and raked all who came near. "Did not your mother have my eyes? Do you not have your father's hair? Your eyes and your hair? What of the softness of your voice?"

"Lies, lies! Silence her! Kill them all and rid them from my sight! You have no right to speak to me in such a way. I order you to silence and if you do not listen, I will deliver your life by my own hand." He grabbed a dagger from another's belt and lunged at

Adrina as she cried out and begged him to remember.

The point of the blade never found its mark although it did meet flesh. Amir's face was not lit by sorrow or fear as he fell, but disbelief. The wielder of the blade backed away; a tiny voice cried out in his thoughts. It knew the truth. He had not always been.

Shchander and Shalimar jumped over Amir as he went down. They struggled to reach Adrina but Xith moved between them and the girl. "This is not your fight," Xith told them.

"Come back to us," Adrina repeated as she fought off her attackers. "What of the boy I once knew?"

"A man, no longer a boy," the other said as he set upon her brutally, swatting away her tiny dragon as it sought to defend her. A savage kick to her stomach brought her to her knees. She would have collapsed to the floor if his followers had not held her. Instead, she doubled over, coughing up blood.

Tnavres returned, clawing at the man's face. He angrily snatched the dragon from the air, squeezing with all his might and then thrusting out, sending the tiny flailing beast flying into the stone chair upon the raised dais. Grinning savagely, he returned his attention to Adrina who was now on her hands and knees, kicking her again and again.

Tears such as she had never known welled up in Adrina's eyes. She cried out, "Please no more, please no more." Her eyes wide and pleading turned to Xith who was no more than a handful of steps away.

The other brought the heel of his boot to her left forearm, crushing bone as he twisted and smashed down with all his might. The vision flowed strongly. He felt the surge of strength within him peak and the power came unbidden to his hands. As he spread his hands, brilliant bolts of blue and white spread between them, arcing wildly.

"Why, oh why?" Adrina cried out. "What have I ever done? Please no more. Please, please no more."

For an instant her pleas touched him, he reached down to her, but as he did so pain swept over him. "No, no, not again," he cried out. He watched as the three circled the other in his mind. "Go away!" he told them but the thoughts would not go.

Seeing the inner turmoil reflected in his eyes, Adrina reached out to him with her good arm, her hand finding his leg. He clasped his ears, pounded the sides of his head until the pain within was replaced by the pain from without, but the voices would not fade.

He pulled her to her feet, grabbed her broken arm, twisted. Adrina's screams of agony intensified. "Stop, Stop!" she yelled.

His eyes wild, he laughed madly. "You are a great fool. The boy is gone."

"Fool?" Adrina screamed back at him, finding sudden anger. "Never underestimate the fool. The fool on the board can capture the king just as easily as any."

She stood firmly, defiantly, despite pain, staring into his wild eyes. She did a thing no one looking on expected of her, he least of all. She raised her broken arm into the air and called Tnavres to her. "Tnavres return," she said as she lunged, wrapping her good arm and both legs around the other, causing both to fall to the stark, gray granite of the dais.

The granite that should have met them cold and full, pulled them in, allowing them to pass by as if they instead met the waters of some gray dark lake. Soon after, they were falling through the air, landing on firm ground in a shadowed land. It was a place Adrina knew though she wished she did not; it was a place the other apparently knew as well for he howled his displeasure in a long stream of angry words. "Not this place, not this place. It is not fair to return. The master promised more. The master promised all. This must be a lie! This is a lie!"

Adrina crab-crawled backward away from him. It never occurred to her as she looked up to him that in this place she had full use of both her arms. As she looked on, one became three and then suddenly there was a fourth in the space between them.

The Dragon King and his queens came winging in. Their great speed surprised Adrina for it seemed that one minute she saw them distant in the gray sky overhead and the next they were landing beside her.

"Dalphan, it is time," the Dragon King said in his firm deep voice.

One of the figures broke from the circle and climbed onto the Dragon King's back. "Has my beloved been found?" he asked.

"She has," replied the Dragon King. "She waits for you."

"On the other side?"

"As ever."

Before the Dragon King took wing, Dalphan called back to those in the circle. "Brother," he spoke firmly.

A dark figure, his face hidden in the cowl of his cloak, turned from the circle. As he climbed onto the back of one of the queens, the skulls and bones in his armor showed clearly. He did not speak as the other had, though he did clench a hand into a fist and wave it defiantly in the air as the queen dragon took to the air.

Tnavres jumped onto Adrina's lap and licked her cheek. To her it felt more like soft lips than the tongue of a dragon. Indeed as she looked on she saw a beautiful lady elf and not a tiny dragon.

The lady elf said in as beautiful a voice as Adrina had ever heard, "I am Adrynne, Servant of the Dragon, as you will one day be again."

"What is happening?" Adrina asked.

Adrynne said, "Take the boy's hand and let us go from this place."

"But what of the other?"

"The Fourth will remain as must be so. Quickly now, we must be away from this place."

As Adrina took the boy's hand, Vilmos' hand, Adrynne took hers. The shadowland faded.

Adrina found herself lying supine on cold, gray granite, her arms and legs wrapped around Vilmos, who looked ever the boy and nothing like the man she had leapt upon.

She squealed with delight when she found herself looking into his eyes. "Vilmos, by the Mother, I have never been so happy to see anyone in all my life."

Vilmos, somewhat dazed and confused, sought to untangle himself from Adrina. Adrina didn't want to let go for fear that if she released him she might find that by some dark twist of fate the other was there and not the boy from Tabborrath Village.

Taking a leap of faith, Adrina released Vilmos and rushed him to his feet. She turned him around and inspected him. "By the Mother, it is you!" she exclaimed, wrapping her arms around him.

"Is Xith here?" Vilmos asked.

"I am," Xith said, stepping to the dais.

"I didn't know what I was doing. I—I—"

"You need say no more. You could not have known what was to

happen. You could have no more turned back the wind. It is done. It has run its course."

"Has it?"

Having dispatched the last of the foes, Shchander, Shalimar and what remained of their band of free men from Solntse pressed suddenly close around Adrina, Vilmos, and Xith.

Aven stepped between the men, moving onto the dais. "It has. It is the start of a new age, an age of hope."

Xith cleared his throat. Aven looked over to Xith and to Amir struggling to his feet. Amir bit back his grimace of pain, his eyes going to Adrina and Vilmos.

"But there is work to be done before it is over," Amir said knowingly.

"True," Aven said, reclaiming the guise of Noman, Keeper of the City of the Sky. Xith added a moment later, "Indeed."

Chapter Thirty Nine

Upon exiting the Great Door, as the Gates of Uver were known to Ærühn's people, Geoffrey, Lord Serant, Captain Brodst and the others found themselves in the frozen wastes of the far north. With the snows all around him, Ærühn, Dragon Man of the Stone Shields, became a different man. He stood tall, eyeing the kingdomers as if he were just now seeing them for what they were. He hissed and spat at them and then raced off. Ayrian took to the air to follow him, but driving snows and loud angry winds made the task all but impossible.

Before long Ayrian was settling to the ground in front of them, emerging from the blowing snows so quickly that he startled Calyin. Calyin slipped on the snow and ice, falling backwards into her lord husband and soon both were lying in the snow. Lord Serant tried to maintain his composure and find his feet, but Calyin would have nothing of it. She rolled on top of him and kissed him full in the lips, laughing like the girl she had once been.

Captain Brodst took the impropriety in stride and a smile almost touched his lips. The hint of a smile, however fleeting, was replaced by his shielding scowl, but his displeasure wasn't due to their actions. He envied them and their love, and this he would never deny. With the mother of his children, he had known a kind of love though the marriage was one of obligation to maintain Elzeth's honor. His second love was a true love but a love that broke the heart of his first love. Elzeth had taken her own life in a moment of weakness, and it was clear to him now how much her death impacted his life and his family.

At the thought of his family, the captain chuckled sardonically. He had no one, no family. His sons were gone. Pyetr betrayed the Kingdom. Emel quit the guard and was off in search of a thing he might never find. He knew Emel was running from a thing he could never outrun, even if Emel himself did not know this. To the captain, it seemed that for the whole of his life he himself had been running from the very same thing—a ghost of the past that he could never truly excise.

He gritted his teeth, maintained his ground, still thinking of the past. Happy times, not sad times. He thought of Emel and the day Emel joined the guard. He thought of the day he first met Elzeth. It was in this way that he came to terms with his captivity and his freedom. A cage could hold a man's body, but it could not keep his mind from soaring or his soul from crying out.

Not two paces away, Midori watched Ansh Brodst. He seemed to be looking through her to Edwar and Calyin who were lying in the snow behind her. She didn't know why there were tears in her eyes and blamed it on the icy winds and snows. Some day, she vowed. Someday, she would tell him. Not this day, likely not any day soon, but one day.

She brushed the frozen tears from her cheeks, and turned away to find Keeper Martin regarding her in almost the same way as she had regarded the captain.

"You must tell him, you know," Keeper Martin said knowingly.

Finding the priestess in her, Midori brushed back her long black her and pulled her robes around her. She eyed the keeper for a moment, then in a tone harsher than intended, she said, "Do you read minds now, keeper?"

"You wear the truth of it. I do not need to read your mind."

Midori's reply was drowned out by Ayrian's shrill call to alarm. The bird man heard and saw things the others couldn't. Those around him heeded his call, drawing their blades, forming a defensive line. Midori and Calyin stood defiantly in the middle of the line, wielding short blades even as the others sought to push them to the rear.

Ærühn emerged from the snowy veil, riding on the back of an enormous black bear. Others of his kind followed, each riding one of the great bears—black, white or brown. Behind them came still more, riding great wolves, either gray or white. Captain Brodst was quick to discern that those riding wolves were an offensive force of outriders, for those on the wolves carried long spears, pikes and bows, and were lightly armored. Those on the bears were heavily armored and wielded clubs and swords.

Ærühn dismounted, hissing and spitting. Keeper Martin stepped forward, explaining that this was a greeting—a greeting of friendship. Smiling, Ærühn nodded and said, "The Great Door is watched. You must come."

Ærühn mounted his bear. Turning back to Martin, he said, "Mount, we shall ride." Martin climbed on the back of Ærühn's black bear. Serant, Brodst, Calyin, Midori, and Geoffrey climbed onto the backs of other bears, each taking up a position behind one of Ærühn's men.

Ayrian looked on. He wanted desperately to take to the skies, to feel the air beneath his wings despite the snow and wind. One of

Ærühn's men dismounted and approached the Eagle Lord, hissing and spitting in a gesture of friendship. Ayrian cast a glum stare to the skies, and then mounted the dragon man's white bear. The dragon man said something then that Ayrian didn't understand. The others' words must have been in a different dialect than Ærühn's.

"He says," said Ærühn moving his bear alongside, "that it is the greatest honor. That he will tell his sons about the day he gave ride to the one of the Lords of the Heavens."

Ayrian was about to explain that he wasn't a lord of anything, but Ærühn called the group to movement and the great white bear loped forward. Ayrian was surprised by the relaxed long strides and swift speed of the bear.

Ærühn led his men north and east. Within an hour, they were passing a most amazing sight and Keeper Martin found that he had to swallow more than a few gasps. From the texts of old, he recognized the giants of the six clans—fire and ice, storm and mountain, stone and hill—but he did not recognize the long-haired peoples that rode atop mammoths whose long curved tusks were covered in polished steel. The steel, inlaid with many intricate designs, glistened as it reflected the bright white of the ice and snow. The giants and the men on mammoths went by six abreast. The thrump, thrump of their boots and hooves and the roar of their trumpets, echoed long in the ear and across the land.

Keeper Martin did not doubt that the giants and men were going to the Great Door. For just as Ærühn's bear troop carried them north and east, the giants and the men upon mammoths went south and west. What they would do when they reached the door, Martin could only guess, but Ærühn had named them watchers. He did not dwell on this thought much longer for the spires of a city grew in the distance. Try as he might, Martin could not recall a telling of such a city this far north.

Soon he could see the majestic, serpentine spires of some enormous building or palace that was within the city. Before he knew it, they were racing down the city's ancient streets. The great bears continued to move in long, easy strides.

At the foot of the palace was a large open square that might have served once as a market for those that dwelt in the city. For now, though, the square was being used as a meeting place and was filled from end to end with the peoples of the north: the many tribes of the dragon men, the wild men who stood their mammoths, some few representatives of the giant clans, and the clansmen of Oshywon.

Much to Martin's surprise, in the center of the assembled mass stood one he thought he might never see again. "Master Keeper," he called out in greeting, surprise evident in his voice. He dismounted somewhat roughly but Ærühn's firm hand kept him steady on his feet.

The crowd around Noman parted. Martin caught sight of the young woman standing behind him, her long black hair flowing freely and her clear, green eyes shining like jewels in the bright sun of the full day. He gripped Noman's forearm as he passed, moving to greet the princess. Another behind him was faster though and he could only look on and smile as Calyin embraced her sister. In a moment, Midori joined in and the three sisters hugged each other while they cried.

He did not know whether they cried tears of joy or sadness, only that he himself was near tears. He had to look away to maintain his composure. Nearby he saw Lord Geoffrey Solntse greet his son

Nijal Solntse, at first formally, and then with unabashed enthusiasm. It was then that he saw the boy, Vilmos, standing alone in the crowd, looking lost and unsure of himself. Martin did then what he knew he must. He took Vilmos' hand, led him toward the great brown bear the captain was still mounted upon.

"Captain," he said firmly. "I've someone I'd like to introduce you to." The captain eyed Vilmos, dismounted expertly, almost as if he had ridden the immense bear all his life. Vilmos looked on. "Captain, this is Vilmos. Vilmos, I would like you to meet King's Knight Captain Ansh Brodst."

"A knight?" Vilmos asked, his voice breaking.

"Indeed and more," Xith said, stepping to Martin's side. Xith looked to Martin before speaking. A silent approval passed between the two. "Do you recall the day we met?" Xith asked.

"I do," Vilmos said, "but it seems many lifetimes ago."

"Do you recall the story I told you of the girl, the one I spirited away to the southlands?"

"My mother," Vilmos said quietly, "You said she was my mother."

Before Xith replied and confirmed this, Captain Brodst realized for the first time who Vilmos was. Vilmos was the son he thought he would never know, the son whose identity was kept from him these many long years. He turned to look for Midori in the crowd only to find she was beside him.

"Vilmos," she said, taking the captain's hand in hers. "Do you remember me?"

"Of course," Vilmos replied without a moment's hesitation. "You are Midori. You were my tutor. You are the one who took me away from my village."

"That is not the full of it, Vilmos—" And this is the part that sent Vilmos' knees to buckling and his heart to soaring. "—The truth of it is that I am your mother and Ansh is your father. Shh... Before you say anything, you must know that I did what I had to do."

"I know this," Vilmos said, speaking truthfully and standing bravely still when all he wanted to do was run, perhaps to her, perhaps away and to the winds.

Seeing and understanding the conflicting emotions playing out on his face, Midori embraced him before he could make up his mind whether to run to her or away from her. Her aim was to calm and sooth him, but she was the one who was calmed and soothed. She was the one who was healed and made whole.

She reached out to Ansh and he to her. Tears rained down her cheeks. One minute she was angry to her core, gnashing her teeth, reeling on the inside from the pain of the past. The next, she was calm, at peace with herself and the past, smiling as she lived life in the moment.

Xith looked on, pleased. He was about to speak to Ayrian when he saw Adrina and Calyin. He moved to her before she could cross to Midori. "You know you want to ask, so ask," Xith told her.

"My brother," Adrina said, "if I am the one with the mark, is he safe?"

Xith removed a glowing sphere from a rough, leather pouch at his side. Adrina recognized it immediately as an orb of power, much like the one Emel had taken from her and gone over mountain with in search of answers.

"Hold the orb and think of him," Xith told her.

Adrina did as told and within the glow of the orb she saw Valam.

He was dressed in battle armor with his great sword strapped on his back. He stood on the balcony of a great tower in a city that was foreign to her. Father Jacob was to his left. The queen of the elves was to his right. Lines of soldiers stood at the base of the tower. She heard shouts and cheers. "To the High Prince!" went the call. In the distance, beyond the walls of the city, she saw a large fleet of ships. Across the dark waters behind the ships, she saw the great black wave of an army tens of thousands strong sweeping in from the plains.

"No, no," Adrina found herself saying, then suddenly she was standing within the glow of the orb itself and Valam seemed so close to her, almost as if she could reach out and touch him.

She wanted to take a step back, away from the flashing world, but Xith's voice beside her kept her still. "Don't move," he said. "Dangerous, often lethal, to do so."

"Where am I?"

"Shh… Look," Xith said, directing her gaze back to the island city of Leklorall.

From high above, she heard a tremendous roar and as she looked up she saw a glowing ball of fire, falling from the sky. She did not doubt, and Xith would later confirm, that this was the object the Dragon King had thrown into the fading image of the prince and his men just before he and his queens set upon Xith, Noman, and Amir.

The enormous ball of fire rushed, hissing, into the dark waters of the lake. Towering waves of water spread out from the impact point, washing over the ships, moving over the land, and nearly emptying the lake. Adrina could see ships lying broken upon the rocks at the bottom of the lake. The grave, gray wall of water rushed across the land. The army turned about in the field. Some found safety; many others did not.

"You are doubly indebted now," Xith told Adrina.

Adrina said only, "I am a Servant of the Dragon, am I not?"

"You are indeed," Xith said, as he took the orb from her and led her to Calyin and Midori whereupon Adrina told her sisters of Valam and the three rejoiced as one.

End Of Book Four

He waits in the shadows.

ABOUT THE AUTHOR

Robert Stanek is the author of many previously published books, including several bestsellers. Currently, he lives in the Pacific Northwest with his wife and children. Robert is proud to have served in the Persian Gulf War as a combat crewmember on an electronic warfare aircraft. During the war, he flew numerous combat and combat support missions, logging over two hundred combat flight hours. His distinguished accomplishments during the Persian Gulf War earned him nine medals, including the United States of America's highest flying honor, the Air Force Distinguished Flying Cross.

As a boy, he dreamed of being a writer. In elementary school, he was a junior editor for the school newspaper. Although he has written many books for professionals since 1994, his works of fiction have quickly become his most popular books. His first novel was Keeper Martin's Tale, which was simultaneously released in adult and children's editions. He describes the book as "a story of mystery, intrigue, magic, and adventure." Many of his other works of fiction are also fantasies, set in incredibly fantastic worlds.

Learn more at
www.robertstanek.com

Enter the world of the books
www.ruinmist.com

Characters in the Books

Adrina Alder	Princess Adrina. Third and youngest daughter of King Andrew.
Alexandria Alder	Queen Alexandria. Former Queen of Great Kingdom; Adrina's mother, now deceased.
Amir	One of the lost. Child of the Race Wars. Son of Ky'el, king of the Titans.
Andrew Alder	King Andrew. Ruler of Great Kingdom, first of that name to reign.
Ansh Brodst	Captain Brodst. Former captain of the guard, palace at Imtal. King's Knight Captain.
Anth S'tryil	Bladesman S'tryil is a ridesman by trade but a bladesman of necessity. He is heir to the Great House of S'tryil.
Antwar Alder	King Antwar. The Alder King. First to rule Great Kingdom.
Ashwar Tae	The 12th son of Oshowyn.
Ayrian	Eagle Lord of the Gray Clan.
Brodst, Captain	See Ansh Brodst.
Br'yan, Brother	Elf of the Red order. Proper Elvish spelling is Br'-än.
Cagan	Sailmaster Cagan. Elven ship captain of the Queen's schooner. Proper Elvish spelling is Ka'gan.
Calyin Alder	Princess Calyin. Eldest daughter of King Andrew.
Catrin Mitr	Sister Catrin. Priestess of Mother-Earth.
Charles Riven	King Charles, former ruler of Sever, North Warden of the Word.
Danyel' Revitt	Lieutenant Danyel'. Former Sergeant Quashan' garrison.
Delinna Alder	See Midori.

De Vit, Chancellor	See Edwar De Vit.
Der, Captain	See Olev Der.
Edwar De Vit	Chancellor De Vit. King Jarom's primary aid and chancellor.
Edwar Serant	Lord Serant. Husband to Princess Calyin. Governor of High Province, also called Governor of the North Watch.
Edward Tallyback	A troant (half troll, half giant) and friend of Xith's. Edward would be the first to tell you that he is only distantly related to the hideous wood trolls and that he is a direct descendant of swamp trolls.
Eldrick	A tree spirit of old.
Emel Brodstson	Emel. Former guardsman palace at Imtal; Son of Ansh Brodst.
Erravane	Queen of the Wolmerrelle.
Evgej, Captain	See Vadan Evgej.
First Brothers	Council made up of the presiding members of each order of the Elven Brotherhood.
Francis Epart	Father Francis. Member of the priesthood of Great Father.
Galan, Brother	Elf of the Red order, second only to Seth.
Geoffrey Solntse	Lord Geoffrey. Lord of the Free City of Solntse. Descendant of Etyr Solntse, first Lord of Solntse.
Great Father	Father of all. He whom we visit at the last.
Imson Adylton	Captain Adylton. Imtal garrison captain.
Isador Froen d'Ga	Lady Isador. Nanny for Adrina; given honorary title of Lady by King.
Jacob Froen d'Ga	Father Jacob. First minister to the king. Head of the priesthood in the capital city of Imtal.
Jarom Tyr'anth	King Jarom, ruler of Vostok, East Warden of the Word.
Jasmine	Sister Jasmine. First priestess of the Mother.

Keeper Martin	See Martin Braddabaggon.
Ky'el	Legendary titan who gave men, elves, and dwarves their freedom at the dawn of the First Age.
Lillath Tabborrath	Mother of Vilmos.
Liyan, Brother	Elf, presiding member of East Reach High Council.
Mark, King	The Elven King of West Reach.
Martin Braddabaggon	Keeper Martin. A lore keeper and head of the Council of Keepers.
Michal Klaive	Baron Klaive. Low-ranking nobleman whose lands are rich in natural resources.
Midori	Sister Midori. The name Princess Delinna Alder earned after joining the priestesses.
Mikhal	Captain Mikhal. Quashan' garrison captain.
Misha	Innkeeper, an old friend of Xith's.
Mother-Earth	The great mother. She who watches over all.
Myrial	Adrina's childhood friend. The current Housemistress of Imtal Palace.
Nijal Solntse	First son of Geoffrey, former day captain city garrison, Free City of Solntse.
Niyomi	Beloved of Dalphan, lost in the Blood Wars.
Noman	Master of Amir. Keeper of the City of the Sky.
Olev Der	2nd Captain Olev Der of the Quashan' garrison. Captain of the City Watch.
Parren	Keeper Parren. Member of the Council of Keepers.
Pyetr Brodst	Second son of Captain Ansh Brodst. Guardsman palace at Imtal.
Queen Mother	The Elven Queen. Queen of East Reach, mother of her people.
Q'yer	Keeper Q'yer. Member of the Council of

Keepers.

Ry'al, Brother	Elf, second of the Blue. Heir to Samyuehl's gift.
Samyuehl, Brother	Elf, first of the Blue order.
Sathar the Dark	He that returned from the dark journey.
Serant, Lord	See Edwar Serant.
Seth, Brother	Elf, first of the Red, protector of Queen Mother.
Shalimar	A warrior of Shchander's company.
Shchander	Old compatriot of Nijal.
S'tryil, Lieutenant	See Anth S'tryil.
Teren, Brother	Elf of the Brown.
Tnavres	Adrina's dragon.
Trailer	A warrior of Shchander's company.
Tsandra, Brother	Elf, first of the Brown order.
Vadan Evgej	Captain Evgej. Former Swordmaster, city garrison at Quashan'.
Valam	Prince Valam. Governor of South Province. King Andrew's only son. Also known as the Lord and Prince of the South.
Van'te Duardin	Chancellor Van'te. Former first adviser to King Andrew, now confidant to Lord Valam in South Province.
Vilmos Tabborrath	An apprentice of the forbidden arcane arts.
Vil Tabborrath	Father of Vilmos and village councilor of Tabborrath.
Volnej Eragol	Chancellor Volnej. High Council member, Great Kingdom.
Willam Ispeth	Duke Ispeth. Ruler of the independent Duchy of Ispeth.
William Riven	King William. King of Sever.
Xith	Last of Watchers, Shaman of Northern

Reaches. He is most definitely a Gnomic Dwarf (Gnome) though there are those that believe he is a creature of a different sort altogether.

Yi Duardin — Chancellor Yi. First adviser to King Andrew. Brother of Van'te.

Ylad', Brother — Elf, first of the White order.

Ylsa Heman — Bowman first rank. A female archer and later a sectional commander.

Learn more about the people, places, and things in Robert Stanek's world of Ruin Mist. Read *Ruin Mist Heroes, Legends & Beyond*—a companion book for *The Kingdoms & the Elves of the Reaches* and *In the Service of Dragons.*

The Reaches

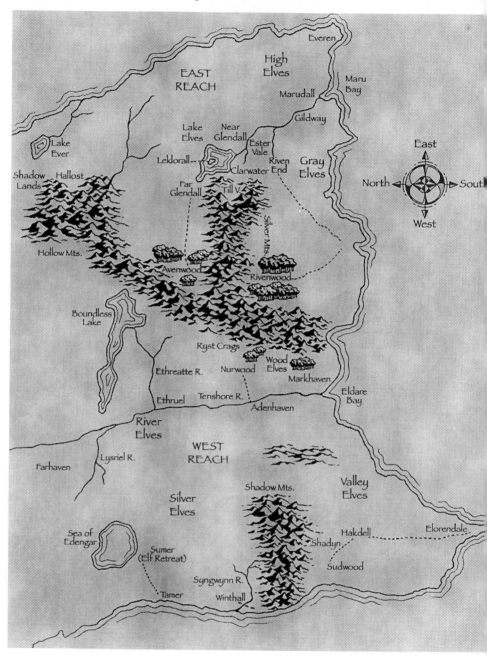

The Kingdoms

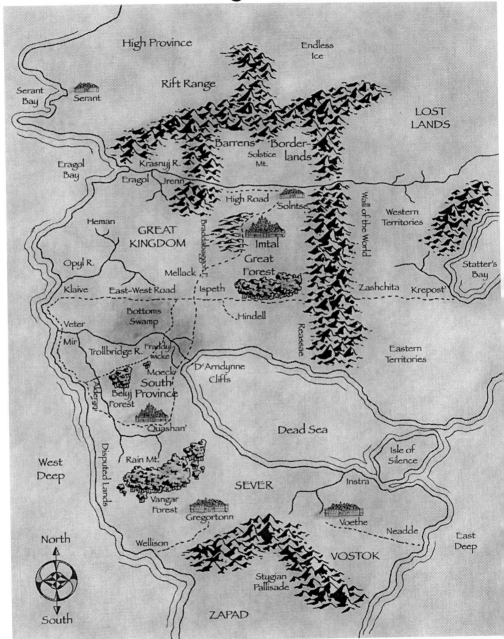

Under-Earth

Uver Region

Samguinne Mts.

Entreatt Shost

B'Him

Zadridos Forest

Zabridos Forest

Var Daren
Lord Vylniul

Lord Zeli

Vytrandyl

Wrenrandyl

Ckrij V.

Abrikos Shost

Qerek

Skunne Daren

Triaran Desert

Lord Ghil

Lord Lozzan

"The Jeshowyn"

Lord Ergej

Lord Chilvr

Azz

Rhylle Plains

Lord Rhil

Pakchek Daren

Lord Yuvloren

Dtanet Shost

Nesryth

Lyudr Hills

Lord Boets

Efrusse River

Njom Mts.

Stranth's Path

Lord Mark

Lord Kylauriel

Lord Kylaurieth

Kastelle Swamp

Lord Lionne

Oshio Damen

Lord Yras

Lord Hettod

Stranth's Wish

Khennet

Stranth's Defeat

Beyet Daren

Lord Ittwar

Kedrette

Papiosse Shost

Adrynne Swamp

Marek Damen

Lord Ryajek

Rill Akh Arr